"Are you saying you're attracted to me, Harper?"

He pushed back thoughts of the ranch and ignored the voice in his head that told him to put his clothes on,

He smiled at her, letting all pretense fall away. "It's about time."

PRAISE FOR A.J. PINE

"A steamy cowboy romance novel that is sure to warm your heart!"
—LovelyLoveday.com on *Hard Loving Cowboy*

"A delightfully sexy read that made me want to go in search of a cowboy of my own."
—KimberlyFayeReads.com on *Hard Loving Cowboy*

"Sweet and engrossing."
—*Publishers Weekly* on *Tough Luck Cowboy*

"Light and witty."
—*Library Journal* on *Saved by the Cowboy*

"A fabulous storyteller who will keep you turning pages and wishing for just one more chapter at the end."
—Carolyn Brown, *New York Times* bestselling author, on *Second Chance Cowboy*

"Cross my heart, this sexy, sweet romance gives a cowboy-at-heart lawyer a second chance at first love and readers a fantastic ride."
—Jennifer Ryan, *New York Times* bestselling author, on *Second Chance Cowboy*

"Ms. Pine's character development, strong family building, and interesting secondary characters add layers to the story that jacked up my enjoyment of *Second Chance Cowboy* to maximum levels."
—*USA Today* "Happy Ever After"

MY ONE *and* ONLY COWBOY

ALSO BY A.J. PINE

Meadow Valley Series

Cowboy to the Rescue (novella)

Crossroads Ranch Series

Second Chance Cowboy

Saved by the Cowboy (novella)

Tough Luck Cowboy

Hard Loving Cowboy

MY ONE *and* ONLY
COWBOY

A Meadow Valley Novel

A.J. PINE

FOREVER

NEW YORK BOSTON

Copyright © 2019 by A.J. Pine
Toughest Cowboy in Texas copyright © 2017 by Carolyn Brown

Cover design by Elizabeth Turner Stokes
Cover copyright © 2019 by Hachette Book Group, Inc.

Forever
Hachette Book Group
1290 Avenue of the Americas, New York, NY 10104
read-forever.com
twitter.com/readforeverpub

First Edition: December 2019

Forever is an imprint of Grand Central Publishing. The Forever name and logo are trademarks of Hachette Book Group, Inc.

The publisher is not responsible for websites (or their content) that are not owned by the publisher.

The Hachette Speakers Bureau provides a wide range of authors for speaking events. To find out more, go to www.hachettespeakersbureau.com or call (866) 376-6591.

ISBNs: 978-1-5387-4979-1 (mass market), 978-1-5387-4980-7 (ebook)

Printed in the United States of America

OPM

10 9 8 7 6 5 4 3 2 1

To those whose minds rebel
and those seeking a cure

ACKNOWLEDGMENTS

When Sam and Ben came into the picture in the Cross-roads Ranch series, I hoped they'd one day get their own stories. Well, here we are! Thank you first and foremost to Forever Romance for giving my California cowboys a home, to my wonderful agent, Emily Sylvan Kim, for finding their wonderful home, and to my fabulous editor, Madeleine Colavita, for bringing out the best in all that is Meadow Valley.

Jen, Chanel, Lia, Megan, and Natalie, you will always be on this page because I could never do this without you. Love you!

To all the readers—thank you for reading, reviewing, and sharing the love of romance. But to one reader in particular, Dawn Scarbeck, whom I should have mentioned a long time ago, THANK YOU for your years of support. It means the world to me.

S and C, I love you three thousand times infinity.

Alzheimer's disease has touched my family for generations. There is no cure yet, but we continue to search. Thank you to Nolan, Sam, Ben, and Barbara Ann Callahan for showing there is dignity and quality of life while we still search.

MY ONE *and* ONLY COWBOY

CHAPTER ONE

S am Callahan stood on the front porch of Meadow
Valley Ranch's registration cabin, the one where he,
his brother Ben, or their buddy Colt greeted each new
guest. They were only in their second month of full operation, though, which meant *new guests* weren't exactly
pouring through the doors. Not yet, anyway. What was
that saying from the baseball movie he loved—*Field of
Dreams*? Something about once you build the thing,
people will come.

*Well, come on, people. We're ready and waiting—and
really need you to spend your money.*

He and his brother Ben sold their family's horse boarding business and sank every penny they owned—and a
few they didn't—into building the thing. The ranch. Their
dream. They'd even let Colt invest as a third partner. Now
it was just a matter of getting the people to come.

Right now he watched as Ben gave a riding lesson to a
young couple celebrating their first anniversary. Colt was
leading a trail ride for the Tanners, a family of four with a

pair of identical twin boys he still couldn't tell apart even after they'd been at the ranch for three days. And Pearl called from the inn to let him know she was sending a handful of folks his way now that she was booked solid.

It was a start, but a slow one to say the least.

Today, though, something felt...off. The guests all seemed happy at breakfast, and everyone headed out to their various activities just fine. But sometimes Sam got an inkling, and for a guy who liked to keep things simple and logical, inklings didn't sit well.

His phone vibrated in his pocket, and he pulled it out to see KITCHEN EMERGENCY in all caps from Luis, Meadow Valley's head chef.

"Shit," he hissed. It was only ten o'clock in the morning. He was hoping to make it until at least noon before any all-caps texts came through. No such luck.

He stepped out from under the protection of the covered porch and was hit head-on by the hottest morning sun they'd had in months. The transition from September to October had brought along mild days and cool nights, but today the temperature was nearing a record high of ninety degrees.

He swore under his breath and swiped his arm across his forehead, where sweat had already started to bead along his hairline. He kept his hair cropped short for this very reason, but on days like today, it didn't matter. Hot was *hot*.

He silently berated himself for insisting that whoever worked the desk in the main cabin wore a collared shirt. Didn't matter that his plaid button-up was paper thin or that his sleeves were rolled to his elbows. There was no relief. It was going to be one heck of a fall festival if these temps held out for the entire week. He had planned to wait until spring to clear the new trail to the swimming hole, but maybe he would add that to his already growing list for this weekend.

But first—kitchen emergency.

He entered the dining cabin to the sound of raised voices, a man's and a woman's, arguing about—apples?

"My apple and spinach salad needs a Granny Smith! I always use a Granny Smith!" Luis bellowed, his arms raised and his round belly straining against his white apron.

"Never trust a cook who looks like he doesn't enjoy his own food," Luis had said when he'd come to interview for the job. "*Cuanto más grande sea la barriga, mejor será la comida.* The bigger the belly, the better the food." It didn't take much more than that—and a tasting menu that had put Sam, Ben, and Colt into a major food coma—to know that Luis was right for the job. He was one of the best chefs Sam knew, running the ranch's kitchen like a well-oiled machine. But when things went wrong—no matter how tiny—it was an all-caps kitchen emergency.

"For the eleventh time," a tall, short-haired brunette yelled, hands gesturing wildly, "the Granny Smith crop was destroyed by a pack of squirrels. But my Honeycrisp are the best you'll ever taste. I charge *more* for the Honeycrisps and am willing to give you the same price for a better apple!" It was Anna, their produce supplier.

She plucked a piece of fruit from the white box sitting on the kitchen's prep island and shoved it in Sam's face. "Here," she said. "Taste. Tell this man he'd be crazy not to use this apple in his precious salad."

The apple was practically touching Sam's lips, and he'd once again forgotten to eat breakfast, so he grabbed the fruit in question and tore off a bite with a satisfying crunch.

Apple juice dribbled onto his chin as his taste buds exploded with the perfect mix of sweet and tangy. Maybe this inkling he was having about the day wasn't such a bad thing after all.

"That's one fine apple, Luis," Sam said around his mouthful. "I'm not much for salads, but I'm thinking this is the fruit you're looking for. And it is less than two hours until we open for lunch." He raised his brows.

Luis narrowed his eyes—a standoff of sorts.

Luis was a few years older than Sam, early thirties. He'd been a sous chef at a resort restaurant on Lake Tahoe. Sam and Ben had a chance meeting with him when they'd made the drive down to Carson City to visit their mom and her husband, Ted. He asked to interview for the job on the spot—while the Callahans were eating at his resort. There was no way Sam could match what Luis was being paid—not yet, at least—but he could offer him his own kitchen and the promise that he, Ben, and Colt would never step on his toes. But it was hotter than Hades out there already, and he guessed the Meadow Valley patrons would be less than happy if they showed up for their second paid meal of the day only to find the kitchen had come to a halt over apples. Sam and Luis were dealing with a ticking clock.

Luis opened his mouth—likely to protest—but Anna shoved an apple between his teeth.

"One bite," she said calmly. "One little bite, and if it's not one of the best apples you've ever tasted, I'll drive across town to that awful touristy orchard that charges an arm and a leg for a bushel of what I could pick from my own trees if those pesky squirrels hadn't broken through my fence, and I will *buy* you your stupid Granny Smiths."

Sam shrugged and bit off another chunk of his own apple.

Luis sighed through his nose and sank his teeth into the forbidden fruit. His eyes fluttered shut, and he groaned.

Anna tossed the apple in the air, caught it bite side up, and grinned, triumphant. "Stubborn man."

Luis swallowed and opened his eyes, reaching for his apple.

"Oh no," Anna said. "Apology first. *Then* you get your fruit."

Luis's jaw tightened.

Sam hopped onto the counter and continued to enjoy his apple. "Don't mind me, folks," he said. "I'm just here for the show."

Anna slid the box of apples farther from Luis's reach, then brandished the one he'd tasted like she was the evil queen tempting Snow White. "Come on, Luis," she taunted. "All you have to do is say, 'I'm sorry, Anna. You were right. You're *always* right.'"

Sam choked back a laugh.

Anna tapped her foot on the tiled floor.

Luis emitted a low growl. "I'm...sorry, Anna. You...were..." He sighed and threw his hands in the air. "Just...give me the apples. I paid for them."

Sam cleared his throat. "Technically, *I* paid for them, and I'd kind of like to see you say the thing she wants you to say."

Luis mumbled something under his breath, which meant he'd likely have some words for Sam when they kicked back with a few beers around the firepit later that evening. In the short time they'd worked together, the two men had become friends. Sam wasn't the type to pull the boss card, but in this case it was worth it.

Veins pulsed in Luis's neck, and Anna beamed.

"I'm sorry, Anna. You were right. You're always right. Give me my apples." Luis spouted the words in rapid succession, snatched the apple he'd tasted from Anna's outstretched hand, and then stormed through the dining hall and out the cabin's front door, likely to finish his apple and cool off—emotionally, at least. Because the temperature was still rising.

Sam laughed and hopped off the counter, tossing his apple core into a nearby composting bin.

"Can I tell you a secret?" Anna said.

"Sure."

"There were no squirrels. The Granny Smiths are fine. But I knew he'd like these better."

Sam shook his head. "Why do you torture him like that?"

Anna shrugged. "Because it's so easy. And fun. I can't help myself." She patted the box of Honeycrisp apples. "I'll email you the invoice. Always a pleasure doing business with you, Sam Callahan."

She held out her hand, and he shook it and grinned. Then she bounded out the back door to her truck. She'd be back the same time next week, likely to mess with Luis again.

"Is there no one else?"

Sam turned to see Luis standing in the doorway that separated the kitchen from the dining hall.

"No one else to what?" Sam asked.

Luis crossed his arms and stared toward the back door. "No one else who can be our produce supplier."

"And dairy supplier." Sam laughed. "Where? Anna's

farm is the best in the county, and she's ten minutes away. If you actually ever had a kitchen emergency, she could be here in a matter of minutes, most likely with whatever you needed."

Luis lifted his Chicago Cubs baseball cap—still a fan of his hometown team—and ran a hand through his overgrown brown hair. "Then we've got a big problem."

"Oh yeah?" Sam said. "What's that?"

Luis shook his head and sighed deeply. "I think I'm in love with her."

Sam rubbed his temples and blew out a breath. "We have a great thing going with Anna," he said. "Affordable prices. On-time delivery. And she even knows what goes better in your salad than you do. Please, Luis. I'm begging you. Don't mess this up."

Luis held a hand over his heart and wistfully stared at the place where Anna once stood. "That's your problem, Sam. You only see the logic. When it comes to Anna, I don't think with my head. I think with my—"

"All right. All right," Sam interrupted. "I don't need to hear about your—"

"*Heart*," Luis said before Sam could finish. He whacked his friend on the shoulder with his baseball cap. "The *heart* doesn't care about logic or what's best for business. Do you think I cook with *logic*?" Luis slapped his knee and howled with laughter. "If you don't start using that rusty old—and I might remind you, *vital*—organ soon, you're going to miss out on the best of all of it."

"All of *what*?" Sam asked.

Luis simply shook his head. "One of these days, my friend, you'll get it."

Sam shook his head and left Luis to his pining. He had a ranch to run.

"Logic," he mumbled as he strode back toward the main cabin. That was how you ran a business. With logic. Not *heart*. Luis could fall for whomever he wanted. But their produce supplier? Maybe Anna didn't exactly work for the ranch, but she worked *with* them. Daily. If things ever truly went south between her and Luis, then Sam, Ben, and Colt would be up one hell of a creek.

Ben was standing against the arena fence while his riders braved a few laps on their own.

"Who's got your panties in a wad?" he called to Sam as he passed.

Sam flipped his brother a good-natured bird and kept on toward his destination.

Didn't Luis get that Sam had to be the logical one? Or Ben or Colt for that matter? Of course they didn't. They all had lives outside the day-to-day running of the ranch. Sam was the one who signed the checks, who balanced the books, and who knew how much they needed to pay the next bill. His life *was* the business. He knew they'd be in the red for a while after getting things off the ground, but he also knew that doing anything to remotely jeopardize the ranch could sink them.

They'd moved north to Meadow Valley, California, from their hometown of Oak Bluff not just because they got the land for a steal but also because it had an exceptional memory care facility where his and Ben's father now lived. So it wasn't just their livelihoods on the line. It was their father's life as well.

"Panties in a wad," he said to himself as he strode back into the main cabin, where his silver pit bull, Scout, was sleeping on the sunny part of the rug where he'd last left her. He'd woken in a pretty good mood this morning, but now he'd gone from enjoying a really good apple—and watching Anna make Luis eat his words—to wondering when the next shoe would drop.

He stepped over his still-lounging pup but stopped short before he could make it to his office. A woman stood at the reception desk, her back to him as she peered over the top so that all he could see were her fitted jeans, her tennis shoes, and the tanned skin at the small of her back where her red tank top rose up.

He cleared his throat, and the woman straightened with a gasp.

"Sorry!" she said, turning to face him so that he now saw the messy strawberry-blond bun on top of her head and the smattering of freckles across her nose and cheeks. Clear hazel eyes stared him down as if she were privy to the biggest secret in the world while he was lost in the dark. Pretty—for a snoop.

"Can I help you with something?" he asked. He planted his feet firmly on the ground and crossed his arms. He didn't take kindly to anyone, pretty or not, looking through his stuff, especially if said stuff belonged to the ranch.

She raised her brows. "That depends. Are you the owner of this place?"

He nodded once, already getting a sinking feeling in his gut. "Sam Callahan. One of three."

She extended her hand, and he shook it without thinking because that was what you did.

"Delaney Harper," she said. "And you mean one of *four*. My ex-husband sold you this place by forging my name on the quitclaim deed, so the way I see it, this place is half mine."

Sam pulled his hand away and laughed. "Ben put you up to this, right?" His brother had been giving him shit all week about loosening up. He'd always been the jokester—spraying Sam with the hose when he was bathing the horses, pushing him off the pond bridge fully clothed. Come to think of it, Ben's pranks usually occurred only when water was around. This was his most sophisticated one yet.

"Who's Ben?" Delaney asked.

"It was Colt?" he said.

But even as he tried to rationalize that it could have been his buddy, her name replayed in his head, and he knew it wasn't a coincidence. The last name was all over the paperwork for the sale of the property—the land, the ramshackle little cottage, and the barn that was in disrepair. Neither structure had been good for anything other than tearing down and rebuilding.

"Delaney *Harper*," he said, emphasizing her last name.

"That's me," she said with a wince. Then she cleared her throat and squared her shoulders. "All I took was the man's name, and he went and took everything from me in return. That changes today."

"You're either kin or you're Wade Harper's wife," he said simply. Wade was the property's former owner. "Either way, still not sure what you're talking about."

"*Ex*-wife," she explained. Her expression turned wistful as her green-eyed gaze traveled to the window that looked out on the stable. "You took down my barn. I know it wasn't much, but I had a hand in building it. Wade and I were underwater when I left him, which was why we didn't unload the property then. It's spelled out in the divorce that when the place was fit to sell, we'd split any profit equally. Guess I shouldn't be surprised he found a way to sell it out from under me before the divorce was even final, but here I am." She sighed. "Glad you kept the English maple on the outskirts. Always did love that tree."

He followed her gaze. Either she was putting on one hell of an act, or she was who she said she was, because the first thing he and his crew did when they started work out here was tear down that barn and replace it with the stable. And no way was he tearing down any trees. The whole point of this place was to appreciate the outdoors. Not destroy it.

"I had a real estate attorney go over everything," he said, more to himself than to her.

She turned her attention back to him, her expression hardening, and shrugged.

"Yeah, well, I'd fire that lawyer, because either they didn't spot the forgery, or they helped push it through. I'll just need to get a copy of the quitclaim deed, give it to *my* lawyer, and then—I don't know—see you in court to figure out which half of the land is mine."

"The quit *what*?" he asked. He knew a thing or two about buying and selling property, but she was speaking another language.

She sighed. "Quit. Claim. Deed. When two people own a piece of land together, the only way one can sell it on their own is for the other to sign over ownership. Which I did *not*. Yet somehow Wade was able to sell you our property. I don't suppose the forgery was included in your paperwork?"

Sam laughed. He was never an asshole intentionally, but this woman sure had some nerve. "You waltz in here telling me what I own isn't really mine, and now you want me to produce the paperwork to prove it?" He was certain her first name was nowhere to be found in his closing documents. Wade Harper was the only person listed as seller. "And why are you coming around now when I bought this place almost two years ago?"

She crossed her arms. "So that's a no to the paper-work?"

He crossed his arms right back. "I'll show you any-thing you want to see because I guarantee your name is nowhere to be found. Now it's your turn to answer my question."

Her shoulders sagged. "I didn't know he sold it," she said, losing some of her steam. "Not until I couldn't sleep last night and decided to google Meadow Valley." She shrugged. "I do that every now and then. This was supposed to be my new home, you know? Guess I'm still not over it. And imagine my surprise when your ranch came up in my search—far, far down the page, by the way. You should work on your analytics."

"Ana—*what*?" he asked, but she waved him off.

"I saw my maple tree in your website photo and figured out what Wade did. Hopped right in my car. Made the drive from Vegas in eight hours flat," she added proudly. "No stopping." She cleared her throat. "Who built your website, anyway? Could use some work if you want to get folks through the door."

Maybe he wasn't a graphic design whiz, but he bought the domain and got some good pictures up there. What else did she expect? He wasn't trying to sell the *site*. And why was he getting so defensive anyway? The ranch was what mattered, and he was proud of what he, his brother, and Colt had built.

"You drove here in the middle of the night?" Sam's brows drew together. "After you *happened* upon our website?"

Delaney groaned. "You ever have your life all planned

out and then have it ripped out from under you? As long as we still owned this land, there was a chance I could get back what I lost. Instead he sold that chance. And do you want to know the worst part?" She didn't wait for him to answer. "He assumed I wouldn't come back to fight for it because what does Delaney do when she can't fix a problem? She runs as far from it as she can get." She mumbled that last part, and he realized she was talking more to herself than to him.

Sam gritted his teeth. "Look. I'm sure you want out of this mess as much as I do. If what you're saying is true, can't we figure out a fair price for me to buy you out?" He didn't know yet where he'd get the money. Maybe the bank would give him an equity loan. He'd cross that bridge when the time came. Hell, he'd move heaven and earth to keep his land and his business intact, not just for himself but for Colt and Ben. For his father too.

"Sorry," she said. "But I want my land back. If you don't have the paperwork for me, I guess that means I'll be heading down to the county courthouse to grab a copy of the forged deed I plan to contest. Sorry to bother you, Mr. Callahan."

She turned on her heel and strode toward the cabin door.

"Whole town's shut down for the week. Autumn festival and all."

"Autumn festival?" she repeated, her brow furrowed.

He nodded, then scratched the back of his neck. "Meadow Valley Harvest Fest. Gourds. Corn maze. Bounce house for the kids. Any of it ringing a bell? You did live here at one point, right?"

Her throat bobbed as she swallowed. "Didn't make it past six weeks before—before I left."

Her eyes flashed with something that looked like fear, but when he blinked, her gaze was nothing more than focused and intent. For a second, though, he saw. He saw that there was more to her story, and he found himself wanting to ask what it was or why she'd gone so soon after arriving.

She spun to face him. "What kind of town closes down for an entire week for pumpkins and bounce houses?"

"Don't forget the corn maze and bobbing for apples," he said with a wink. "We go all out."

She gritted her teeth and let out an exasperated groan. "Very well," she said, chin held high. "Then I guess you'll be hearing from my lawyer when the town is back in business."

He fought the urge to follow her to the door, some inexplicable need rising—a need to stop her from leaving, especially in her state of distress.

"Why not just take this up with your ex-husband?" he asked. "Doesn't that make the most sense?"

Her shoulders sagged as he watched her bravado deflate. "Because I don't know where he is. I tried calling the only number I had for him, but it rang and rang until it finally went to a generic voicemail. Not sure the phone is even still his."

"You leave a message?" Sam asked.

She shook her head. "Didn't see the point since I wasn't sure who I was leaving it for." She paused. "I thought if we fixed this place up together and made something out of it that I could somehow fix *him*. But I learned my lesson."

This mess wasn't her fault. She was just as blindsided as he was, and it wasn't fair to put the blame on her.

"Let me get you a cold drink, maybe something to

eat?" he said. "You have to be starving after driving all night and into the morning."

She pressed her full pink lips together, and he couldn't tell if she was considering his offer or trying to keep herself from yelling at him. Wade Harper was the one to blame. Not either of them. But Wade wasn't here, so it was up to the two of them to figure it out, which meant he had to ignore the lips he realized he'd been staring at.

Logic. Not whatever it was that drove Luis's decisions. *Lo-gic.* Yet he found himself gritting his teeth, waiting for her reply. Did he want her to say yes? No? Why couldn't he reconcile the thoughts swirling around his head?

"I can't," she finally said.

And with that she stepped through the door, letting it slam behind her, the sound jolting him back to reality.

He breathed a sigh of relief, yet every muscle in his body was still as tense as the day his mother walked out on their father.

It was only then that Sam realized the white-knuckle grip he had on the reception desk's wood trim—and that he had torn it free from its nails.

Luis, Anna, and the so-called kitchen emergency were already a distant memory. His stupid inkling had nothing to do with them. No, sir. It was all about Delaney Harper—the woman who would be his undoing.

This wasn't the other shoe dropping. It was a steel-toed boot pummeling him into the dirt. He had to figure out how to fix this before Colt and Ben found out—before all three of them lost everything they'd given up to build their dream.

CHAPTER TWO

Delaney slammed the key into the ignition and peeled off of the ranch property in a matter of seconds, her heart thudding against her chest, her eyes burning with the threat of tears.

Her lawyer—a.k.a. her aunt Debra—said she couldn't promise anything without seeing the forged deed. What was she thinking waltzing onto someone else's property and thinking he'd just hand it over? And what kind of town closed down for an entire week when the rest of the world kept on keeping on?

Meadow Valley, California.

It had been over two years since she left. She'd loved the small town when she and Wade were newlyweds— and when she'd been so close to getting the animal shelter up and running. Now, though, when she needed the town to behave for her, it left her in the dust.

A stop sign loomed ahead, so she pressed her foot to the brake. Something popped. She yelped as the car lurched. Then instinct took over and she steered the vehicle into the grass before it came to a complete halt, smoke pouring up from the hood.

"No, no, no, no, no!" she growled at the traitor of a vehicle.

She sat there for several long minutes, half hoping that whatever happened to the car would right itself if she just waited it out. When that didn't seem to fix it, she pulled out her phone and googled the number for the town's auto repair shop. It rang four times before the voicemail picked up.

"Welcome to Meadow Valley Motors. Just like the rest of the town, we're closing shop until after the festival. Leave a message, and we'll return your call in about a week."

She tossed the phone onto the passenger seat and groaned, whacking her head against her seat back.

"A week? I'm stuck like this until Monday of the following week? That's—that's *ten* days!" Her voice rose both in volume and pitch.

She looked down at her phone and saw the seconds still ticking by on the timer.

Great, she hadn't ended the call, which meant her building tantrum was recorded for posterity. She vigorously pressed her index finger again and again over the red icon on the screen, just in case the first try didn't take.

This wasn't the plan. She was supposed to breeze into town, get a copy of Wade's forged deed, and get the ball rolling on reclaiming her land. Now she was stuck in her busted-up car with a busted-up plan on an October morning that felt like the middle of July.

A hand rapped against the driver's side window, and Delaney yelped for the second time in ten minutes. She looked out to see Sam Callahan standing on the road next to her, his arms crossed and a cowboy hat casting a shadow over his eyes.

He seemed to tower over the vehicle like a movie villain ready to take down his rival.

She tried to open the window so she could talk to him from the relative safety of the car but realized that a car that wouldn't move was also a car whose windows wouldn't open. It was also growing hotter by the second. For all intents and purposes, Delaney was sitting inside a slowly heating oven, which meant she had no choice but to open the door and get out.

She stood, brushing nonexistent dust off her jeans, then mirrored Sam Callahan's stance, arms crossed and everything.

"Ms. Harper," he said with a nod.

"Mr. Callahan," she said coolly, nodding back. "How'd you know I was here?"

He glanced back toward the guest quarters, which were easily visible from the road.

"Heard your car give up on you. Heck, everyone did. All that sputtering spooked the horses. It's lucky Ben was done giving his lesson or we mighta had an emergency on our hands."

Delaney threw her hands in the air. "Does this not look like an emergency? Not that it matters because Meadow Valley is not dealing with any emergencies until sometime by the end of the day a week from Monday. *Monday*!"

Sam cleared his throat. "County sheriff and deputies are on call the whole time. So's the fire department. All our firefighters are trained EMTs. You got an emergency that needs policing or medical attention?"

She squinted into the sun, trying to gauge his

shuttered expression. But it looked like he was biting back a grin.

"I suppose you think this is funny? The big bad landowner comes back to claim what's hers and gets stranded on the side of the road in an October heat wave."

He scratched the back of his neck. "It's not *un*funny."

She gritted her teeth and fought the urge to scream.

"Look," he said, "I got a towing hitch and trailer I can put on the back of my truck. I can take you and your car to Pearl's inn—I'm assuming you have a reservation at the most popular and *only* place to stay in the center of town—and someone from the shop will come grab it next Monday morning."

Delaney winced. "Reservation?"

Sam nodded. "Meadow Valley Harvest Festival, remember? It's the biggest thing next to the Fourth of July. Lots of family reunions. Inn fills up real fast. We got a little bit of their overflow, but most people here for the festival like to stay in town. We're a bit off the beaten path."

She glanced back at the car, then at Sam again. "It cools off at night, doesn't it? I can just recline the seat and—"

"You're kidding, right?" he interrupted. "You're not actually considering sleeping in your car."

She shrugged. "Look, I wasn't planning on being in town overnight. So, no, I didn't make any sort of reservation. Not like I can really afford it anyway, so if you don't mind, the car will suit me just fine."

Sam rolled his eyes. "Will you just get in the truck?"

"Where are you taking me?" She didn't like being at this guy's mercy. She didn't like being at anyone's mercy. All she wanted was to stand on her own two feet, and she'd been trying to do that for years now. She thought coming back to Meadow Valley was the answer, but it wasn't that easy. Now here was this big bad cowboy who'd built his business on *her* land thinking he could swoop in and save the day.

"I've got an empty room in the guest quarters," he said. "You can stay there until next week when you either get this thing fixed or put it to rest for good."

She opened her mouth to protest, but he cut her off.

"No charge, of course. Think what you want of me, Vegas, but I'm not leaving you stranded. Especially if that land is half yours like you say it is."

She narrowed her eyes. "It *is*."

He shrugged. "Well then, looks like I have some time to convince you to let me buy you out. Seeing as how you're in financial straits, it seems to be a win-win for both of us."

Delaney jutted out her chin. "Thank you, but I don't take handouts. I'll stay at the ranch, but you'll let me earn my keep. Whatever needs doing, I'll do it. And my financial *straits* are none of your business. Once my land is officially *my* land again, I'll get back on my feet. So there will be no need to convince me of anything. I'm sure your little business can survive on half the land."

She grabbed her phone, purse, and keys from the car and sauntered off toward his truck, not waiting for a response. Sam seemed like a nice enough guy. But they were on opposite sides of the property line, so to speak. She didn't want to argue with him, especially since he wasn't the one she was angry with.

Only when she was sure he couldn't see her face anymore did she blow out a long, shaky breath.

She could do this. It wasn't like she was looking to

steal Sam's business from him. She was just looking to get hers back.

She yanked on the door handle and hopped inside the silver Ford truck. It was still running, and the air conditioner poured out from the vents in heavenly gusts. She couldn't help the small moan that escaped her lips or the smile that spread across her face. Growing up in the desert, she was no stranger to the heat. But she'd always hated it. She'd begged her parents year after year to take her and her sister somewhere cold for a family vacation. But it was always the same excuse.

"If we shut down the motel, we shut down our income, and you know we can't afford to do that," her father had said every time she asked. So vacations were relegated to an overnight stay at the Bellagio when they could scrape together enough money to check out the competition—a quick trip to the Grand Canyon or the Hoover Dam when they couldn't. Wade had promised her a honeymoon in Colorado, replete with ski lessons, as soon as they had enough money. But she learned early on that "enough" meant poker funds or Wade's next no-fail business venture that always failed, and soon, *enough* equaled *in debt*. So here she was, twenty-nine years old, and she'd still never seen snow.

"You all right there, Vegas?" Sam asked, sliding into the driver's seat.

She pointed toward his door. "Close it. You're letting all the beautiful cold air out."

He chuckled. "And you expect me to believe you were going to spend the night in your car? I doubt you'd have lasted five minutes, let alone more than a week out there. No air, no plumbing, no change of clothes?"

She crossed her arms. "Just because I like cool air doesn't mean I can't rough it when necessary."

He threw his hat in the back seat of the cab, put on a pair of aviators, and set the truck into gear, pulling onto the road and around her stranded vehicle.

"Wait!" she cried. "What about towing my car?"

He shook his head. "I said I *had* the gear. Not that it was hitched and ready to go. Plus, it's hot as hell right now. Figure I'll wait until dusk and then come back." He cleared his throat, but it sounded very much like a stifled laugh. "I don't think you have to worry about anyone stealing it."

She blew out a breath. He had her there. Mildred—or Millie for short—was the affectionate name she'd given the red Honda Civic when she'd bought it used eleven years ago. She saved every tip she'd earned working nights and weekends all throughout high school and while she'd commuted to Pima Medical Institute, where she earned her associate degree as a veterinary technician. Millie—named for the mutt her family rescued from a kill shelter when Delaney and her sister Beth were kids— was the one thing she truly owned, and now she was just a heap of metal on the side of the road, left to bake in the blistering sun.

"Fair enough," she finally said. "But I don't want to leave her—I mean it—too long."

The corner of his mouth twitched. "That old beater has a name, doesn't it? Or should I say *she*?"

"She might," Delaney admitted. "It's Millie."

He nodded and then gave his dashboard an affectionate pat. "Revolver here hasn't let me down yet." He paused, and when she didn't say anything to the not-so-obvious Beatles reference, he added, "Your car's in good hands—at the ranch and when the shop opens up after the festival."

Her shoulders relaxed. She and Sam were in opposition when it came to the piece of land they both wanted, but she guessed that didn't mean they were enemies.

He pulled back up the main drive of the guest ranch but passed the cabin where they'd first met, rolling to a stop in front of a stable instead.

"Come on," he said, pulling the key from the ignition. He grabbed his cattleman out of the back seat and set it on his head.

Her brow furrowed. "Where are we going?"

He took off his sunglasses. Finally, after all this time playing it straight, he grinned, and holy hell, was he that good looking when they'd met? His chocolate-brown eyes darkened with mischief, and his teeth—straight and white—had the tiniest gap between the front two. She liked perfect little imperfections like that. They gave a person character. It was what drew her to Wade—his crooked smile and asymmetrical nose. She should have seen the red flag when he'd told her his nose had been broken one too many times to be properly set. She'd eventually seen firsthand what a broken nose looked like when Wade couldn't pay one of his "associates" back for the money he'd lost.

The line of Sam's nose was nice and straight. That alone told her he wasn't the type of guy other men messed with.

"Look," he said. "I have empty rooms to spare. Rooms with thermostats that you can make as cold as you want. Why don't you get situated, rest, do whatever needs doing after that overnight drive? It's really no trouble."

She shook her head. She wasn't going to take advantage

of his hospitality or—or let him be so nice to her. She was on a mission, and she was going to show him that she was up to the task, even if the thought of diving headfirst onto a fluffy pillow in an air-conditioned room did sound heavenly.

"Put me to work," she insisted. Ugh. Why did she have to be so stubborn?

He sighed. "Suit yourself, but don't say I didn't offer."

All the tension that had left her body on the short ride over came back as he led her into the stable and straight to a wall where a large pair of dirty overalls hung on a hook. He pulled them down and tossed them to her. She coughed as she caught them, a puff of dust invading her air space.

"Huh," he mused. "We should probably wash those sometime this month."

Delaney's eyes widened. *This month?*

"We've got five horses. They're all outside enjoying the warm weather, so it's the best time to muck out the stalls. Pitchfork is hanging against the side of the first stall. Gloves and wheelbarrow are over there." He pointed over her shoulder. "Make sure you really scrape under the shavings to get rid of anything that's wet. I'll let one of our stable boys take care of the wheelbarrow and add fresh bedding after the stalls are dry. I'll even send someone over with a thermos full of ice water. I hear mucking is thirsty work."

She stared at him for several long seconds, but he said nothing. He was serious. And she had no one to blame but herself. This was what she'd asked for.

Fine. No big deal. When she did her clinical at a Vegas petting zoo, she did everything from grooming llamas to catheterizing a goat with a urinary obstruction. Hell, she grew up taking care of the family's two dogs and three cats. This was nothing. A horse stall was nothing more than a giant litter box. A giant, foul-smelling, filled-with-larger-than-cat-sized-waste litter box.

She dropped her bag on the ground, raised her brows, and wriggled into the overalls. She grabbed the gloves from where they hung and put those on too. She should have been exhausted, but she was riding on adrenaline now.

"Anything else, Mr. Callahan?"

He shrugged and was gentleman enough to hand her the pitchfork. It took everything in her not to growl in response, even if said growl would have been meant for *her* and not him. Instead she smiled pleasantly.

"Thank you for your generous hospitality."

He winked. "You're welcome, Vegas. Happy mucking." He sauntered out the stable door. When Delaney heard the roar of his truck's engine and was sure he was out of earshot, she gritted her teeth and finally let loose a guttural sound that would have raised a cat's haunches or sent a pit bull to cower in a corner.

Pitchfork in hand, she pushed open the first stall door and winced at the mess inside.

What Sam Callahan didn't realize was that Delaney's spirit had already been broken by one man too many. He didn't have that kind of power over her. She'd muck his stalls and take whatever else he threw at her, but she wasn't backing down. She'd come for what was hers, and she wasn't going anywhere until she got it back.

CHAPTER THREE

S am spent the rest of the morning calling anyone in town who might know where Wade Harper had run off to. He didn't get very far, especially because he didn't need the whole town knowing that Wade's ex was here trying to contest the sale of the land he, Ben, and Colt thought they owned. The last thing he wanted was his business partners finding out the ranch was at risk for more than just getting the books into the black.

He'd never met Wade Harper and already disliked him not only for putting him in this precarious situation but also for leaving his ex-wife high and dry. No one deserved to be cheated out of what was rightfully theirs. But if he could convince her how hard they all worked to keep the ranch afloat, she'd give up her claim. Wouldn't she?

He drove over to the stable at half past one o'clock. Delaney was sitting on the bench outside the structure with the bib of her overalls hanging open onto her lap as she drank ferociously from the thermos he'd sneaked inside and set down by her bag when she was deep into mucking.

Tendrils of hair had loosened from her bun, and they were dark with sweat. Her cheeks were pink.

He stepped through the stable door, taking a peek inside.

"Finished a half hour ago," she called after him.

He gave the first couple of stalls a quick glance, then headed back outside.

He tilted the brim of his hat over his eyes, attempting to hide his surprise. The stable boy who lucked out with a morning off would have taken twice as long. Sam needed to start either paying him less or giving him more to do on the days he was here.

"Why didn't you tell me?" he asked, hoping he looked unfazed.

She set the thermos down next to her and crossed her arms. "You sorta left me stranded. And it's not like I knew where you were or how to get a hold of you. So I waited."

Damn. He wanted her to see what it took to run a ranch, but he hadn't meant to abandon her.

"You hungry?" he asked. Then he remembered she'd driven through the night. "Or tired? Guess I could have at least given you a room key before putting you to work—which you insisted I do, by the way."

She shrugged. "I'm a big girl. I can ask for what I need when I need it. When I want to sleep, I'll sleep. Right now I'm starved," she admitted. "And downright dirty. Speaking of things I need, I'd say a shower is top of the list."

He scratched the back of his neck. He had a room ready

for her but sort of forgot she'd need to eat, and Luis was already cleaning up the kitchen since lunch only ran until one p.m. "I'll take you to your room. Then, um, you can swing by the dining hall, and we'll find you something to eat." The truth was, he'd been so intent on finding information about Wade Harper's whereabouts that he'd forgotten to eat too.

She stood, slid the rest of the way out of the overalls, and then pressed both the overworn garment and the thermos against his chest. "Thanks, boss."

He clenched his teeth. Something about that word rankled. It brought back memories of his father's long-winded speeches about being a self-made man, his own boss, someone who called all the shots. He'd worked his way through college and had gone on to study veterinary medicine. Soon he was one of the most sought-after equine vets and breeders in San Luis Obispo County, which often meant travel to other farms and ranches. But to Nolan Callahan, calling the shots had meant mistresses on business-related trips and his wife leaving to find a new man and a new life.

For years now, ever since his father's mental health had started to deteriorate, Sam had been his own boss. He answered to no one but himself—and his brother and Colt. But they were equals. Even when it came to his actual employees, he insisted they only ever call him by his first name. His brother was the only one at the ranch related by blood, but to Sam everyone here was his family, which meant no one took liberties that exploited anyone else.

"You don't need to call me that, you know," he said coolly, wrapping an arm around the thermos and the denim that was much in need of a wash.

Delaney shrugged. "And you don't need to call me Vegas, but you do."

She had him there. "How about I just call you Harper?" he asked.

Her brow furrowed. "How about Delaney?"

First names were personal, and he wasn't getting anywhere near personal with the woman who wanted half his land—half of what he'd built from the ground up with his bare hands.

"Harper it is," he said, and nodded toward his truck. "Shall we?"

She rolled her eyes. "Lead the way...Callahan."

Satisfied, he strode to the driver's side of the truck and she to the passenger door. They both climbed wordlessly into the cab of the truck. He traded the hat for his sunglasses again, then slid the key into the ignition and immediately lowered the windows.

"I know you prefer the air-conditioning—" he started, but Delaney interrupted.

"Yeah, no. I stink." She snorted, then laughed—the sound so light and carefree that he couldn't help but smile.

"You really do," he said as he pulled away from the stable and onto the small inner road that wound through the property. "But...you did a damn good job. So, thanks for that."

She gave him a self-satisfied grin and crossed her arms. "You're welcome." Then, after several moments of silence, she added, "And thank *you*. For giving me a place to stay until I can get my car fixed."

And until she could pull the rug out from under him. He had to remind himself that no matter how sexy he found her bare shoulders or her infectious laugh, she was here to take what he thought had been his since he signed away his life to the bank.

He cleared his throat. "It's just business, Harper." He pulled to a stop in front of the guest quarters, where a bedroom had been cleaned and prepared for their *business* transaction. He'd purposely built the registration cabin separate from where the guests stayed so the main office was centrally located among the stable, arena, dining hall, and guest quarters. Now he sort of regretted leaving her here and heading back to the office, which made zero sense. She was going to shower. She certainly didn't want him around for that.

Sam handed her a key card from the center console. "Here you go. Room 210. Head up the stairs. Make a right, and it's at the end of the hall. Dining cabin is the building next door. Head on over when you're ready. I...um...had Ivy run you over something to wear." He'd at least had the forethought to realize she would want nothing to do with her clothes after mucking out the stalls.

She narrowed her eyes. "Ivy? Is she your—"

"No," he said, cutting her off. He and Ivy weren't a thing. She was engaged to Carter Bowen, a lieutenant at the fire station who moonlighted at the ranch leading trail rides. Sam wasn't a thing with anyone because serious relationships weren't his *thing*. Not when his future was so uncertain. He didn't see the point of getting close to someone he'd likely push away.

"Ivy's a friend. She owns a small boutique thingy in town. She dropped by with a few donations off her sale rack. But even her sale stuff is good. I mean that's what I hear. I don't have much occasion to go shopping for women's clothing." He rolled his eyes at himself, grateful for the mask of his sunglasses. *I don't have much occasion to go shopping for women's clothing?* Why was he fumbling for words around her?

Delaney raised her brows. "You know, there's nothing wrong if you wanted to trade your plaid or flannel for something that feels a little softer against the skin." She snatched the key card from between his fingers. "Tell Ivy I said thanks. I'll meet you for some food in about thirty minutes."

She hopped out of the truck and sauntered toward the guest cabin's main entrance. His gaze followed her, trained on her like a magnet to the nearest piece of metal. He told himself it was because he was examining her motive—trying to figure her out. But even his silent thoughts knew he was full of shit. Every part of his being filled with an inexplicable heat as he watched her walk away, her hips swaying and that damned top riding up again to expose her lower back.

He shook his head, then let out a mirthless laugh.

Things weren't any easier before he'd left Oak Bluff. Back then he and Ben were their father's main caretakers while they worked to both sell the family business and start Callahan Contracting. Somehow, Ben had always found room for a social life. Maybe that was because Sam was there to hold down the fort whether he wanted to be or not.

Some things never changed, which meant Sam had no business feeling any sort of physical stirrings for *any* woman, let alone Delaney Harper.

He stopped back by his office where Scout was now taking her afternoon nap.

"Hey, girl," he whispered, and her ears perked up before she opened her eyes. "You want to go for a walk?"

She was up on all fours, tail wagging and tongue hanging out of her mouth, before he could grab her leash and clip it to her collar. Once she was all hooked up, she tugged him toward the door.

He laughed.

This—him and his dog, a walk on the ranch, and fall festival underway—this was all he needed. And maybe a few more bookings in the guest quarters. What he didn't need was for him, his brother, and his friend to be wrapped up in some sort of scandal that could cost them everything. And he certainly didn't need Delaney Harper threatening to tear his livelihood in two, even if her ex-husband was the one to blame.

"Just you, girl," he said as Scout pulled him along. "You, a stable full of horses, and money in the bank so we can do it all again tomorrow." A simple life with no complications.

After their walk, he dropped Scout back at his office where she curled up in the sun once more. *She* certainly got what he meant about simple.

He left her there and strode to the back of the dining cabin and entered the door that opened straight into the kitchen.

Luis sat on a stool at the counter, pounding away at his laptop.

"Are we breaking even yet?" Sam asked his chef, knowing the man was likely balancing the kitchen books like he did after every meal.

Luis shook his head slowly before looking up. "It's only been a couple of months. It's still too early to tell. But maybe I should cut back next week. At the rate we're going, I'll have to toss more produce than I'll use—though you know that'll piss Anna off if we cut the order in half."

Sam felt the tension start in his shoulders and quickly move to the back of his neck. He was so sure that with the Meadow Valley Inn selling out for the festival, the ranch would get much of the overflow. The rooms were ready. He'd already committed to paying their two stable hands overtime for working during the festival, yet now it looked as if it'd be business as usual, which meant he, Ben, and Colt could have handled it on their own—even if Ben disappeared for an overnight rendezvous or two.

"Half?" he said. "It's that bad?"

Luis winced. "I'm already going to have to freeze some of the meat and poultry, and you know how I like my kitchen to be fresh and never frozen."

Fresh versus frozen was the least of his worries right now.

All the contracting work in Oak Bluff came via word-of-mouth. He'd never needed to advertise his services because everyone knew the Callahan brothers would get the job done. But he wasn't catering to just the locals anymore, and he wasn't sure how else to get customers through the door other than a fancy website—which had set them back a few grand—and hopefully some long-distance referrals. He hadn't expected it to be easy, but he certainly hadn't banked on it being this hard.

"Skim a quarter off all your next orders, and we'll take it from there," Sam said.

"Only a quarter?" Luis protested, but before he could get another word out of his mouth, he was cut off by the sound of a woman's voice coming from the dining room.

"Hello?" she called out. "Sam?"

Luis's brows rose, and his worried expression morphed into a grin.

"You got a lady friend out there, boss man?" Luis teased.

Sam groaned. "You know I hate that word."

"*Lady friend*?" Luis asked, his smile growing wider. "I don't remember you saying anything about *lady friend*. Also don't remember you having one, but that's beside the point."

Sam started toward the swinging doors that led to the dining room, but Luis was off his stool, breaking into a near sprint before Sam had the chance to pick up his own pace.

Luis didn't push through the doors. Instead he peered through the slats, squinting. Seconds later he turned to Sam, his mouth hanging open.

"She's here to see *you*?" Luis asked.

Sam rolled his eyes. "Why is that so hard to believe?" And why was he getting defensive? Delaney wasn't here to see him in *that* capacity, but he didn't think it would be so hard to fathom if she was.

"Because no woman is ever here to see *you*," Luis reminded him. "Not that I'm assuming your heterosexuality or anything, but no guy has ever come looking for you either."

Good lord. What was he thinking moving from one small town to an even smaller one? He'd thought living a few miles outside would give him some semblance of privacy, but that was obviously a crock.

"She's a business acquaintance," Sam said. "Helping out at the ranch while she's here."

Luis's smile fell. "I need to cut one quarter off my produce order, but you got extra cash for this—*acquaintance*—of yours?"

"I'm not paying her anything other than room and

board, and right now I need to feed her, so tell me what I can use."

Luis narrowed his eyes. "Are you sure this is just business? Because in the food world, making a meal for someone is a very intimate gesture. It's almost as sensual as sex."

"You make food for people three times a day," Sam said. "Does that mean you're having intimate relations with all our patrons?"

Luis doubled over laughing, and Sam took that as an opportunity to nudge him out of the way of the swinging doors. "Just leave me something I can fix her and myself for lunch, okay?"

Luis was still laughing when Sam pushed through the doors to find Delaney brushing her hand along the knotty pine of a rocking chair in front of the unlit fireplace.

He strode up behind her. "A friend of mine from back home made that," he said, and she spun to face him, hands behind her back as if she were a child who'd gotten caught with her hand in the cookie jar.

"You snuck up on me," she said. "Figured you were the one laughing his ass off back there." Luis was still at it. "Guess I was wrong."

Her hair was damp, resting on the shoulders of a flowy white top that hung just below the button of a pair of frayed denim shorts that had flowers sewn into the material—Ivy's design signature. A pink sheen covered her full lips, and where there had once been an old pair of tennis shoes, there was now a pair of honest-to-goodness cowboy boots, brown with white stitching.

"You look...clean," he said, immediately wanting

to kick his own ass for his lack of complimentary vocabulary.

She smoothed out her top even though he didn't see any wrinkles. "Not too shabby when I don't smell like the inside of a stable, huh?"

From behind the doors, Luis—who'd gone quiet for several seconds—burst out laughing again.

Sam's jaw tightened, but he forced a smile. "Don't mind him," he said, loud enough for Luis to hear. "He was just leaving, because I'm sure as hell not paying him overtime to eavesdrop."

"I'm salaried!" Luis called back. Then the laughter faded into the distance, which Sam hoped meant he had the kitchen to himself.

He scrubbed a hand across his jaw. "Sorry about that. Luis—our chef—has a hard time keeping his nose out of other people's business. But he's heading out for his own lunch break now." He called out the last sentence toward the kitchen and got no response.

"Wait a second," Delaney said. "You had me meet you here for lunch but sent your chef home?"

He raised a brow. "What's the matter? You think I don't know my way around a kitchen?"

Delaney shrugged. "I guess we're about to find out, aren't we?"

"After you," Sam said, gesturing toward the swinging doors and hoping to hell Luis left him something easy enough to work with. He wasn't at a complete loss when it came to food, but he was by no means a professional either.

He followed her in and let out a sigh of relief when he saw a loaf of bread and a block of cheddar cheese sitting on the steel prep island next to a bowl of apples. He brushed past Delaney to survey the ingredients closer and found a sticky note atop the sourdough's plastic bakery bag.

> *Slice up a Honeycrisp nice and thin and layer*
> *between the extra-sharp cheddar. You'll thank*
> *me!* —Luis

"What's that?" Delaney asked over his shoulder.

Startled, he snatched the note and crumpled it into his palm.

"Nothing," he said. "Just Luis letting me know he doesn't need this stuff for dinner prep. It's all ours."

He spun to face her, loaf of sourdough in hand.

"You want to cut the bread, and I'll do the apples and cheese?" he asked.

She took the bread willingly. "*Apples*? Knows his way around a kitchen *and* is a bit of a gourmet with the grilled cheese, huh?"

The corner of his mouth quirked up. "I haven't fired up the griddle yet. There's still time to burn the cheese."

"Mmm," she said, her eyes fluttering shut. The sound was almost sensual, and Luis's stupid words about cooking and intimacy flooded his brain, making it hard to think straight. "I *love* when the cheese burns against the crust."

He cleared his throat, and her eyes shot open. "Sorry," she said. "I'm just really hungry, and grilled cheese is one of my favorites. My empty belly kind of got the better of me."

He pulled two cutting boards from the shelf under the island and two large knives from a drawer. Wordlessly the two stood side by side, slicing.

It was quiet. *Too* quiet. He could hear the soft sound of her breath as she exhaled.

"Music!" he blurted, pointing his knife at her, and Delaney practically threw hers across the island. Before he had time to say anything else, her hands clenched into fists. One slammed into his wrist while the other careened toward his face. Thanks to expert reflexes, though, he pivoted out of the way just in time so that her fist connected with nothing but air.

"What the hell was that?" he asked.

Her chest heaved as she inhaled and exhaled. "Me? What about you? Are you insane?" she asked. "You don't yell at someone while they're operating extremely sharp cutlery! And—and you don't *point* extremely sharp cutlery at those who are operating said tools."

She lowered both of her hands, and he scanned them, making sure all fingers were present and accounted for. Then, feeling like an idiot, he slowly lowered his own knife.

"I'm sorry," he said. "I wasn't thinking. Just thought we could cut the tension with a little music."

"What tension?" she asked, arms crossed. "We're making lunch."

He nodded to where her knife lay across the island, the blade teetering over the edge.

"That was a little *in*tense, if you ask me. You almost clocked me in the jaw." He raised his brows. "*Almost.*"

Delaney exhaled. "How'd you know I was gonna hit you? Not that I *wanted* to, by the way. Knee-jerk reaction."

He chuckled. "The fist headed for my face was a pretty good clue."

This time she groaned. "I meant your reflexes. Why

wasn't I fast enough? Not that I'm sorry I missed—I mean, now that it's clear I may have overreacted."

He shrugged. "Our firefighter-paramedics work long shifts, especially with no hospital in town. I think they spend more time providing ambulance services than they do putting out fires."

She nodded. "I know. I used to live here." She let out a bitter laugh. "Ambulance had to come pick up Wade once when he couldn't pay up on a *friendly* loan." She made air quotes around the word *friendly*.

"Does that have something to do with that knee-jerk reaction of yours?" he asked warily.

"No," she said. "Maybe. You're changing the subject. I was asking about *you*, remember?"

Yeah. He remembered. He also remembered using the same sort of evasion a time or two when he didn't want to talk about himself. Funny how he didn't feel the need to use it now.

"Right. So the firehouse... They put together a little gym out back, even built a boxing ring." He shrugged. "I never fought for sport but have trained for years for fun. Sometimes the guys let me spar with them." It was only then that something clicked into place. His reflexes were good, but she almost had him. That was no amateur left hook she threw at him.

"You've trained, too, haven't you? Delaney, did Wade ever—"

"No." She cut him off. "He stole my money, but he never raised a hand to me. Some of the jerks who came after him, though... I learned real quick that the only person who was going to protect me was me."

He got that, but her determination didn't hide the tremor in her voice. It didn't stop him from finishing the thought in his head. *Did Wade ever hurt you?* Simply thinking the words brought on a fierce desire to be the one who protected her from even the possibility of something like that happening.

He cleared his throat. "What about your family back in Vegas?"

"Why all these questions about me? What about you? Don't you have enough around here to do for fun?"

Aah, the masterful art of misdirection—not just a boxing technique. He was well versed in it both inside and outside the ring.

"You first," he said, buying himself some more time.

She sighed. "My parents work seven days a week. And they've been protecting me long enough. I have a younger sister, Beth. And she sometimes still needs my protecting, though not the physical kind. It's more about making good life decisions."

"So you want to fix her," Sam said.

Delaney scoffed. "*No.* Sometimes people need a little help figuring out their path. There's nothing wrong with that, especially when it comes to family."

Or ex-husbands. He felt like a jerk just for thinking it, but she'd said it herself. She couldn't fix Wade. He knew the type. His mom was a fixer and couldn't fix his father, so she left. He never wanted to be anyone's "project" other than his own.

"Hey," she said, snapping him out of his thoughts. "Your turn."

She wasn't letting him off the hook. "I have a lot on my mind." The muscles in his neck and shoulders tensed. "Sometimes I need something a little more cathartic than a trail ride or toasting marshmallows around a bonfire."

Ben and Colt didn't even know how he spent the occasional night off. As long as it didn't interfere with the ranch, they didn't bother one another about what they did with their time away. Ben was still working on the whole not-interfering-with-the-ranch part, but he and Colt seemed to have it under control.

"Fair enough." She pulled her phone out of the back pocket of her denim shorts. "You want music? Fine. But I get to pick."

She fired up a playlist that started with Eminem's "Lose Yourself."

He stifled a laugh, guessing this was likely some sort of workout playlist. He had a similar one.

She retrieved her knife from the opposite end of the island and went back to work slicing the bread.

"Maybe while I'm stuck here—" she started, but he jumped in before she could finish.

"Oh no you don't, Vegas. While you're stuck here, you're working off your free room and board, remember? Besides, my time in the ring is *my* time in the ring, and I'm not about to . . . to share my time in the ring."

Her nostrils flared and she slid the stack of sliced sourdough in his direction.

"And I'm not about to share my land, so I guess we're at a standstill, aren't we?"

He gritted his teeth. Minutes ago he was this close to taking her in his arms and telling her everything would be all right. Lucky for him, she reminded them both why she was here.

After that, he let the music fill the space between them—everything from Slim Shady to Pistol Annies. He slathered butter on one side of each slice of bread and pieced the sandwiches together while the griddle heated.

Then, spatula in hand, he made what he thought looked like the best damned grilled cheese he'd ever cooked. But their taste buds would be the judge of that.

He plated and sliced each of the two masterpieces in half, gooey extra-sharp cheddar mixed with Honeycrisp apple spilling like lava from the center. He retrieved a pitcher of iced tea from the beverage cooler and poured them each a glass. Then he took the liberty of tapping the pause icon on her phone, the sudden absence of music tossing them into an abrupt silence.

He cleared his throat. "Eat up. You'll need your strength."

She rolled her eyes. "Let me guess. More earning my keep?"

He nodded. "Checking out a possible new trail this afternoon. One that supposedly ends at a swimming hole that I think our guests would like. Just gotta make sure the terrain is safe for all riders, regardless of skill level. How are you on a horse?"

"I can hold my own," she said, then sank her teeth into her sandwich. "Oh mah Gah."

Her words didn't come out quite right with the food in her mouth, but it was enough for Sam to know he'd exceeded her expectations as far as his kitchen competence was concerned.

"And to think you doubted my abilities," he bragged, unable to suppress a self-satisfied grin. Then he bit into his sandwich and had to keep himself from moaning with pleasure. "Damn," he said under his breath after he swallowed. "Luis better not mess up our professional relationship with Anna."

"Who's Anna?" Delaney asked. "I mean, not that I care about any women you know. I'm just curious. Making conversation. Since we have to sit here and eat."

Sam's brow furrowed, and she took a larger bite than her first, effectively shutting down her ability to say any more.

"Anna's farm supplies the dining hall with pretty much all our dairy and produce. And Luis—my chef and the laughing eavesdropper from before—has a thing for her."

She nodded. "And I'm guessing you're a no-fraternizing-in-the-workplace kind of guy? Even though, if you want to get technical about it, she doesn't exactly work for you."

Sam brandished his almost-devoured half sandwich. "Everything you're eating right now—except for the bread—is Anna's. The butter, the cheese, the damned Honeycrisp apples? All hers. If the next kitchen emergency text I get from Luis is the one where he tells me he messed this up—"

Delaney snatched the sandwich from his hand, tore off a chunk between her thumb and forefinger, and shoved it into his open mouth. Her fingers lingered on his bottom lip, and her eyes grew wide with something like confusion or surprise or a mix of the two until he finally closed his mouth, and she snatched her fingers away.

"Sorry," she said. "But there was this vein in your forehead that was sort of pulsing, and—do you ever just take a few seconds to relax?"

No, he didn't relax. This place—the ranch—it was his life. It occupied his waking hours, and he dreamed about running the place when he slept. Nothing else mattered. Because the second he stopped moving full steam ahead, he'd be alone with his thoughts, and that was not something he enjoyed.

He chewed his food, then swallowed. "I'll tell you

what," he said coolly. "You find me an extra few seconds in the day, and I'll do just that. Until then"—he snagged what was left of his lunch in one hand, picked up his iced tea with the other, and downed the whole glass—"we got work to do. Grab whatever you need for the trail ride and meet me at the stable in thirty. I should warn you though. No air-conditioning on the back of a horse."

She narrowed her eyes at him. "I told you I can rough it, Callahan. So you're going to have to find another way to break me if that's what you're trying to do."

Break her? No. He wasn't a jerk, even if his brother and Colt tended to disagree. She asked for him to put her to work, so he had. Maybe he came on too strong, but he just wanted her to see it all—what they'd built from nothing—and convince her to change her mind. Maybe she'd let him buy her out in interest-free installments so he didn't have to get the bank involved.

"Just helping you earn your keep, Harper." He winked at her. "See ya in thirty."

He strode out the kitchen's back door, sandwich still in hand, and took another bite. But it didn't matter how good the thing tasted—and it was damned good. He couldn't shake the memory of her fingers resting on his lip or the heat that passed from her skin to his.

Forget air-conditioning. After helping his new guest earn her keep, Sam Callahan was going to need one heck of a cold shower.

CHAPTER FOUR

So much for washing herself clean from the stable. Delaney was spending the rest of the afternoon on the back of a horse. In the heat. With Sam Callahan likely making her hop off her saddle to clean up after their trusty steeds along the way.

Luckily, Ivy had also sent over a pair of jeans in her generous donation, so Delaney didn't have to put her dirty ones back on. Delaney wasn't sure what Sam had told her, but they fit better than the ones she owned. There was a plain white ribbed tank and a gray hooded sweatshirt in with the lot of clothes, so she changed out of her nice top and into the tank, tying the hoodie around her waist. It was almost as if Sam had given Ivy a list of what they'd be doing today, and she had pulled the perfect clothes to match. Why was he being so considerate?

Delaney wrinkled her nose. Why did she even care? He was a high-strung, selfish jerk who cared only about getting her out of his hair as quickly as possible. He fed her only because it would have been overly cruel not to.

And he clothed her only because he probably couldn't stand to be near her in her stable clothes. And he was giving her a free place to stay because...

She groaned and dropped onto the foot of the queen-sized bed.

She couldn't make Sam Callahan out to be the bad guy no matter how hard she tried, even after he made her muck out the filthy stable. She'd challenged him to put her to work, and he'd simply complied. Maybe he wasn't the worst guy after all.

Who was she kidding? She'd *married* the worst guy. Sam Callahan was just protecting what was his. She couldn't fault him for that. Not until the courthouse opened, anyway. Maybe they could call a truce until then. Otherwise it was going to be one hell of a long weekend.

She dumped her bag out onto the bed. She didn't want to carry anything she wouldn't need on the trail. Her wallet weighed a ton, thanks to her never getting rid of loose change. She wouldn't need that on the ride. Her hairbrush and the stack of folded mortgage documents she hoped would prove she still owned the property when Wade sold it.

She was about to set her phone aside when it rang with an unfamiliar number. She stared at the screen, waiting to see if the call went to voicemail so she could listen to which telemarketer was scamming her today and then block yet another number.

The ringing stopped, and she waited several seconds for the voicemail notification. But it didn't come—not until at least thirty seconds more had passed, and she'd set the phone on the don't-need-it-on-the-trail pile.

She picked it back up and pressed Play.

"Hey there, sunshine."

She gasped at the sound of Wade's voice.

"Imagine my surprise when I saw that you called and didn't leave a message. That hurts, darlin'. Thought maybe you'd finally come to your senses and wanted to give it another go. Even popped into your parents' place to let you know how much I'd like that to happen, what do you know? They said you'd skipped town. Where'd you go, sunshine? I may be real good at not being found, but I can always find my way back to you, can't I? This is my new number. How about we catch up soon?"

Delaney's hand shook as she stared at the screen.

She hadn't given herself time enough to think or wonder if Wade would be here when she got to town. She hadn't even considered there'd be a consequence to calling him. All she'd cared about was her land and doing what she had to do to get it back. She had figured she would deal with Wade when she got here, and she was relieved to find he was long gone. Except now he wasn't.

She closed out of the call carefully, as if holding the phone the wrong way or pressing the wrong button would summon her ex-husband to her door, and scrolled through her contacts until she found her sister, then tapped the name.

Beth picked up after the first ring.

"Delaney? Oh my God. You'll never guess who was at the front desk looking for you."

Delaney cleared her throat. "Wade," she said flatly. "He just called. No one told him I'm back in Meadow Valley, did they?"

She wasn't afraid of Wade on his own. But she'd learned in the end that he was a package deal with the kind of trouble she wanted no part of, and she certainly didn't want to bring that trouble back to Meadow Valley.

"Mom said you went away for the weekend. Dad threatened to call the police on him if he didn't get the hell out, and I gave him the best stink-eye I could."

Delaney let out a breath. "Okay. Good. Look, I'm gonna be gone awhile straightening things out here. The whole town is shut down for this fall festival, and Millie broke down. But if all goes according to plan—"

"You're moving back to Small Town, USA, for good?"

She could hear the thinly masked disappointment in her sister's voice. Beth was two years younger than Delaney, and while they were close, they were miles apart as far as what they wanted out of life. Beth loved the glitz and glamour of the Vegas nightlife. A born performer, she worked days at the motel check-in desk and nights as a dancer in everything from magicians' acts to themed nightclubs. The only way she was leaving Sin City was if she landed a dancing gig on Broadway or as a backup performer for a recording artist. As much as Delaney urged her to at least get an associate's degree, to have something to fall back on if dancing didn't work out, Beth wouldn't hear it. She was the type of dreamer who shot for the stars.

All Delaney had ever wanted was her own piece of land, to be able to build and run an animal shelter, and a little bit of quiet away from city lights and oxygen-infused casinos. When she had found Meadow Valley, she was sure it was *the* place. But when leaving town was the only real way to leave her husband, it also meant putting her dream on hold until she had the finances to get it off the ground again. It had made sense *not* to sell when she'd left. They'd have made nothing back, possibly would have lost money on the sale. At least if they were splitting the profit, it would have been negligible.

But Wade selling it on his own? Looked like he'd done all right while she'd bided her time the past couple of years, working whatever motel shifts her parents couldn't fill, which often meant overnight. It meant living at home, socking away every penny, and waiting for the day when she could claim that dream again.

She didn't have the funds yet. Heck, she wasn't sure what she would do once the land was rightfully hers. All she knew was she was done sitting on the sidelines, waiting for life to do right by her.

"I don't know what I'm gonna do," she finally said. "But as long as Wade isn't here, I have a little bit of time to figure things out."

She heard her sister sigh. "Just be careful, okay, Lanes? I know you know Wade is bad news when you get your distance, but that man is a charmer. I don't want to see him charming his way back into your good graces just to screw you over again."

Delaney's jaw tightened. Maybe she'd been young and naive when she let him sweep her off her feet. But she was on solid ground now. Had been for the better part of the past couple of years. There was no way he was weaseling his way back into her life again.

"Thanks for your faith in me, sis," she said coolly. "But I came here to get back what he took from me and nothing more."

"*Lanes*," Beth said, and she could hear the regret in her sister's tone. "You know I think you're the strongest woman I know, but..."

But.

But she also couldn't blame Beth for the lack of trust. She *had* been strong. A straight-A student in high school, she'd won enough grants to put herself through her vet tech program for almost nothing. Wade asked *her* to pick any place on the map, not knowing she'd already researched and found the land for the shelter. It was big enough that they could rescue animals small and large. She'd envisioned dogs and cats as much as goats and sheep. She'd even found a local vet to donate his time. She and Wade contributed equally to the down payment, had bought the place together, and were supposed to build a happy life. That was the only reason she'd put up with his business ventures and lack of money management for as long as she did. She spent most of her life building up a dream in her head only to lose it as quickly as blinking.

"I know," she finally said, then swallowed the knot in her throat. "I gotta go. Call you in a few days, okay?"

She wasn't leaving Meadow Valley with her tail between her legs again.

"Love ya, Lanes," her sister said.

"Love ya, Beth."

She ended the call, deleted Wade's voicemail, and then hurriedly threw the few items she thought she'd need on the trail back into her bag. The faster she got out of this room, the better.

Sam was leaning against the stable door, arms crossed and hat tilted over his eyes so that all she could see was his stubbled jaw peeking out from the shadows. She knew cowboys were a real thing but never thought she'd run into one in Meadow Valley, let alone be just about ready to hop on the back of a horse and ride off into the sunset with him. Not that their sunset ride was going to be like some sort of Hollywood movie ending. It would be work. Another item added to the list of ways she'd earn her keep.

What about him cooking for her, though? He could

have handed her a loaf of bread and some peanut butter and jelly and called it a day. But he'd cooked for her, had shown concern for her when she'd nearly knocked his block off. And the clothes from Ivy? Sam Callahan was more than a rancher in a cowboy hat. He was a gentleman, chivalrous as a medieval knight in more ways than one—and completely at odds with her plan to take her land back. Still, she did enjoy the few seconds of fantasizing that he was some sort of romance hero.

Had she really thought she could turn Wade Harper into someone like that? Or had she simply been too young and naive and blinded by what could have been rather than what was? Either way, she had no one to blame but herself for her questionable judge of character and even more questionable willingness to put her trust in a man who was only ever going to break her heart.

"You ready?" he asked.

"As I'll ever be."

Sam shook his head.

She set her hands on her hips. "What now? Did I not clean the stalls to your liking? Got another task for me to complete before his highness steps onto his horse?"

She was well aware that he didn't deserve her outburst, but someone had to bear the brunt of her anger, fear, frustration—whatever it was—and it might as well be Sam Callahan. Wasn't as though she could stand in front of a mirror and yell at herself. Well, she could, but people might worry about her if she did.

He strode toward the bench and picked up a straw cowboy hat she hadn't noticed a few seconds ago. Then he approached her slowly, pausing when he was only inches from her.

"May I?" he asked, and something in that simple

gesture—asking for her permission—made her stomach flip.

She tucked her hair behind her ears and nodded.

He set the hat on top of her head. "By the way," he said, his deep voice sending tingles from head to toe, "I only shook my head at you because I can't figure you out. I'd have crashed face-first on my pillow about ten times already if I were you, but your battery doesn't seem to quit."

"Vegas is the real city that never sleeps," she said with a nervous laugh. "Guess I brought a little bit of home here with me. Also thanks for the hat," she added, realizing she'd left her sunglasses in her car.

Her car!

"Hey," she said, less venom in her tone. "You haven't forgotten about my car, have you?"

He grinned. "You mean ol' Millie? Already talked my buddy Colt into towing her for you. Turns out he has some spare time before dinner and offered to help."

She smiled warily. "And he knows what he's doing with your truck and the towing hitch and everything?"

Sam laughed. "He's the one who installed the hitch on the truck in the first place. Only thing the guy knows better than horses is cars." She opened her mouth to respond, but he cut her off. "And before you ask why I don't just have *him* fix your car, it's because any work Colt does on my truck or anyone else's vehicle, he does outta Meadow Valley Motors, which is—"

"Closed," she said, finishing his sentence. "I get it. Whole town's asleep until..." Something clicked together in her head, and she narrowed her eyes at him.

"What did I do now?" he asked, backing away from her glare.

"If the whole town is shut down for over a week, how'd you get Ivy to send over all these clothes?"

He shrugged. "I called in a favor."

"And you couldn't call in a favor to get my car fixed?"

He tilted the brim of his hat up so she could see his brown eyes darken and his jaw tighten. "Are you leaving town before the courthouse opens and you file a claim to get your land back?"

He had her there. "Well...no."

"Then I guess I'm about all out of favors. Let's go."

He turned on his heel and stalked back toward the stable door, disappearing inside.

Shoot. She'd actually hoped this afternoon might be a little fun. She hadn't been on the back of a horse in a while, but she loved riding. She'd done some volunteer hours with an equine veterinarian and had earned herself some free riding lessons from the owner of one of their patients.

But she and Sam were at odds again, and she knew she was the one who got them off on the wrong foot. Maybe this ridiculous attraction that so wasn't part of her plan wasn't one-sided. Maybe *he* was waging the same internal battle, which seemed to result in friction, keeping either one from being truly civil toward the other. She wondered if they could go more than a few minutes without running hot and cold on each other. Looked like they had a whole afternoon to find out.

She followed him inside a few moments later but found the stable as empty as it had been when she was cleaning it. Then she noticed a door on the opposite end was open to the fenced-in arena, so she headed back out into the sun to find Sam patting the flank of a gorgeous black-and-white-spotted horse. Tied to the fence next to them was a second horse, chocolate brown from head to toe, the color of Sam's eyes. The animal paced back and forth, seemingly impatient to get on the trail.

"Hey, girl," she said, approaching the brown mare and stroking a palm from her eyes to her nose.

The horse stopped moving and gave an approving whinny.

"How did you know it was a girl?" Sam asked.

She shrugged. "I'm a registered veterinary technician. Did one of my clinicals with horses. I can sense these things."

His brows raised. "Really?"

Delaney laughed. "Nah. Her tail went up when she was dancing back and forth. Saw all I needed to see."

Sam smiled and shook his head. "So what's a Vegas vet tech want in Meadow Valley—other than your land, of course?"

"Open my own animal rescue," she said. "That's what the land was for. "Had a vet lined up and everything. Before we left Las Vegas, Wade and I ran a crowdfunding campaign for initial donations to get the whole operation up and running. I was surprised at how successful it was, but I guess a lot of people have a soft spot for an animal in need of a home."

Sam went to work securing a couple of travel packs to the male horse.

"What happened?" he asked.

"Wade used the money for one of his no-fail business deals—that failed miserably. It was the last straw. I'd forgiven him for so much along the way. But he took my dream. So I finally left, used every penny I could scrape up to divorce him. So now you know why it's taking me some time to get back on my feet financially."

Sam came back around the horse to face her. He

lifted his hat, swiping the beads of sweat that dotted his forehead.

"I'm sorry, Delaney." His words were suffused with a sincerity she wasn't anticipating.

"Thank you," she said. "I appreciate that." She looked at her bag slung across her torso and suddenly felt under-prepared. "Should I have brought more than this?"

Sam laughed and shook his head. "We should only be gone a few hours. But a good trail leader always plans for the unexpected. Not that I'm expecting anything—unexpected."

He suddenly sounded flustered.

Her brows drew together. "That's why it's called unexpected. You don't expect it. Should I be worried about whether or not you know what you're doing, Sam Callahan?"

He patted the brown horse's nose. "Only thing you need to worry about is whether you and Barbara Ann can keep up with me and Ace. Do you ride as well as you identify a horse's gender?"

Delaney untied Barbara Ann's reins, hooked her boot in the stirrup, and hoisted herself into the saddle.

He raised his brows.

"Impressed?" she asked.

He nodded. "Every time I learn something new about you."

Heat crept up her neck. They needed to get moving before she started getting ideas about riding cowboys instead of horses.

"Lead the way, Callahan."

Sam walked Ace across the grass expanse of the arena to where the fence opened in the direction of the woods, and Delaney followed on Barbara Ann's back. The mare moved with an easy grace, and Delaney breathed a sigh of relief that she hadn't spooked the animal by climbing into the saddle without warning. Once outside the gate, Sam made sure it was closed securely, then climbed into Ace's saddle like it was as easy as breathing.

God he looked good up there, so sure of himself, so in control. Even when she pushed his buttons—and she'd been pushing them—he had this steadiness that did anything but steady her. Instead she felt off-kilter and out of sorts.

"You ready?" he asked, breaking into an ear-to-ear grin.

Her head swam, and her pulse quickened. *No.* That was the honest answer now. But it was too late to turn back. Plus, she was still earning her keep, wasn't she?

"You bet!" she replied with more enthusiasm than necessary. "Let's hit the trail."

Sam took the lead, which made sense since he was the one who knew where he was going. But that left her with a perfect view of what she realized was a pretty perfect cowboy butt sitting perfectly in well-worn jeans atop Ace's saddle.

"Hey!" she called out, then tapped her heels against Barbara Ann's sides until she caught up with him. "Is this trail big enough to ride side by side?"

He nodded, then gave her a once-over.

"You look good on top of a horse, Harper," he said. "I gotta say, it's kinda hard to picture you in Sin City."

"I know," she said.

But picturing something sinful with Sam Callahan and those jeans? Unfortunately, that wasn't hard at all.

CHAPTER FIVE

Sam kept looking over his shoulder to make sure Delaney was still there. Riding side by side had lasted for only about fifteen minutes. Once he and Delaney had headed into the shade of the trees, the trail narrowed enough that she had no choice but to fall behind.

It wasn't just the density of the trees that worried him. The terrain was untrodden, grass having grown over roots so that a less experienced horse—or rider—might take a nasty tumble. If they were going to add this trail to their list, he, Ben, and Colt would have to come through and clean it up. This particular rider worried him more than others. After he heard her story, that fierce desire to protect her had reared its inconvenient head again. He couldn't protect her from the fallout of what might happen with their land war of sorts, not when he was the opponent. The only thing he could do was make sure she stayed on her horse.

"I'm *fine*," she said. "That's, like, the third time you've checked on me in the past thirty minutes."

"It's how I do trails," he told her. "Every ten minutes—especially if my riders get too quiet. I gotta make sure no one fell off a ledge or into a creek."

"So far, I've seen zero ledges or creeks. Plus, I'm not some newbie rider, you know," she added.

He laughed. She was right. The way she'd hopped so naturally onto the mare's back threw him for one hell of a loop, though he did his best to mask his surprise. The thing was, Delaney Harper surprised him at every turn. A vet tech who could muck out the stalls in half the time it took his stable hand *and* ride a horse she'd never met like she'd been doing it for years? It was—it was so... He turned his gaze back to the trail ahead and blew out a breath.

It was so damned sexy. Only he had no business finding this woman the least bit attractive. Yet here he was, making her ride with him to "earn her keep" when what she'd done in the stable was more than enough, especially when he'd have given her the room for free. But she wanted to be put to work—and as much as he knew it was a bad idea, he wanted a reason to spend more time with her.

He decided to lay off on the checking in for a bit, especially since he was no longer sure whether he was doing it to make sure she was okay or because he was hungry for a glimpse of her.

He groaned. He damned well knew his motivation was more self-serving than altruistic.

He started mumbling the lyrics to the Beatles' "Yellow Submarine" under his breath, anything to distract himself from thoughts that were not going to get him anywhere he wanted to be. Mumbling turned to singing—singing he *thought* no one but he and Ace could hear.

"Oooh!" he heard Delaney call from behind him. "Are we doing a trail-ride sing-along?" She belted out a line of the chorus, overemphasizing the *"Hey!"* many liked to yell after each line. His shoulders tightened, and he inadvertently pulled up on the reins, which brought Ace to a halt.

"Whoa, girl," Delaney blurted, and he turned over his shoulder to see her bring her own horse to an abrupt stop. Her eyes met his, and she raised a brow. "Just a solo, then, I guess? Sounds like you got some nice pipes on you, Callahan." She motioned for him to keep moving. "Why don't you take us to the second verse and into that clearing up ahead?"

He turned forward again and squinted. She was right. The foliage parted several yards ahead. Had they already made it? They'd been riding over an hour, but he'd thought it would take closer to two. With a group of tourists it probably would—even after he and Delaney cleared a safer path—but Delaney Harper was no tourist.

He'd heard about the swimming hole from folks in town, but it was unreachable by car. If he could get there by horse, and it looked like they just had, he'd be able to add another feature to the list that would hopefully attract another tourist or ten to the ranch.

He gave Ace a nudge with his heels and motioned for Delaney to follow. He stopped right after Ace broke through the trees, and Delaney did the same with Barbara Ann once she reached his side.

"Oh my God," she said, her voice full of wonder.

He couldn't even speak. He just stared at the clear, shallow water, at the small waterfall pouring over outcroppings of rock. His breath caught in his throat.

How the hell had he not been here yet? What he'd

heard about the place didn't hold a candle to what he was looking at.

"We're going in, right?" she asked, a smile spread across her face. "We didn't come all this way *not* to take advantage of cooling off during this heat wave."

"You bring a suit?"

She shook her head, her grin tinged with mischief. "The only difference between undergarments and a bathing suit is how long it takes the fabric to dry. And in this heat, that's not going to be an issue."

She hopped off her horse and tied Barbara Ann to the branch of a tree. In seconds her bag was on the ground, as was the hoodie tied around her waist. She kicked off her boots, stuffed her socks inside, and then glanced up to where he still sat on top of Ace, his arms crossed and a bemused smile playing on his lips.

"Are you enjoying the show?"

He tipped his hat. "Yes, ma'am. Looks like you're more Vegas than you thought."

She narrowed her eyes at him, then backed up, ensuring he could see her clearly from head to toe. She gripped the bottom of her tank, like she was ready to pull it over her head, then halted.

"You *are* joining me, yes?"

He cleared his throat, trying to buy himself some more time. The thing was, he'd had every intention of *finding* the swimming hole. But he hadn't planned on using it. If he were alone, it'd be a no-brainer.

"Here's the thing," he started. "You know what you said about 'the only difference' and 'how long it takes the fabric to dry'...?"

He paused, hoping to hell she wasn't going to make him spell it out for her. It wasn't that he had any issue with the fabric under his jeans—or lack thereof. But it made the situation they were in a tad more delicate.

Recognition seemed to bloom as her eyes widened and her jaw fell open. But she recovered just as quickly.

"Sam Callahan...are you going commando?"

He hopped off of Ace, tying him to his own branch, then spun to face her and grinned. "Like you said, it's a heat wave, and sometimes a man doesn't want to feel so...so constricted."

Her eyes widened. "Didn't take someone so straight and narrow for a rule breaker."

He rolled his shoulder, his muscles tensing. "The only rules I follow are the ones I set for myself."

She was right. It was hotter than Hades out here, and he deserved to cool off every bit as much as she did. If she was fine with his seeing her in nothing but her bra and panties, then she'd have to deal with seeing him in nothing but his—well, *nothing*. Maybe it was time to bend the rules just a little bit.

And with that, he unbuttoned his shirt and shrugged it off.

Her throat bobbed as she swallowed. "Wait. What are you doing?"

He kicked off his boots, then lost the socks. He tipped his hat once again, then dropped it on top of his shirt. All that was left were the jeans.

"Living by my own rules," he said. "You can cover your eyes if you want." He winked at her. Then one button and one zipper later, he left a wide-eyed Delaney Harper standing frozen as a statue as he strode past her, buck naked, and waded into the pool.

Once he was deep enough, he dove under, letting himself sink until the cool water washed away the stress of the ranch, if only for a few seconds. When he popped back up for air, Delaney was gone.

"What the—?" he said, scanning the immediate landscape. The horses were still there, but she clearly wasn't. "Vegas?" he said warily. "You messing with me?"

But all he could hear was the waterfall breaking the water's surface behind him.

"Harper!" he called again. "This isn't funny!"

"Woo-hoo!" he suddenly heard from the direction of the fall.

He spun to see her treading water a yard away, a triumphant grin lighting up her face.

"Damn, Delaney!" he yelled. "I thought—" Hell, he didn't know what he thought. All he knew was that his heart was hammering in his chest, and he was trying to reconcile his anger with his relief that she was okay.

She swam toward him, keeping her head above the water so he could see that gorgeous, victorious smile taunting him. When she reached him, she stood just inches away, and he realized her shoulders were devoid of bra straps. He did his best to keep his face expressionless, but beneath the surface of the water, his body betrayed him as he grew hard in a fraction of a second.

"What's the matter?" she teased. "Were you *worried*—about little ol' me?"

He ran a wet hand through his hair and blew out a breath. "How do you think it woulda looked if you blew into town planning to take half my land and wound up at the bottom of a swimming hole...on my watch?"

Her smile fell, her brows drawing together. "So you were only worried about people thinking you murdered me." It was a statement, not a question. "Wow. I can't believe they say chivalry is dead when right before me is a cowboy in shining armor." Her cheeks turned pink, and she chewed her bottom lip. "I mean, figuratively speaking, of course. Since, you know, you're not wearing—"

"Neither are you," he said, interrupting her.

She shrugged. "Wasn't going to let you have all the fun. Besides, I've never been skinny-dipping before."

His erection throbbed in response, but he hoped his expression remained impassive.

"That's a real shame," he said. "And—I wasn't worried about what people would think if something happened to you. I was worried about *you*."

She pressed her lips together, and he could tell she was fighting off a grin.

"Why is it that I'm only attracted to men who will royally complicate my life?"

He took a step closer to her, and she sucked in a tiny breath.

"Are you saying you're attracted to me, Harper?"

He pushed back thoughts of the ranch and ignored the voice in his head that told him to put his clothes on, get back on his horse, and put as much distance between himself and Delaney Harper as was humanly possible. Instead he stood there, his jaw tight as he held his breath, waiting for her response.

She took the next step. Their mouths were still inches apart, but her breasts grazed his skin, and it took every ounce of his will not to kiss her. Despite her misgivings, he liked to think some modern version of chivalry did still exist. And that meant not making a colossal mistake.

"This doesn't change anything," she finally said. "I still want my land."

He nodded. "And I still want my ranch." He tucked a

clump of wet hair behind her ear and stroked his thumb across her cheek. She shivered. "But heck if I don't want you too."

"I dare you to kiss me," she said, a challenge in her tone.

He smiled at her, letting all pretense fall away. "It's about damned time."

She pressed her hands to his chest, then leaned in. They could pretend for a little while, couldn't they? Reality was back at the ranch. But here...

Sam dipped his head, and her lips swept softly over his...just in time for the sky to darken and the first crash of thunder to startle them out of their little pocket of make-believe.

Delaney yelped.

Sam swore under his breath. "We need to get out of the water. *Now.*"

For the first time, it seemed, Delaney Harper didn't argue with him.

They pushed through the water as fast as they could. When Sam started to gain the lead, he reached out his hand, and she grabbed hold, allowing him to buoy her forward with his longer strides.

"Rain hasn't hit yet!" he called out. "But it's close. And from the sound of it, a pretty big storm as well."

The two of them scrambled onto the pebbly bank and ran straight for the grass where Ace and Barbara Ann were tied to their respective trees, whinnying as they both paced at the startling noise.

Sam and Delaney fumbled their way back into their clothes. It was no small feat getting jeans onto wet legs, but Sam managed with a few seconds to spare, which meant he could sneak a glance at Delaney trying to do the same. She'd thrown on her tank, then her underwear, and was using her hoodie to dry off her legs.

"You're gonna want to keep that dry," he said. "Temperature's probably gonna drop once the rain hits, which means good-bye, heat wave and hello, autumn."

She looked up at the sky, which was growing increasingly gray. "We can outride it, though, right? I mean now that we know the trail and—"

She was cut off by another clap of thunder and the gray sky illuminating with the first visible lightning.

Sam shook his head. "We're going to need to set up camp. And quick."

He didn't bother with his shirt. Instead he went to work unpacking his supplies from where they were attached to Ace's saddle.

"Grab me a few long branches!" he called as the first drops of rain began to fall. "Nothing smaller than two feet." He reached into his back pocket and tossed her his Leatherman multi-tool. "You okay with using a pocketknife?"

She nodded and ran off toward a nearby tree with the exact thin, spindly wood he needed.

Sam gave Ace a reassuring pat on the nose and retied Barbara Ann so she was closer to Ace. They were good horses, but thunder and lightning spooked the best of them.

He was less than thrilled to be in a forest during a storm, but at least they were in a small valley of land. The taller trees lay inward, back the way they came. He hoped that meant they were safe from a nearby lightning strike.

Yeah, he wasn't going to dwell on that idea right now.

He busied himself unrolling the tarp and fastening the center around a branch above Ace's and Barbara Ann's heads. Using a couple of tent spikes, he hooked the corners of the same edge to two different tree trunks.

Delaney returned with a handful of branches, the rain coming down hard now. Using them as makeshift poles, he transformed the tarp into the best version of a tent that he could while Delaney gathered the rest of their belongings and brought them inside.

"This is amazing," she said, her teeth chattering as goose bumps dotted her skin.

"And you're freezing," he said. "Come here."

He grabbed a rolled-up blanket from the ground and wrapped it around her shoulders. She shivered beneath his hands. He wanted to pull her to his chest, to warm her with his own body heat, but somehow—even after what had just happened in the water—it felt too intimate. It was something a man who cared about a woman did, but he'd known Delaney Harper for only a matter of hours. Caring didn't come that quickly.

"How did you know to bring all this? I checked the weather earlier, and it said clear skies until early evening. Storms weren't supposed to hit before five o'clock."

Her teeth chattered, so he pulled the blanket tighter and rubbed her upper arms with the heavy material, hoping to warm her without coming across as too concerned.

"I bring a pack whenever I hit the trail. Just in case." He raised his brows and glanced around their poor excuse for shelter. "Welcome to just in case."

She laughed, even as her teeth clacked together. "Let me guess," she said. "M-m-my lips are blue, aren't they?"

He nodded once. "As a corpse. It's kind of freaking me out."

She snorted, then swatted his shoulder with a blanket-covered hand. "It feels like the temperature dropped more than twenty degrees. And I'm not exactly dressed under here."

Right. And he was standing there in nothing but his jeans.

He opened his mouth to say something, but she must have read the change in his expression, and beat him to it.

"We don't have to talk. I mean, what almost happened before, out there..."

She trailed off without finishing her thought, which meant he had zero clue how she actually felt about what almost happened—before.

"There's an attraction," he said coolly, hoping his voice didn't betray how strong that attraction was. What would be the point? Nothing could come of it long term, even if he wanted it to. He wouldn't risk hurting someone who'd already been hurt enough. "We would have acted on it if not for the storm, but we didn't. Since nothing happened, there's nothing to discuss. It doesn't have to mean anything."

She blew out a shaky breath. "Oh, thank goodness. I was so worried you were going to think it was a thing, but it obviously can't be a thing because, well, I'm me and you're you and we want *really* different things— when it comes to the land, I mean. I don't know what you want when it comes to relationships, and you certainly don't know what I want, and I don't even know why I'm bringing up relationships when I obviously have no idea how to have a healthy one, so I'm just going put an end to this verbal—"

Boom!

The thunder shook the ground, and the royal-blue tarp lit up in an electrifying hue.

Ace let out a groaning neigh while Barbara Ann seemed to dance in place.

Delaney screamed and launched herself at Sam. On a normal day, he'd have caught her, no problem. But his feet were bare, the grass was wet, and he wasn't exactly expecting her. So he stumbled backward, slamming against the trunk of a tree.

"Damn it," he growled.

"Oh my God!" she said. "I'm sorry. Did I hurt you?"

He narrowed his eyes. "*You* didn't. The tree, on the other hand . . ."

She backed away, giving him room to step forward. "Let me see."

"I'm fine," he said. "Just caught off guard."

She pulled the blanket tight over her shoulders, and he guessed she was trying to cross her arms.

He rolled his eyes and turned around.

"I've got good news and bad news," she said. "Which do you want first?"

He shook his head. "I can take whatever you want to dish out."

"Well, you're a little scratched up," she said.

"And the good news?"

She laughed nervously. "The *bad* news is there's a wasp on your shoulder that must have taken shelter from the rain."

He chuckled. "I've been stung before. I can handle it." He looked over his shoulder to where the insect perched on his skin, and readied himself to flick it away.

"Don't!" Delaney shouted. "I've been stung before, too, and I went into anaphylactic shock and almost died."

Well, that sure as heck changed things.

"Do you have one of those—"

"An EpiPen? Yep." She bent down slowly and picked up her bag. Then she clumsily rifled through it while trying to keep the blanket up. A few seconds later she looked up at him, her eyes wide with horror. "I dumped out my bag on the bed and repacked it so I'd just have the essentials. It must have been buried under something else. I got sidetracked by a phone call, and…" Her eyes shone with the threat of tears.

"Delaney," he said evenly, "are you telling me that if you get stung while we're out here, you might die?"

She shook her head and worried her bottom lip between her teeth. "Actually, it's pretty much a sure thing, me dying if I get stung and don't get a shot of adrenaline within about fifteen minutes."

He carefully cupped his hand over the insect, then moved slowly toward an opening in the tarp. Lightning struck, and although Delaney gasped, she held still as he kept backing closer to the open air.

He was an outdoorsman, knew the importance of wasps when it came to the ecosystem, especially when it came to someone like Anna's crops, but if he was forced to choose between the little six-legged gal and Delaney, he was choosing Delaney. And here he was worried she'd wind up at the bottom of the swimming hole.

He stepped out into the rain and, as suspected, the wasp stung him as soon as it was startled by the downpour. He wasn't sure whether or not it survived, but at least Delaney would—for now.

He reentered the shelter and ran a hand through his hair, brushing out some of the wetness.

"Don't say I never do anything nice for you," he said, half-teasing, half-angry.

She winced. "Did it sting you?"

He nodded. He wasn't angry because he'd been stung, though. He was angry at her carelessness. He already had a younger brother to worry about on that front. But his protective instincts kept kicking in whenever it seemed Delaney needed protecting. Now he'd spend the next ten days worrying about whether or not she had her EpiPen on her.

"How could you..." He paced back and forth in their tiny space. "I mean, what would I have done if...Do you have any idea—"

"Hey!" she said, and he halted midpace. "I think I understand the consequences of my actions. And no offense to how awful it would be for *you* if I had been stung, but at least you'd live to tell the tale."

He opened his mouth to throw a comeback at her, then thought better of it. She was right. But he was still furious, maybe not at her but at the idea of what could have transpired. His stomach twisted in knots. He couldn't keep his mom from leaving, couldn't stop his father's brain from deteriorating—or the same from possibly happening to him when he was older. Heck, he wasn't even sure he could keep half of the land he thought he owned. But with Delaney Harper he was completely out of control—and not just when it came to how much he still wanted her.

She raised her brows. "Stumped ya, didn't I?"

"Yeah, Vegas. I guess you did."

CHAPTER SIX

It rained for the better part of an hour while they sat huddled under the tarp. After the whole wasp incident, Sam hadn't seemed much in the mood for trading barbs with Delaney. No matter how she'd tried to push his buttons and defuse the situation, he wouldn't take the bait.

"Sounds like it's quieting down out there," she said after a short period of silence. "Maybe we should head back." It was either that or she would keep thinking about what they'd almost done in the swimming hole and what she wished they were still doing to while away the time in their little shelter. Though Ace and Barbara Ann looking on would have been less than favorable.

He rose from where they were sitting on the damp blanket—both of them fully clothed now—and stepped outside the tarp.

"Looks pretty good," he called to her. "The sky, that is. Not sure I can say the same about the trail."

He came back inside, brow furrowed. "I'm not sure what's safer: waiting until morning and hoping things dry up a bit, or riding back in the sun when all the life-threatening insects will be back in full swing."

Delaney rolled her eyes. "I rode all the way here without incident," she insisted. "Not that I'm looking forward to a night under a tarp with nothing to keep me warm other than..."

Other than body heat.

She swallowed, then cleared her throat. Sam broke eye contact and scratched the back of his neck. His mind had apparently gone to the same naughty place hers had.

"We should go now," they both blurted at the same time.

"There's still enough daylight to make it back," he added. "Plus, Ace and Barbara Ann are seasoned trail riders. They should be able to navigate the terrain well enough. If we pack up now, we'll make it back in time for dinner."

Food. God, she was starved.

"You mean to tell me you didn't add food to your little Boy Scout kit there?" she teased. Wait, what was she doing? If he had food, that would make it easy to stay. And they shouldn't stay. But if they did...

Nope. Bad idea. Stop thinking with your libido, Delaney.

He shrugged. "If you want to dine on jerky and protein bars, sure. We're all set."

She *did* like jerky. "Do you know what's on the menu for tonight?" She had to weigh her options. If they were going to slog through the mud just to get back to something like mushroom risotto—because she had a strict policy against fungi—she'd be slightly disappointed.

He raised a brow. "I do believe it's taco Friday—beef, chicken, and fish. I know it's not Tuesday, but—"

"Say no more," Delaney said, zipping her hoodie and

throwing her bag over her shoulders. "I've always said that Tuesday shouldn't get to have all the fun. *Every* day is worthy of tacos."

They were packed up and on their horses in ten minutes flat. She guessed Sam was as hungry as she was. They had been on their way to working up quite an appetite when the storm hit. Not that she was still thinking about that as Barbara Ann took her first few steps back into the woods. If nothing happened, there wasn't actually anything to think about. Except her imagination couldn't let go of what *could* have happened if there were no storm, which meant she couldn't steer her brain away from the subject even if she tried.

What would it have felt like to kiss him, to touch him intimately, for him to touch her? An ache spread from her belly out to the very tips of her fingers and toes.

It would have felt good. *Really* good.

She squirmed in her saddle. This train of thought was going to get her nowhere. Maybe Sam had the right idea when they were headed toward the swimming hole. She started humming, but she could barely hear herself over her horse's hooves clomping against the terrain. The tree cover had helped save the trail from getting too muddy, but that just meant each of Barbara Ann's steps was louder than the last.

So she started singing aloud, a song she loved because it reminded her of the trip she and Beth went on with their dad on one of the rare weekends he took off from work. They drove to Arizona for a Diamondbacks game. The Diamondbacks lost, but she hadn't cared. All she remembered was eating ice cream, drinking her ice-cold soda, and singing "Take Me Out to the Ball Game" with her dad and sister during the seventh inning stretch.

"Take me out to the ball game," she started, a little bit louder than her humming but not quite loud enough to drown out Barbara Ann. So she increased the volume a bit more. By the time she got to *One! Two! Three strikes you're out*, she was shouting at the top of her lungs. She couldn't help it. It was just the nature of the song. But it was enough that Ace slowed to a stop, and Sam twisted in his saddle to face her.

"Vegas?" he said, his eyes shaded by his cowboy hat.

"Yeah?"

"I don't recommend you pursue a career in the musical field." He tilted his hat up and winked at her.

She narrowed her eyes and crossed her arms. "I'm not *that* bad." But she knew she was. Tone-deaf as the day was long no matter what the song or how well she knew it. When her elementary school put on the fourth-grade music class concert for the holidays, she knew well enough to mouth the words. She'd hoped that as her voice matured, so too would her ability to sing on key.

No such luck.

"I don't mind it," Sam said. "I can hear the effort along with the missed notes. It's kind of cute."

She shooed him along. "Yeah, well, no more cute for you, mister. I want my tacos, so how about you keep on keepin' on."

He chuckled and then did as she requested.

It took longer to get back to the ranch than it had taken them to get to the swimming hole, but according to Sam, dinner would still be in full swing for another forty-five minutes. Technically, he said Luis wouldn't close the kitchen before eight, especially if there were guests lingering. She was a guest, right? And she definitely wanted to linger wherever there was food, but they were both still a little damp and a lot dirty. Not for the first time today, Delaney *really* needed a shower.

"We should eat now if we want there to be anything left," Sam said as they exited the stable after getting Ace and Barbara Ann situated. "When Luis makes a taco bar, there are never any leftovers, even if we're barely booked. They're that good." He laughed. "Also, my brother, Colt, and I can *eat*."

Her mouth watered. "Can we walk in there like this?" Her jeans and boots were splattered with mud, as were Sam's. Her borrowed cowboy hat couldn't hide that her hair was matted and plastered to her cheeks. She guessed his hair was nice and dry, not that it mattered. He looked like he'd stepped off the pages of some country and western magazine. On him the caked-on dirt looked sexy.

He nudged her arm with his elbow. "You forget I own the place. It's okay to go anywhere in any condition so long as it's not offensive to the patrons. Looking like we do, we've got a story to tell. Stories sell excursions. Excursions show guests there's more to the ranch than meets the eye, and then they hopefully spread the word so we get more guests."

She nodded as they started walking toward the dining cabin, her lips pursed as she processed his logic. Then she laughed.

"That's a crock of you-know-what if I ever heard one," she said. "Please tell me you have better marketing ideas than that."

His eyes widened. "Excuse me?"

"It's not enough that the guests you already have enjoy their stay. Sure, you can ask them to write testimonials you can quote on your website. Maybe you can even get them to write a review on TripAdvisor or some Wild

West travel site if it exists. But what about something a little more proactive for the next guests? You need to get out there and *advertise* for them. Word of mouth and pretty pictures on a website will only get you so far. I'm guessing you aren't the only guest ranch in California. So what's going to make someone searching for the ranch experience choose you over someone else?"

Sam stared at her blankly.

She groaned. "There's a festival happening this week, right? Bounce houses and gourds and all that?"

He nodded, but it was clear he still wasn't following.

"You got a booth at that festival?" she asked.

"No, but—"

"You got pamphlets someone can pass around, maybe with a coupon for incentive?"

This time he shook his head. "We've barely got our feet wet. You think I can afford to start discounting? Like what, a free room?" He raised his brows, and she knew he meant her. Even if the vacation business wasn't her thing, she grew up in it. She watched all the tricks her parents used to get people in the door of their "upscale" motel. That was what they'd called it in a flyer she and Beth had helped create and pass out to the tourists who would watch the Bellagio's water show.

She stopped as he was about to pull open the door to the dining hall. She could see the buffet through the window, and it took all her mental resolve not to push him out of the way so she could forget about business and gorge until she was in a food coma.

"I'm not saying you should *give* away a free room. Also, if you asked—which you haven't—I'd be confident in saying I've done a heck of a lot already to prove myself a worthy boarder. But I'm going to take it a step further and give you some advice free of charge. Talk to whoever runs this little festival and see if you can squeeze in having a booth or table or whatever where you can pass out pamphlets and let people bid on an auction item."

He slapped his palm against the side of the door, then pointed at her like she'd just said the magic words. "There's a silent auction to benefit the firehouse. It goes on all week, and then the winners are announced on the final night right before the fireworks." His brow furrowed. "What am I auctioning?"

"Wait," she said. "Fireworks? Why?"

He shrugged. "Why not? From what I've learned about Meadow Valley, when the town celebrates, it celebrates *big*."

"So, fireworks and shutting down for a full week?" she asked.

Sam grinned. "Now you're catching on."

Delaney sighed. "Fine. Fireworks in October it is. Back to the auction. How about a weekend stay for two, excursions and meals included?"

He shook his head and opened his mouth to argue, but she cut him off.

"It's for a good cause, remember?" she said. "That's good PR too. Plus, if rooms are sitting empty now anyway, shelling out a few hundred or so to bring people in the door is hardly any skin off your back."

Shoot. Now she was thinking about the skin on his back, how close she was to raking her fingernails against it before the storm. For the love of air-conditioning, they'd skinny-dipped and almost kissed. She was thinking about more than just his back.

Advertise the ranch. Advertise the ranch. Advertise the—

"You okay there, Vegas?"

"Huh? What? Sorry. Lost in thought about . . . about the amazing brochure we can put together so people can grab one when they bid."

"You'd help me do that?" he asked, and his earnest brown eyes threatened to melt her into a puddle right then and there.

She shrugged, thankful for the hat that kept half her face in shadow, hoping he hadn't seen the heat rush to her cheeks. "As long as you have a color printer and some decent paper, that's all we need."

"I do," he said.

She extended her hand. "Then it's a deal."

They shook, his skin warm against hers.

Her mouth watered, but this time it was for more than the taco bar that waited for them on the other side of the door.

"Why are you helping me?" he asked, and she realized she wasn't sure.

"If someone offered me help when I was in danger of losing what I loved, I'd have taken it in a heartbeat." They were still holding hands even though they were no longer shaking. "I'm not here to run you out of business, Sam. I just want my life back."

The land *was* his business. But it was hers, too, long before the Meadow Valley Ranch existed.

"We should eat," he said.

She nodded.

"And I haven't exactly told Ben and Colt about, um, your situation," Sam added. "So this might be a little awkward."

"Don't tell them," she blurted without thinking. "I mean, it's a holiday of sorts. I'm stuck here, and we've got work to do. I don't want to ruin anyone's week.

Besides, I still have several days to convince you that you don't need all this space to run a ranch."

She forced a smile. He'd already built on the property. Whichever way they divided it, he'd lose something he built with his own hands. He'd lose the money he invested. But none of that was her fault. She'd lost *everything*. She was only asking for a portion of it back.

He smiled, too, but she could tell it was just as difficult for him as it was for her. "And I still have several days to convince *you* to let me buy you out."

She wasn't going to call his bluff and ask what money he was planning to use to do so. Sam Callahan was definitely a resourceful man. She'd known him for only the better part of a day and was already convinced that if he wanted something bad enough, he'd find a way to get it.

The door flew open before she could think of what to say next, and they both had to jump out of the way of two young parents and their brood of children as they loudly and laughingly headed off to whatever they were going to do next, barely taking notice of her and Sam.

"Guess that's our cue," he said with a chuckle, and took off his hat and held the door open so she could finally step through. And once she smelled the aroma coming from inside, it wasn't a minute too soon.

"Look what the cat...dragged through the mud," a man called from across the room, where he seemed to be schmoozing with a table of guests like he owned the place. Actually, he looked like a younger, less tightly wound version of Sam.

"Callahan number two?" she asked as the other man approached them. He wore an unassuming black T-shirt and jeans, but there was nothing unassuming about the man himself. He was Sam's height and build, but he walked with swagger that said he knew how good-looking he was while Sam—sexy as could be—either didn't know it or didn't think it mattered. She guessed it was the latter, which unfortunately made him even sexier to her.

"That obvious, huh?" he asked.

"What happened to you, big brother?" the other man asked. He crossed his arms, his smile widening when he looked at Delaney. "And who is your lovely friend?" He winked at her. "Ben Callahan." He extended a hand, his biceps flexing as he did. "How did I miss *you* on the list of guests?"

She shook his hand quickly and looked at Sam and then back at his overtly flirtatious brother. "Delaney," she said, purposely omitting her last name in case he recognized it. "My car broke down on the way through Meadow Valley, so I'm staying at the ranch for the week. Can't quite afford a week's stay," she said with a wince, "so I'm earning my keep. Mucking out stalls, testing new trails in the rain, putting together a marketing plan for the festival auction." She gasped and clapped her hands. "We can set up a mailing list for those who bid—and even those who don't—so you can start sending out monthly mailers of what's new at the ranch, share pictures of excursions, and—"

"Whoa, there, Miss—what did you say your last name was?" Ben asked.

Shoot. Nothing was getting past this guy. Or maybe it was the nervous word vomit that made him suspicious.

"I didn't," she admitted. "It's Spence. Delaney Spence." Which wasn't entirely a lie. Before she married Wade Harper, that *was* her last name. And as soon as this whole quitclaim deed forgery situation was behind her, it would be her last name once more. All she knew was that, right now, the most important thing to do was protect Sam from whatever the fallout would be when she won her half of the land back. Maybe by the time it came to that, it wouldn't be such a big deal. She had a little over a week to fix the situation so everyone would come out a winner.

"You had Colt and me tow her car, and now you're giving away my job to the first person to pass through town?" Ben turned his attention to Sam. "I thought you were happy with the website. If you wanted brochures and auction items and whatever else you think I'm not doing for the ranch, feel free to speak up."

Shoot.

Shoot, shoot, shoot, shoot, shoot.

Her intent was to *not* ruffle this guy's feathers, but apparently the preening peacock was sufficiently ruffled.

"We didn't think about the festival," Sam said evenly. Just from that one sentence she could tell there was friction between the two that stemmed from something further back than this particular incident.

Ben crossed his arms again, setting up a wall of defiance that Delaney—and anyone else who grew up with a younger sibling—was all too familiar with.

"No," Ben said. "We agreed we didn't need to advertise to the locals. They know we're here."

Delaney cleared her throat, and both men raised their brows, turning their attention to her. Sam and Ben stood with the exact same posture—backs straight and arms crossed over their chests—their expressions identical. The only difference was the places where their faces held the slightest clues they might no longer be in their twenties. Ben had the finest crow's-feet at the

corners of his eyes. They were more prominent when
he smiled. Sam's almost imperceptible sign of wear
and tear were the twin creases between his brows, as
if he furrowed them too often. It gave her heart a little
squeeze to think about all that Sam must carry on his
shoulders running this place.

"It's a holiday week, right?" she asked them. "If
celebrating autumn were an actual holiday."

Both men nodded in unison, and she stifled a laugh.
They really were two peas in a pod, even if they were at
odds with each other for the time being.

"And holidays are a good time for family reunions and
such. Sam told me the inn was booked, which is why I'm
staying here rather than in town."

She could see the wheels turning in both their heads,
and then—*bingo*! Their eyes widened with realization.

"Out-of-towners," Ben said, his ego seeming to deflate. "I just kept thinking about the town shutting down
and the festival being a local thing. Kinda ignored the
potential for new guests."

Sam clapped a hand on his brother's shoulder. "I
didn't think of it either. We all have a lot on our plates
right now. Delaney's stuck in town, so how about we just
let her roll with this?"

"Yeah, sure. Sounds like a good idea," Ben said.

"Where's Colt, by the way?" Sam asked.

Ben winced and scratched the back of his neck. "I,
uh, had some unexpected plans come up tonight. So he's
setting up the bonfire."

Sam shook his head and huffed out a bitter laugh.
Before he came up with any sort of retort for his brother,
she decided this was her cue to exit.

"So, I'm starved, and there's a taco bar. I'm gonna go

load up a plate and you can meet me at that conveniently open table just to the right of said bar?"

Sam nodded absently. "There in a minute. This won't take long."

Ben rolled his eyes, but Delaney put on her best customer service smile. "It was really nice meeting you, Ben," she said.

Then she escaped to the oasis of the taco bar.

She tossed her hat on the chair next to her and was a taco and a half in by the time Sam sat down across from her with his plate, tossing his hat on the empty chair next to him. She didn't even apologize. Her appetite waited for no one.

She had to finish chewing and swallowing before she spoke. "Why aren't you shoveling the contents of your plate into your face like I am?"

His plate was piled with food, but he wasn't touching it.

"What do I have to do?" he asked. But his gaze was straight ahead rather than on her. She followed his line of sight to where Ben was back at it, ingratiating himself with the ranch's remaining dinner guests, and they were eating up his charm as if it were just as good as the tacos, which was bullshit. *Nothing* was as good as the tacos.

"About what?" she asked, the next bite of her fish taco already halfway into her mouth.

He leaned back in his chair and placed his palms on the table. "You know, if I told him this second that the real reason you're here is to take half our land away, I don't even think he'd bat an eye. He has no damned clue what that would cost us. All he'd see is more time for '*unexpected plans*' to come up."

Delaney put her taco down and placed a hand on his forearm, giving him a gentle squeeze. "I know you're all bent out of shape right now, which is why I'm not even going to touch the 'take half our land away' comment. So do yourself a favor and just eat."

"But I—"

"*Eat*, Sam. Lunch was hours ago, and you worked your ass off building us that shelter for the storm."

"But he's such a—"

She picked up one of his tacos and held it to his mouth.

"Either you eat this of your own volition, or I'm going to feed it to you like you're a child having a tantrum because he doesn't realize how *hangry* he is."

His jaw tightened, and his nostrils flared. If he were a cartoon character, she was pretty sure smoke would puff right out of his nose.

"Give me the damned taco," he mumbled, so she handed it over. He ate half of it in one bite. He closed his eyes as he swallowed, and his shoulders relaxed. "Thank you. I needed that."

"Yeah," Delaney said. "I know. That's my version of slapping you across the face to snap you out of your hysteria. Except I'm not a big fan of violence, so my weapon is food."

He polished off the rest of the taco, then drained the contents of his water glass in mere seconds. "Is that why you tried to break my nose earlier today?"

She rolled her eyes. "You were a complete stranger who was pointing a knife at me."

"While I was making you the best grilled cheese sandwich you ever tasted. I can see how that might have confused you."

She fidgeted in her seat. "I didn't *want* to hit you. I don't want to hit anyone. But I'll do what I have to do to protect myself if the time ever comes." Not from

Wade. She knew he wouldn't lay a hand on her. But her ex-husband mixed with the wrong people. It was what had landed him in the ER more than once and what taught Delaney that the world wasn't all puppy dogs and rainbows, even in what she thought was a haven like Meadow Valley.

Sam looked at her appraisingly but didn't say anything.

"So. Siblings, huh? I have a younger sister. Born and raised in the same home by the same parents, and it's like we're from two different planets." Here, at least, she and Sam had some common ground.

"Sometimes I'd like to send my brother to another planet. Do you know any that have an all-female population? He'd leave on the next flight out."

She laughed. "He does seem to be quite the charmer."

Sam groaned. "That is what everyone seems to think. Helps him get away with a *lot*."

She shrugged, her next taco in her hand and at the ready. "I don't know. I like a guy who's steadier. Reliable. Hell, I'll even throw in responsible. Much sexier than a charmer who's out the door the next morning." Or who charms her right out of her life savings *and* investment money.

The corner of Sam's mouth twitched, but he didn't exactly smile. It didn't matter. He knew she meant him.

Despite their attraction to each other, she knew nothing could happen between the two of them beyond this week. The whole land situation was just plain sticky. If she got her half back, it would mean dismantling some of what he and his partners built. She was pretty sure that messing with someone's livelihood would douse any sort of flame between them. Wade messed with hers, and that was the last straw. There was no taking him back after that.

If she didn't walk away from the courthouse next week with some sort of guarantee her land *was*, in fact, *her* land, well, then it was back to Vegas to continue pinching her pennies and putting her dream on hold for a while longer.

No matter what happened at the courthouse, her stay in Meadow Valley would end either in Sam hating her or in Delaney trudging back home looking like a fool.

It was too bad. Delaney had a serious thing for the whole responsible, hardworking, kind, and damn-I-can-make-a-good-sandwich vibe Sam Callahan was giving off. Not to mention what she'd seen at the swimming hole. Responsible *was* sexy, but tall, dark, and naked didn't hurt either.

She blew out a breath and looked around the room and out the window to where the setting sun painted the sky a brilliant orange and pink. She reminded herself what it felt like to lose all that Wade had taken from her, and tried to imagine if she'd have forgiven *him* if he took only half the crowdfunded money and half of what she'd put in their savings account. If he'd sold only half the land without telling her.

She shook her head softly to herself. She'd still have left him, which meant Sam Callahan and everyone who was a part of this ranch would always see her as the person who took what they believed was theirs.

She set her taco down and pushed her plate forward, her ravenous appetite suddenly disappearing.

"Done already?"

She pressed her lips into a closed-mouth smile. "I'm just realizing how much I could use a shower, some dry clothes, and a good night's sleep. We can get to work on the brochure bright and early in the morning.

Maybe you could take me around to some of the best spots for photos? Might not hurt to head into town as well. A ranch just outside a quaint small town could be a good draw for those who don't want to be totally off the grid. Plus it's been ages since I took a stroll down First Street. I know everything is pretty much closed, but—"

"The inn's always open. We could start there with some coffee. Morning's a great time to take photos in town. The sun lights the place up like you wouldn't believe."

She laughed softly.

"What?" he asked.

"Nothing. You just seem a little sentimental. And I know you're not a local since, well, your land was once mine."

He shook his head. "Been in Meadow Valley almost two years, but no. Not a local. I did grow up in a small town not much different from here. Guess that's why I picked the area. Reminds me of home."

Her eyes burned, and a lump formed in her throat. All she'd ever wanted was to leave the hustle and bustle of Vegas for someplace else. For someplace like *this*. What if Sam *had* been here before, when she was married to Wade? Then a guy like him would still have been beyond her reach.

"Timing," she mumbled.

"What's that?" he asked.

"Time to head out," she said more clearly. "Dinner was great. Tell your brother thanks for towing my car." She pushed her chair out, and he stood as well. *They really broke the mold when they made him, didn't they?* "Have a good rest of your evening, I guess." And because she had no clue what an appropriate parting would be for a man she'd almost kissed under a waterfall, she awkwardly offered her hand, and he awkwardly shook it.

"Good night, Vegas." He grinned.

This morning the nickname had annoyed the heck out of her, but tonight—tonight it made a warmth spread through her that she hadn't felt before.

She smiled back. "Goodnight, cowboy."

Delaney waited until after a long shower to check the time on her phone. It was nearing nine o'clock. The exhaustion of the overnight drive had finally caught up with her, but it was more than that. It was one thing to step foot on a ranch owned by a nameless, faceless entity that seemingly took what was hers. It was another to spend the day with Sam Callahan, to put a face to that entity— a face she still saw when she squeezed her eyes shut and begged for sleep, only to realize he'd likely be the first person she saw the next morning.

Good night, Vegas.

Delaney groaned as she stared at the ceiling, sleep more elusive than ever.

No matter which way she sliced it, Delaney Harper was in way over her head. But until she saw this week through, she had no intention of coming up for air.

CHAPTER SEVEN

Sam raised his hand to knock on Delaney's door, then lowered it. Even though they'd settled on starting the day in town with coffee at the inn, they hadn't exactly discussed a time.

He checked his watch. Maybe 7:30 a.m. was too early to go knocking on someone's door. On any other day he'd have been up for hours already. Usually he took a trip into town around 4:30 a.m. to spar with the guys at the station, but he'd slept like shit last night, tossing and turning, wondering why Delaney had just up and left in the middle of dinner. And then tossing and turning some more, wondering why it mattered so much.

Knock on the damned door, idiot.

He was about to do just that when instead the door swung open and Delaney Harper barreled straight into him.

She yelped, jumped back into her room, and then slammed the door in his face.

"Sam?" she called.

"Yeah?" He stared at the white number 210 painted on the polished brown wood.

"What are you doing here?"

He laughed softly and shook his head. "Picking you up for coffee. But seeing as how I'm talking to a door, I'm thinking it's going to be more difficult than I thought."

The door opened slowly. She stood there in a blue sundress dotted with tiny pink and yellow flowers. Thanks to the cooler temperatures after the storm, she carried a denim jacket to wear over the dress. The boots that were encased in mud the last time he saw them now looked almost brand new.

"You startled me," she said to him. "Again."

That made two of them, because his first reaction when she opened the door was to kiss her, but they didn't do kissing. They didn't do anything of that sort, and agreed that what had almost happened at the swimming hole was best left at *almost*.

He scrubbed a hand across his jaw and realized he'd forgotten to shave.

"Appreciate the absence of your left hook this morning. Not sure I'm awake enough to have blocked it this time. You clean up pretty darn good, by the way."

She slung her purse across her body, smoothed out the dress, and shrugged. "What, this old thing?" Then she laughed. "I know she's closed today, but I really need to meet Ivy and thank her. I can't believe she just *gave* me all of this."

He clenched his teeth and tried to cloak his reaction, but Delaney noticed and her brow furrowed.

"She didn't give it to me, did she?"

He scratched the back of his neck and winced. "She did. I mean, she would have. But I know how hard she works, and money can get tight. I might have run a check over to her yesterday while you were mucking out the stalls."

Delaney went from bubbly to deflated in the time it took him to blink.

"*Sam.* I may not be in the best financial situation, but I didn't come to Meadow Valley to freeload. I'm paying you back. For the clothes. The room. I realize that once this week is through, you and I might not be on the best of terms, but I'd once planned on making Meadow Valley my home. And that was still the plan when I came here yesterday..."

She trailed off, and he thought he noted a tremor in her voice.

"Vegas...?" He wasn't sure if his reaction was one of hope or dread. "Are you changing your mind about contesting the deed?"

She squared her shoulders and sniffed, then shook her head, her hazel eyes bright as daylight.

"No." Her tone was firm. "Just coming to the realization that you are pretty well liked around here, which is not surprising." She let out a nervous laugh. "I might make a few enemies in town if I set up shop here, so I don't want to start off on the wrong foot with anyone thinking I'm here to collect freebies."

His chest tightened. "I'm not your enemy, Vegas. And you're not mine."

She skimmed her teeth over her top lip. "Well, then what the hell are we?"

He pressed his palm against the doorframe and sighed.

"We're bad timing," he said, going for as much honesty as he could. There was no use digging any deeper into his hang-ups about commitment. Maybe he and Delaney weren't right for each other because of the whole land situation. But Sam didn't know if he was living on borrowed time or not. It was easier to simply play it safe—to keep to himself, to work the ranch, to do what he loved for as long as he could, even if he fell asleep last night looking forward to seeing her again.

She cleared her throat and forced a smile. "And a whole lot of sexual tension."

He laughed. Looked like Delaney Harper wasn't pulling any punches this morning either.

"Yeah. That too," he said. "So how about we not think about what comes after this week and enjoy the morning. Colt has things under control, and my brother actually offered to start working on clearing a path for the new trail."

She gave his shoulder a playful push. "See? You got through to him last night."

Sam shook his head. "Nah. It most likely means he's going to bail on us again tonight."

"And you're not mad?"

He blew out a breath. "Actually, I'm furious. Things weren't always like this, but then again, we never ran a twenty-four-hour business before. I'm starting to wonder if he really knew what he was getting into." Sam shook his head. "Doesn't matter. And to be quite honest, I don't have the energy for Ben's crap today."

"That's mighty enlightened of you, Sam Callahan," she said, rocking on her heels. Her loose strawberry-blond waves bounced on her bare shoulders. He thought about tangling his fingers in that hair, and again about doing the things they didn't do, like kissing every freckle that dotted her exposed skin. Seemed he couldn't stop thinking about what he shouldn't be doing.

Why'd she have to go and mention their sexual tension?

"So," she started, rescuing him from any further thoughts about freckles and exposed skin. "Did you get yourself set up for the auction?" She stepped back, putting at least six inches of space between them, as if proximity determined whether or not the tension remained.

He sighed. "Made some calls last night. Gonna auction off a weekend stay for two, and anyone who signs up for our newsletter gets a voucher for one day of breakfast, lunch, and dinner on the house." When Colt asked if they could afford to do it, Sam had told him they couldn't afford not to. They needed beds occupied and excursions booked. It was as simple as that.

But for Sam it was something more. His father's illness changed the man he looked up to into a man he didn't recognize. When Sam was young, his parents seemed blissfully happy. He remembered wanting what they had someday. Years later, his father started returning from business trips and lobbing hurtful accusations at his wife, accusing her of cheating while he was away when she was rarely out of Sam's or Ben's sight. Before anyone knew his paranoia was a symptom of early onset Alzheimer's, Nolan Callahan began to act on his delusions. He cheated to punish their mother for what she never did. He pushed her to the brink until she'd had enough and finally left, leaving Sam and Ben to deal with the fallout. Meadow Valley Ranch was more than a dream. It was Sam's new family, the permanence he'd longed for in a life that felt as though it had been in a slow-moving state of chaos since he was a teen.

There was nothing at all simple about that. Delaney hooked her arm through his, and he shook away the thought of what he really stood to lose. "Well, come on, then," she said. "We've got a busy day if we're going to put this brochure together and have it ready for tomorrow. Are you sure it's okay to be away from the ranch for a few hours?"

He nodded. "We trade off who's on-site running the show. Today's sort of my day off."

She narrowed her eyes. "Yet you're still working. Why doesn't that surprise me?"

He shrugged. "It's a twenty-four-hour ranch, so I guess that makes me a twenty-four-hour rancher."

She smiled in unexpected understanding. "That's what the shelter would have been. I mean, it's what it *will* be. Animal rescue can happen anytime, right? Always gotta be ready for new guests."

He glanced down at her bag. "You got everything you need in there today?" He'd never worried that a stroll through a small town could be life threatening, but Delaney Harper changed that.

"Yep. I swear yesterday was the first time I've ever forgotten my EpiPen. And I learned my lesson. I will never leave the room without it again, even if I'm only heading down to the front desk to ask for the Wi-Fi password." She laughed. "Thank you, again, for...you know...saving my life."

He smiled. "I don't volunteer myself for a wasp sting for just anyone, you know."

"Well, don't I feel special."

She laughed and tugged him forward. He followed, albeit reluctantly, but not because he didn't want to do what needed to get done. For the first time in a long while, Sam Callahan wanted to procrastinate his entire workday. Tension or no, being in the presence of Delaney Harper had certain side effects, like Sam smiling more and worrying less, which made zero sense when she might end up with half his land. But before the wasp sting and the storm, he'd enjoyed the trail ride more than any other simply because she was there. Showing off his culinary skills to someone who appreciated a good sandwich— even if it almost ended with her breaking his nose—was another highlight of the day. Maybe for once he wanted to be the brother who shirked responsibility and had a little fun instead. But wanting and doing were two different things, and Sam always let his sense of duty win out.

It was a short drive into town, but they had to park a block southeast of First Street since it was already closed off for the festival setup. When they finally made it onto the main drag, Delaney stopped dead in her tracks and stood there silent and motionless for several long seconds.

"You all right there, Vegas?" Sam finally asked.

Delaney nodded, but her wistful expression said otherwise.

"The courthouse," she said.

Sam followed her line of sight to where the sun shone on the redbrick building, its white pillars standing with regal elegance on a street that otherwise seemed perfectly ordinary. "That's where Wade and I got married. I mean, we had a small reception in Vegas, but we made it legal here, in our new home." She huffed out a laugh. "I know it doesn't make any sense. Where I come from, there's a chapel every fifty feet, but we eloped here. I knew Wade had made some questionable choices before we got married, but I got swept up in it all. I thought that if he was really committed to me, I could get him to commit to a different kind of life. But love makes you stupid, you know?"

Sam tilted his hat down so it covered his eyes. "Can't say I *do* know. Never been down that road myself," he said, then quickly steered the subject away from his lack of relationship experience. "You don't miss being married to him, do you?" he asked. "I mean, after everything he did?"

Delaney laughed loud. Guffawed was more like it. "Miss *Wade*? Wade *Harper*? The man who stole from me, divorced me, and then stole again? Okay technically *I* divorced *him*, but that's beside the point." She shook her head hard. "No, screw it. It's *not* beside the point. *I* divorced him because it wasn't love. It was some conjured-up dream of what I'd hoped love was, and I was trying to make him fit the mold. What I *miss* is the hope I felt after we signed the marriage license. What I *miss* is putting my finger on a map and saying, 'Here. Here's where I'm going to realize my dream.' But instead I left with my tail between my legs."

She poked a finger at the brim of his hat, freeing him from the safety of its shadow.

"Looking for something?" he asked.

"Yeah." Her brows drew together. "I'm looking for an explanation to the part of the conversation I think you think I missed."

He cocked his head to the side, playing dumb and hoping it was working.

"You've *never* been in love?" she asked.

Nope. It wasn't working.

He shrugged. "It's just not something I've ever looked for. It doesn't exactly fit into my life." It was more that he didn't *let* it fit, but that was for his own protection as well as the protection of any woman he might fall for.

She laughed again. "You don't find love by looking for it. It sneaks up on you when you least expect it, and then, *bam*! It hits you right in the face."

He shrugged. "Guess it's a good thing I'm trained in the ring. Now how do you feel about eggs Benedict?" He needed more than a subject change. He needed a diversion.

"But you didn't—" she stammered. "I mean, that's not really an answer, Sam Callahan." She crossed her arms and blew out a breath. "I can see you like to remain a bit of an enigma—and that you've already learned my weakness when it comes to redirecting me."

His smile broadened, yet his facial muscles felt tight and unyielding. He shook his head and laughed softly.

"I don't think my love of all things delicious is anything to laugh at," she said. "We all have our own Achilles' heel."

She was right. His was the ranch and taking care of his family. The two went hand in hand. But in pouring so much of himself into both, he'd forgotten what it was like to be in the moment—to simply smile and enjoy himself. Yet here was this woman who threatened everything he'd worked for, and she'd slapped that grin back on his face without any sort of warning.

"Don't worry, Vegas. I wasn't laughing at *you*. But I'm happy to know I figured you out so quickly. Now how about we go fill our bellies and get to work?"

They walked down First Street side by side but kept a safe distance. He was spot on about the way it looked in the morning light. The high end of the sloping street dead-ended at the courthouse. The low end looked as if it were cut off by a dense wall of lush fir trees, but really it curved to the right, seeming to disappear.

The narrow storefronts and other buildings ranged in color from pale yellow to sky blue to the deepest reds and browns. The sun lit the place with Technicolor brilliance, but Sam wasn't sure it had ever looked like this before.

Delaney stopped and pulled her phone from her bag. "Granted I was only here for about six weeks, but I don't remember the view ever looking like this," she said as she snapped one photo, then two, then three. "Maybe it's a trick of the light or something?"

"Both," Sam said. *Or something.*

It was three blocks before they hit the Meadow Valley Inn.

"Something's different," she said, her eyes wide as she stared at the refinished pillars and the new balcony rail. "I mean, the place was always pretty, but it's... The only word I have for it is 'majestic.'"

She backed into the street to get a wider shot. When she returned to the sidewalk, Sam took his hat off, held it to his chest, and gave her an exaggerated bow.

"Appreciate the compliment, Miss Harper," he said, straightening, "but make sure you don't flaunt the competition too much in your brochure. I've got rooms to fill. Pearl here has to turn guests away on weeks like this."

Delaney shoved her phone back in her bag and stared at him, arms crossed. "*You* did that?" she asked. "You made the place look like it would have if it was brand new two hundred years ago?"

Sam shoved his hands in his front pockets. "Had to wait for a lot of permits to go through when we first got up here from Oak Bluff. Needed some way to pass the time for a couple weeks—and put a little extra in the bank."

"Wow. You've really made your mark here, haven't you?" she asked.

He shrugged. "I'm just lucky I'm good enough at what I do that people want to pay me for it. Not that it matters anymore. Don't do much contracting now that I have the ranch."

"Twenty-four-hour cowboy. I get it," she said, her smile fading. "Now, about the eggs Benedict..."

He pushed open the front gate and gestured for her to walk through. He followed her up the front steps, then stopped her before she opened the door to the inn's main entrance.

"Here," he said, gesturing to the left. "This goes straight to the café."

He led her through the door—waving and saying hello to people he knew and those he didn't—across a small café space, and out to a back patio hidden from street view. Atop red brick pavers sat six round tables made from rustic-looking wood with matching high-backed chairs. Only two of them were occupied so far, but the place would be packed soon enough.

She let out a nervous laugh as he pulled out a chair, gesturing for her to sit.

"Let me guess," she said as he sat down across from her. "You crafted these beautiful chairs and tables too."

He waved her off. "Nah, but a buddy of mine— Walker Everett—did. I got him the gig, and he cut me a small commission. So I guess, indirectly, I had a little something to do with it."

"Sam Callahan, I thought that was you!"

Sam stood as quickly as he'd sat down.

Pearl strode toward him with arms open wide. Her chin-length gray hair was pulled back from her face, her signature blue-framed glasses perched on her nose. "It's been over a week since I've seen you, which in my book is far too long."

"Morning, Pearl," he said as she pulled him into a hug.

She looked him up and down as she stepped back. "You're not eating enough," she said, eyes narrowed.

"I'm eating plenty," he assured her. "I've got Luis to make sure of that. Just been busy. You know how that goes. Sometimes I forget breakfast or don't have time to stop for lunch."

She set her hands on her hips. "If you're forgetting to eat, Luis isn't doing his job. No wonder you're here." She cleared her throat and raised her brows as Delaney stood from her chair. "And who might this be? You've been here almost two years already, and I cannot think of one time you've brought a guest to breakfast." She slid her glasses to the tip of her nose and looked over them as Delaney held out a hand.

"Hi, Pearl, it's nice to—"

"Wait a minute. I know *you*." The older woman's eyes narrowed. "You're the Harper girl, aren't you? I never forget a face, especially one that brought trouble to our town." She glanced around nervously. "Where is he? Where is that no-good husband of yours? He's still got an unpaid tab *and* a bad reputation. Thought when he sold that land he was gone for good."

Delaney's expression fell. "He's not with me," she assured the other woman. "I mean I'm not with..." She cleared her throat. "We're divorced." She looked at Sam. "I should probably go."

Pearl looked Delaney up and down, scrutinizing her. In the time that he'd known Pearl, he'd never seen her so distrusting.

"Pearl," Sam said, a defensive hint in his tone. "I promise you Delaney is here alone. She hasn't had contact with him since she left Meadow Valley. Isn't that right?" he asked, turning to Delaney.

She nodded. "I was just passing through, but Millie—my car—had other plans. I'm sort of stuck here for the week."

Pearl crossed her arms and nodded slowly. "Okay. Maybe I was too quick to judge, especially if Sam here will vouch for you. But that man wreaked havoc on this town, and it's my job to protect it."

"And I thought it was the county sheriff's job to do that," Sam said, relieved. "But what the heck do I know? I'm still pretty new around here."

Delaney's shoulders relaxed, and she forced a smile.

Pearl turned to Sam. "I guess you're right," she said. "Besides, it's really none of my concern. I'm not one to meddle in other people's business."

Sam tried to shield his laugh with a cough, but Pearl simply pressed her lips together and shot daggers at him with her gaze.

"Other people's business when I don't know them well enough," Pearl corrected. "You weren't here longer than the blink of an eye. Thought you might have been a good egg. You were going into business with Eli Murphy, weren't you? The vet outside of town? But that husband of yours..."

"*Ex*-husband," Delaney said. "And yes! Eli was so wonderful. He was going to volunteer his time at the rescue shelter I never got the chance to open." There was that forced smile again. Sam wondered how hard this really was for her—being here but feeling unwelcome, rehashing a painful past. He got it. He had a past of his own to contend with—and quite possibly an equally painful future. It took guts for her to come back and face it all, which only made him admire her more.

"I'd love to stop by and say hi to Eli and Tess,"

Delaney added. "But I'm stranded in town until my car gets fixed."

"Wait, you know Dr. Murphy? He's Scout's vet," Sam said. "He was the one who was going to volunteer at the shelter?"

Delaney nodded, and her eyes lit up. "Before I officially chose Meadow Valley as the place to open the shelter, I looked around for a veterinarian. Eli didn't even hesitate before saying yes."

Pearl's expression fell. "I guess you didn't hear about his wife," she said. "Got thrown from a horse a little over a year ago. Hit her head and never woke up."

Delaney gasped. "Oh no. I feel terrible. As soon as my car's fixed, I'm going to pay him a visit. They were both so supportive of the shelter."

Sam cleared his throat at the sobering thought. "I didn't know he'd been married."

Pearl nodded. "He's not the type to advertise being a young widower. Keeps to himself, his farm, and his practice." She sighed. "I'm hoping when he's up for it, though, that I can introduce him to my granddaughter, Charlotte. Been trying to convince her to move out this way, but the first job she got after her residency was at a pediatric practice out in New York, and she claims to love it out there." Pearl scoffed. "I don't know what she sees in city living. I blame her mother. My daughter did her own residency in LA and never looked back. It's bad enough the most I got to see Charlotte when she was growing up was during the summers she spent with me here. Now she's across the whole darned country. Maybe if she met the right man, though..."

The older woman's gaze turned wistful for a moment.

Then she blinked, seemingly bringing Sam and Delaney back into focus.

"I'll go get some coffee and let you two get settled in," she said.

"It's just business," Sam blurted before Pearl turned away. "Delaney and me, I mean. She was passing through, got stranded, so she's helping me and Ben and Colt put something together for the auction."

Pearl smiled. "Sure, honey. Just business. Your secret's safe with me." Then she spun on her heel and headed back inside.

Delaney and Sam sat back down, her worried expression mirroring how he felt.

"I know to her it looks like we're—" Delaney said.

"But *we* know we're not," Sam interrupted.

"Right." She picked up her menu.

Yet what they were or were not seemed to be all that any of them could think about. There was something between him and Delaney. They both admitted as much but also decided *not* to act on it. Yet here he was, doing some of that procrastinating he'd thought about before. He wasn't thinking about work or his father or anything other than being in the moment. With her.

Her eyes darted over the top of her menu, and he realized he was staring.

"What?" she asked.

He went for honesty since he really didn't know any other way. "I guess I'm having a hard time keeping my eyes off you, Vegas."

Her cheeks turned crimson, and she went back to studying the menu.

"We barely know each other anyway," she said. "It should be easy enough to forget about . . . you know . . . and move on. Shouldn't it? It's not like we know what we're missing. *Not* that I think I'm missing anything."

"It should. Like I said, I don't really look for..." He trailed off and picked up his menu, too, even though he already knew what he wanted. He wasn't going to say it—the L-word. That wasn't what was potentially brewing between them. He almost laughed at the impossibility of it. He met her yesterday. *Yesterday.* When she blew into his office to inform him she owned half his land. "And there's the whole property situation," he reminded her. Because it felt as if they both were forgetting a really big obstacle that was already in their way on top of Sam's personal resolve to fly solo when it came to relationships.

Still, he couldn't help himself. He sneaked a peek over the top of her menu to see Delaney worrying her bottom lip between her teeth. He almost kissed that lip. And the other one too. All he'd have to do was lean over the table and...

"Right. You don't look for...and I didn't come here to... We're obviously the wrongest wrong that two people could be," she said, adjusting herself in her seat, the toe of her boot accidentally nudging his.

"Sorry!" She straightened in her chair, eyes wide. Had she felt it too? That jolt when her boot hit his that felt anything but wrong?

He picked up the glass of ice water sitting in front of his place setting and downed it in one long gulp.

"We should order." He waved at Pearl, who was greeting another couple who'd just been seated.

"Yes!" Delaney slammed her menu down on the table in front of her. "Food. Eat. Perfect."

Pearl sauntered back over with a knowing grin on her

face and a pitcher of water in her hand. "What'll it be, you two?" She refilled Sam's glass.

A room? Sam thought. *Or just five minutes alone with the woman I've been dying to kiss since yesterday's storm?* They were better off here, with Pearl as their chaperone, but it didn't change the fact that what Sam wanted to order wasn't anywhere on the menu.

"Eggs Benedict!" Delaney blurted, and he guessed her thought process might be similar to his own.

"Same for me," Sam said, lifting his glass. "And maybe leave the pitcher." In case he needed to dump it over his own head.

"You got it," Pearl said with a wink.

It was going to be a long week.

CHAPTER EIGHT

Sam watched Delaney polish off the last of her eggs. With her mouth still full, she closed her eyes and hummed a soft *mmm*.

Sam laughed. "The best, right? Don't tell Luis I said that, though."

Delaney swallowed and held up her right hand as if swearing an oath. "I promise not to tell Luis that you're cheating on his cooking with Pearl's. Though if he isn't putting avocado on his eggs Benedict, someone should tell him. I mean, that was a religious experience."

"So is watching you enjoy it."

She wiped her mouth with the cloth napkin, then smiled sheepishly. "My mom is an amazing cook. Even when money was tight, she found a way to throw something together that felt decadent, you know? Like chicken potpie made mostly with frozen vegetables and a can of soup. She just had this sort of magic that totally skipped a generation. My sister and I are both the worst in the kitchen. So, I don't know. I guess good food makes me think of home and family—the stuff I want to have some-day." She laughed. "Also, good food is good food. Did you get your cooking gene from your mom?"

Sam's jaw tightened. Aside from the occasional visit, he hadn't had much of a relationship with his mom since he was a teen. She'd wanted to take him and Ben with her when she left Oak Bluff, but back then he couldn't imagine leaving the only home he'd ever known. They'd chosen to stay, not knowing then what was in store for their father's health—for what it might mean for their own futures. And a little part of him always blamed her for that, as if she'd known and had left anyway. She couldn't have known, but she also could have worked harder to keep him and Ben in her life. She hadn't.

He tossed his napkin onto his empty plate, stood, and deposited a pile of bills on the table. "Come on," he said. "We should get a few more shots while the lighting is still good."

He strode toward the indoor portion of the restaurant and then back out onto the inn's front porch.

"What the heck was that?" Delaney asked as she burst through the door a few paces behind him. "We were having a lovely conversation about my favorite thing—food—and then you up and leave the table? Did I offend you with my talk of avocado?"

He blocked out her line of questions and focused solely on the task at hand. He strode down the steps to the sidewalk and then pointed across the street. "I think if we head to the other side, you can get a good angle of the sun coming through the firs. Maybe grab a few more storefronts, and then we can—"

Delaney ran down the steps, grabbed his still-outstretched arm, and pressed it back to his side. "I'll get the photos, but first you have to tell me what I said because you're being weird and standoffish—more so than usual."

"Standoffish? When the heck have I ever been—"

She was smiling triumphantly. "There. See? I broke your train of thought. Now do you maybe want to tell me what set you off back there? If it wasn't the avocado, then I can only guess it was me mentioning your mom. Was it your mom?"

He was saved by his phone vibrating in his pocket. Who was calling him so early in the morning? So help him if Ben was trying to get out of leading the trail ride after breakfast, he was going to seriously lose it.

He answered the phone without looking at the screen. "Hello?"

"Mr. Callahan, this is Denise Foster from Quincy Long-Term Care. We're experiencing a situation with your father's meds and—"

"I'm on my way," Sam said. "Be there in ten minutes."

He ended the call and shoved the phone back in his pocket.

"We need to go," he said, then grabbed Delaney's hand, not caring who was watching. He just needed to get her to the truck. Now.

She must have read the situation loud and clear because she didn't ask him any more questions about avocados or his mother or why they were speeding out of town and onto the county road. He was grateful for the silence on the ride as well. He needed to think. Last time his dad wouldn't take his meds it was because he thought it was twenty years ago and that he was running late for Ben's soccer game. Spoiler alert: The man showed up late to every one of their sporting events and sometimes—a majority of the time—not at all. There was always an excuse, just like there were excuses for his infidelity. None of them knew that it all boiled down to Nolan Callahan's brain rebelling against him. None of them knew anything until their mother left and it was too late to salvage what had once been a happy family. .

Sam barely let his foot off the gas until they pulled into a parking spot, at which time he maybe slammed a bit too hard on the brakes, causing him and Delaney to lurch forward against their seat belts.

"Well," Delaney finally said, coughing. "Now I know what getting in a head-on collision might feel like."

Sam blew out a shaky breath. "Sorry. Look, I'm not going to be a prick and tell you to wait in the car, but I also don't really know how to prep you for what you're going to see in there."

Delaney nodded. "Whatever you need, Sam."

He hopped out of the truck, then rounded the bed to help Delaney, but she was already slamming her door shut and on her way to join him. She laced her fingers through his and gave his hand a squeeze.

He didn't pull away. Together they approached the main entrance of a stucco building that was trying to look like a resort, and for many residents, it was. Dear old Dad, though, liked to shake things up every now and then. Lucky for Sam, today was one of those days.

He took his hat off as he pushed through the door and nodded at the young man behind the front desk. "Morning, Thaddeus."

"Morning, Mr. Callahan. They're in the game room."

Of course they were. Dad couldn't have a meltdown in private. It had to be with an audience.

He could hear the yelling as they got closer.

"You idiots are making me late for a meeting. Do you know I'm the most sought-after breeder in California? Do you know what it will cost me if I don't land this account?"

"Mr. Callahan," he heard someone say. "You can leave for your appointment as soon as you take your meds."

Sam steeled himself for whatever he and Delaney were about to see.

They rounded the corner to a room that was usually warm and inviting—two circular wooden game tables and chairs, two sofas with a rectangular coffee table between them, and a fireplace with a television mounted above the mantel. Whenever Sam came to visit, no matter what time of day it was, the room would be packed with residents enjoying a game of backgammon, euchre, or good old-fashioned Trivial Pursuit. This morning, though, the room must have been cleared out because the only people there were two nurses—and his father standing on top of one of the game tables, holding the Trivial Pursuit board above his head as if it were Thor's hammer.

Jacob was the nurse trying to reason with his father while Trish stood behind him readying a syringe.

"Hey, Dad," Sam said evenly. "How's it going?"

Nolan Callahan directed his attention toward his older son. His brow furrowed, but he didn't lower the game board.

"You look like hell, son."

Sam let out a bitter laugh. "Thanks, Dad."

"You have a big exam this week or something? Or did the Everetts' mare keep everyone up all night again? Your mother said she's a feisty one."

Sam approached the man slowly, leaving Delaney where she stood.

"No exam this week, Dad. I'm thirty-two now, remember? Ben and I run a ranch just a few miles from here. It's a tough job getting a new business off the ground. Might be why I look like hell."

The man stared long and hard at his son, his brows raising as his confusion morphed to recognition. He lowered the board. "Thirty-two?" He shook his head. "Your mother left when you were fifteen."

Sam nodded. "And Ben was thirteen."

"We don't board the horses anymore?" It was half statement, half question.

"You're done breeding them too," Sam said. "You retired and came to live here."

Sometimes all it took was a familiar detail to jar Nolan back to the present, and Sam hoped this was working. The last time they had to sedate him, he sat in his room, virtually catatonic, for four hours. No man deserved that.

"What's with the medication?" his father asked.

Sam approached the table slowly and held out a hand for the older man to grab.

He used to be such an imposing figure, his father. Sometimes he seemed larger than life. But now, as he climbed down with Sam's assistance, he was just a man— thin but not frail, and barely taller than his son, his once dark hair now salt-and-pepper and in need of a trim.

"Sometimes you get confused, Dad. Like today. The medication helps with that."

Nolan Callahan leaned over and whispered in his son's ear. "That one behind me—she wants to stick me in the ass with a needle. Hope she's not disappointed."

Sam rolled his eyes. "You're a dirty SOB, you know that?"

His dad laughed, then held out a palm for the small white cup of pills.

Maybe Sam didn't always approve of the man's methods, but he liked seeing his father laugh. Nolan's illness robbed him of his marriage and his ability to take care of himself. Sam wanted some semblance of happiness for him, but if he didn't keep up with his medication, he'd only deteriorate.

The older man tossed the pills into his mouth, then held out a hand for the accompanying cup of water, draining the whole thing in one long gulp as he washed the meds down.

"Okay," Nolan said with a grin. "How about we bust out of here and grab a couple of longnecks?"

Sam's heart squeezed so tight it hurt. "It's not even ten a.m., Dad. And drinking is probably not the best idea right now."

Nolan waved him off. "Live a little, Sammy. Barbara Ann and I are always talking about how we wish you'd do more of that."

Sam's brows drew together. He'd thought his father had come back to the present, but if he was remembering conversations with Sam and Ben's mom, Nolan wasn't quite here yet.

"Mom's in Tahoe, remember?" Sam said.

"Yeah, yeah. Tahoe. That's right," Nolan said. "Fine. No longnecks. What do you say, then? You and your pretty friend over there want to stay for a game? Already got the board out."

And as if he hadn't been standing on top of a table ninety seconds ago threatening to bludgeon his nurses with a Trivial Pursuit board, Nolan Callahan was ready to get back to his regularly scheduled programming.

Sam gave his father a reassuring squeeze on the shoulder. "Sure, Dad. But maybe something a little simpler. How about Uno?"

His father looked at the game board in his hands and shrugged. "Your mother loves Uno. Maybe she'll want to join. We can always use a fourth." He looked around for the woman Sam knew wasn't there. This was how it went sometimes—lucid one minute and living in the past the next. And despite Nolan Callahan having been a crappy husband before anyone knew he was ill, it still killed Sam to see the hope in his father's eyes—the hope Sam always had to crush whenever the man forgot what had happened over fifteen years ago.

"Ma's not here, Dad. Remember? She moved to Carson City to be near her sister, and then she met Ted. Lake Tahoe?"

Delaney was standing next to him now, and she placed a hand on Sam's forearm. "I'm sorry, Sam," she said softly. "You should have told me to wait in the car. I had no idea—"

"Ted," Sam's father said, more to himself than anyone else. "Ted from Tahoe. Ted. From. Tahoe." He shook his head, then looked at Sam with dawning realization. "She left when you were fifteen," he said once more, and Sam nodded. "But she still loves Uno when I see her."

"You're right, Dad. Mom has always loved Uno."

He and Ben had only seen their mother a handful of times since she moved out. Lake Tahoe was almost a seven-hour drive from their hometown of Oak Bluff, which had made regular visits difficult. Now that he and Ben had moved closer, Sam thought they'd see her more often. But the physical distance had forged an emotional one that felt too hard to travel. She'd come out to see the ranch a couple of times, and he and Ben went to Tahoe once or twice as well. But their relationship with her now was more like that of distant cousins, and even though his father was right here, it was as if he were a million miles away. Nolan's illness changed everything about their family, and since coming to Meadow Valley, Sam was finally accepting that he couldn't get any of it back.

"I'll wait in the lobby," Delaney said, her hand still on his arm. "Take all the time you need."

Nolan's head shot up, his eyes on the young woman next to his son. "I thought we were playing Uno. You can't play with just two people. The game'll be over in minutes."

Delaney stared at Sam for several long seconds. She'd seen the worst of the episode. A quick game of Uno couldn't make things any worse.

"Stay," Sam finally said to her, his voice low and his throat dry. He thanked the medical staff, and they left the room, trusting that Nolan was no longer a threat to himself or anyone else.

"I have to warn you, though," he added. "My father is ruthless when it comes to laying down the Draw Four cards."

Sam's father tossed the Trivial Pursuit game board back in its box, then snagged a deck of Uno cards from a nearby game shelf.

The three of them sat around the table Nolan had been standing on only minutes before, and he shuffled and dealt the cards with the precision of a Vegas dealer.

"I'm Nolan Callahan, by the way," he said to Delaney after setting the extra cards down in a pile in the center of the table. "Sam didn't tell me he was seeing anyone."

"Delaney Harper," she said, shaking his hand. "And Sam and I just work together."

"She does some marketing for the ranch," Sam added. "I don't mix business and pleasure." The second sentence came out with more bite than he'd intended. Sometimes immature, resentful teenage Sam forgot that Nolan's behavior all those years ago was a result of the early-onset dementia. *Sometimes* he wanted to still be the innocent kid instead of having the roles reversed.

Delaney picked up and stared at her cards, but she kicked his boot under the table, letting him know she not only picked up on his tone but didn't approve.

"He means me," Nolan said, laying down a yellow two on the started discard pile. "My mixing of *business and pleasure* is why his mother divorced me. I loved her, you know. Still do. Sometimes, though, I forget things." He sighed. "And then I do things that don't make sense."

Nolan's episodes of confusion were hard, but sometimes the periods of lucidity were even harder—to see his father realize again and again what he'd lost.

Sam threw a green two onto his father's card, and Delaney followed up with a green Reverse card.

"Sorry," she said to Nolan. "It's the only green I had."

The older man shook his head. "Don't apologize for something you wanted to do. The way I see it, apology doesn't change anything. What's done is done. You can't take it back."

"I know a lot about empty apologies," Delaney said, and both men looked up to meet her gaze. "It's one thing to let someone down once. But soon actions speak a heck of a lot louder than words, and you realize that no matter what you once felt for a person, they aren't who you thought they were, and you have to leave. Even if it costs you everything."

She raised her brows and bit her lip. *Sam* knew she

was talking about Wade, but for all intents and purposes, she very well could have been talking about Nolan and Barbara Ann Callahan.

Sam's father blew out a long breath. "Your mother's gonna love her," he said to his son, a knowing grin on his face.

"Just play the game, Dad. Whose turn is it?"

Delaney slammed down a Wild Draw Four card, and Sam stared at her wide-eyed.

"Red," she said, informing him of the color change. "And I can be ruthless too."

Sam's father yelped with laughter while Sam gritted his teeth and drew his four cards. The three of them went on like that for another half hour until Delaney finally won the game. Sam admired her strategy as they played—smart and calculating yet never boastful when she outmaneuvered either of the men. She had the best poker face he'd ever seen, and he realized that while you could take the girl out of Sin City, she never quite lost that Vegas touch.

"What was it you said you did for the ranch?" Sam's father asked as they were cleaning up the game.

Delaney cleared her throat. "Marketing," she said with enough surety that Sam would have been convinced had he not known the truth. "But my first love is animals. You boarded horses, right?"

Nolan smiled and perked up. "Boarded 'em. Bred 'em. Started out as an equine veterinarian, and everything sort of took off from there. You ever work with horses?"

Delaney nodded. "Helped a mare give birth once when I was in school."

The older man's brow furrowed. "You helped a mare foal in marketing school? Something isn't adding up."

She laughed. "I went to school to be a veterinary technician. When that didn't pan out, I sort of fell into the marketing thing."

"And she's damned good at it too," Sam added.

His father crossed his arms. "Foaling or marketing?"

All three of them laughed, and for a few moments, Sam's life felt easy and normal rather than like a race to put out one metaphorical fire before the next one started.

"Maybe you could talk your business partner into bringing me by the ranch to see Ace. I'd love to take him for a ride. Did my son tell you he rescued him from abandonment? Owner dropped him off to board and never came back for him. Ben wanted to sell him, but Sam didn't have the heart."

Delaney's hand flew to her chest, and she smiled so endearingly at Sam that he had to look away.

"So I like animals," he said matter-of-factly. "It's not a big deal."

She opened her mouth to say something else, but he cut her off before any other sort of emotional connection took place. This morning had already been a doozy, and he wasn't sure he could take much more.

"We should go, Dad. I mean, you're doing okay, right? I'll be back on Monday like usual."

His father answered with a plaintive nod. "Of course, son. We should stick to the schedule." He tapped his temple with his index finger and winked at Delaney. "Routine keeps the mind sharp, and Sam was always good at routine."

"Maybe we'll come by for a rematch sometime," Sam said, and gave his father's shoulder a squeeze. "Take it easy, Dad."

The older man stood as Sam and Delaney did the same. She leaned over and gave his father a kiss on the cheek.

"It was lovely meeting you, Mr. Callahan," she said.

He chuckled. "She's a keeper, Sammy. Especially if she can stand to be in the same room as your old man when"—his smile faltered—"when I'm having one of my less stellar mornings."

"It's just—"

"Business," his father said, finishing Sam's thought. "Sure, son. Whatever you want to call it."

"See you Monday, Dad."

He waited for Delaney to step away from the table first, then followed her out into the late morning sun.

He said nothing as he opened the door on her side of the truck, and still nothing as he backed out of the parking spot and made his way onto the street. He'd have driven the whole way back to the ranch in the safety of such silence, but Delaney seemed to have other plans.

"Sam, I'm so sorry. I had no idea," she said.

He kept his eyes on the road. "About what? Him being a workaholic when I was growing up? A crappy husband? Or that all of it wasn't really his fault? He was sick, and no one knew it. Our mom left. Ben and I resented the hell out of him. We all basically punished him in our own ways when we could have helped."

"Oh, Sam...," she said, her tone mixed with pity and something else he couldn't quite put his finger on. "You can't blame yourself."

Couldn't he, though? He and Ben hadn't made things easy for their dad when their mom left. Maybe if they'd paid better attention to his behavior...maybe if Nolan had seen a doctor earlier...

When Sam didn't say anything in response, she let out a long breath, and he steeled himself for what was coming.

"Are you scared?" she asked. "I mean with the possibility of heredity and your dad being so young."

His knuckles whitened around the steering wheel. "I'd be one hell of an idiot not to worry, wouldn't I?" he said coolly. Yet he'd never said it out loud—not to his brother, not to any of the doctors who might have answers for him, and certainly not to any woman he'd ever been with. No one had ever gotten close enough to see what he dealt with—partly because he never let them. But Delaney Harper had done it in a matter of hours. Somehow this woman blew into his careful life and threw everything into chaos in one single day.

"Mind if I drop you off at my office?" he asked before she had a chance to respond. "I've got some image files of the ranch on my laptop that you can use along with what you took in town. Figure that will be enough for the pamphlet. How long do you need to work on something like that?"

"I could throw something together in about an hour, actually. I'm pretty good," she mused, and Sam could tell she was trying to lighten the mood.

He was a jerk for not even cracking a smile, but he knew what he needed to get out of his funk, and talking wasn't the answer. Sam was a doer, not a talker.

"Maybe you can work on it while I take care of a few things and meet you back at the ranch for lunch," he said.

He remained focused on the road but glanced at her through his peripheral vision. She was staring straight ahead, too, her hand tucking a strawberry-blond lock behind her ear.

"Sure," she said. "That sounds great."

But she wasn't smiling, and nor did she do anything to hide the disappointment in her voice.

He pulled up in front of the main cabin and got her situated in his office when Scout bounded in after them.

"This is Scout," he said flatly. "Do you mind if—," but before he could finish the introduction, Scout had curled up at Delaney's feet.

She leaned over and gave the pooch a scratch behind the ear. "I don't mind at all," she said. "The more animals, the better. You got a cat too? Maybe a goat? I get along with them all."

"See you at lunch, Ms. Harper," he said, his tone more formal than he'd intended.

Delaney forced a smile. "Good-bye, Sam."

When he picked her up this morning, all he could think about was kissing her—and then some. Now what he needed was to get as far away as possible from the woman who saw him too clearly—who'd already seen too much.

CHAPTER NINE

"Delaney Harper, *you* are a genius!"

Delaney grinned at the finished brochure in her hand, not caring that she was speaking aloud to herself.

Scout rolled onto her back and wiggled her bottom, howling for a belly rub.

Delaney laughed. "I told you I was almost done." She dropped the brochure onto Sam's desk and dropped down to a squat, rewarding her graphic design companion with not just a rub on the belly, but also a well-deserved scratch behind the ears.

"Who's a good girl?" she asked, and Scout answered by hopping up and giving Delaney a sloppy kiss on the cheek.

"Okay, okay," Delaney said. "Are you as hungry as I am?"

Scout answered with a bark, which meant it was feeding time for both of them.

The clock on Delaney's phone said it was already

twenty past one. She'd expected Sam around noon but hadn't thought much of it since she was still deep in the design trenches. But now she was done, and he was nowhere to be seen.

Her brow furrowed. "Maybe we were supposed to meet him at the dining hall." She didn't see a food or water bowl for the dog, but she did see a leash sitting on a corner of the cluttered desk.

"Come on, girl. Looks like we're going for a walk."

Scout sat willingly and waited for Delaney to clip on the leash. Then the two headed out into the bright afternoon sun.

Delaney fished her sunglasses out of her bag and wished she had the cowboy hat Sam had loaned her the day before. She could always buy one for keeps. After all, if she was going to spend most of her days outdoors taking care of rescue animals, such a hat would be fitting, right? Wanting the hat had nothing to do with how it reminded her of Sam or their ride to and from the swimming hole, she told herself.

"What's with that human of yours, anyway?" she asked Scout as they weaved around the property, the pit's curious nose leading them off the official path more than a few times. "He's so—stubborn."

Scout barked at a grasshopper, but Delaney took it as Scout's agreeing with her opinion of one Mr. Sam Callahan.

"He's also pretty wonderful with his dad, considering their past, you know?"

The leash yanked out of Delaney's hand as Scout bounded after the insect. She had to run to catch up before the dog chased the grasshopper clear into the woods.

"Whoa, there," she said laughing, and Scout whimpered

as her prey got away. "Keep your eye on the prize, girl. *Lunch.*"

She decided not to distract her companion with further talk about Sam's deep brown eyes or the way he wore his stubble so damned well. It seemed she and Sam had come to an unspoken agreement to ignore Wade's forged deed until they had to deal with it, which she guessed was good. After this morning she could see that Sam had enough on his plate already. Maybe, though, their land war didn't have to be a war at all. The property wasn't huge, but he could build the dining hall up and make that the guest quarters too. And the stable wasn't full. It could be cut in half and the arena shrunk down to allow for another structure. They could be neighbors. *Very* close neighbors who hopefully would find a way to get along when all was said and done.

Delaney groaned. All of that would cost money and labor she guessed Sam didn't have, especially if he was still working to get people through the door in the first place. No matter which way she sliced it, dividing the land meant something would be lost. She needed to think. And an empty stomach was only making matters worse.

Five minutes later, Delaney and Scout pushed through the doors and into the modest dining hall. She scanned the tables one by one, but Sam was nowhere to be seen.

"Can I help you?" someone asked from behind.

She turned to see a sandy-haired man in the doorway, spinning a cowboy hat on his fingers.

He spoke around a toothpick sticking out the side of his mouth. He was tall and lean, like Sam and his brother, but other than that, he bore no resemblance to the Callahan men—aside from the air of authority he carried that assured her he knew this ranch inside and out.

"You must be Colt," she said, taking a guess.

"And you must be our stranded guest who's convinced my partners they don't know a lick about advertising." He grinned and held out his right hand. "Colt Morgan."

"Delaney Spence," she said, remembering that she'd given Ben her maiden name. "Thank you so much for your help with the car. Millie's never given up on me before, so I'm hoping it's not yet time to give up on her."

Colt laughed.

A fire truck's siren sounded in the distance.

Scout whined.

"You two must be close," Colt said. "You and the car, I mean. I'm guessing you and Scout here are just getting to know each other."

"I think she's hungry," Delaney said, and her own stomach growled. "We both are. Sam was supposed to meet us..."

Colt winced. "I think you're stranded again, Ms. Spence. Sam peeled off in his truck a few hours ago. Something about taking care of unfinished business in town for the start of the festival." He shrugged. "The guy never takes a break."

Delaney scanned the dining room once more, then the outside landscape beyond Colt's broad shoulders.

"Speaking of town, how far is the walk? I could really use some fresh air," she asked him. In Delaney's short time as a Meadow Valley resident, Millie had been as reliable as Delaney's next breath, so she'd always driven, especially since going to town meant she was shopping for groceries or something else to bring back to the property. The trip this morning with Sam had felt instantaneous, so she guessed it couldn't be too bad.

Colt's brows drew together. "It's not very long, but

even with the cooler temps, the sun's likely to do you in once you get moving. If you want a ride—"

"Thanks," she said, interrupting him. "But I've been sitting for hours. I need to stretch my legs. After Scout and I get some food, of course."

"Suit yourself," he said, gesturing for her to lead the way into the kitchen. "I'm sure Luis has something in back for Scout."

Turned out Scout got to enjoy as good a meal as Delaney did. The canine feasted on grilled chicken and carrots while Delaney satiated herself with a chicken salad sandwich and the sweetest, juiciest sliced watermelon she'd had in ages. After changing into her tennis shoes and dropping Scout back at Sam's office, she was ready to hit the pavement.

Colt had been right about two things. The walk wasn't that long—about twenty minutes—and even though it was barely sixty-five degrees outside, after she got going, the sun felt hotter than Channing Tatum. She'd tied the denim jacket around her waist, but it didn't matter. By the time she hit First Street, she was cursing herself for her bravado and for not bringing a bottle of water.

Closed signs hung in shop windows, but the street bustled with who she guessed were the shops' proprietors setting up booths and tents for the festival. She walked slowly, scanning the signs until she found what she was looking for.

IVY'S

In front of the clothing boutique, a woman struggled with a plastic pole and the canopy into which it was supposed to fit.

"Need some help?" Delaney asked, and the woman

looked up from beneath a veil of dark fringe, blowing the hair out of her eyes as she did.

"*Please*," she said. "My fiancé was supposed to help me put this thing together, but he was on call. And wouldn't you know it? He got called. Some reckless kids decided to set off some pre-festival fireworks and lit a poor tree on fire." She shook her head. "At least they had the sense to call the fire department rather than flee."

"Must have been the siren I heard earlier," Delaney said, taking hold of the canopy's corner and keeping it steady as the other woman threaded the pole and locked it into position. "I'm Delaney, by the way. Any chance you're Ivy?"

The other woman's brown eyes brightened. She dusted off her hands and surprised Delaney with a hug. "I'm so happy to finally meet you!"

Delaney stiffened at first. She'd been expecting a reception more like Pearl's. But then she realized Ivy was genuinely happy to see her, and Delaney hugged her right back.

Ivy laughed and gently pushed her an arm's length away.

"I knew I recognized that dress! It looks great on you!" she said. "If anyone back home tells you they like it, you let them know it's an Ivy original. Only available online or in Meadow Valley."

Delaney's brows rose as she smoothed out the dress. "You design the clothes in your shop?"

Ivy nodded. "Not all the pieces I sell. A girl's gotta sleep. But yeah. Flowers are kind of my thing. You really like it?" Ivy's cheeks flushed pink.

"It's beautiful," Delaney said. "You and Sam...Colt towing my car and Luis feeding me and—" An unexpected wave of emotion swept through her. "You've all been lifesavers. Well, Sam literally was." She let out a nervous laugh. "Took a wasp sting for me and everything."

Ivy smiled warmly as the two women went to work putting the rest of the canopy together until it stood perfectly over Ivy's festival territory. "He's a good man, that Sam Callahan. Even though he didn't grow up here, he's one of those people you feel like you've known your whole life. He just sort of fits here."

"Oh?" Delaney said. "So you *are* from Meadow Valley?" She didn't remember the woman or the store from the last time she was here.

"Born and raised," Ivy said. "But there was college. And then my older brother moved out east for a job. And a girl. They had a kid, and my parents flocked to where the grandbaby was, as grandparents tend to do." She laughed, but Delaney detected a note of sadness in the woman's eyes. "My brother was a firefighter. Lost his life in the line of duty. I stayed in Boston for a while after that with my family, but I always knew I'd come back home when the time was right." She swiped a tear from under her eye.

Delaney's throat tightened. "I'm so sorry. I didn't know."

Ivy pressed her lips into a smile. "Thank you. I didn't expect Sam to tell you. He's private enough about his own life, which means he's not one to go gossiping about others." She blew out a breath. "Want to come inside for a few? I can grab you something cold to drink."

A drink sounded heavenly, but before she could say yes, she saw something glinting in the sun out of the corner of her eye—a silver truck parked around the corner from the firehouse.

"Thank you, but I think I need to take a rain check," she said, curiosity winning out over her thirst.

Ivy followed her gaze and grinned. "How about I get you that drink to go, then?"

She was in and out of her shop in a flash, returning with two perspiring bottles of cold water. "There's a recycling bin at the fire station," she said.

"Thanks." Delaney took the offering before the rest of Ivy's words registered. "I mean, I wasn't going—" She sighed. "Am I that obvious?"

Ivy shrugged. "I meant what I said. Sam's one of the best. But odds are if he's at the fire station—and his truck's been there awhile—he's dealing with *something*, and either the speed bag or one of the guys on call is paying the price." She laughed. "Might even be Carter if they're done saving that tree."

Delaney's cheeks burned. She hoped her reaction was hidden by the fact that she was also flushed from her walk. She understood that what happened this morning was rough on Sam, probably more so because she was there to witness it. But they'd connected over the incident, too, hadn't they? Enough so that the least he could have done was give her some notice that he wasn't coming back for lunch—or likely any part of the day.

Delaney took a swig from her water and smiled at Ivy. "Thank you for this and the clothes and understanding why I can't stay."

Ivy beamed. "I'll see you tomorrow at the festival opening, right?"

Delaney nodded as she backed away from the canopy. "Can't wait."

Then she spun on her heel and crossed the street, making a beeline for the Meadow Valley fire station.

People waved at Delaney as she passed, and she smiled and waved right back, wondering if those who looked familiar thought the same of her.

Her destination was situated on the corner of the street, offering two easy exits for emergency vehicles. She made a right turn where she saw Sam's truck, expecting to hear loud, thumping music or something reminiscent of a gym in use, but the air around her seemed to grow quieter instead, stiller than all the activity on the town's main street.

Just like he'd told her, there was a small outdoor gym under a carport-type roof. She unlatched the waist-high gate and stepped through, the ring straight ahead. But Sam wasn't there. Behind it, though, she caught a glimpse of a dark swath of hair, bare shoulders, and a speed bag being given no mercy by the gloves beating against it.

"Hey," she said as she rounded the boxing ring. She was only a few feet from him, but he didn't turn around, didn't even acknowledge her presence. She should have been angry, even indignant, but she couldn't take her eyes off his back, off the sculpted muscles that seemed to move with a quiet grace that juxtaposed the violence of each fist pounding against the bag. All he wore were a pair of basketball shorts and his gloves.

Delaney's throat went dry, and she had to swallow more than once to regain the ability to speak.

"Sam," she finally said, louder this time. "I know you're upset, but we were supposed to have lunch. Your *dog* needed to be walked and fed, and I had no idea where you were."

Still nothing. Just his incessant pounding.

She took a step to the right, ready to give him hell, and saw the wireless earbuds.

She blew out a breath. Okay. *Not* ignoring her.

With another careful step, she moved into his peripheral vision.

He glanced at her for a fraction of a second, then returned his intense gaze to the speed bag. Several seconds later—though it felt like hours—he finally slowed to a stop. He used his teeth to tear one glove from his wrist, tucked it under his arm, and pulled his phone from the pocket of his shorts.

He pressed Stop on whatever song had drowned out her voice and, likely, the rest of Sam's world.

Sweat trickled down the sides of his face. His hair was drenched.

Delaney was having a hard time remembering why she was angry.

"What are you doing here?" he asked coolly.

She crossed her arms, her indignation returning.

"I know I'm not technically a *guest* at the ranch and that the work I'm doing for you is to pay off a room that I *know* you offered me for free. You don't owe me anything, Sam Callahan. But I'm stranded in a town where I'm basically a stranger. *You* are my only connection right now. And it's obvious after this morning that you're dealing with a heck of a lot more than just some woman coming to town to claim her land." She paused and took a steadying breath. He didn't deserve her anger, but she also didn't deserve being left stranded. "We're all dealing with something, aren't we? And I get it if you needed some time to yourself. But my experience has been that when someone disappears without so much as a heads-up, something's wrong."

They stared at each other for several long seconds. "Look," she finally said. "I know there's no label on whatever this is or isn't." She motioned between them. "But I was worried."

There. She'd said it. Because when the anger and indignation melted away, the root of it all was that like it or not, Delaney cared what happened to Sam Callahan.

He glanced down at the phone still in his palm, then back at her. "Guess I lost track of time."

That was it? He guessed he lost track of time?

"That's all you have for me? Come on, Sam. Beating the crap out of that bag obviously hasn't helped much. Maybe if you talk about it—"

"I'm not a talker," he interrupted. "I just need to work it out of me and I'll be fine."

Yeah, he sounded really convincing.

"Fine," she said. "Work it out on me."

His brows rose.

She groaned. "I didn't mean ... Where can I get a pair of those?" She nodded at his gloves.

"In the bin against the building, but—"

She rotated in the direction he was looking, marched over to the bin marked *Equipment*, and rummaged for a pair of gloves that might fit her smaller hands.

"Jackpot!" she whispered.

Maybe he didn't want to talk, but hours out here alone weren't doing the trick. She could be here. She could help him without the words. Sometimes all it took was knowing someone was on your side. She could be on his—or on the opposing end of his gloves.

Delaney tossed her jacket, bag, and bottle of water on the ground and pulled on one glove, then used her teeth to tug on the other. She smacked her fists together to make sure the gloves were on securely.

"Let's go," she said, nodding toward the ring. She didn't wait for him to respond as she climbed between the ropes, positioned herself in the center, and began bouncing on her toes, readying herself to spar.

Sam rolled his eyes. "I'm *not* fighting you, Delaney."

"What's the matter?" she asked, rolling her shoulders one at a time. "Afraid of a little friendly competition?"

He approached the ring carefully and stood against the ropes, but didn't enter. "Look, it's not a man-woman thing. I'm not sexist or anti-feminist, or whatever you want to call it. But I'm bigger than you, faster than you, and I've been at this a long time. I could *hurt* you."

She moved toward him, gloves at the ready. "Bigger and faster, huh? *Because* you're a man? Hate to break it to you, Sam, but that is some sexist BS right there. I told you I train. I may be smaller, but that doesn't mean I'm weaker. It doesn't mean you have better moves. I'll make you a deal though. I'll get out of this ring if you talk to me about why you've been here, probably for hours, beating that poor bag to smithereens."

The muscle in his jaw twitched.

"There's nothing to talk about."

"Well, I'm not going away, so..." She punched him lightly in the ribs.

He narrowed his eyes. "Is that one of your moves? Breaking the rules of the sport?"

"What's it gonna be?" She opened her arms wide. "Work off some steam or tell me why today is getting the best of you." His eyes darkened. "I know what happened with your dad this morning was hard on you, but I also know it's probably not the first time. So talk to me."

"You're wearing a dress," he said matter-of-factly.

She shrugged. "And tennis shoes. And gloves. I'm good to go. Besides, what's wardrobe got to do with how good I am?"

Instead of answering her, he climbed into the ring and slipped his other glove back on.

"I'm not going to hit you, Delaney."

She bumped her gloved fists together. "Okay. Let's see how fast those reflexes of yours really are."

She threw an uppercut to his chin without so much as the ding of a bell.

He pivoted to the right so that all she hit was air.

He *was* fast.

She threw a flurry of jabs at his torso, and he blocked them with ease. And was that—was Sam Callahan smiling?

"Are you *laughing* at me?" she asked.

Sam shook his head as he blocked another jab, then another.

"I just think it's important to point out that weight classes in boxing exist for a reason. There has to be some way to level the playing field so that the sport is more about skill and dedication than who is bigger than whom."

Delaney threw her hands in the air. "It's also not a fair fight if only one person is fighting. Come on, Sam. *Fight.*"

She feinted left, then hooked right—and nailed him in the ribs.

Sam's eyes widened, and he rubbed his side with his glove. "Maybe you *do* know what you're doing, Vegas." He grinned. Then he tossed a jab her way.

She could tell he used little force, but he moved

with swift precision—and she pivoted out of his reach as if she'd known the whole time which punch he would throw.

He raised his brows.

She jabbed right back.

For several minutes they danced like this. Maybe they weren't talking out his issues, but he also wasn't alone. She cared and he knew it, and she hoped she'd thrown him some semblance of a lifeline, just like he'd done for her the second she got stranded in town.

True, he was being careful not to actually hit her, but she had a couple of close calls, so she allowed herself to believe that her own skill was part of the reason she was still in the ring—until she rolled her ankle during a pivot.

"Ow!" she yelped. Sam's hook grazed her side as her knee buckled, but she righted herself before she went down, planting her good foot firm as she retaliated with a right cross.

Only she hadn't realized Sam had dropped his hands or that he was stepping toward her, and her glove connected firmly with his face.

"Oh my God!" she cried as blood trickled from his perfect nose.

Sam stood there for several seconds, eyes wide. Then he shook his head and stumbled a few steps back before righting himself.

"Did you just break my nose?" he asked calmly.

"Oh my God," Delaney said again, unable to think of any other words.

All she'd wanted was to be there for him, to maybe distract him from what was weighing him down, but all she'd done was make it worse. She was pretty sure breaking someone's nose was never the way to say, *Hey. Just want you to know I'm here for you.*

She tore off her gloves and moved toward him, the pain in her ankle having already subsided.

"I'll drive you to the hospital," she said, pulling his gloves from his hands.

He was still just standing there, stunned and bleeding, and, oh God, *she* did this to him.

"No," he said, swiping his arm across his face, blood smearing. "Carter is inside. All the firefighters here are paramedics. He'll know what to do."

She tried to grab hold of his arm, to help him out of the ring, but he shook her off.

"I'm fine," he insisted as he climbed through the ropes, but once on solid ground, he stumbled backward again, the base of the ring stopping him before he fell.

"You're *dizzy,*" she said, climbing down beside him.

He groaned. "I might be."

She wrapped an arm around his waist, and this time he didn't object. Instead he rested an arm over her shoulder.

They walked toward the sliding door that led into the back of the firehouse.

"You really don't like accepting help, do you?" she asked.

"Help is fine," he said. "What I don't like is getting punched in the face. There's a difference."

Delaney bit back a grin. She still felt bad for hitting him, but she couldn't help her amusement. He was charming and funny even when he was mad at her.

She slid the door open with her free hand, and they entered the firehouse's kitchen. A man with auburn hair stood rinsing a dish at the sink. He was dressed in a short-sleeved black firefighter uniform. When he made eye contact with Sam, he dropped the plate in the sink and rushed over.

"What the hell happened to you, Callahan? You piss off a speed bag?"

Sam nodded toward Delaney, who still hadn't let go of him. "*She* happened. I tried to help her when it looked like she landed wrong on her ankle, and this was the thanks I got."

"You must be Carter," Delaney said. "I'm Delaney. We were only sparring. It was a total accident. Did I break his nose? He's dizzy and bleeding, but it might only be a contusion, right? It's starting to swell a little but doesn't look crooked. That's a good sign, isn't it?"

Carter and Delaney helped Sam into a chair at the kitchen table.

"You work in medicine?" Carter asked her.

Delaney shook her head. "I mean, not *people* medicine. I'm a veterinary technician. During one of my clinicals, the vet I was working with treated a dog who had some facial trauma from a car accident."

"So I'm a dog now?" Sam asked, unamused.

"I wasn't finished." Delaney raised her brows and cleared her throat. "We discussed the difference between the canine facial bones and human bones." She shrugged. "Guess I've learned a few things about humans by studying animals."

Medically speaking, that was. She had great intuition when it came to dogs, cats, or horses. But with humans—more specifically *men*—she was still a novice.

"The bleeding's not too heavy," Carter said. He snagged a napkin from a holder on the table. "Use this for now. I need to get you cleaned up so I can take a closer look. Let me just grab a few supplies. In the meantime, Delaney, there should be some soft ice packs in the freezer. Never hurts to minimize swelling."

"I'm on it!" She rushed toward the freezer as Carter slipped out of the room. She threw open the door and found the packs stored in a bin on the bottom shelf. "Figured there'd be more hustle and bustle in here," she said, turning to face Sam.

"Folks are upstairs watching TV or supervising the fireworks setup for the festival," Sam said. "The fact that you already heard a siren today means Meadow Valley is full up on emergencies for at least another six months to a year."

She held out the ice pack, and he took it.

"Thanks," he said, but his voice was still tinged with irritation.

He placed the pack gingerly over the bridge of his nose, wincing at first, but then closing his eyes and letting out a long sigh.

Even though she knew the cold felt good, he looked so uncomfortable holding the napkin under his nose with one hand and the ice pack over it with the other.

She rounded the back of his chair and placed a hand gingerly over his.

"I'll hold it," she said.

She expected him to protest, but he nodded and slid his hand out from under hers, letting his head fall back against her torso.

On instinct, she skimmed her other hand over the hair at his temple, and his shoulders relaxed.

"You were really stopping to help me?" she asked. "That's why you let your guard down?"

"I thought you were hurt," he said. "But I guess it was a feint I hadn't counted on."

She laughed. "I don't fight dirty. I *did* twist my ankle. But I was so determined to show you that even though I'm smaller I'm not weaker that I didn't want to let *my* guard down, even for a second." She blew out a breath. "I never wanted to hurt you, Sam. All I wanted was for you to talk to me instead of bottling up how much what happened with your dad got to you this morning."

Sam's shoulders tensed again, but he was saved from responding by Carter as he strode back into the room with a blue canvas medical bag.

"Okay, Callahan. Let's see how good Delaney clocked you."

Delaney lifted the ice from Sam's face and winced. She wasn't squeamish about the sight of blood—just at the sight of an injury *she'd* caused. She stepped away from him so as not to get in Carter's way, but Sam reached back and grabbed her wrist.

"Stay," he said. "If you don't mind. I kind of like the headrest."

She smiled and moved back into position, her hands on his bare shoulders as he leaned against her torso once more.

Carter pulled on a pair of blue nitrile gloves and went to work cleaning the blood from Sam's face.

She let out a breath. Even from her vantage point, she could tell the swelling was minimal. His nose wasn't crooked. All good signs. But she needed Carter's seal of approval.

Carter shone a penlight up each nostril, then at each of Sam's eyes.

"Okay," he said. "Now for the part you're not going to like."

Sam nodded once. "I'm ready when you are."

Carter started by placing a hand on either side of Sam's head, then pressed his thumbs against his cheeks and under his eyes. He did the same to each side of Sam's nose as well as the bridge.

Sam gritted his teeth and hissed in a breath when Carter hit a particular spot on the bridge under his left eye.

"Right hook, huh?" he said to Delaney, brows raised. "Nice shot."

"Um, thanks?" she said.

Sam rolled his eyes. "Anyone want to tell me how much damage that nice shot did?"

Carter grinned. "I see no obstructions inside. How's your breathing?"

Sam sucked in a careful breath through his nose. "A little congested on the left side, but I can still breathe."

Carter removed and disposed of his gloves, then crossed his arms. "It's not broken. Everything looks good. The bleeding has stopped, and you can breathe. The tender spot on the left doesn't feel like anything is out of place, so my money is on contusion rather than fracture. You can head to the ER if you want a second opinion. Put some ice on it, ten to twenty minutes a pop, every hour or two. Pick your favorite over-the-counter pain med, and maybe snag yourself Sudafed if the congestion is bothering you." He glanced up at Delaney. "Can I count on you to make sure he does all this and doesn't head straight back to work, at least for the rest of the day?"

Delaney nodded, unable to wipe the relieved grin from her face. "You have my word."

Carter narrowed his eyes at Sam. "Do I have *your* word,

Callahan? I can shoot a call over to Ben and Colt to make sure they don't see you in the stable, the arena...Heck, I don't even want you in the dining hall because you're likely to get bent out of shape about something Luis did or Ben didn't do."

It sounded as though everyone in town knew Sam Callahan was a twenty-four-hour rancher. She wasn't happy she'd hurt him, but maybe this would give him a chance to take a second to breathe.

"He's really got you pegged," she said.

Sam stood and crossed his arms over his bare chest. "Are we done here?"

Carter stood and mirrored Sam's gesture. "As soon as you tell me you're going home to rest."

Sam groaned. "I'm going home to rest."

Carter smiled. "That's all I wanted to hear. I'll text you to check in tomorrow." He looked at his watch. "But I am officially not on duty anymore, which means I get to go see my girl."

"Say hi to Ivy for me," Delaney said. "We met just before I came here."

"Will do," he said. "It was nice to meet you, Delaney. Hope we'll see more of you this week."

He left Sam and Delaney alone in the kitchen, an awkward silence stretching between them. Sam washed his hands and face at the sink, wincing as he patted himself dry with a paper towel. She still stood behind the chair, not sure what their next move was. Maybe she'd butted in when she shouldn't have. Maybe he did just need some space.

"Give me a lift back to the ranch? Actually, I should probably drive your truck anyway," she said. "Then I'll let you be."

His brow furrowed as he strode back toward her. "You walked here? Looking for me?"

"Is that so hard to believe?"

He ran a hand through his hair. "I should have shown up for lunch like I said I would. I'm sorry I left you stranded."

She smiled and reached toward him, resting a hand gently on his cheek. "I'm sorry I almost broke your nose."

"What if..." He paused. "I'm really not good at this."

"Good at what?" she asked.

He blew out a long breath. "Letting someone care about me. *Wanting* someone to care about me."

Her throat tightened. All she'd asked for was for him to be vulnerable with her. But now that she got her wish, it made her chest ache. She could give him ice for his nose, a couple of pills for the physical pain. But whatever he was working through today, she couldn't fix. Yet all she wanted right now was to do just that.

Her hand slid from his cheek to his shoulder, then down his arm until she laced her fingers with his.

"I care," she said softly.

He nodded and squeezed her hand. "Then maybe I don't want you to let me be."

"What do you want?" she asked.

"I want you to take us back to your place," he said. "*If* you want that too."

"I do," she said, a weight lifting from her chest. "I really, really do."

CHAPTER TEN

S am let Delaney drive the truck, which was the surest sign he wasn't himself. No one got behind the wheel of Revolver when he was in the vehicle other than him.

"You wait here," she said when she parked in front of the Rite Aid outside of town—the only place nearby that was actually open. Her tone was authoritative and stern.

He reclined his seat and closed his eyes. "I'm not arguing with you, Vegas. There should be a tote bag or two in the back of the cab." His T-shirt was in the back of the cab, too, but he was too worn out to bother pulling it back on. "Plus—no shirt, no service."

She laughed. "Glad I didn't knock your sense of humor out of you."

He smiled but didn't say anything else. His head throbbed. No, his whole face throbbed.

Even though he could tell she was trying to do it softly, he still flinched when the driver's side door shut. Noise was definitely not my friend at the moment.

He shook his head and chuckled.

Delaney Harper.

Yesterday he was doing fine, running full speed ahead at whatever life threw at him, whether it was Luis and his dangerous crush on Anna, or his brother skipping out on yet another night on duty. He was stressed, overextended, and exhausted, but he was *fine*. As long as he kept moving, he didn't worry about the big picture of his life, only what needed to be done next.

Now he was laid up in the passenger seat of his truck with an ice pack over his face and too much time to think about his father's episode that morning—and what it meant as far as the big picture. Because despite his best intentions, he hadn't obliterated the experience with hours at the speed bag.

He added yesterday's wasp sting to the list. Not that he was keeping score, but if he was, the wasp sting totally counted.

At every single turn, since the moment she stepped onto his property—or was it *their* property?—Delaney had disrupted the status quo by exponential proportions. And he hadn't even told Ben and Colt who she was or why she was really in town.

He squeezed his eyes harder, trying to shut out thoughts that only made his head pound more. Maybe she had disrupted his life, but despite what happened in the boxing ring, all he wanted right now was to be in Delaney Harper's presence. Something about the nearness of her did what the speed bag couldn't. She didn't solve all his problems, but she somehow made them feel less like they were going to swallow him whole. He simply wanted more of whatever it was she did to him.

"How ya doing, sleepyhead?" he heard from a voice that sounded a lot like Delaney's.

"Huh?" he cracked one eye open and saw her situating herself in the driver's seat. She tossed one tote bag on the floor behind her, dropped another one on his lap, and set a bottle of water in the center console cup holder. Whatever was in the bag was cold as ice.

"I've been gone fifteen minutes. You must have fallen asleep. I think I even see a bit of drool..."

He swiped a hand across his mouth. "I was *not* drooling." But he also hadn't realized he'd fallen asleep, which meant that even when he was unconscious he was thinking about Delaney Harper.

She grinned. "I know, but I made you think you were."

He straightened his seat and looked inside the bag.

"I bought myself a few necessaries to get me through the next few days. For you, I got some ibuprofen and a decongestant, just like Carter suggested. Also a couple of bags of frozen peas since I don't have any ice packs. The decongestant might speed up your heart rate though. So I'd wait on that if you can. You could probably use a nap."

He grunted. "I said I'd rest. But I'm not in kinder-garten."

She shrugged. "Suit yourself, but once we get to my room, I'm not letting you off the bed. I mean...shoot, you know what I mean."

"Whatever you say, Vegas."

A blush traveled up her neck and into her cheeks.

He hadn't meant to flirt, but then he didn't regret that he had. Despite the physical injuries he'd sustained since Delaney Harper blew into town and the reason she was here to begin with, he was finding it harder and harder to fight the pull he felt whenever she was near.

He lowered the visor, realizing he'd yet to assess the

damage for himself. The skin under his left eye was starting to purple, and the bridge of his nose was noticeably swollen, but he'd seen worse.

He sat back and caught Delaney glancing at him out of the corner of her eye.

"I know," she said, as if reading his thoughts. "It's already bruising. I can't believe I did that to you."

He slapped the visor shut and rested his head against his seat. "I'm just glad you were wearing gloves. Hopefully you'll be gentler with me when we get back to your place," he teased.

She shook her head and reversed out of the parking spot but didn't respond. Maybe she was done fighting the pull too.

He popped a couple of pain relievers in his mouth and washed them down with the water, following them up with a Sudafed because the swelling was making it harder to breathe.

"You really do have a nice hook," he said, breaking the silence once they'd made it out onto the road. "You want to elaborate on why you box so well?"

She swallowed, and her throat bobbed.

"It's good exercise. Isn't that why you do it?" Her tone was light, but it sounded forced, and he knew she was as full of shit as he'd be if he said yes.

"Sure. But it also clears my head," he admitted. "Sometimes, like today, it takes a little longer to get clear."

She blew out a breath. "I guess after the whole knife thing yesterday and almost breaking your nose today, I owe you a little more of an explanation."

He shrugged. "You don't owe me anything, Vegas. What happened today was an accident, but we've got fifteen minutes before we're back in Meadow Valley.

I might not be the best at talking, but I sure as heck can listen."

Her cheeks reddened again, but he knew this wasn't an embarrassed flush, not when he saw her jaw tighten and her shoulders tense.

She cleared her throat. "Before we got the idea to crowdfund the shelter, Wade used to deal with more face-to-face investors."

Sam groaned. "You mean loan sharks?"

She nodded. "I didn't know the first time he got involved with one—not until everything fell through and he came home from a 'meeting' with a split lip." She put air quotes around *meeting*. "And when I flipped, he apologized backward and forward saying he'd learned his lesson and that he'd never deal with anyone like that again. His next venture was being a silent partner in his buddy's food truck business. He even showed me the loan documents that were in Theo's name. The guy was a real good cook too. Gourmet tacos." She let out a bitter laugh. "At least I didn't lose my love of tacos." She paused for a few moments.

"Food truck went belly-up?" he asked.

"Yup. And that's when we left town. I wanted to move north where even if it's one hundred and ten in the summer, I might actually see snow come December."

His shoulders tensed now because he knew what was coming next. But he wouldn't interrupt her again.

She gripped the steering wheel tighter, her knuckles growing white.

"You know about the crowdfunding, so there was no one shady involved. We put a down payment on the property. Dr. Murphy was on board to volunteer his services. Everything was lining up. After barely six weeks in the new place, we got a knock on the door one night." She shrugged. "It's a small town, good reputation. I thought nothing of it. Until three guys barged in, pushed me out of the way, and messed Wade up really badly."

She pulled onto the outskirts of the ranch's property, but she still wouldn't spare him a glance. It was probably a good thing. Because he was seething at the thought of anyone laying a hand on her.

"Did they hurt you?" he asked, afraid of the answer.

She shook her head as they came to a stop in front of the guest quarters. Then she swiped a finger under her eye.

"They held me back and made me watch. Said if he didn't come up with what they owed him that I'd be next."

She finally turned to face him, tears pooling in both eyes.

"He must have shown me fake papers for the food truck—something he probably printed from the internet— and I was stupid enough to believe him. I mean, he was my *husband*. There *were* good things about him. I like to think I wasn't that naive, but..."

"And the money for the shelter?" Sam asked.

She let out a bitter laugh. "I was actually worried about him, about what they did to him. But he managed to empty our account while he was getting stitched up in the ER without breathing a word of it to me." She laughed. "Gotta love online banking."

Sam reached for her hand, wanting to do something to make this better even though he knew he couldn't. She shook her head. "I put myself through school. I put together what would have been that shelter. I'm *not* any- one's damsel in distress." She forced a smile. "Unless, of course, wasps are involved. Or my broken-down car. I let him *rescue* me from a life where I felt stuck. I thought I needed someone to be my reason to leave Las Vegas and chase a dream. But despite how things might look, I can take care of myself. That's why I started training at a gym when I went back home. If anyone ever busted through my door like that again, I was going to be ready and able to kick some serious butt. It's why I'm counting every penny. And it's why the second I learned what Wade did, I drove all night without exactly thinking through what I'd do once I got here."

He crossed the invisible boundary between them and cupped her cheek in his palm, ready to retreat if she wanted him to. But when he pressed his skin to hers, she leaned into his touch. He couldn't articulate what it felt like imagining her opening that door, those men scaring and threatening her. He wanted to tell her what *he* would have done if he were there. How *he* would treat her if she'd chosen him as the person to trust with her life. But this wasn't about him.

"Vegas," he said with the utmost certainty. "If there's one thing I know, it's that you're quite capable of kicking some serious ass. I speak from *very* recent experience."

She laughed, even as another tear fell. "Thank you for listening. I never told my parents or sister the whole story. I guess that's the first time I said it all out loud."

His brows drew together. "Why?"

She shrugged. "It's humiliating—how blinded I was by this supposed knight in shining armor. I trusted him and fell for his BS more than once. Guess it's easier to tell a stranger than those who know me best."

He tucked her hair behind her ear. "You think a man can't know a woman after only a couple of days?" It had barely been that long, yet now he couldn't imagine *not* knowing her.

"Then I guess it's your lucky week because you've got a whole handful of days to get to know me better, whether you want to or not."

He grinned. "I guess you're right." *Lucky* was not the word he would have used when she showed up two days ago. But he wasn't so sure anymore.

Her room was small—only enough space for a bed, nightstand, and dresser—but tidy. They didn't have a maid service at the ranch. Part of the rustic feel of the place was taking care of your own quarters. Plus, it just wasn't in their budget to hire anyone else. But each room got clean towels and sheets upon request. There was also a washer and dryer on the main floor, free of charge. Every time a room was vacated, they'd send one of their stable hands in to vacuum and give the place a once-over, but during anyone's stay, the room was the guest's responsibility. So far it had worked out well.

Sam glanced down at his bare torso and remembered how long he'd been at the speed bag. "Mind if I use your shower?" he asked. An unexpected yawn punctuated his question.

She raised a brow. "Sure you don't want that nap first?"

"I'm *not* tired." He was exhausted. But also stubborn as heck, not that he'd admit it out loud. "But I am pretty dirty."

She pointed toward the bathroom's open doorway. "It's all yours."

"Vegas?"

"Yeah?"

"I have a confession to make." He blew out a breath.

Here went nothing. Or everything. "I've been thinking about kissing you for two days now, and I don't know if I'm going to be able to *stop* thinking about kissing you until I know what I missed out on because of that damned storm."

She stared at him, and he watched her chest rise and fall with each breath she took. It was a risk just to say the words, to admit what he wanted. What would they be risking if they acted on what he guessed they both were feeling?

She fidgeted with the material of her dress.

"I still want my half of the land," she said.

He nodded. "I know." Once it was rightfully hers—and he had no doubt it would be—it would mean dismantling property and rebuilding, neither of which he had the time or money to do. Yet it didn't change him wanting—no, *needing*—to kiss her. The sooner the better.

"So it's just a kiss?" she asked. "We get it out of our systems and that's that?"

Encouraged, he took a step closer, wrapping his hand around hers.

"That might be all it takes to free us from this tension we keep running into," he said with a grin, but it was a lie. He knew the second his lips touched hers he'd already be counting the minutes until he could kiss her again. And he also knew he couldn't give her what she deserved, even if the timing of their meeting had been different. "But if it's not," he continued, "I need you to know that while I'd never do what Wade did, I'm not a forever kind of guy, Delaney. You saw my father. You saw what my future might look like, and I can't—I *won't* put someone through that."

His father's illness tore his family apart. He wouldn't chance doing the same to a family of his own.

She let his hand go and pressed both her palms to his chest.

He held his breath as she rose onto her toes, her lips a breath away from his.

"Maybe we could just enjoy the week and not worry about what comes next until we get there?"

He wrapped her in his arms and pulled her close.

"You deserve better," he said.

"I've had worse." She winked at him. "I like you, Sam. You're a good man with a lot on his plate, and I'd be a lucky girl to get to spend the week with you."

They were stuck in limbo until the courthouse opened back up, and she wanted to spend that time in limbo together.

"You're sure about this?" he asked.

She nodded.

"All I've been able to think about for two days is kissing you, Vegas." Even when he'd left her stranded, he didn't forget about her. Not every jab at the speed bag was to work through what happened with his father that morning. Some were in the hopes of clearing his mind of her—of wanting her when he knew it couldn't end well for either of them.

It hadn't worked.

Delaney swallowed. "It's all I've thought about too."

"What if we stopped thinking about it?" he asked, tucking her hair behind her ear.

She nodded. "Thinking is totally overrated. I'm more of a doer."

He dipped his head and let his bottom lip lightly brush hers, and either another storm was brewing or they'd just created an electricity all their own.

She sucked in a sharp breath, and his heart raced. She had to have felt it too.

"You sure?" he asked. There was no question in Sam's mind that he wanted this, wanted *her*.

"Mm-hmm," she hummed.

Maybe she couldn't carry a tune, but that sound was absolute music to his ears.

Finally, after two days that felt like as many lifetimes, he kissed her.

Sam's heart raced. He tried to take it slow—to protect his nose, for crying out loud—but two days of wondering and wanting and *needing* took over when she parted her lips and let her tongue slip past his.

All he'd wanted today was to escape. If only he'd realized sooner that *she* was the answer. Her soft skin. Her warm lips. She tasted like sweet release. Like salvation. Like everything he never knew he needed.

"Vegas," he whispered, wondering if she could hear that need.

"Sam," she answered, breathless.

He slid his hands beneath her thighs and lifted her onto his hips.

She yelped with laughter.

"Keep me company," he said, glancing back toward the bathroom door where the shower beckoned.

Her eyes grew wide. "I promised Carter—I mean, you're supposed to rest."

"I'm *fine*," he insisted. "Just bruised, remember?"

"That was Carter's educated guess. You didn't get a second opinion. What if it *is* broken?"

He backed slowly toward the bathroom. "Then the treatment would be exactly the same. Unless, of course,

it heals crooked. I guess we'll have to wait and see."
Broken, not broken. He didn't care. The only thing that
mattered right now was showing her that despite his aban-
doning her earlier—despite her excellent right hook—the
day wasn't a total wash.

"Sam..."

"Vegas?"

"You need to ice your nose, and rest, and that kiss was
amazing but—"

"It's just a shower," he said. "We've already seen each
other naked, so it's not like this is anything new." He
smiled, but it was absolutely something new. What happened at the swimming hole—or what *almost* happened—
was spontaneous. Now they were talking, being logical,
and deciding.

She brushed a soft kiss against his lips, humming a
delicious *mmm* as she did.

"So you're not suggesting we—"

He shook his head. "Not yet, at least. Don't get me
wrong. I want to..."

"But we should wait," she said.

He heard the question in her voice and nodded his
agreement. He'd follow her lead and take it slow. After
all, they had over a whole week. Right now, he just
wanted to be close to her. To touch her. To kiss her until
their lips were swollen.

He set her down on the rug and started the water.
They kicked off their shoes and toed off their socks
as though it were a dance they'd performed a hundred
times.

She pulled her dress over her head, and his eyes
widened.

"Vegas, are *you* going commando today?"

She skimmed her teeth over her bottom lip and smiled.

That tidbit of knowledge had him hard in a fraction of a second.

She glanced down at his shorts and back up at him, brows raised.

"Just because we're waiting for...you know," she said, "doesn't mean I can't help you with...you know."

She pressed her palm between his legs, and he groaned. Seconds later she had his shorts on the floor and was leading him into the steam-filled shower.

Once under the warm spray of water, she kissed him hard, stroking him from root to tip. He slipped a hand between her legs, dipping one finger inside her. She sucked in a sharp breath.

She looked at him, her eyes earnest and full of longing, and he wondered if she saw the same in his. Because good lord he longed for every part of her to be touching every part of him.

She gripped him tighter, and he hissed in a breath.

"Did I hurt you?" she asked, eyes wide.

He laughed. "No, Vegas. You just drive me so damned crazy, I don't know what to do with myself."

"Good." She smiled. "All I want to do right now is make you feel better."

She spun him toward the shower spray. The water hit his back in warm, massaging relief, and he let out a long breath.

She combed her fingers through his wet hair, then planted a trail of kisses from his chest up to his neck until she had to stand on the tips of her toes to reach his lips. Her tongue slipped into his mouth, and she smiled against him.

"Are you sure about this week?" he asked.

"I'm not sure about anything," she said. "Not one single thing in my life except this—us—in this moment."

That was when it hit him, how long it had been since he'd simply lived in the moment instead of worrying about the next bill, his father's next episode, or whether he was about to lose half his land to the woman in his arms.

He kissed her, slow and deep, until it felt as if she were melting into him.

"I know exactly what you mean, Vegas."

He felt the shared understanding between them. Something he couldn't name. He'd been with women he'd known for less time than he'd known Delaney, but this was different.

"Stop thinking," he growled before realizing he'd said it out loud.

Delaney's eyes fluttered open. Then she smiled and kissed him.

"Stop thinking, Sam," she said, her voice pleading as she repeated his words. "Be here with me. Right now."

So he stopped thinking altogether and kissed her, letting his unquestionable need take the wheel.

When the hot water was long gone, they retreated, naked, to Delaney's bed.

She burrowed into the space between Sam's arm and the rest of his body. Sam stroked his fingers through her wet hair, wondering how long they could stay like this before he had to start thinking again.

"That is probably *not* what Carter meant about you heading home to rest."

She stroked his chest, and he picked up her hand, kissed her palm.

"This was way better than rest," he said, his last word swallowed by a yawn.

Delaney laughed. "Bet that nap is sounding awfully good right about now."

It was getting harder to argue against the suggestion. His body felt heavy, his head foggy.

"Sleep," she said, pulling the bedding up over his waist before sliding out of the bed.

"I'm just going to close my eyes for a few minutes," he insisted.

He heard the bathroom door snick shut and let out a long, satisfied sigh.

"Just a few minutes," he mumbled once more, then drifted off before reality invaded his world again.

CHAPTER ELEVEN

Sam had been sleeping for almost an hour already, but Delaney couldn't relax—couldn't keep her mind from racing. So she left him in bed and headed to the guest house's laundry room, throwing in her muddy clothes from the day before, everything she'd worn since, and the package of cotton underwear she bought at Rite Aid—minus the pair she'd thrown on under her sundress. She found an ice machine down the hall and filled the tote bag containing the thawing frozen peas with enough ice to keep them cold for at least another hour or two—until the bag became a leaky mess. She could do this, right? Spend a week with a man she really liked and then part as friends in a war over land.

She grimaced. Everything that led her to this point in her life happened because she let herself get swept away by a man who made promises he couldn't keep. But Sam had been honest, had told her what he could give and what his limits were. There would be no getting swept away if she already knew Sam wasn't the sort to sweep.

She'd almost convinced herself, when her phone vibrated on top of the washer, and Delaney jumped when she saw the same number as the call she received the day before.

He can't hurt me anymore.

She pushed back the fear and mustered all the anger and indignation her ex-husband deserved.

"What do you want, Wade?" she asked, answering with no more greeting than that.

"Sunshine," he said. "Is that any way to talk to the man you promised to be with till death do us part?"

She gritted her teeth. "That was when I was still falling for your tall tales. I'm not so naive anymore."

He chuckled, and she heard something sinister in his laugh she'd never noticed before.

"I just want to catch up, darlin'. Why not tell me where you are—or why your aunt Deb is asking around about me after all this time? I'm not a big fan of lawyers, you know."

Her stomach lurched. That arrogant son of a—he didn't even care if she knew he sold their property out from under her. He committed a felony, which could send him to jail, and he had the nerve to laugh.

"I needed a break from Vegas, so I'm visiting some friends in LA. Not that I owe you any explanation," she said. "What's *your* excuse for being so hard to find?" She winced as soon as the words left her mouth.

"So you *do* want to see me. I missed you, too, sunshine."

Her skin crawled. How? *How* had she been so blind? Wade's top priority was only ever himself.

"I divorced you, Wade. Or don't you remember?"

He chuckled again. "It's only paper, sunshine. What we had was stronger than that, and you know it."

Her throat tightened. "You're wrong," she said. "And I'm not looking for *you* anymore, Wade. I have everything I need. So do me a favor and stay away from me and my family."

"Have fun visiting your *friends*, sunshine."

She ended the call without another word.

She had renewed purpose now. She would get her hands on a copy of that quitclaim deed, take it back to Vegas, and prove she had never signed it, before Wade knew what hit him. She would figure everything else out—what that meant for her, for Sam—after that.

She waited until the wash cycle was done and the clothes were in the dryer before heading back to the room. She'd come back for the laundry once it was done. She laughed softly as she slipped quietly through the door to find him still out like a light.

"Doesn't nap," she said under her breath. "You sure showed me, cowboy."

But as she got closer to the bed, her desire to tease disintegrated. The late afternoon sun peeked in from the side of the window's drawn shade, so even though the room was dark, she could see Sam's bruised face.

It was a small enough bruise, just under the inside corner of his eye, but it seemed to darken by the hour so that now anyone who looked at him would not be able to miss it.

"You gonna stare at me all day, Vegas?" he said groggily, eyes still closed. "Heard these things called pictures last a heck of a lot longer."

"I wasn't staring." She turned on the bedside lamp, and

he opened those beautiful dark eyes, squinting as they adjusted to the light. Delaney groaned and sat down on the edge of the bed. "Okay, fine, I was staring, but it's only because the bruising is getting worse, and you haven't iced since the fire station. Are you in any pain?"

He propped himself up on his elbows and grinned. "If I am, are you gonna play doctor and take care of me?" The blanket and sheet she'd covered him with slipped down his chest, and she remembered that he was 100 percent naked beneath it.

She grabbed a bag of peas out of the melting ice, dried it off on the bedspread, and pressed it gently over his nose and eye.

He dropped back onto the pillow and moaned. "Hell, that feels good."

She raised a brow. "You *are* in pain. You know, you don't lose any credibility in admitting it."

He shook his head. "You don't get it, Vegas. I'm the guy who takes care of things. I don't get taken care *of.*" He bolted upright. "Scout. I forgot about her when we— damn it. I gotta get out of here and back to work."

She cleared her throat—the sound intentional and exaggerated. "Scout's fine. I walked her and made sure she was fed before I came looking for you. You're welcome, by the way."

"Wow," he said sheepishly. "Thank you."

She raised her brows. "And I'm not letting you out of this bed until you've iced for ten to twenty minutes like Carter said."

He gritted his teeth and groaned, all flirtation gone.

"You don't even have any clothes to get back to work *in.* So how about slowing down that brain of yours and taking care of *you* so you're well enough to take care of everything and everyone else." She stood and crossed her arms. "Now sit up."

"What?" he asked. "First I have to rest and now I need to sit up? How about *you* make up your mind?"

She narrowed her eyes at him, and he pushed himself up with the hand that wasn't holding the peas to his face. She propped the pillows against the headboard, then crawled into the bed behind him, pulling him back so he rested against her chest.

He let out a long breath, and she snaked her arms under his and pressed a soft kiss to his bare shoulder.

"Is this an acceptable way to spend the next ten to twenty minutes?" she asked.

"I suppose," he said, and she laughed. She'd meant to come back to the room and tell Sam about Wade's call. But he had too much on his mind to worry about her issues with the ex-husband she just wanted out of her life for good. Wade wasn't Sam's problem. He was *hers*. All that mattered now was taking care of a man who spent his life taking care of everyone and everything else.

She clasped her hands around his torso and gave him a gentle squeeze, and she felt the tension leave his body as he relaxed against her.

"I think you're adapting quite nicely to letting someone take care of you," she said softly. And even though he was in *her* arms, she felt just as cared for too. She didn't know it could be like this—the mere touch of someone else enough to assure her that she meant something. But somehow, with Sam, she knew it was more than acting on the pent-up chemistry that had been brewing between them. If they'd met under other circumstances, they might have actually had a shot at something real.

Maybe they only had this week, but it was a week where both could be what the other needed. Where was the harm in that?

He moved the bag of peas out of the way and tilted his head up to press his lips to hers.

"I think I might actually like it," he said, then went back to icing his face.

That was the problem—how much she liked it too.

After a good half hour of *actual rest*, they hopped in Sam's truck and headed back to the small registration building. They could have walked, but Sam didn't want anyone speculating about why his truck was parked outside the guest quarters for an extended period of time.

"I'm fine to drive for thirty seconds," he insisted, holding his hand out for the keys she still had in her bag. "Painkillers are doing their job, and in case you forgot what transpired this afternoon, Vegas, I think my body can handle driving from point A to point B."

She scoffed, but he could tell she knew he was right.

He laughed, palm still upturned. "The keys?"

She finally relented and handed them over. The swelling had actually gone down, reaffirming her trust in Carter's firehouse diagnosis that Sam's nose had only been bruised. In fact, other than the purple skin under his left eye, he almost looked like himself again. She credited that to her excellent bedside manner.

Once inside the truck she asked the question that had been plaguing her since the incident. "What are you going to say, I mean...when people ask what happened?"

He picked up his phone from the center console and unlocked it to show a string of text messages.

"News travels fast in a small town, Vegas. Everybody already knows."

Delaney's jaw dropped as they read through the texts together.

Ben: Heard you had your first TKO in the ring today.

Colt: So our stranded guest laid you out pretty good, huh? Let me know if you need me to cover you at the festival opening tomorrow.

Luis: Anna said la chica bella whose car broke down broke your nose! But no worries, compañero. Anna's the only chica bella for me.

Ben: Wait, she broke your nose? Luis just told me! 😄

Colt: Hey man, let me know if you want me to walk Scout for you.

Pearl: Carter told me about your nose! I'm sorry to say it, Sam, but I think it's a sign. Be careful with that girl. Any connection to Wade Harper is a bad connection.

Sam quickly closed out of the texting app, and Delaney's throat tightened.

"Ignore her," Sam said. "You know Pearl. She's everyone's mama whether they want her to be or not. You told me everything I need to know about Wade, right?"

She nodded slowly, reminding herself that Wade was *her* problem, not Sam's. The only problem they had to figure out together was the land.

"Then don't let Pearl get to you," he said. "She's just being overprotective."

Delaney nodded again and forced a smile. "I was in and out of this town faster than you can blink. I didn't think *I* left an impression at all, let alone a bad one." She blew out a breath. "Pearl's not all wrong, you know. There is the issue of the land."

He shook his head. "We're not talking about that now. We agreed. We can't do anything about it until next week, so let's enjoy ourselves and deal with it then."

She swallowed a lump in her throat. He was right. But if she was being totally honest with herself, it felt kind of crappy that he could so easily detach from a life-changing issue—from *her*. Plus Pearl's comment niggled at her. She didn't want to prove the woman right by waltzing into town and ultimately wreaking havoc in Sam's carefully built life. No matter what happened with the land, Delaney wanted to leave some sort of impression on Sam that showed how much she cared about him.

"Have you ever thought about getting tested?" she asked after a long pause. "So you wouldn't have to wonder how your future might turn out?"

Sam's knuckles whitened as he gripped the steering wheel harder, but he forced a smile.

"Now where's the enjoyment in that, Vegas?" he asked.

She swallowed the lump in her throat. "Sam, please," she said softly. "I just want you to be happy. But in the two days I've known you, I've watched you run yourself ragged with the ranch and beat a speed bag senseless when work wasn't enough to distract you. I know it's scary to see what life might look like for you one day, but the not knowing . . ." She laid her hand on his arm.

The truck came to a stop in front of the registration cabin, the vehicle idling.

Sam pulled himself from her gentle grip and crossed his arms over his chest.

"I'm not looking to be your next project, Delaney."

Delaney. Not Vegas.

She flinched at the sound of her own name.

"That's not what I—" she started, but he cut her off.

"Really?" he said, his tone biting. "You married a man who wasn't up to snuff and thought you could fix him. Now you're getting tangled up with me. I may be different than Wade in a lot of ways, but I'm just as much of a mess. The only difference is I'm not making promises I can't keep."

The words hit her like an uppercut right to the jaw. Maybe she pushed when she shouldn't have, but defensive Sam was not a Sam she liked.

She sniffed back the threat of tears and held her head high. "I'm sorry if I overstepped," she said. "Maybe I was out of line. But that doesn't give you the right to box me up and throw on a label like you know *exactly* who I am."

He wouldn't look at her and instead stared straight out the windshield. They just sat there in the aching silence for what felt like days. Finally, Sam glanced at the clock on his phone. "Dinner starts soon. I'm sure you're hungry," he said, a hint of defeat in his tone. "I'm going to head inside and get dressed."

He hopped out of the truck without another word, leaving her there to wonder how she'd let herself believe that she could keep from getting emotionally involved. Because she was one big basket of emotions right now, and that basket said Sam Callahan all over it.

It was one thing to *be* an outsider in a town she'd once hoped to call home. But Sam Callahan had an impeccable knack for making her feel welcome one minute and like he wished she'd never step foot in Meadow Valley the next.

Of course, *she* had the impeccable knack for saying whatever the heck she felt whenever she felt like saying it, which wasn't her most ingratiating quality.

"Damn it," she mumbled. After the day he'd had—from his father's episode to her delivering her best right hook to his face—she maybe should have cut him some slack. And he maybe shouldn't have retaliated with hurtful anger.

She exited the vehicle and strode through the registration cabin's door to find Scout curled up on the rug in front of the check-in desk, Sam's office door wide open, but no Sam to be found.

Scout's ears perked up when the door clicked shut behind Delaney.

"Hey, girl," she said, squatting in front of the animal as she basked in the pool of sun on the rug.

Scout sprang to her feet at the sound of Delaney's voice, tail wagging as Delaney gave her a good scratch behind both ears.

"Where is that human of yours, huh?" she asked. "I'm getting awfully tired of his disappearing act. Plus, I sort of owe him an apology."

Scout gave her a sloppy wet kiss right on her cheek, and Delaney laughed.

"You think you could tell me where he is?"

Scout danced back and forth in front of the desk, then scrambled down a narrow hallway to the right, where she wagged her tail proudly in front of a door.

Delaney blew out a breath. "Yeah, yeah. I'll let you out," she said. Looked like all Scout really knew how to communicate was whether she was hungry or needed to do her business. So Delaney opened the door she assumed led to the back of the cabin and jumped when she realized it was, instead, what looked like an apartment.

Scout scrambled inside. From behind an interior door, Delaney heard music blaring. She didn't recognize the tune but could tell it was classic rock.

Sam.

She set her bag on the round wooden table that sat outside a small galley kitchen. Scout ran into the kitchen and whined at something on the counter. Delaney found a canister of dog treats sitting just above Scout's head, so she took the liberty of giving her one as thanks for leading her to Sam.

She'd give him his space while he drowned out the rest of the world with his playlist. But she wasn't leaving without apologizing for putting her foot in her mouth. They'd agreed to go the week without letting reality ruin a good thing. After all, they only had next week, and the thought of spending it without Sam? Well, it was a thought she certainly didn't want to think. So she collapsed onto a chair at the table and decided to wait.

She scanned the apartment's surroundings—a rustic wooden coffee table framed by a tan sectional. A modest flat-screen television was bolted to the wall above a short bookcase with shelves boasting everything from DVDs to books to the occasional picture frame. DVDs? Really? Didn't everyone stream movies these days? She laughed. The place was sparse but at the same time homey, much like her room in the guest quarters. She guessed that was Sam's design, and she felt that much closer to him knowing this.

She left her spot and strolled cautiously toward the bookshelves, lowering herself to her knees once she got there.

It wouldn't be snooping to look at the pictures, right? After all, pictures were on display because they were meant to be seen. Anyone Sam invited into his living space would also be invited to view what was on display. So she wasn't *exactly* invited inside. She wasn't uninvited either.

The first frame she grabbed was one of Scout sitting in the bed of Sam's truck, staring right at the camera as if she knew she was the star of the show. In Sam Callahan's life, Delaney guessed that was exactly what Scout was.

The second frame was of a woman and two young boys outside, stretched out on a blanket staring up at the stars. Absent was the photographer, who she guessed was Sam's father, realizing the boys were unmistakably younger versions of him and Ben. She picked it up and traced a finger lightly over the outline of the taller boy's frame, knowing it was Sam. He looked so happy. They all did. It broke her heart to know that the family no longer existed in this capacity—that he kept the photo on display, even now.

This *was* an invasion. She hadn't meant it to be, but now it was.

She swallowed the lump in her throat and put the photo back on the shelf before pushing herself to her feet. That was when she spotted the black file folder on top of the shelf, its existence camouflaged against the dark wood. The label on it read *Alzheimer's Articles*.

"You might as well read what's inside."

She yelped at the sound of Sam's voice, turning to find him standing right next to her. She hadn't realized the music had stopped, or heard the door open.

"My heart just leapt all the way up my throat," she said.

He stood there in a black Rolling Stones concert T-shirt and well-worn but clean pair of jeans, dusty work boots on his feet. She guessed he was ready to throw himself back into work.

"I'm sorry," she said. "I didn't mean to snoop. And you don't really think I was going to read a private file, do you?"

He shrugged, his expression impassive. "You barged into my apartment, gave my dog an unearned treat, and are clearly nosing through my stuff. The thought did cross my mind."

Delaney narrowed her eyes at Scout, who lay curled on the ceramic tile floor, the telltale crumbs framing her muzzle.

"She earned it," Delaney said with a pout. "And I'm not *nosing*. Photographs are fair game."

He grabbed the folder and handed it to her. "Go ahead. Proof I'm not living my life as some sort of distraction from my inevitable future." He backed toward the sectional and sat down on the edge.

Delaney shook her head. "That's not why I barged in here." She groaned. "I mean, I didn't *barge*. You were right. We made an agreement to enjoy the week, and I get that a slew of things that happened to you today— minus what happened in my room, because I think we can both agree that was pretty spectacular—were pretty much crap. I came to find you to apologize."

He scratched the back of his neck and sighed.

"I shouldn't have snapped at you like that," he said. "You might have overstepped, but you didn't deserve what I said about you making me your project. You haven't had the easiest time of it either. But I'm not used to letting anyone else see this much. Hell, not even my brother has witnessed our father standing on a table and threatening to use a board game as a weapon. I don't know how to do this."

She sat down on the floor and crossed her legs, dropping the folder onto her lap.

"Do what?" she asked.

"Let someone in."

She laughed. "Actually, I let myself in."

This, at least, got him to smile. "Read it," he said. "It's okay. Someone else might as well know."

So she opened the folder, first to a printout of an online article about genetic testing and counseling. He'd included the comments, one by a person who was thrilled to have tested negative only to find out her sister tested positive. Another commenter was awaiting results, claiming if he had the gene mutation he wasn't going to have children for fear of passing it on.

There was a second printout outlining statistics for each possible gene mutation. Sometimes the inheritance skipped a generation, while at the same time having a parent with any of the mutations meant that the child or children of that parent had a 50 percent chance of also having the gene. Those with early-onset Alzheimer's could start exhibiting symptoms as early as their thirties.

"Oh, Sam," she said, looking up at him, her eyes burning. "I had no idea."

For the first time since she'd met him, she saw past the rugged exterior—and the recently bruised eye—to what lay underneath. Fear. Here was a man who had everything going for him, and his own genetic makeup could snatch it away as early as sometime in the next decade.

"How old was your dad when he was diagnosed?" she asked.

"It's been about a decade since the official diagnosis, so...forty-eight. But things started going south years before that. We just never thought—I mean, he was so young. He still is. I guess you could call him lucky. His dementia is pretty slow as far as progression. Ben and I moved him into the facility because he wanders off sometimes, and if it's a bad day, he gets lost. Ben and I just aren't around enough to keep him safe." He scrubbed a hand across his jaw. "A lot of what happened between him and my mom had to do with his own damned mind revolting against him. It started with paranoia and strange accusations. He accused my mom of infidelity. He accused *me* of doing something to his son."

Her brows drew together. "I don't understand."

He shook his head. "Neither did I. There was a day my freshman year when I came home from school and he was working out one of the horses we were boarding. When I stepped into the arena to say hi, ask if he needed a hand, he stared at me with this blank expression. 'Can I help you?' he asked, and I thought he was messing with me. I told him it was me, Sam, and he got angry, asking what I did with his boy. I kept insisting I was me, and he kept yelling until I freaked out and ran into the house. When he followed me in a few minutes later, he was different— upset still, but remorseful. He apologized and blamed it on the sun—said he'd been outside too long and just got a little confused."

He stared straight at her, his brown eyes fierce with

something she hadn't seen in him before, something she couldn't name. But what happened to his father—and what could happen to his own future—had broken something inside him.

She dropped the folder onto the floor and rose to her knees in front of him, pressing her palms to his chest. "I'm so sorry," she said. "You must have been so scared. I know it wasn't easy to tell me that, but I'm so grateful you did."

She wanted to comfort him, to tell him that everything would be okay. But she didn't have the ability to do that. This wasn't something that could be fixed. He had either one kind of future to look forward to or another.

"I was scared, but also…he was my dad. I trusted him," he said. "So I didn't say anything to my brother or my mom. I believed him when I shouldn't have. Now I wonder what would have happened if I'd told someone. If we'd figured it out sooner."

She cupped his face in her palms, his stubble rough against her skin. "Hey," she said. "I don't know a whole lot about this disease, but I know enough to be certain that you were just a kid who had no idea what he was up against. So whatever happened with him, with your mom? That's not on you."

He wrapped his hands around her wrists, gripping her as if she were his lifeline.

"I'm not getting tested," he said firmly.

Delaney lowered her hands. "But if you knew—"

He shook his head. "My father carries one of the mutations. You read the statistics. That gives me and Ben a one-in-two chance of having it too. That's pretty crappy odds for both of us. So we decided neither of us would find out. We'd just live our lives until the inevitable happened—or didn't."

She glanced around his apartment, at Scout sitting tentatively, watching them, as if she knew any second one of them was going to jump up and take her outside to play.

This was his whole life—the ranch, his dog, and his father.

"I know you have a lot to fulfill you, but is it really living, Sam?"

She thought he was your typical workaholic, throwing himself into his business because that was all he knew how to do. But it was what he *wanted* to do. What he needed.

He let out a bitter laugh. "I don't have a choice whether or not I'll get the disease. But I do get to choose how I live until I do."

"*If* you do," she argued. "And if you knew, you could prepare. I don't know how, but there are medications. Diets. There are options, and everyone's prognosis is different. If you knew—"

"If I knew I had the gene, I'd live my life exactly the same as I am now—keeping my nose to the grindstone, doing what I love, and leaving personal connections at the door."

His words hit her like a punch to the gut.

She cleared her throat and stood up, brushing non-existent lint from her dress.

"Delaney, I didn't mean..." But he didn't finish the sentence.

"Yes, you did." She forced a smile. "It's okay. I get it. This was only ever going to be a weeklong thing anyway. I overstepped, and you set the record straight. End of story."

What the hell was she thinking, that after who-knew-how-many years of his living with that mentality that she'd come in and change his mind after *two* days?

"You were right. I'm pretty hungry. I'm going to head to dinner," she said, and turned toward the door.

"Wait," he said, his rough hand wrapping around hers. "Please."

She turned back to him, her heart in her throat.

He was standing now, towering over her with those pleading eyes that just about did her in.

"If I could have dreamed up the kind of girl I'd let myself fall for—"

"She'd have been just like me. Blah, blah, blah. I'm a big girl, Sam. I don't need you to protect my feelings."

He huffed out a laugh. "You really are impossible, you know that?"

She opened her mouth to protest again, but he raised a brow, and she thought better of it.

"If I could have dreamed her up," he started again, "the girl in my head wouldn't hold a candle to you."

"Oh," she said, and that was the extent of her vocabulary.

He slid his fingers into her hair, her head resting against his hands. And then he kissed her, his touch achingly gentle, even as his tongue slid past her parted lips.

In that moment, Delaney didn't care about her shelter or his ranch or anything that sent her peeling off from Vegas on the fastest route to Meadow Valley, California. All she cared about was his lips on hers, his hands in her hair, her heart thumping against her chest.

She didn't have the same control as he did. There was no *letting* herself when it came to falling in love. And maybe two days was far too quick to truly know, but something started on that trail ride yesterday, and she couldn't stop it now no matter how hard she tried. So she'd see these few days through, soaking up every second she could with this man.

Maybe they didn't have a future, but they had today, and tomorrow, and a handful of days after that. For now it would have to be enough.

CHAPTER TWELVE

After dinner, Sam took Delaney back to his office so she could show him the fruits of her labor.

He thumbed through the stack of brochures she'd printed on firm, glossy paper he hadn't even known he owned.

"These are amazing," he said. "Consider your room and board paid in full from here on out."

She laughed, but the sound of it felt off. He'd dropped a bomb on her earlier, the seriousness of his situation and what he planned to do—or *not* do—about it. But his mind was made up, had been for years. It wasn't simply a matter of knowing if he had the gene mutation, but there was Ben to consider too. As much as his brother drove him up the wall, he knew Ben's way of life was his own way of coping with the situation. If Delaney thought Sam was barely living, then he guessed she'd describe Ben as living too much.

It was hard enough not knowing what his own future held, but knowing his little brother had the same weight on his shoulders was almost too much to bear. Colt knew the whole story. He also knew stipulations were in place for him to take over Sam's or Ben's third of the business should one or both of them no longer be fit to run it.

"I'm hedging my bets on you being around for a long time, Callahan," Colt had said when Sam laid everything on the table before anyone signed on a dotted line.

As much as he hoped his friend was right, it was enough to know the ranch would be in good hands no matter what happened in the years to come.

"About my room and board...," Delaney said, bringing him back to the moment.

He raised his brows.

"I was wondering if maybe there was any chance I wouldn't have to sleep in that big bed all alone tonight."

He grinned, happy she'd let the whole issue of his future go. He'd meant what he said, that she blew into his life like nothing he could have expected. And he knew that if she stayed in Meadow Valley, he'd have to let her go. He'd have to watch her fall in love with someone else and find the happiness and future she deserved. After what Wade Harper took from her, Sam wasn't about to take anything else or offer more than he could ever give. He could give her tonight, though. He could be in the moment for the time they had, even when they both knew it would eventually end.

"You know, Vegas. Come to think of it, I don't think you should sleep in that bed at all."

He was sitting in the office chair while she leaned on the desk, facing him. He gave her arm a gentle tug, but it was enough for her to slip off her perch and into his lap.

She yelped with laughter and wrapped her arms around his neck.

"Stay at my place," he said.

"But what about your brother? And Colt? They might see us together."

Sam shrugged. "To hell with what anyone thinks. We have a week to make the most of this. We don't need to hide from them." He had this amazing woman in his arms who, despite their differences—despite knowing they had no future beyond these next few days—was willing to offer him more than he deserved. He wasn't going to waste another minute.

"As far as they know, you're Delaney Spence, stranded traveler. No way they'd begrudge me a few days of fun. In fact, I'm pretty sure Ben's actual profession is 'a few days of fun.' They might be surprised, but that's it."

Her smile faltered, only for a second, but he caught it before she painted the mask back on.

"Hey," he said. "We're going to figure this land thing out."

"But not right now," she conceded, her expression brightening. "So you really want me to spend the night, huh?"

He slid a hand under her dress and up her thigh, his thumb stroking her at the tender spot where leg met pelvis. And heck if he didn't want to play the role of Ben tonight and shirk his evening duties. But he'd already been gone the whole day, which was rare for him even if he did have the time off.

She sucked in a breath.

"I really do," he said. "But first, you have to head back to your room and find something warmer to wear. We have a bonfire to attend."

She smacked him on the shoulder. "You *tease*!"

He laughed. "I just want to make sure you're aware that your stay tonight will be very worth your while."

She dipped her head and kissed him, palming him over his jeans. She smiled against his lips, ran her hand up his length, and then hopped off his lap.

"One good tease deserves another, doesn't it?"

"Fair enough." His head fell back against the chair, and he groaned. Delaney backed toward the door. "Meet me back here in thirty minutes, Vegas."

She was halfway out the door and into the reception area, her back to him now. She waved at him over her shoulder. "Hope that's enough time for you to cool off, cowboy. See you in thirty."

She sauntered out of sight.

Sam shook his head and laughed. When it came to Delaney Harper, he doubted he'd ever be able to be around her and completely in control. For tonight, he wouldn't have it any other way.

Backyard s'mores couldn't hold a candle to what Luis and Anna put together for a Meadow Valley Ranch bonfire. Because Luis insisted the berries be fresh, he'd asked Anna to deliver them specially for the evening activity, though Sam guessed the man had ulterior motives for requesting Anna's presence at the ranch's evening event.

Guests lined up at a picnic table covered in a red-and-white-checked cloth, the s'mores fixings that ranged from Anna's fresh berries to organic peanut butter to gourmet chocolate to Luis's homemade marshmallows organized to create an assembly line for the decadent creations.

Luis was giving lessons on how to perfectly toast a jumbo marshmallow when Anna interrupted, shoving her stick straight into the fire.

"Or you could burn the sucker just like this," she said, pulling her stick back to reveal the flaming torch that was once a marshmallow. "Nice and crispy on the outside and not too gooey on the inside."

Luis's jaw dropped in horror. "That's not how we do things in *my* kitchen."

Anna blew out her marshmallow, stalked to the table, and picked up the bowl of fresh blueberries, strawberries, and raspberries. She glanced from Luis to Sam. "You haven't paid me for this delivery yet. I can take it back."

Some guests watched the interaction with suppressed smiles—much like Sam and Delaney were doing—while others on the opposite side of the fire were oblivious to the escalating row.

"You wouldn't," Luis said, calling her bluff.

Anna knew the best way to push Luis's buttons was to threaten his food.

She tilted the stainless steel bowl, and a couple of berries tipped over the edge and into the dirt.

Luis gasped. Then he let loose in rapid-fire Spanish that Sam couldn't understand, punctuating his tirade by brandishing his stick at her, the perfectly toasted marshmallow flying off the end and landing with a gooey splat right on Anna's chest.

"Oh my God," Delaney finally said. "This is amazing."

Sam tilted his head down toward hers. "I should probably do something," he said under his breath.

Delaney shook her head. "Are you kidding? Look around you. The guests are eating this up. *Literally.*"

Sam laughed as he saw what Delaney meant. Guests' rapt faces—both young and old—bore smiles as they devoured their s'mores and enjoyed the show.

"What's the worst that could happen if I don't intervene?" he asked.

He didn't have to wait for his answer. Anna had

already rested her marshmallow-topped stick gingerly on the corner of the table and was now facing Luis—no more than two inches between them—with a handful of berries.

"*Diablo*," Luis said with a growl.

Devil. That one Sam knew.

"You would waste your stock just to spite me?" he added.

Anna smashed the berries against his chest, purple and red juices running down his apron and staining the skin under his neck.

"At this rate," Sam said, "no one will even notice you messed up my face."

Delaney elbowed him in the side, and he stifled a laugh.

"Why do I keep coming back here?" Anna asked, her berry-stained hand fisting the collar of Luis's T-shirt. "Other than a paycheck, I get nothing but your nagging mouth. Your full-lipped, never-shuts-up, nagging mouth."

"*Cállame*," Luis said, his voice low.

"What the hell does that mean?" Sam whispered.

"'Shut me up,'" Delaney answered. "Thank you, AP Spanish."

And that was exactly what Anna did, planting one square on Luis's stunned lips.

Whoops, hollers, and applause rang out from the guests along with a few grumbles and *ew*s from some of the younger members of the crowd.

Sam laughed. He surveyed the scene—the happy guests, the people he worked with who were more friends than anything else, and the amazing woman beside him who would warm his bed tonight.

This was what he was fighting to protect. It was more than money or preserving the integrity of the ranch. He'd built the best life he could imagine for himself in Meadow Valley, and that meant everything to him.

"You're like a little family here, aren't you?" Delaney asked. "You and everyone who works for the ranch."

Sam nodded. This was it now. Him, Ben, Colt, Luis, the rest of their small team—and hopefully Anna if Luis didn't screw up. He still had both his parents, and he was grateful for that, but they weren't a family anymore, not in the traditional sense at least.

Anna relinquished the berries back to their rightful spot on the s'mores assembly line.

"Hey, Sam," Luis said, but Sam waved him off.

"We're good here, Luis. Take the rest of the night off."

His temperamental chef grinned as he grabbed Anna's hand and led her from the bonfire.

"You still owe me for the evening delivery!" Anna called over her shoulder.

Sam laughed. He'd never admit it, but it was he who owed them for showing him—*and* Delaney—what this all truly meant.

"Okay," Delaney said. "When do *I* get to make a s'more?"

Sam gestured toward the picnic table. "Right this way, ma'am." He grabbed two sticks from the pile on the bench and handed one to her.

She bounced on her toes and smiled as she chose a suitable marshmallow. "I haven't done this since I was a kid. Is that weird? We could never take long family trips, but we'd camp one night here or one night there. This reminds me of that."

They grabbed a couple of open spots on large rocks that served as chairs around the fire.

"Are you a slow roaster or a burner?" Sam asked,

MY ONE AND ONLY COWBOY   183

holding his marshmallow just out of reach from the lick of the flames.

"Hmm," she mused. "I think maybe I'm a combo of the two, a slow burn."

She kept her focus on the fire, but he could see the blush in her cheeks lit up by the campfire's glow.

Slow burn? Right. Delaney Harper was a blazing inferno he couldn't extinguish. The more he tried to douse the flames, the stronger they grew.

They sat in silence, the two of them turning their sticks until both their marshmallows started to droop.

"Time to make a masterpiece," she said, rising from her rock.

Sam followed her to the table. Of course, Luis didn't serve the guests store-bought graham crackers. He baked them from scratch. The cinnamon and sugar coated Sam's fingers as he put two of them on his plate.

"Oh my God," Delaney said, licking the sweetness from her own fingers. "Did he *make* these?"

"Mm-hmm" was all he said, watching her slide the gooey marshmallow off her stick and directly onto one of the graham squares. She carefully placed a smattering of berries on next, then topped off her creation with a block of dark chocolate.

The ranch hosted bonfires every weekend, but they were simple. Store-bought grahams—much to Luis's chagrin—as well as any other fixings. Not like this one. They'd gone all out for the festival. Sam had never brought anyone along before now. The guests were none the wiser, but had Ben or Colt been working tonight, they would haze him something good because when it came to matters of the heart, men were always thirteen-year-old boys on the inside.

"What?" she said, looking up at him. "Do I have something on my butt? Did I sit on a marshmallow?" She strained to look over her shoulder to confirm her suspicions.

"No." He laughed. "I've just never done this with anyone before. It's—different."

She sandwiched her s'more together and stared at the two bare grahams on his plate, then looked down, where his roasting stick hung at his side, his perfectly toasted marshmallow now a sticky puddle in the dirt.

"Damn it," he said when he followed her gaze. He used the stick to scrape as much of it as he could onto his plate, then threw the whole mess in the trash bin on the other side of the table. "Guess I got distracted," he said, dusting off his hands.

Delaney picked up her s'more—the marshmallow dripping with warm berry juice.

"So, is me being here *good* different?" she asked. "Because the right answer might get you a bite, seeing as how you're now completely without dessert."

He wasn't exactly sure how to articulate what it was like having her here, sharing something that was normally just a routine part of his job. But nothing about tonight felt routine, especially the idea of her feeding him her s'more.

"Yeah," he admitted. "I guess it is *good* different. Did I pass the test?"

She bit her lip and grinned. "You get an A plus, Mr. Callahan. I guess you've earned your reward."

She lifted the s'more to his lips and held her plate under his chin. He bit into the confection, and berry juice dribbled down his chin.

Delaney snorted and tried to catch the juice with

her plate. "You've also got a big glob of chocolate right—"

He stuck his tongue out and licked the corner of his mouth, right where he could feel the warm, melted chocolate.

She pouted.

"What's the matter?" he asked.

She shrugged. "Maybe *I* wanted to clean that off for you."

Sam's whole body filled with heat as he imagined her doing just that. He wanted it, too, wanted so badly to let go of everything holding him back from being here in this moment. But letting go meant admitting that while the ranch and everyone who was a part of it were his family, something was missing—something he hadn't realized until Delaney Harper blew into town.

He let out a nervous laugh, and she raised her brows.

"You don't want to kiss me in front of the guests." The words were an accusation, but she was still smiling. "I dare you, Sam Callahan. I dare you to break all your rules and plant one on me right in front of a big old audience."

He glanced around at the various couples and families, and the group of women who all came to celebrate their fiftieth birthdays. After witnessing Luis and Anna's fervent display of both contempt and affection, the guests had turned their interest back to enjoying their own conversations and desserts. Still, he was one of three owners of the establishment and the most visible, what with living on the property while Colt and Ben shared an apartment in town. They each crashed in the guest cabin if they had a late night or early morning on duty. Or, if it was Ben, sometimes that crashing was *with* a guest or someone else in town. If Colt was doing the same, he made less of a show of it. Which brought him back to the case at hand.

Sam Callahan was not one to make a show of things, least of all his personal life.

"Wow," Delaney said. "Those wheels are really turning. Don't worry about it, cowboy. Some people are the dare-accepting kind. Some people aren't. Consider yourself off the hook. You don't need to kiss me in front of the clientele. I get keeping the business side of your life separate from the personal side. Or whatever this is." She took a bite of her s'more, her lips now covered in marshmallow and chocolate.

His brow furrowed. "There's no difference," he said, realization in his tone. Every part of his life was right here at this bonfire. It was in the stable and the dining hall and the guest residence. It was walking Scout on one of the horse trails or hopping into the saddle and riding Ace to the swimming hole—with a beautiful stranger close behind.

Except she wasn't a stranger anymore.

"I don't follow," Delaney said after swallowing.

If that one bite of her s'more was any indication of what those lips of hers would taste like now…He shook his head, momentarily freeing himself from the thought.

"The business side and personal side of my life. You were right about me throwing myself into my work. But it's not a distraction. It's what I love."

She nodded. "I know. I was out of line."

"No. That's not what I meant. With you here—aw, screw it," he said, snatching Delaney's plate from one hand, the s'more from the other, and tossing both into a pile on the picnic table.

"Hey!" she cried. "What do you think you're—"

He threw his arms around her, lifted her onto his hips, and waited the split second for her to wrap her legs around his waist before kissing her with everything he had and then some.

He guessed people were likely staring, and perhaps there was a hoot and holler or two. But for the first time in—he couldn't remember how long, he didn't give a shit about who caught a glimpse behind the curtain, not when it meant he got to kiss the woman in his arms, to feel her body pressed against his, warm and soft and tasting of chocolate and berries and something so inherently *her* he'd know it even if he were blindfolded.

He lifted his head to see her staring at him wide-eyed, a smile spread from ear to ear.

"Wow," she said. "I should dare you to do stuff more often. Oooh, I have another one. I dare you to cop a feel. No, wait! I dare you to swipe your hand across that picnic table, knocking all of Luis's treats to the dirt, and take me right there!" She squeezed her legs around him, and he had half a mind to call her bluff. But the other half of his mind reminded him that throwing caution to the wind and kissing her senseless in front of an audience was about as far as his *screw it!* mentality could go.

"Can we keep a mental list of all those things?" he asked. "Because as soon as we clean up here and get back to my place—"

She cut him off with another kiss, and they spent the remainder of the bonfire enjoying Luis and Anna's gourmet spread along with the guests while stealing kisses whenever they thought no one else was looking—or even when they knew they were.

As the fire dwindled and guests started heading back to their rooms, Delaney grabbed the trash bin and winked at him. "I'm going to expedite the process, if that's okay. We've got a list to take care of."

"Who's got trash?" she called out to the crowd. "Don't worry. You don't need to get up. I'll come to you!"

She rounded the circle of guests, collecting offered remnants of their s'mores, even doing so much as to stack the paper plates and drop them in a smaller paper bag for composting back at the ranch.

Sam shook his head and laughed. Not that he wanted any of his guests to feel rushed, but if Delaney's trash collection meant the two of them would be alone sooner rather than later, so be it.

They waited as the last of the guests made their way down the path and back toward the guest headquarters until they were the only two left. Sam went for the jugs of water Luis had wheeled over on the dolly along with the s'mores fixings.

"Wait," Delaney said, grabbing his hand and pulling him back to his rock. "Can we sit here awhile longer, just the two of us?"

But our list.

She narrowed her eyes at him, likely having read his mind. "*Sit.*"

He sat.

"Are you officially off duty now? Other than putting out the fire and bringing back all the kitchen stuff."

He nodded but patted his cell phone in his pocket. "But I'm on call." Always on call. For the ranch, for his father, for just about everything.

Delaney held her hands out toward the fire. She'd followed his advice and wore a hoodie and jeans, but the air still had a bite at night, sometimes getting as low as fifty degrees.

"Are you cold?" he asked.

She shrugged. "A little. But you know how I like the cooler temps." She bumped her knee against his. "You know, we're the only ones here now. If you wanted to cop a feel, no one would see."

He tilted his head toward the star-studded sky and laughed. "You make it sound like we're meeting under the bleachers at a high school football game. Kinda takes all the romance out of it when you put it that way, doesn't it?"

She spun on her rock, straddling it so she could face him. "Well now, cowboy. I don't believe I was aware that I was being *romanced*."

He pivoted, too, mirroring her position, his knees brushing against hers. He slid his hands under her thighs, tugging her closer to the edge of her rock. The warmth the fire brought earlier had nothing on the spark that jolted through him when his body touched hers. "Maybe I don't have time to wine and dine you or take you on an actual date, but I like to think my moves tend toward the romantic."

She snorted. "Saying the word 'moves' doesn't really help either."

Sam was out of his element. He wanted her—yes. But he also wanted her to know that she meant something. That what they were possibly about to do *meant* more than two people satisfying a mutual need.

"I have never met anyone like you, Delaney Harper. And I'm not sure I ever will again."

She narrowed her eyes. "I'm not sure if that's a compliment or an insult."

He laughed. "You're smart and funny and spontaneous and sexier than anyone else who's ever leveled me with a right hook."

Her eyes widened, and she sucked in a breath.

"*Sam* . . ." was all she said, but it was all he needed.

It was out there. She knew without his spelling it out. Even if he couldn't give her a future, he could give as much of himself as possible tonight.

He gently grabbed the bottom of her hoodie, his fingers playing with the material.

"Are you teasing me again, Callahan?" she asked, trying to lighten the mood.

He raised a brow. "That depends on whether or not you find teasing to be one of my more successful *moves*."

His pinkie slipped under the thick cotton, tickling her abdomen over the ribbed tank she wore beneath.

She wrapped a hand around his wrist, guiding it upward toward her breast. "That depends on your follow-through. Teasing me and leaving me wanting? Not a successful move. But teasing me and following through . . ."

He felt the hardened peak of her breast beneath the tank, and his eyes widened.

"Commando up top, Vegas?"

She bit her lip and grinned. "Guess you could say my move is not wasting time with extra layers."

He pulled the loose tank down over her breast, her soft, warm skin enveloped in his palm.

He detected a tremor in her next inhale.

"I really, really like your moves," he said, giving her a gentle squeeze.

She hummed softly, then unzipped the hoodie so he could see her in the glow of the firelight—her creamy skin with its smattering of freckles, the pink circle of her areola, and the dark pebbled flesh ripe for a tiny, teasing taste.

He pinched her between his thumb and forefinger, then dipped his head and flicked his tongue against her taut skin.

She gasped, and he grazed her with his teeth.

Her back arched as she whispered his name.

There was no way he wanted to stop now, douse the fire, and clean up before he could give her what she needed—what they both needed—back at his place. Sam wanted her now. Here. Under the stars.

He looked up and scanned his surroundings. The path out of the clearing and back to the main building was several yards long, and even after that the guest house was at least another thirty yards off, if not more. And the picnic table was on the far end of the bonfire, nowhere near the footpath.

He pinched her again, and she cried out.

"Dare me," he said.

"What?" she asked, her breath ragged.

He eyed the picnic table, then met her gaze again.

"*Dare* me, Vegas."

Her jaw dropped, and the reflection of the flames danced in her eyes.

"I dare you to swipe your hand across that table and take me right here."

He swallowed. This was so far from taking it slow, but now he wanted to squeeze in every possible experience with her before their week was up.

"Are you sure?" he asked. "I know what I want, which is not to waste any of the time we have left. But it has to be what you want too." Whatever happened, he'd follow her lead. They were in this together.

She shook her head. "I want to soak up every minute with you that I can." She paused. "And I want *you*, Sam. All of you. No matter what happens next."

His throat tightened. Would she want him if he turned out like his father—if he forgot her name in twenty years or that they spent this inexplicable evening together?

"I want all of you, too, Vegas" was all he said.

Then he stood and held out his hand. She took it, letting him lead her to the table where, after one swoop of his forearm, the remnants of the s'mores fixings scattered across the dirt.

"We should probably clean that up after," she said with a smile.

"Noted."

Then he laid her out on her back—his own veritable feast—and peeled off her hoodie and top.

Her chest heaved with each breath, and he bent over her, his tongue licking a trail from her navel to her chest. He cupped one breast in his palm, laved her nipple with expert, tender care.

"Does it taste as good as the other?" she teased, her words peppered with tiny gasps.

"Better," he said, his voice rough with need. "Every bit is better than the last. I don't know how you do it."

He couldn't get enough of her, couldn't satisfy the ache in the pit of his stomach. With every nibble, every lap of his tongue, he simply wanted more.

He wouldn't think about the week ending or who owned what part of the land—only her and the fact that, if only for a little while, she was his and he was hers.

Delaney Harper woke him up when he hadn't even known he was sleeping, and for the first time in his life, reality was better than the dream.

He kissed his way up her neck and felt her go to work with the button of his jeans. His lips reached hers right as she freed his erection from its confines, her hand wrapping firm around his pulsing length. She stroked him from root to tip, squeezing—not enough to inflict pain but just enough to drive him absolutely mad.

"Damn, Vegas," he growled between gritted teeth. Then he kissed her hard, his tongue plunging past her parted lips. He wanted to devour her, to satiate the unyielding need his body had for hers.

His kisses were unrelenting, and she drank in all that he offered.

"How can we…?" she said between breaths. "I didn't bring…"

"Back pocket," he said, his voice hoarse.

She curved her hand around his ass, her fingers plunging into each pocket until one came away holding a small square wrapper.

"Was this your plan all along, Mr. Callahan? To have your way with me in the wilderness?"

He grinned. "Not exactly. But I should probably tell you that I was a Boy Scout once upon a time. If there's one thing I remembered, it's to—"

"Always be prepared," she finished. "I do love a man who plans ahead. Not that I *love*—I mean, I just meant—"

"It's okay," he said gently and smiled.

She pinched the packet between the thumb and forefinger of each hand, but Sam shook his head.

"Also, I haven't quite made *all* the necessary preparations," he said. "I mean, you're still wearing pants."

She barked out a laugh, then threw a hand over her mouth.

"Don't worry," he said, his voice low. He slipped the button of her jeans through the hole and unzipped the fly. "I'm ninety-eight percent sure no one can hear us."

"What about the other two percent?"

He shrugged, yanked her pants below her ass, and rested his palm between her legs. "Either take your chances or try to come quietly." He sank a finger between her folds, and she pressed her lips together, suppressing a whimper.

She dropped the condom onto the table and retaliated by grabbing his erection, sliding her fist over his wet tip and down to the base. He buried his face in her neck to stifle his groan.

"Challenge accepted," she breathed into his ear. "But are you up to the task as well?"

He knew if anyone came looking for them—if a guest wandered back to the bonfire having forgotten a jacket or having lost a room key—he'd be toast. Bare assed with his dick out was so far out of the realm of professional behavior. Yet logic failed him at every turn. He was willing to risk his reputation and possibly his livelihood for her. And it wasn't simply because he couldn't keep his jeans zipped when he was around her. It was everything from her teasing and dares to climbing into a boxing ring when he didn't have the words to say what he was feeling.

Kind of like right now.

"Fine," he said smiling. "Challenge accepted. Condom. Please."

She skimmed her teeth over her bottom lip and then let go of him. He let out a shaky breath as she pushed herself up to sitting and tore open the packet. Then she deftly slid the condom over his length, a shudder running through him as she did.

He tore off her shoes, tossing them to the ground. He did the same with her underwear and jeans. She yelped, covered her mouth again, and laughed.

Sam raised a brow, and she swatted him on the shoulder.

"You said *come* quietly. I wasn't—you know."

"Not *yet*, Vegas."

He wrapped his hands around her thighs and yanked her to the table's edge. He stood, the table the perfect height for him to nudge her opening, the ultimate tease.

She braced her hands on the edge and whimpered softly, her head falling back.

With a delicate thrust of his hips, he penetrated enough to dip into her warmth but exited just as quickly.

Delaney sat up and hooked her legs around his waist, her eyes meeting his with a gaze full of a need so primal he guessed its only match was his own. She flashed him a wicked grin, her only warning before she wrapped her arms around his torso and he sank, root to tip, into her intoxicating heat.

He kissed her hard to silence his groan, teeth clacking and tongues tangling. He'd meant to go slow, to restrain what had been building inside. But all bets were off now. The dam had burst, and he was diving headfirst into the flood.

He rocked against her, filling her with everything he had. Their lips still joined, her muffled cries propelled him, guided him, undid him. Each thrust pushed her farther from the edge of the table until he had to climb over her to maintain their connection.

Harder, faster, he plunged deep inside her, his urgency fed by the ticking clock. What would it be like to have a lifetime to get to know this woman, to give her all she deserved and more? He wouldn't be able to answer those questions, so he gave her everything, right here, right now, to make up for the future he couldn't offer her.

Again and again he buried himself to the hilt, doing what he could to commit every touch, sound, and scent to memory. No matter what happened after tonight, there was no way he'd forget this, no way he could forget *her*. No way his brain would be so cruel as to take this night away from him.

He'd let himself believe the lie for tonight.

She cried out his name as her muscles contracted around him, triggering his own climax. Something savage tore from his chest, their challenge to stay silent a thing of the past, and it all came crashing down.

CHAPTER THIRTEEN

L iterally.

The sound of wood snapping registered a second too late—not that Sam could have done anything to save them—and the picnic table collapsed beneath them, Delaney slamming to the ground on her back and Sam braced above her, the impact rocketing a jolt of pain from his palms all the way up to his shoulders.

Delaney shrieked, and he was sure she must have been injured—until she erupted in peals of laughter.

"You're not hurt?" he asked in a loud whisper, then realized muffling his voice at this point was futile. If no one heard the crash, no one was going to hear him speak. But if someone *did* hear the crash...

He sprang to his feet, peeling off and tossing the condom in the trash, then tugged his jeans up from his ankles, a quick button and zip taking care of his biggest worry.

He held a hand out for Delaney, who was still roaring with laughter, and pulled her to her feet. Together they scrambled to find her jeans and shoes. She was fully dressed except for one shoe when two figures burst into the clearing from the footpath and rounded the dying bonfire. One of them sprayed what Sam knew was a Super Soaker, and the other shone a handheld strobe light.

Delaney yelped as she was nailed in the side with a blast of water.

"Hey!" Sam called out, but whoever was wielding the water gun had already hit him square in the chest with an icy burst. "It's just me! Call off the damned wildlife prevention squad!"

The strobe light fell dark, and the other figure lowered his toy-store weapon. After Sam's eyes adjusted and he could make out Ben's and Colt's features, his suspicions were confirmed.

Ben pointed at the collapsed table with his gun. "What the heck happened here? We got a bunch of city folk thinking the property is about to be attacked by mountain lions."

Sam raised a brow and nodded at the toy weapons in each of the men's hands. "You sure it's only the city folk afraid of an animal that hasn't been seen in these parts in over a decade?"

Ben pointed the Super Soaker at his brother once more. "You're the one who told us we always had to be prepared for the unexpected. You even shared the website with us claiming bright lights and water would do the trick without harming the animal."

Colt brandished his powered-down flashlight. "He's right, Sam. This was *your* suggestion. Ben's the one who found everything in the storage shed."

Sam crossed his arms. He was the one who had bought the items, trying to cover any and all just-in-case scenarios. He just hadn't realized his brother had been listening.

"What are you two doing at the ranch tonight anyway? You both have the night off."

"Festival's tomorrow," Colt said.

"Figured you could use a hand getting everyone to town after breakfast," Ben added.

It wasn't like they were booked solid, but with only his truck, it would take Sam a few trips to get everyone to town who didn't want to walk. But with Ben's truck and Colt's hybrid SUV, they'd be able to cut that time in half.

Sam scratched the back of his neck. "This is pretty unexpected. I don't know what to say."

Ben shrugged. "It was Colt's idea. But since I didn't have any other plans..."

Sam chuckled. "He finally get shot down?"

"Hard," Colt said. "By Pearl's granddaughter. The doctor. It was painful to watch."

"Hey," Ben said. "I'm right here. And *no*. I didn't get shot down because *I* don't get shot down. I'm seeing Charlotte. Just not until later. She was catching up with Ivy and Carter."

Colt laughed, but he stopped short when he saw that his friend wasn't smiling.

Ben fired a blast of water at an unsuspecting Colt.

"Hey!" Colt yelled. "You're a real jackass, Callahan. You know that?"

Ben didn't respond. Sam and Colt's ribbing had hit him where it hurt, and all three men knew it.

"Hey," Delaney said, breaking the silence. "Not that I know this girl at all or anyone who *hasn't* shot Ben down, but maybe she likes the fact that Ben doesn't want to be tied down. There's nothing wrong with enjoying yourself outside the realm of commitment."

Sam cleared his throat.

Ben laughed.

Colt hung his head and swore under his breath. "You're right," he said, chagrined, his eyes meeting hers. "My apologies, Ms...."

"Har—" Sam froze as she caught herself midway through the word. "Spence," she corrected. "Delaney *Spence*."

She was still protecting her identity, protecting the fantasy of their week together before having to deal with why she was really here—and why he couldn't say to hell with the deed and ask her to stay.

"We were, uh..." Sam wasn't sure what to say next.

"About to pitch that tablecloth and the rest of the mess you made?" Ben asked.

Delaney groaned, dropping her face into her hands. Colt shook his head at Ben, and Sam gritted his teeth.

"Think you two can head back and let the guests know it was a false alarm?" Sam asked. "Better yet, maybe tell them it was some kindling falling while I doused the fire. I'll find us a new picnic table this week."

"We'll take the foodstuffs back to the dining hall," Colt said. "You can have the dolly for the water jugs and trash bin—and what's left of the table."

"I trust you won't be frightening the guests any more this evening, big bro?" Ben asked as he and Colt started piling what was left of the food supplies to carry back.

Delaney doused the fire while Sam rolled up the tablecloth and stuffed it into the trash. Then he loaded the pieces of the collapsed table onto the dolly with the garbage can.

"What are you going to do with that?" she asked.

He shrugged. "Chop it into kindling and use it for a future bonfire—long after anyone might remember where the wood had come from."

She laughed. While their night had come to a comical end, there was nothing funny about everything that happened before the table collapsed.

It was everything she promised herself she'd avoid. Sam Callahan was sweeping her off her feet, and despite knowing he couldn't give her forever, she was letting him.

He used his Maglite to guide them along the darkened footpath, pushing the dolly as she walked silently beside him, both seemingly not knowing what to say after all that had transpired.

Hey, Sam, so that was amazing, huh? I might fall in love with you by the end of the week.

Or *Hey, Sam, I'm having these feelings for you that might be outside our little agreement. How about you?*

Or the absolute truth. *Hey, Sam, I know the future might be extra scary for you and anyone you let into your life, but you'd be worth the risk.*

Was she crazy to think of the possibility of more after only a couple of days? Or was it possible to know in your heart that something could be so right if only given the chance?

It didn't matter. She'd scare him off for sure if she said any of that out loud. Only when they could see the lights of the main ranch building ahead did she break the silence.

"So I guess I'll see you for the festival opening tomorrow?" she asked, the question masked with an air of nonchalance she hoped he believed.

He clicked off the flashlight and stuck it in his back pocket, then took her cheeks in his palms and kissed her.

"What was that for?" she asked.

Sam blew out a breath. "Thought it might remind you about me asking you to spend the night."

Her breath caught in her throat, and a warmth spread through her that was quite different from what she felt when Sam's skin was pressed against hers. He still wanted her in his bed, even after they'd already done what they'd planned to do at his place.

She let out a nervous laugh. "Yeah, but we just—I mean, I figured since we already..."

He stroked her soft cheeks with his thumbs, her skin growing hot against his touch.

"Maybe I want to wake up with you," he said. "See what it's like to have you close by without the heightened adrenaline of a thunderstorm or boxing match or a table collapsing beside a bonfire."

Her heart squeezed in her chest at the thought of sleeping in his arms, of his gorgeous, currently battered face being the first thing she saw in the morning.

She slid her arms around his waist and breathed a soft sigh. "Don't forget my car backfiring and dying on the road." She laughed again.

His brow furrowed. "I didn't realize it was *that* funny."

She shook her head. "Not funny 'ha ha' but more funny like, 'Wow...I never realized that.' There's this action movie from the nineties where at the end the cop falls for the girl after saving her from this runaway bus, and she kinda puts it perfectly, that relationships that start under intense circumstances never last. Guess it's a good thing this isn't a relationship."

Again she went for breezy, but her heart raced in anticipation of his reaction.

Sam tilted his head back and raised his brows, his gaze meeting hers.

"A Keanu Reeves fan, huh?" he said.

She gasped. "You've seen *Speed*? And heck yeah. I'm a proud Keanu fangirl. That beautiful man does *not* age. He can save me from a speeding bus any day."

"See?" Sam said. "I have so much to learn about you in so little time. You're going to have to spend the night."

So they dropped the dolly at the shed.

"I'll deal with what's on the cart in the morning," he said.

When they got back to his place, he offered Delaney an uninterrupted shower while he took Scout for a walk. Afterward, when she was relaxing on the couch in a pair of his basketball shorts and a clean T-shirt with the dog and the glass of red wine he'd poured for her, he cleaned himself up as well.

When he was out of sight, she lifted the collar of his T-shirt over her nose and breathed in. Even though the garment was clean, it still held traces of Sam—a clean, outdoorsy scent she could breathe from here until the end of time.

He emerged from his bedroom in nothing but a pair of sweats—sexy as can be—then grabbed a DVD from his bookshelf and popped it into the player before taking the empty spot next to her. A few seconds later, the opening scene of the movie—actor Dennis Hopper messing with elevator wiring in the basement of a building—filled the television screen.

Delaney beamed. "Shut *up*! You *have* Speed? And here I judged you for having a DVD collection at all."

His eyes widened.

"Not to your face, silly," she added, then burrowed into his side, careful not to spill her wine. "There he is!" she exclaimed giddily when Keanu Reeves entered the frame as Officer Jack Traven. "This is the best night!"

Sam laughed. "Yeah," he said. "I guess it is. I've got two hours of Sandra Bullock ahead and an even more beautiful woman snuggled tight against my side. Can't say I have anything to complain about."

Delaney's heart fluttered.

She felt safe in his arms. Cared for. Known—feelings she'd never realized were missing with Wade until now.

"Sam," she said, keeping her gaze focused on the television screen.

"Yeah?" he asked, doing the same.

"Thank you." Her throat tightened, preventing her from saying more without letting her emotions get the best of her.

He squeezed her tight against him and let out a long sigh.

"You're welcome," he said, not asking her what she meant.

So she let herself believe he felt it, too, a shift in the air around them. Things were different now. Maybe the week could end differently too.

CHAPTER FOURTEEN

Delaney roused to soft kisses peppering her cheek. She smiled and let out a sleepy sigh, eyes still not ready to open. The kisses continued, but they were getting...wetter. There was also the absence of Sam's signature scruff.

Her eyes flew open so she was face-to-face with a certain dog's snout.

"*Scout*!" She loved doggy affection as much as the next person, but first thing in the morning after last night—an *amazing* last night—she was kind of hoping for more human affection from a certain very human man.

She rolled toward the other side of the bed to find it empty, the spot where her body had fit so perfectly against Sam's now cool to the touch, which meant he'd been gone for some time.

Scout barked, startling Delaney to fully awake mode. Well, as fully awake as she could be without coffee.

"Okay, okay, Lassie. We'll get Timmy out of that well."

She rolled out of bed, still wearing Sam's T-shirt and

shorts. She didn't want to change out of his clothes, not if it meant being surrounded by his scent for a little while longer.

"That is one fine-smelling human you have, sweet girl."

She knelt down and scratched Scout behind the ears, and her tail tapped against the floor in canine appreciation.

Delaney padded groggily into the bathroom, rubbing her eyes and smoothing down her bed head. She wasn't sure what she expected to find, but it certainly wasn't a brand-new toothbrush, still in its package, a sticky note attached that read: *Had an extra. It's yours if you want.*

She wanted.

After finishing the bare minimum of her morning bathroom routine, she made her way toward the kitchen. The closer she got, the stronger the scent of coffee became, and she perked up when she saw a fresh pot on the counter. Above it a sticky note hung from the cabinet.

Mornin', Vegas. Had to take care of some business before the festivities began. Made you some coffee. Breakfast is hiding from Scout in the microwave. DON'T give her any more bacon. She already stole more than her share. See you soon. —Sam

"Bacon?" she said aloud, sidling over to the microwave. She opened it to find a plate with avocado toast, a pile of crispy bacon, and fresh fruit. "The man made me coffee *and* bacon?" And remembered her love of the spreadable green fruit. She glanced down to where Scout waited with her tongue out and eyes wide, and slipped her a piece of bacon despite her human's request. "If I'm not careful," she said, popping a piece into her own mouth, "I might fall in lo—"

The front door flew open, and Sam—dressed in jeans, boots, and a gray T-shirt, basically looking devastatingly handsome while she was still rumpled and sleepy-eyed—strode through.

Delaney coughed as she swallowed her bacon.

"You all right, Vegas?" He was at her side, patting her on the back.

She nodded, coughed again, and then swallowed. "Wrong pipe." She grabbed one of the rinsed wineglasses sitting next to the sink, filled it with water, and downed it without coming up for breath.

Water dribbled down her chin as she set the glass back on the counter. She didn't want to imagine what she looked like now—or what Sam had almost heard her say in a bacon-induced euphoria. Because it was absolutely the bacon talking. Nothing else.

He swiped his thumb across her chin. "You had a little something..." His eyes dipped to where Scout lay on the floor, licking her chops. "You gave her more bacon, didn't you?" he asked, half-playful and half-accusing.

Delaney opened her mouth to protest—because how was she supposed to look at that puppy's sweet eyes and *not* share her breakfast—but Sam silenced her with a bone-melting kiss.

She wrapped her arms around his neck, her body sinking into his.

"Now that's what I call a *good* morning," she said. "Instead I got the romantic treatment from the other woman in your life, though now I'm guessing it's because she knew about the bacon."

Sam narrowed his eyes at his pooch. "And here I thought I'd be the first to kiss you today."

Delaney slid back toward the open microwave, pulled out her plate, and lifted a piece of avocado toast to her mouth. "Mmm," she said after a bite. "I could get used to this. I mean, to avocado toast on the regular. With bacon." She took another bite even though she hadn't swallowed, realizing that on this particular morning she was safer eating than talking. Why was she so flummoxed by waking up in a man's apartment? It wasn't the first time she'd done such a thing, and it certainly wouldn't be the last.

Sam's brow furrowed as she shoved the rest of the piece of toast into an already full mouth. "I can make you more if you want. It's just toast."

She shook her head and tried to smile without food crumbling over her lips. When that proved less than successful, they both stood in awkward silence as she finished chewing, swallowing, and guzzling another wineglass full of water.

She swiped her forearm across her mouth. "So, where'd you rush off to so early? Was sort of hoping we'd maybe do some things in there"—she nodded back toward Sam's bedroom—"before doing coffee-and-food-type things in here."

"Boring business stuff," Sam said. "But if you want to head back to bed and 'do some things in there,' I think we've still got some time." He used air quotes around her *do some things in there*. Then he swiped a piece of bacon from her plate and popped it into his mouth.

"Hey!" She backhanded him on the shoulder. "I thought that was for me."

He shrugged. "If you can share with the dog, you can share with the chef. It's an unwritten rule."

She set the plate on the counter and poured herself a

cup of much-needed coffee, wrapped her hands around the steaming mug, and sipped.

"There we go," she said. "Now I'm officially awake." Everything seemed clearer—more in focus—after that first sip of coffee. Including Sam's bruised face. Yesterday the purple bruise was confined to the corner of his eye, but today the bridge of his nose had a bluish hue as well.

Yet he was smiling. And stealing her bacon. They were sort of, kind of acting like a couple, and it scared her how much she liked it. Still, she didn't want Sam's flirty playfulness to end.

She set the coffee aside. "Does it still hurt?" she asked, reaching a hesitant hand for his cheek.

"Only when you touch it," he teased, but he didn't pull away.

"I still can't believe I hit you."

"When I was trying to help you," he reminded her.

She pouted. "Yeah, well, now I know a man's weakness is assuming a woman can't hold her own. I'll make a mental note to use the damsel-in-distress feint next time."

He shook his head and laughed. "Oh no you don't, Vegas. I learned my lesson. I'm not getting in the ring with you again." He cleared his throat. "Also I got some good news. Bumped into Boone Murphy, owner of Meadow Valley Motors, on my way back through town. Dr. Murphy's brother, in case you haven't met. He was supposed to join Eli on a cattle drive this week—missing the festival entirely—but plans fell through. Which means that even though the town is still technically in shutdown mode, he said he'd take a look at your car as a favor to me. The courthouse is another story. But at least you won't be stranded anymore—in case you wanted to head back to Vegas instead of waiting out the festival here."

"Garage owner and cattle driver? Is *every* man in this town part cowboy?" she asked.

Sam laughed. "Just about."

"And it looks like you're pretty good at getting people to do favors for you. But not the courthouse, huh?"

She fought the urge to clap her hand over her mouth. Sure, if her car were fixed and Sam could get a favor from a court clerk, she could be out of here sooner rather than later. But what if she didn't want sooner anymore?

She stared at him, her chest heavy and her throat tight. She was suddenly overcome by the realization that their fairy tale might come to an end, possibly sooner than expected. If she wasn't stranded, what was her excuse to stay when she didn't have to?

"I guess—if Millie is good to go by tomorrow—"

"Boone might have to order parts," Sam said. "I mean, we don't know for sure."

She nodded. Tiptoeing around the issue was going to drive her mad, so she dove in headfirst. "What if I wanted to stay? For the week, I mean."

She held her breath waiting for his answer, but Sam didn't leave her hanging for longer than a second.

"Hell yes, Vegas."

She clasped her hands around his neck, tugging his head down as she stood on her toes. She kissed him, both of them smiling against each other.

"I wanted it to be your choice," Sam said. "Because even though it might not make sense—"

"I'm not ready for this to end," she interrupted.

He shook his head. "Me either."

She brushed a soft kiss under his bruised eye.

"I never wanted to hurt you," she whispered. "Not with coming back here or getting you in the ring or any of it. I hope you realize that was never my intent."

"I know," he said, his breath warm against her ear. "And you want to know what really doesn't hurt, not one bit at all?"

"What's that?" she asked.

He threw another piece of bacon on the floor to distract the dog, then scooped her into his arms. She yelped with laughter, her worry a thing of the past as he strode with quick, easy glides back toward the bedroom. He kicked the door shut behind him, then dropped her onto the bed.

He checked his phone, then set it on the nightstand. "We've got just under an hour before I need you dressed and ready to go."

She tucked her hands under her head and smiled. "Then you best get to work, sir. There's lots to do between now and then."

She'd had little more than twenty minutes to shower and get dressed, but it was worth it. She threw on a pair of jeans and the red tank she wore on her drive from Vegas—now clean thanks to the load of laundry she did the day before. She pulled a brush through her wet hair, slapped on some lip gloss, and tied her hoodie around her waist for when things cooled off later. By the time she headed back outside, Sam was waiting in his truck.

He hopped out and rounded the cab to open her door, one hand behind his back.

"You hiding something, cowboy?" she asked. In his T-shirt, jeans, and aviators, he looked more like someone she'd see walking the strip in Vegas than the rancher she knew he was.

He slid his sunglasses to the top of his head so she could see the glint in his chocolate-brown eyes. "Funny you should mention that..." He pulled his hand from behind his back and dropped a straw cowboy hat onto her head, the same one he'd given her on their trail ride and that had come back from said ride quite muddy and worse for wear. She'd looked for it in her room but couldn't find it.

"Hey. Where'd that come from?" she asked.

He shrugged. "Saw what a mess it was yesterday. So I grabbed it while you were showering and cleaned it off for you."

She narrowed her eyes. "You came into my room *uninvited*?"

"To do you a favor."

"How'd you get in?" she asked.

He laughed. "I own the property. I have access to all the rooms."

She placed her hands on her hips. "Do you make a habit of sneaking into guests' rooms without them knowing?"

He shook his head. "Only yours, Vegas. I did knock first, but I could hear the water running. You still mad?" The smile on his face told her that he knew she wasn't.

Not that she'd have been jealous if he *had* spent time with other guests before her, but it still made her happy to know she was the only one. Okay, fine. She'd have been jealous as hell.

"No," she told him. "But next time you better not sneak back *out*."

He tipped the brim of her hat up so he could kiss her.

"Deal," he said, then opened her door. "Are you ready to see Meadow Valley at its *most* Meadow Valley? It's my second autumn festival, so I'm pretty much a seasoned veteran."

Delaney adjusted the hat on her head. "You know, as much as I've complained about the whole town being shut down, this kind of thing is what I love about small towns. In the short time I was here, I didn't get to experience any of it."

Sam laughed. "Been a small-town man my whole life, and I can tell you that Meadow Valley has given my hometown a run for its money when it comes to holidays and celebrations. You should see what this place looks like come Thanksgiving and through the New Year—the snow and the light? I've never seen anything like it."

She smiled wistfully. "I've literally dreamed about it."

"You like snow?" he asked, amusement in his tone. He hooked a finger around one of her belt loops and urged her closer.

Her eyes widened. "A display of affection right here in front of anyone who passes by?"

He tipped her hat up and kissed her. "Right here in front of anyone," he said.

"And to answer your question, I don't really know if I like winter, but I've always wanted to live in a place where the seasons change more than they do in Vegas. And I *really* want to see snow."

He nodded. "The hills covered in white are pretty spectacular," he said. "Yet it never gets too cold for the animals. Meadow Valley gets the best of all the seasons, if you ask me."

She swallowed a knot in her throat. Thanksgiving wasn't too far off. She could picture herself in a small house on her land—a table set with a feast she'd have to learn how to cook. She closed her eyes and envisioned the table replete with a turkey and all the trimmings. And there was Sam, toasting Ben and Colt with a glass of wine.

She smiled at the fantasy—until she was snapped back to reality by Sam clearing his throat.

Her eyes flew open.

"Everything okay, Vegas?"

"Yeah. We should go," she said, not wanting to let her imagination go any further, like to thoughts of Meadow Valley blanketed in snow, of her and Sam walking down a First Street aglow in holiday lights or the two of them ducking into Pearl's for the gourmet hot cocoa she knew the woman would serve.

She climbed into the truck without another word and pulled the door shut, leaving Sam scratching his head before he finally joined her in the cab.

She was startled by a dog barking as the door clicked shut. Then she laughed, spinning to find Scout perched on the shallow back seat.

"I didn't know we had company," she said, reaching back to pat the dog on the head. Scout nuzzled into Delaney's touch, and her heart just about melted. It had been nearly two years since she'd almost realized her dream of spending each and every day with animals like Scout. Now she had the chance to get back what she'd lost. The problem was losing Sam in the fallout.

He doesn't do permanent, she reminded herself. No matter what she felt for him now—or by the end of the week—she was still going to lose him. Even if she could convince him that she could handle whatever the future brought for them, for Sam's health, there was still the land. If getting a portion of her property back meant dismantling the ranch in any way, her gain would mean his loss as well as a loss for his brother and Colt. Would any of them be able to forgive her?

"Don't you have to drive the guests to town?" she asked, shifting her attention to something less complicated.

Sam turned the key in the ignition, then put the truck in drive. "I took the first load a few minutes ago. Ben and Colt will do the rest. I told them about something I had to do before heading back to town, and they were happy to oblige."

Delaney's brow furrowed. "So we're *not* heading to town?"

He smiled. "Not yet. Gotta make a stop first."

She could tell by his teasing tone that he wasn't going to let on where they were going until they got there. So she took the liberty of turning on the radio and cycling through Sam's presets until she found what she knew would be there—classic rock. She relaxed into her seat as Eric Clapton crooned "Wonderful Tonight," letting herself get lost in the lyrics. She must have dozed off because before the song ended—or in reality three songs after it did—she felt a hand gently nudge her shoulder.

"Got a long day ahead, Vegas. Hope I haven't worn you out already."

She opened her eyes and squinted when she was hit with the bright morning sun. When her vision adjusted, she was able to make out the sign to the right of where they were parked. QUINCY LONG-TERM CARE.

"Your dad?" she asked. "We're visiting your dad?" She wasn't sure what that meant, that he was doing this. *With* her. She'd been with him by accident yesterday. It was either leave her stranded in town or take her along for the ride. But this was Sam's choice. She was here with him because he wanted her to be.

Sam shook his head. "We're taking him to the festival. I called ahead and made all the arrangements. It might be too much for him to stay all day, but I figured we'd cross that bridge when we got to it. Ben knows. He's on board. So between him and me, I think we can manage."

Hope surged through her. Maybe Sam was starting to see his father's illness differently—as something they all could live with given the right support. And if he could see that, maybe it also meant he could envision a different future for himself.

She pressed her hands to his shoulders and kissed him, a quick, soft brush of her lips, lingering for only a second or two.

Even behind his sunglasses, she could see his eyes widen. "What was that for?"

"For being a good man. A good son. For wanting me to be a part of it."

He smiled. "I'm not sure I got the full extent of your message. You might need to tell me again."

This time she flung her arms around his neck and kissed him hard. Her hip jammed into the center console, but she didn't care. She could feel Sam Callahan's mouth smiling against hers, and she let the possibility of what today might bring fill her with hope. If Sam's dad had a good day—if good days were possible—then they were possible for Sam, too, even if his prognosis was the same.

The more she got to know Sam Callahan, the more she believed a man like him would be worth the fight. She just didn't know how to convince him to fight for himself. Wade certainly didn't fight for a better future. He simply looked for the easy way out. There was no easy way out for Sam, but there was possibility. It didn't matter whether he got tested or didn't. He could still choose more—if he'd let himself believe he deserved it no matter what happened twenty or thirty years from now.

Delaney could see it. Why couldn't he?

Her lips were raw when she pulled away. She brushed a palm over the scruff that was starting to look more like a beard.

"I usually shave each morning," he said, peering into her thoughts. "Guess I've been a little distracted this weekend."

"I like it," she said. "Shows you know how to loosen the reins and let go a little."

"Are you saying I don't know how to give up control?"

She nodded without the least bit of hesitation. "That's exactly what I'm saying. I know a few days don't make a whole lot of difference in a person's life, but since I got to town, you've been skinny-dipping, had amazing sex by a bonfire, and watched one of the greatest Keanu Reeves movies of all time. Tell me the last time you let yourself have fun like that in one weekend."

"You forgot I almost got my nose broken."

She groaned. "Yeah, well, you let your guard down. Any trained fighter should know better than that."

He shook his head and laughed.

"Does that mean I'm right?" she asked. "That you *haven't* had this much fun in a while?" Because she liked to think that a few days *could* make a difference, even if it was a small one.

He swatted the brim of her hat. "You might be onto something, Vegas. What about you? You always let go and have a good time?"

That was the thing. She *could* let go. But she hadn't. Not in a long while.

"Only with someone who's worth it." Someone she trusted, who made her feel safe. She hadn't felt safe since she called 911 the night those men made her watch as they beat Wade bloody. She'd waited long enough to make sure he was okay, and then she'd packed her things and driven back to Vegas for good.

"Hmm," he said but didn't offer any further comment. "We should go grab Nolan before he ends up on top of a table again."

He smiled, but she could see the effort it took to do it.

"Hey." She rested a hand on his forearm. "Today's going to be great. I'm here. Ben's gonna be there. I'm guessing this is probably the most control you've given up in a while, so just know you've got people in your corner to help."

He let out a breath. She didn't need him to remove his sunglasses to know the conflict she'd see in his dark eyes. Sam Callahan kept everything in his life in neat little compartments, and today he was throwing it all in a blender without any clue what the final result would be.

He pressed a palm to her cheek, stroked her skin with his thumb. For a second she thought he might kiss her, but instead he pulled away without another word, opening his door and hopping out of the truck, leaving the windows down for Scout.

Delaney met him at the back end of the vehicle, and together they strode toward the care facility's entrance.

Before they made it to the door, Sam threaded his fingers through hers and squeezed.

Her stomach flip-flopped, and a goofy grin spread across her face.

Keep it together, Harper, she told herself. So he was holding her hand. So what? She'd been swept up in a whirlwind romance before, and look where that had gotten her. No matter what she thought she was feeling for Sam, she needed to keep a level head, to think clearly, to remind herself that they were playing at this relationship thing until they had to face the real world—the one where Sam was too afraid to commit, where he shouldered the burden of his future in silence.

"Here goes nothing," he said as he ushered her through the revolving door.

Nolan Callahan sat on a bench in the lobby in faded jeans and a white T-shirt. Aside from his graying hair and thinner frame, he looked so much like Sam today that she had to do a double take. He smiled when he saw her and Sam. He didn't look confused to see them there or as if he was suffering from a disease that was taking over his mind, one day at a time.

"I thought they were joking when they told me my son was coming to pick me up," he said, standing to shake Sam's hand. "And to a big public festival. You sure you're not afraid I'll embarrass you?"

"Having a pretty good morning, huh, Dad?" Sam dropped her hand to shake his father's. "And yeah. I'm nervous as hell about how today's gonna go. But it's the first day of the autumn festival. You should be there with us."

The older man's brow furrowed. "Ben know I'm coming to the festival?"

Sam nodded. "He's looking forward to seeing you."

"What happened to your face?" Nolan added. "You stand behind the wrong horse?"

Sam chuckled. "A little sparring accident in the ring

yesterday." He winked at Delaney. "Looks worse than it feels."

Delaney hoped that was true.

Nolan held a hand out for her. "*Work* friend, right?" he asked, remembering how Sam had introduced her when they'd met.

Delaney opened her mouth to say yes, but Sam cut her off.

"No, Dad." He paused. "Delaney's more than a work friend. At least for the following week."

He slid an arm around her waist, and she smiled. Ben and Colt catching them at the bonfire last night could have just been swept under the rug, but he was telling his father that she was something more, which only made her *hope* more. She was beginning to think that wasn't such a bad thing.

"For another day or two?" Nolan asked. "What the hell does that mean?"

"It's complicated," Sam told his father while Delaney bit her lip and let the conversation play out.

"Complicated?" Nolan crossed his arms. "That's a social media status. Not an explanation."

"It's the only explanation I got." Sam strode to the front desk and signed something Delaney guessed was permission for Nolan to leave the facility.

Delaney shrugged when Sam's father looked to her for further clarification. Right now, she was good with complicated if complicated meant today they could simply be whatever it was they were.

"Ready?" Sam asked on his way back from the desk. "Because Luis is kicking the morning off at the crepe stand with Anna's produce, and I can't wait to see if they hate each other or love each other today. If it's the former, I may be out one damned good produce supplier."

He was smiling, but Delaney caught the hint of worry in his tone.

"And I read in the paper tonight's a great night to see the Orionids before it gets too late," Nolan said. "You won't bring me home before that, will you? It'll be like when you and Ben were kids." He shook his head. "I should have told your mother. She'd have driven up to join us."

Sam's jaw tightened, and Delaney remembered the photo in his apartment—the one of him, Ben, and their mom doing just that—Nolan the man behind the camera.

"Sure," Sam said. "We won't head back before that. But you know Mom wouldn't be coming no matter what, right? She's in Carson City now."

Nolan nodded. "Sure, sure. Carson City with Ted. Poor Ted."

Both she and Sam looked at each other with the same confused expression, but Sam shrugged it off. Nolan seemed a little confused about his relationship with his ex-wife, but other than that, Delaney thought he was in good shape for the festival, and it looked like Sam felt the same.

Nothing about this day was going to be easy for him, but they were here, all of them together, which meant Sam didn't have to shoulder the weight alone.

"Today's going to be great," Delaney assured him, linking her elbow through his. On instinct she reached out a hand for Nolan, and he shocked them all by linking *his* elbow with *hers*.

"Lead the way, darlin'. I've got a day with my sons."

They had to break apart for the revolving door, but

after that the three of them walked arm in arm back to the truck, like she was Dorothy and they were the Tin Man and Scarecrow, the three of them on the way to Oz for a heart, a brain, and a home.

She happily crawled into the back seat with Scout. Looked like they had a Toto too. All they were missing was the Cowardly Lion, which was fine by her. Sam taking a chance on his dad—on being open with her like a couple—was brave enough for all of them today.

CHAPTER FIFTEEN

Everything looked fine at the auction table. Even though it was the start of the festival, the weekend stay at the ranch already had a few bids.

Sam held his breath as they approached the tented crepe stand, Scout running ahead of them and his father happily chasing after the dog. There was a line of people waiting, but he could see that both Luis and Anna stood behind the booth, Anna gesticulating wildly while Luis flipped a crepe.

Were they smiling? He couldn't tell. *Please let them be smiling.*

He glanced at Delaney, who had lifted her hat up and was squinting in the same direction. "Do they look happy or ready to rip each other's throats out?"

Delaney shook her head. "I can't tell. The line keeps moving and obscuring my view."

She sounded just as worried as he felt, which wasn't a good sign.

He started taking longer strides, picking up his pace.

Delaney had to jog to keep up, but at the moment he didn't care. All that mattered was having a happy chef who deserved a much better salary than Sam could give him and not losing his produce supplier.

Finally they made it to the end of the line, which had turned into a crowd—a crowd who was *watching*, but Sam couldn't see what. He could hear it, though.

"See? You added the fruit too early, and now it's a pile of mush!" Anna yelled.

"*No*body has complained about my crepes yet! And look at that line, you crazy fruit diva! It's only getting longer because they *love* my cooking."

"Shit," Sam hissed.

He pushed through the crowd as the bickering continued. By the time he made it to the front, Luis and Anna were—kissing.

Sam heard murmurs from the throngs of people.

"I hope my husband takes a hint from them," one woman said to another.

"Are we gonna have to wait longer for the crepes? He probably burned this batch," someone else said.

"Weren't they the ones kissing at the bonfire last night? They should rename the place the Love Shack or something."

Okay, that was the last straw. His ranch was *not* a love shack.

He opened his mouth to let everyone know this fact, when Delaney's hand covered it up before he could speak.

"Slow down there, cowboy," she said, wrapping an arm around his waist and pulling him away from his front row seat to whatever Luis and Anna did next.

He scanned the crowd and found his father and Scout

waiting patiently with the rest for a crepe, so he let out a breath.

"But they were—"

"Giving the ranch publicity?" she asked.

"That kind of behavior is unprofessional."

She cleared her throat. "And what were we doing last night after everyone else left the bonfire? Conducting a board meeting?"

His jaw tightened as he pushed his aviators onto his forehead, and he pinched the bridge of his nose.

"Ow. Damn it." He squeezed his eyes shut and hissed in a breath. She was right. It wasn't Luis and Anna that were the problem. It was *him*. The anticipation of whether or not things with his father would turn south was keeping him from enjoying a beautiful day with a beautiful woman.

"Sorry!"

"Can you maybe remind me not to do that?" he said, gritting his teeth.

Delaney giggled, then threw her hand over her mouth. "Sorry," she said again, her voice muffled by her hand. "But maybe if you take a deep breath before overreacting next time…"

His eyes narrowed. She had him pegged again, but it didn't mean he liked being called on his own BS. *He* was the one who called BS on everyone else, and it was disconcerting to have the shoe on the other foot.

Delaney held her arms out and spun slowly, forcing him to take in their surroundings.

"Look," she said. "All these people are here having fun. And they're in line for food from *your* chef talking about *your* ranch. So Luis and Anna are a little volatile and don't care about the PDA." She shrugged. "It would also seem they're falling in love, which could actually be good for business."

Sam raised a brow, but she waved him off.

"It's *publicity*." Then she turned toward the crepe crowd, whistling so loud that nearly everyone's heads turned. "Listen up, folks! If you want to spend some time at the Love Shack, head on over to the silent auction after you get your crepes. My friend Sam here and the rest of the Meadow Valley crew are auctioning off a weekend stay, passion-inducing bonfire included!"

Some people applauded. Others whistled their approval right back. And Sam watched with amazement as people began to scurry, plated crepes in hand, toward the auction tent.

Delaney spun back to face him, arms crossed and a self-satisfied grin on her face.

"You're right," he finally admitted.

She opened her mouth to say something but stopped before any words came out.

"What's the matter?" he asked. "Did I render the great Delaney Harper speechless?"

He smiled, and his shoulders relaxed. He was ready to let go and finally enjoy the day.

"Did you say I was *right*, cowboy?" she asked, her eyes wide. "Because I think I need to hear that again."

He laughed and pulled her to him. "You were right, Vegas." Then he dipped her, planting a kiss on her lips that was worthy of a romance movie close-up. At least he hoped it was.

When he straightened and backed away, she stared at him wide-eyed, fingers pressed to her freshly kissed lips.

"See?" he said, setting her hat back on her strawberry-blond waves. "I can PDA with the best of them."

Her cheeks were flushed. She smiled coyly and hooked a finger in his belt loop. "When was the last time you publicly displayed your affection, Mr. Callahan?"

He shrugged. "I think I kissed Tanya Hogan at her locker before trig my junior year."

Delaney dropped her face into her hands and shook her head.

"Oh my goodness," she said. "I had no idea how desperately you needed my help."

"For what?" he asked, laughing.

"For opening up and living a little. I'm not saying you have to relegate yourself to outdoor sex and grandiose kissing gestures in front of an audience—though I wholeheartedly approve of both so long as there's a sturdier table next time around—but maybe it's okay to enjoy your life every now and then, no matter what the future holds."

She pressed her lips together, eyes expectant as she waited for his reaction.

Enjoy his life.

He thought he'd been doing that. He'd resigned himself to his uncertain future, but he'd been happy enough with the ranch, his makeshift family, and the limits he'd placed on his personal life—until he met Delaney. Now his definition of *enough* was changing and growing, and he wished there was a way it could include her.

"I'm sorry," she said, breaking the silence and pulling him out of his head. "I said I'd let it go for the week, and I didn't let it go. It's just that things are going so well. Your dad's getting crepes, the ranch is getting excellent publicity, and you're getting lucky pretty much for the rest of the week. If I asked a Magic 8 Ball if things were

looking up for Sam Callahan, it would say, 'Signs point
to yes.'"

He'd snapped at her the last time she broached the subject. And he still maintained that most women he might
bring into his life would have no clue what it was like
to be in his position. But Delaney wasn't most women.
She was...Delaney. She knew about his situation and it
hadn't scared her away. Maybe there was more to this
thing between them than just the rest of the week.

"You're right again," he said.

Her mouth fell open, and she blinked once. Twice.

"Speechless again, huh?" he asked. He squinted, looking over Delaney's shoulder as a figure appeared, a
four-legged companion trailing not too far behind.

"Hey, Dad," he said as his father and Scout sidled
up next to Delaney. He nodded toward his father's
chocolate-smeared plate that had only a few bites left of
whatever crepe he'd ordered. "You didn't give Scout any
of that, did you? Because dogs can get seriously ill from
chocolate."

Nolan Callahan waved his son off with a chocolate-
coated plastic fork. "I've got Alzheimer's, but I'm not
an idiot."

Sam lost his footing and stumbled back a step. Should
he laugh? *Could* he laugh? If and when he was in his
father's position, would he get to a point where he found
humor in a very humorless situation?

He didn't have the answer, or any words at all. *He'd*
been rendered speechless now, and Delaney's wide-eyed
expression mirrored his own.

Nolan looked back and forth between his stunned son
and an equally stunned Delaney. Then he burst into a fit
of laughter.

When he regained his composure, he clapped a hand on Sam's shoulder. "Lighten up, son. Someday I won't know enough to make jokes about this. Hell, I might not be able to control my own body let alone my own thoughts. I gotta have a little fun while I can."

"Hey, Pop."

Sam glanced over his own shoulder to find his brother approaching.

His father's expression went from jovial to something almost reverential. Sam saw his father on a regular basis, but ever since they moved him into the assisted living facility, Ben had pulled back. If Delaney thought Sam brushed everything under the rug, it was only because she hadn't gotten to know the master of avoidance—Ben Callahan.

"Ben," Nolan said, and Sam heard a tremor in the older man's voice. "Get the hell over here and give your old man a hug."

Ben did as the man asked, but his body was stiff, his shoulders tight. Either their father didn't notice or he didn't care. He wrapped his younger son into the biggest of bear hugs despite his empty paper plate in one hand, his plastic fork in the other.

"Let me take that, Nolan," Delaney said, grabbing their father's trash and taking it to a nearby bin.

This allowed the man to clasp Ben's shoulders, holding him an arm's length away.

"God damn," he said. "Look at you."

Sam looked away. He didn't begrudge his brother and father their moment. He knew Nolan's reaction was because Ben rarely stepped foot inside the facility. But it still stung to see his brother get such a reception when Sam was the one who got the call when their father had an episode, and Sam was the one who was there each Monday for a game of Uno. Even though both brothers had the same terrifying future ahead of them, Ben pretended none of it existed, which only drove home the fact that Sam was in this thing alone.

Then Delaney stepped into view.

She was too good to them, this brood of three men who were about as scared and dysfunctional as they come. Seeing the way she fell so seamlessly into their rhythm made him want so many things he'd been able to push aside before now. Things like time—with his family, with the ranch, with *her*. It made him want to know if there was the slightest chance for a future with someone like her.

Holy shit. Had it taken a punch to the face to knock some sense into him?

He wanted to get tested. He wanted to *know*.

His eyes locked on Delaney as she made her way back from the trash bin.

She cocked her head to the side, and her brow furrowed.

"With your glasses back on, I can't tell if you're looking at me or not. If you are, I think you might be staring, so now I'm wondering if I have food on my face or something even though I haven't gotten my crepe yet!"

She swiped at her nose and then rubbed her chin, and all Sam could do was laugh. He wanted to tell her. But this wasn't the time or place. And he'd have to tell his brother. Whatever Ben decided was Ben's choice. All Sam knew was that he had to take some sort of step to show her that even if he didn't know what his future held, he could see her in it. Telling his brother and Colt about the possibility of giving up half their land was another story. If Delaney felt the same about him that he did about her, though, she'd want the best for the ranch, wouldn't she? They'd work it out. But first he had to know that she wanted the same thing. Then everything else would fall into place.

"There's nothing on your face, Vegas. Nothing but a beautiful smile I can't look away from. That's all."

She blushed hard, from her neck all the way up to her cheeks.

"What's gotten into you?" she asked.

Nothing. Everything. The tornado of thoughts rushing around his head was almost too much to take.

"You're spending the night again, right?" he asked.

She nodded. "I'd like that."

"I'll tell you what's gotten into me then."

She still looked puzzled, but the answer seemed to satisfy her because she slid her hand into his and tugged him back toward Anna and Luis.

"Well then, Mr. Callahan, allow me to buy you a crepe."

He strode toward the tent, his hand locked with hers, as a weight lifted from his shoulders, one he'd been carrying for years.

Signs point to yes.

Sam had never been a believer in signs, but it was hard to ignore the ones Delaney pointed out. Maybe things were starting to shift in a direction he hadn't anticipated. And maybe, *just* maybe, that path led straight to her.

CHAPTER SIXTEEN

Delaney stretched out on the picnic blanket Sam had thrown in the bed of his truck. She was in a blissful food coma. No, scratch that. She was simply in sheer, utter bliss.

Something had shifted in Sam after Anna and Luis and the crepes—something good. And it had spilled over into the rest of what she could only describe as her most perfect day.

They'd eaten everything from crepes to butternut squash ravioli to grilled corn on the cob. She'd participated in—and *won*—an adult hula-hooping contest. She had soaked Sam's T-shirt when they *lost* the water balloon toss, though she might have lobbed it with extra force on purpose, bursting into laughter when it exploded against his chest.

She'd thoroughly enjoyed how his shirt had clung to his torso for the short time it had been wet before the sun baked it dry. With all the food, playing games, mingling with Meadow Valley's residents and visitors, and Sam by her side every step of the way, the day had been nothing short of perfect.

Sam had something to tell her tonight, and she was going to do the same. She wanted her animal shelter. And she wanted it here, in Meadow Valley. But she also wanted it with him in her life. The land thing didn't have to be a deal breaker, did it? Especially not after they'd crossed some invisible boundary today.

Sam strode toward the blanket with Scout in tow.

"I told her that's the last walk for the evening," he said once he was within earshot. "She never has to go this much when we're at the ranch. I think she's overexcited."

Delaney smiled and sat up. She crossed her legs, patting the spot on the blanket next to her. Scout scampered over and curled up, laying her head in Delaney's lap.

"And here I thought you were saving that spot for me," Sam said.

Delaney shrugged. "We girls have to stick together. I scratch her belly, and she falls asleep on my leg. It's a win-win."

Sam dropped down onto the blanket, lying back on his elbows. "What if I wanted to fall asleep on your leg?"

She laughed. "Ladies first. But you'll get your turn a little later."

His pinkie brushed against hers, and she shivered.

"Are you cold?" he asked.

The temperature had dropped significantly, but she had her hoodie on. The goose bumps up and down her arms had nothing to do with the crisp night air and everything to do with Sam Callahan.

"A little," she lied, scratching behind Scout's ear. "It feels good, though."

"I might have a jacket in the truck. I can grab it for you," he told her, but she shook her head.

"No way." She pointed up toward the clear night sky studded with constellations, scanning the landscape until she found Orion's belt, the focal point of the meteor shower. "I don't want you to miss it." She turned her gaze back to Sam. "Wait, where's your dad?"

"Don't worry," Sam said. "He's with my brother grabbing some more food. They'll be right back. I swear, either they're not feeding him at the home, or he has a hollow leg. I've never seen the guy eat so much."

Scout stretched and repositioned herself, her head no longer on Delaney's leg. So Delaney seized the opportunity to crawl behind Sam and wrap her arms around his chest.

"Looks like later came a bit sooner," she said. She carefully slid his sunglasses off his nose. "It's not sunny anymore, and I want to see those puppy-dog brown eyes of yours."

He nestled into her chest and looked up at her, dramatically batting his dark lashes. "Like what you see?"

"Very much so." She kissed his forehead. "Are you sure you're okay with all this? I know it brings up a lot of memories."

He pulled her arms tighter around him. "I'm sure, Vegas."

The look in his mischievous eyes grew serious. She waited, expecting some sort of explanation, but if one might have been coming, it was cut off by Ben and Nolan dropping down next to them, plates of honey-drizzled corn bread in both of their hands.

"Who wants a bite?" Ben asked.

"Speak for yourself," Nolan said, guarding his plate. "I'm not sharing."

They all laughed, and Delaney swore nothing other than being with her own immediate family had ever felt so right. She imagined bringing Beth here—despite her preference for the big city—and showing her how special it was. Meadow Valley was close enough that her parents could take weekend trips during the off-season. Other blankets with other families peppered the grassy hill, and she longed for all of it to last more than a week.

She gasped. "Look! It's starting!"

"Would you look at that?" Nolan said, his voice cracking. "The Orionids."

Ben nodded toward his brother, and Sam nodded back. Neither of them smiled, but they didn't look sad either. Delaney hoped the silent communication had been one of understanding. Of contentment. Of possibly seeing their father in a new, more hopeful light.

Sam reached a hand behind him and placed it on the nape of her neck. "We did good today, Vegas," he said. "We make a pretty good team." He kissed her softly, and Delaney's heart felt like it would burst right out of her chest. "Thank you."

She beamed and drew in a shaky breath. "You're welcome."

Despite the chill in the air, warmth spread from where his lips had touched hers all the way to the tips of her toes. Sam Callahan wasn't the reason she'd returned to Meadow Valley—but now he was the reason she wanted to stay. Experiencing this festival, watching him connect with his father and brother, caring for someone who cared for her—it was everything she'd hoped to find when she came here the first time around. She'd just come here with the wrong person.

"I don't want us to end," she whispered, but her admission was drowned out by Nolan whooping and clapping when another flash of light streaked across the sky.

Maybe they didn't have to—end, that was. Sam might have an emotional hurdle or two to overcome before letting her into his life completely, but there was one obstacle she could remove—the land.

She kissed the top of his head and held him tight.

I'm going to fix everything. And for once, she truly believed she could.

They drove in a comfortable, fulfilled silence to bring Nolan home, Sam's hand linked with hers on the center console. She'd tried to give Nolan the front seat, but he'd insisted he preferred the back of the cab with Scout—who was now curled up with her muzzle in his lap.

It was almost midnight, and Delaney's eyes were heavy. She let them fall shut, the rhythm of the vehicle lulling her to sleep.

When they rolled to a stop in front of the facility door, she woke with a start, then laughed.

"I wasn't drooling, was I?" she asked, recalling Sam's short nap in the passenger seat the day before.

Sam smiled and winked at her. "Don't worry, Vegas. Your secret's safe with me."

She wiped the corners of her mouth only to find them dry and then swatted him on the shoulder. "You're terrible."

"Get a room already," Nolan called from the back seat.

Sam rolled his eyes. "Nice, Dad." But Delaney could

tell he was suppressing a grin. "I'll walk him in, if that's okay. You can stay here with Scout."

She nodded, and Sam hopped out of the car as Nolan exited too.

A second later, the older man knocked on her window, and she lowered it.

"You're good for him," he said softly, then leaned down and kissed her on the cheek. "Don't let him make the same mistakes I made."

"Come on, Dad," Sam said from behind Nolan. "It's late, and you need a good night's sleep after such a long day."

"He's good for me too," she admitted with a grin.

Nolan straightened and smiled a smile so full of love and pride that it made her heart ache. Then he turned toward his son and followed him inside.

Delaney closed the window, pulled out her phone, and opened her recent call list to the number she knew was Wade's. The land issue didn't have to be Sam's problem. The land didn't have to be an issue at all if Wade for once did the right thing, and if anyone could talk him into it, she wanted to think that she maybe still could.

She drew in a steadying breath and initiated the call. It rang five times, her heart pounding in her chest as she waited, before finally going to voicemail.

"It's me," she said. "I don't want to play games any-more. Let's talk. For real. About the land. I know about the sale, Wade, and I just want my half of the money." She couldn't do anything about the money they'd raised for the shelter because it was in a joint account. In the eyes of the law, he didn't exactly steal that time. But this was different, and she wasn't going to be afraid anymore of how he could hurt her next. "I can contest the deed you know I didn't sign, or you can do what's right. For me. For both of us. Call me, okay?"

She hung up and exhaled. She was light-headed. It was possible she'd said all of that in one breath.

When Sam opened the driver's side door, she startled.

"Whoa there, Vegas. You okay?"

She nodded. "Yeah. Sorry. Didn't see you walk out is all."

He sat down, and she leaned over the center console and kissed him.

"What was that for?" he asked. "Not that I'm complaining."

She bounced in her seat, giddy and nervous and everything all at once.

"I'm better than okay," she said. "I'm perfect. *Tonight* was perfect." It was the truth. Everything tonight felt right. *More* than right. She'd watched Sam be brave and do with his father what he might not have felt was possible yesterday. Now it was her turn to be brave.

"I called Wade," she said.

Sam pulled the door shut. "Okay," he said, drawing out the second syllable as if he was worried about what would come next. He stuck the key in the ignition, and the truck roared back to life.

Delaney placed a hand on his shoulder and gave him a reassuring squeeze. "I don't want to contest the deed," she said. "It's your land now. I don't want to mess with that. I just want my share of the profit, and that has nothing to do with you, your brother, Colt, or the ranch. This is between me and Wade."

He stared at her, eyes wide. "Why?" he asked. "The whole reason you came here was for your land."

She shrugged. "There's plenty of land in Meadow

Valley. I'm still going to get a copy of the deed as insurance, but if I can convince Wade to do right by me, then we both win. I thought running here was the way to face my problems head-on. But it's Wade I need to face to get what I want—what I deserve." Her stomach tied itself in knots and she held her breath.

She'd said it. *She* wanted to stay and build the life she'd dreamed of two years ago. But what did Sam want? What did that mean for him and her?

"I'm going to get tested," he finally said. "I wanted to wait until we got home to tell you, but I guess after the day we've had—the amazing, perfect day I didn't think was possible—this seems like the right place. I want to know what my future holds so I know if there's a possible future..." He cleared his throat. "A possible future for us."

Her breath caught, and she smiled so hard she thought her face might freeze in that expression.

Sam smiled, too, a smile like the younger version of him in the photo back at his apartment.

"I dare you to kiss me, Sam Callahan," she finally said. "Right here in front of no one."

He leaned over the center console and cradled her head in his hands.

"I do love a good dare," he said. Then he did exactly as she'd asked.

They stayed that way for several minutes—his lips on hers and the taste of him on her tongue—until the windows started to fog.

Scout howled from the back seat.

He chuckled when they both came up for air and realized what they had done.

"I guess we do have a tiny audience," he said, and

she laughed too. "Why don't we continue this back at my place?"

"That sounds like an excellent idea," she said.

He put the car in gear, and they rode slowly out of the parking lot and onto the street.

She rested her hand on his thigh and gave him a gentle squeeze. "Drive safely, cowboy, but drive quick. I can think of all kinds of ways to celebrate."

His foot fell heavy on the gas—but kept them well within the speed limit.

Delaney closed her eyes, letting her head fall back against the seat as her smile took permanent hold of her features.

Everything was falling into place, even more so than she could have imagined. She might very well fall in love with Sam Callahan by week's end, and the thought didn't scare her anymore. Not one little bit.

She saw the future she'd imagined taking shape, and nothing would throw her off track this time.

CHAPTER SEVENTEEN

Sam was on stable and arena duty for the bulk of Monday's daylight hours, so Delaney had spent the day with Ivy at the festival, helping staff her booth on First Street. He'd just finished his last lesson and was taking Ace for a leisurely couple of laps around the circle while he unwound from a busy day.

He was a sweaty, dusty mess when she showed up outside the arena gate, yet he'd never felt better in his life.

"Hey there, cowboy!" She waved. "What time are you off the clock?"

He rounded the corner and brought Ace to a stop on the other side of where she stood. He checked the non-existent watch on his wrist.

"After Nolan's great day yesterday, he decided he wanted to participate in the facility's movie outing tonight, which means I've got the whole night to myself. Looks like it's quitting time," he said. He laughed when he saw she wore a Midtown Sluggers T-shirt along with her jeans. "Did Ivy recruit you for the Midtown Tavern softball team?"

He couldn't help but smile at how seamlessly Delaney was fitting into not only his world but also the town itself.

Delaney crossed her arms. "Not exactly. I sort of spilled my apple cider on the top I was wearing, and Ivy let me borrow it."

Sam hopped down from Ace's saddle and strode toward his side of the fence, reins in hand.

"Meadow Valley looks good on you, Vegas." He took his hat off and perched it on the fence post. Then he stepped onto the bottom slat and leaned over for a quick kiss.

"Looks like we've both been working hard today," she said. She brushed a finger lightly under his eye. She winced. "So the bruise is still there. Does it still hurt?"

"Not when you kiss me," he said with a wink. "So you're just gonna have to keep doing that."

He dropped back onto the ground, the dusty dirt kicking up around his boots.

"Guess I could use some cleaning up. Then I want to show you something. You got some time before dinner?" he asked.

She checked the invisible watch on her own wrist and glanced back up at him with a grin. "I'm all yours whenever you're good and ready. How about I walk Scout while you clean up?"

"You got yourself a deal," he said. "Meet you on the other side as soon as I get Ace situated."

He might have been tied up on the ranch today, but that didn't stop him from making a call to Mrs. Davis—bookshop owner and kitten foster mother—to set up a visit.

Delaney was waiting when he exited the stable. His chest tightened when he saw her this time, when he realized that after not having seen her for several hours, he'd *missed* her.

He strode toward her, then stopped himself, brushing his hands off on his dirty T-shirt.

"You have no idea how much I want to scoop you into my arms right now, but I am one heck of a mess," he said.

She looked him up and down, then took the final few steps to close the distance between them and wrapped her arms around his neck.

"Scoop away, cowboy. Because there's nothing sexier than a man after a hard day's work."

She kissed him without hesitation, and he wrapped his arms around her thighs and hoisted her effortlessly onto his waist.

"I think we're giving Luis and Anna a run for their money," she said when they both paused for a breath.

He set her back on her feet, his hands sliding into the back pockets of her jeans.

"I guess we are," he agreed. "I am under your spell, Delaney Harper. Not much I can do but simply accept my fate."

She smiled, and he grabbed her hand, threading his fingers through hers.

"Heard anything back from Wade?" he asked as they headed toward his place.

Delaney shook her head. "Not yet. And you know what? I'm not going to let it bother me. In fact, we have *six* more days to not let it bother me. If I haven't heard back from him, then I grab the deed, give it to my aunt— who's my lawyer—and take it from there. Either way, he has to answer for what he did. He can take the easy way out and give me my share of the profit, or it becomes a legal matter. My goal hasn't changed. I want my land. I just want it somewhere that isn't your ranch."

Sam squeezed her hand. "You're sexy when you stick to your goals. Do you know that?"

She laughed and swatted him on the shoulder, then pushed him toward the registration entrance. "Let's go get that beautiful pit of yours, and you can make your goal cleaning up."

Her cheeks were flushed pink. The small reaction filled him with warmth, and he smiled the whole way inside.

Scout bounded out from Sam's bedroom when he opened the apartment door. He dropped down to a squat to receive his pooch's welcome, but she scampered right past him and stopped at Delaney's feet, pacing back and forth with her tail wagging.

"Hey, girl," Delaney said, bending down to scratch the canine behind her ears. "I'm excited to see you too."

Scout panted excitedly as Delaney kissed her square on the nose.

"And here I thought *I* was her favorite," Sam grumbled as he stood and crossed his arms. "Funny how quickly that changed."

Delaney laughed but continued showering Scout with affection.

"I think your human's a little jealous," she said. "Maybe I should tell him that he's *my* favorite." Scout whimpered, and Delaney laughed again. "Okay fine. *You're* number one and the humans both come in second place. I see how things work around here."

She straightened and wrapped her arms around Sam's waist.

"You *are* my favorite," she whispered, then kissed him on the nose too. "I'm just humoring her."

Sam grabbed Scout's leash off a hook by the door and clipped it to Scout's collar, then handed the lead to Delaney.

He kissed her on the cheek. "Your secret's safe with me."

"See you in about ten minutes?" she said.

"Perfect."

And then both his girls were out the door.

His girls.

The thought was at once completely foreign and at the same time the most natural thought in the world.

He showered, grinning like an idiot the whole time and wanting to kick himself for thinking he didn't deserve something like this—like her—simply because his future was less certain than others.

By the time he toweled off and had thrown on a clean T-shirt and jeans, *his girls* were both curled up on the couch. Delaney sipped a bottle of beer and had a second one waiting on the coffee table for him.

He grabbed the bottle and took a long, slow sip. Then he dropped down to his knees in front of Delaney and the dog. He gave Scout a quick belly rub and then gave his other girl a soft kiss just as a knock sounded on the door.

Scout's ears perked up and Delaney's brows rose. "Expecting company?" she asked.

"I am," he said. Then he sprang up and strode toward the door.

"Hey!" she called after him. "That's all you're going to tell me?"

He laughed but didn't give her the satisfaction of a response. A surprise wasn't a surprise if he gave it away.

He threw open the door and was greeted with Mrs. Davis's warm smile.

"I'd hug you," she said, "but I don't have a free arm."

She wore a T-shirt that read *Thyme to Garden*, jeans, and her ever-present green Crocs. Her salt-and-pepper hair was piled into a messy bun on top of her head, and both of her hands gripped the handles of large pet carriers, the sound of high-pitched meows emanating from each.

"Kittens?" he heard Delaney exclaim. She and Scout were standing only a few feet behind him.

The dog barked excitedly. She'd interacted with Mrs. Davis's rescues before, but these were new. He grabbed the pet carriers from Mrs. Davis's hands and set them on the dining room table. He quickly let Scout out into the backyard, then came back for introductions.

"Sorry about that, ladies," he said as Delaney peeked into each carrier. "Mrs. Davis, this is Delaney. Delaney, Mrs. Davis."

The older woman waved Sam off and then shook Delaney's hand. "Please," she said. "Call me Trudy. All the young folks around here who grew up in this town called me Mrs. when they were kids and can't seem to let go of it." She put her hands on her hips and glanced at Sam. "You're practically new around here. I need you to set the precedent."

Sam laughed. "I'll do my best Mrs.—I mean, *Trudy*."

The older woman gave him a satisfied nod.

"Now, Delaney," she said. "Sam told me you're thinking of opening up an animal rescue here in town. Thought you might want to meet a few little friends who could use a place like that." She set the first carrier onto the ground and unlocked its small door.

Delaney clasped her hands under her chin like a birthday girl about to open her most anticipated gift.

The door swung open, and five palm-sized balls of fur tumbled out. There were two orange tabbies, a calico, and two gray-and-white kittens.

Delaney gasped and dropped down to her knees.

"Are these all rescues?" she asked. She waited patiently, letting the kittens sniff around and hopefully—Sam guessed—come to her.

Trudy set the other carrier on the ground.

"Sure are," she said. "No one knows what happened to the mama or what breed she and her mates were. All we know is *this* is the litter."

The second carrier opened, and out sprang three calico-tabby mixes, all black, white, and brown.

"That's all of them," Trudy said. "But this case felt a heck of a lot heavier than just three kittens." She stuck her head down and peered inside. Then she laughed. "Looks like someone else hitched a ride with the litter."

She reached inside and pulled out what sounded like a reluctant stowaway.

The pile of kittens Delaney had amassed on her scurried when they heard the hissing and agitated meows of the full-grown black cat in Trudy's hand.

"Hey there, Butch," Trudy said. "If you come along for the ride, you need to come say hello. Nothing to be scared of here."

Delaney threw a hand over her mouth, then reached for the skittish feline. Sam crouched down next to her and marveled at how the cat relaxed and went right to her.

"What happened to his leg?" Sam asked.

Trudy shrugged. "Nothing. He was born that way. He and another from his litter were inseparable, so we named them Butch Catsidy and the Sundance Kitten. Sundance got adopted. Butch didn't. He's never been the same since."

Delaney cradled Butch in her arms, and Sam heard the fur ball start to purr.

"I helped deliver a couple litters back when I was in school," Delaney said. "I know birth abnormalities occur, but I've never seen one." She rubbed Butch's belly and the spot where his left front paw would have been. "No one wanted him?" she asked Trudy.

Trudy shook her head. "I foster for a humane society over in the next county—closest rescue shelter we've got. Usually I just get them through the critical first weeks, take care of their vaccinations and surgeries to fix 'em from making more litters. By the time that's all said and done, pretty much everyone's spoken for. Butch came to me a few years ago, and I didn't have the heart to send him back to the shelter." She scratched the cat behind his ears. "Never saw him take to anyone like he's taken to you, though."

Sam reached a hand for the cat, and he hissed, swatting at Sam with claws out. He pulled his hand back just in time to not get Freddy Kruegered.

"Hey," Delaney said, stern but gentle. She laid a hand over his extended paw. "He's a friend." Then she looked up at Sam. "Hold your hand like this first, knuckles out, and let him sniff. Once he realizes you're not a threat, he'll let you pet him."

Kittens rubbed at his ankles. One nibbled his toes. They *loved* him. Yet here he was trying to win over the one feline in the room who wanted to tear his face off.

"Only for you, Vegas," he said, and then he held out the back of his hand for Butch to either sniff or rip to smithereens. He hoped for the former. He might have been squeezing his eyes shut to avoid witnessing the carnage, should carnage ensue.

Delaney snorted. "You have a pit bull out roaming your yard, and you're scared of a little cat?"

His eyes flew open to find Butch sniffing but not scratching. "Hey," he said. "Pit bulls get a bad rap, but Scout's a sweetheart and you know it. This guy right here—"

The rest of his words failed him as Butch licked his knuckles with his sandpaper tongue and then proceeded to rub his head beneath Sam's open palm.

"Ha!" he said. "Did you see that? He likes me!"

The next thing he knew, Butch was crawling off Delaney's lap and onto his.

"Huh," Trudy finally said. "He usually takes to women much better. Part of the reason I haven't been able to adopt him out is that he scratches the heck out of any man that gets near him. I guess he sees something in you, Sam."

Sam narrowed his eyes at Trudy. "You could have told me that *before* I marched into battle unarmed."

Both women laughed.

"Maybe Trudy saw something in you, too, and knew you were safe."

Trudy patted Delaney on the knee. "Nice save, honey. I appreciate it." She looked at Sam. "I brought the kittens over so Delaney could see we've got animals in town already who could use a place of rescue, but it looks like I might be here to see if you're interested in adopting a three-legged cat."

Sam's eyes widened. "Me?"

Delaney gasped. "You'd give him up?"

"I don't know anything about cats," Sam said.

"It'd be hard to say good-bye," Trudy admitted. "But I think he's been waiting for you two."

Sam's chest tightened. They'd known each other four days. He hoped he and Delaney had a future, but adopting a pet together was permanent. And permanent still scared the pants off him.

"I'm going to let Sam off the hook," Delaney said, laughing. "We're—I mean, things are very new. But if everything works out the way I hope it does, I'll have a home here in Meadow Valley with plenty of room for a furry friend or two."

Sam blew out a breath. "You're not mad?" he asked. "He could stay here until you get situated." Then he smiled. "And you could visit."

Trudy cleared her throat, then rose to her knees. "Okay, I'm going to collect the little critters. And this thing with Butch can be a trial run. If things don't pan out like they're supposed to, he's always got a place in town with me."

Butch scampered out of Sam's lap and chased after one of those critters.

"Wow," he said. "You'd never know anything was different about him from the way he gets around."

Trudy took off after him, pet carriers in hand.

Delaney leaned over and kissed Sam on the cheek. "Different doesn't necessarily mean broken. It just means learning to cope."

Then she got up and followed Trudy around the room, helping her wrangle the kittens.

Learning to cope, huh? Did that mean she'd be willing to cope with his uncertain future? Or was she trying to tell him to do exactly that? Either way, he'd never considered the possibility that someone might want a future with him even after knowing the risk. But after only a few days with Delaney Harper in town, he was starting to see everything through a different lens.

That night, they lay in bed, his body spooning hers—Scout sprawled across their feet and Butch curled up on Sam's pillow above his head.

"How in the world did you do it?" he asked softly, his lips a breath away from her ear.

She pulled his arms tighter around her. "Do what?" she asked sleepily. "And your cat's purring too loud. Tell him I'm sleepy."

Sam chuckled. "He's *your* cat."

"Do what?" she asked again, tired but insistent.

"Turn my world upside down and make me see it all differently."

"I am pretty special." She sighed dreamily as he chuckled. "Dare you not to fall in love with me, cowboy."

He felt her stomach constrict. He couldn't see her face, but she was holding her breath.

"I don't want to take that dare," he admitted after a long pause.

She rolled over to face him and pressed her palms to his cheeks, her eyes shining with what he hoped were happy tears.

"Good," she said. "I didn't want you to."

Then she kissed him. Or maybe he kissed her. It didn't matter who started it—only that they stayed this way until sleep finally came—despite the blissfully loud, three-legged cat who saw something in him, perched above their heads.

CHAPTER EIGHTEEN

Delaney stood in between Sam and Nolan Callahan—the two men bookending a perfect week. Okay, *maybe* it started off a little rocky with Delaney and Sam in a bit of a land war. Then there was Sam's wasp sting, the right hook to his nose, *and* almost watching him get mauled by a cat—a cat she knew he now loved. But now here they all were, at the festival's closing, where the auction winners would be revealed and then the fireworks display would start.

She still hadn't heard back from Wade, but it didn't matter. Millie was fixed. Tomorrow the courthouse would open. And she'd get her insurance that would either bring Wade out of the woodwork or take him to court. It was out of her hands for one more night, and she wasn't going to let it get to her.

She glanced up at Sam, and the corner of his mouth turned up before returning her gaze, as though he sensed she was looking at him.

Butch Catsidy wasn't the only one head over heels for the guy.

"What?" he asked. "Do I have something on my face?"

She shook her head. "I just like looking at you."

He laughed. "Right back at ya, Vegas."

"How you doing, Dad?" Sam called over Delaney's head.

The older man crossed his arms. "Good. Good. Though I can smell that grilled corn from that stand over there." He pointed to the vendor. "It's driving me crazy. Making my stomach growl."

Sam shook his head ruefully. "Are you really still hungry?"

Nolan shrugged. "I don't get out much. Gotta live it up while I can."

Sam's smile faltered, but only for a second. Sam had taken a chance on bringing Nolan back to the festival, and the day had been another success. But when Nolan made his little self-deprecating jokes about the disease, it likely reminded Sam that they were on borrowed time for days like this.

"I can see the stand from here," Sam said. "Why don't you go grab some."

Nolan's brows rose. "An unchaperoned trip to the grilled corn stand? Son, how can I *ever* thank you?"

Sam rolled his eyes. "Go already, Dad. Before I change my mind."

Nolan bounced on his heels and then strode toward the food stand.

Delaney threaded her fingers through his.

"He's going to remember this week," she said. "Maybe not always, but it'll be there, popping up every now and then to make him smile. *You* did that. You and your brother."

Sam's brow furrowed. "Have you seen Ben lately?"

Delaney laughed nervously. "He and Charlotte—Pearl's granddaughter? They were sort of bobbing for apples when I ran to get a cider."

Sam narrowed his gaze. "Does 'bobbing for apples' mean 'bobbing for apples,' or is that a euphemism?"

She winced. "They were making out on the side of the apple bobbing booth. I pretended not to see them, but they were *really* hard not to see."

"Can you all hear me?" a female voice asked over a loudspeaker, and Delaney was momentarily saved from having to rat on Ben and Charlotte any more than necessary.

There was a small platform at the bottom of the grassy hill, and on it stood Ivy and Carter.

"I can hear you," Carter said into the mic. "Isn't that that all that matters?"

Ivy laughed. "That depends. Hearing is one thing. *Listening* to what I say is another."

"For the last time," Carter said. "You did *not* ask me to pick up a carton of eggs. My mind is a steel trap, and that request was not trapped in there."

There was playful exasperation in his tone, and Delaney could tell this was an act for the crowd, but she also guessed there was some truth to it.

Ivy swatted Carter on the shoulder. "You are so lucky I love you," she said.

"Luckiest man in the world."

A ripple of laughter and *aw*s emanated from the growing crowd settling on the hill. Delaney uttered one of the *aw*s.

"I hope that's us one day," she mumbled under her breath.

"Huh?" Sam asked.

"Nothing," she told him. "I think this is it. You ready to see who's the proud recipient of an all-expenses-paid stay at a guest ranch?"

Sam answered by squeezing her hand.

First they announced the winner of a book basket from Trudy's bookstore. After that came a night of free drinks and appetizers at the Midtown Tavern. A young couple and their twin six-year-old boys won an exclusive tour of the firehouse *and* the station's main engine.

"And now for our final and *top* bidder of the evening, the winner of the weekend stay at Meadow Valley Ranch, generously donated by our very own Sam Callahan, Ben Callahan, and Colt Morgan, the strapping young lads who own and run Meadow Valley Ranch. Excursions included and *no* blackout dates. And our highest bidder, donating one thousand dollars to the Meadow Valley Firehouse, is—oh yay!—Charlotte North! Thanks, Charlotte! Please make sure you stop by the fire station either after the fireworks or sometime tomorrow to claim your certificate for a weekend stay at Meadow Valley Ranch."

"*And* to drop off your generous donation," Carter said with a chuckle. "The Meadow Valley Firehouse and all the Meadow Valley residents thank you for your kindness and generosity."

Delaney giggled. "Guess she and your brother got more done today than just making out. That was actually really sweet of her. I'm sorry it couldn't have been me who made the bid."

"Are you kidding?" he asked, wrapping his arms around her. "You're the reason we're in that auction to begin with. None of this would have happened without you."

Over her shoulder, she saw Ben Callahan approaching.

"Hey, Ben," she said, and Sam released her from his embrace.

He nodded toward his younger brother. "You have something to do with Pearl's granddaughter making that donation?"

Ben gave his brother a self-satisfied grin. "It's not my problem if a week with me isn't enough. She's heading off to New York tomorrow, but she'll be back at some point. What better place to stay than a guest ranch run by yours truly?"

Sam groaned, and Delaney laughed.

"Hey," Ben said. "Where's Dad?"

"Corn," was Sam's only response. But all their heads turned toward the stand, and Delaney's heart sank.

"Where the hell is he?" Sam asked.

"You *lost* him?" Ben asked, his voice tinged with anger.

"He was right there. I turned my back for one second and..." He started pacing. Delaney reached for his shoulder. "Sam. I'm sorry. What do we need to—"

"Not *now*, Delaney. Sorry isn't going to fix this. I need to think." He ran his hands through his hair. "We need to find him before he hurts himself—or someone else."

Delaney flinched. She knew he hadn't meant to sound cruel, that he was scared, but his snapping at her still stung.

"What do you need me to do?" Ben asked.

"Comb the area and find him before it gets dark. If we don't find him before the fireworks start, he'll never hear us. He could be miles away by the time we catch up to him."

Sam stalked off in one direction without giving Delaney or Ben another glance. Ben spun and strode off the other way. And she was left there, mouth agape, not knowing what to do.

Sam had gone in the direction of the woods and Ben toward the food and game booths from where he'd come, so Delaney headed toward First Street in the heart of town, where the shop owners were closing down their booths as night began to fall over Meadow Valley.

"Excuse me," she said, approaching a middle-aged woman who was cleaning up her merchandise from her table in front of a craft and gift shop. "Have you seen a man—in his late fifties—good-looking, salt-and-pepper hair, a T-shirt and jeans? He might be lost."

The woman tucked a lock of dark hair behind her ear and shook her head. "Sorry, sweetheart. But if you find him, feel free to send him my way. You had me at 'good-looking' and 'salt-and-pepper.'"

Delaney forced a smile. She wasn't expecting this to be easy, but she was crossing her fingers for some sort of miracle anyway. "Thanks," she said as she moved on to the next booth, a young man and woman in front of a bookshop called Storyland.

"Hi," she said. "Sorry to bother you right before the fireworks—*wait*, is this Trudy's shop? Anyway, have you seen a man wandering by himself, late fifties, probably looking a little lost?"

The guy scratched his head. "I don't think so. And *yes*. This is Trudy's shop. She's the boss. We just do the dirty work."

Then the young woman's eyes brightened. "What about that guy who asked us if we'd seen his Barbara Ann? Said he'd just gotten back from a business trip and was looking for whoever his Barbara Ann was."

"Oh yeah," the man said. "We didn't recognize him,

and we don't know a Barbara Ann in town, so we thought maybe she was staying at Pearl's inn."

Delaney's heart sped up. "Barbara Ann?" That was the name of the horse she'd ridden with Sam. Was Nolan Callahan looking for the horse? Or was the horse named for someone he cared about, like his ex-wife?

Both strangers nodded.

"Thank you!" Delaney said, hope creeping in. If Nolan was at the inn, he was safe. Everything would be fine.

She heard a faint whistle in the air, then realized the sky had gone from dusk to dark without her even noticing. Seconds later the sky lit up with pink sparks that crackled and fizzled before fading into the black, followed by a heart-stopping *bang*.

Delaney sprinted up the steps of the inn's front porch.

Pearl stood there as if she'd been waiting for Delaney, and gestured her inside. "You looking for Sam's father?"

Delaney nodded.

"He's in the common room," the older woman said. "I called Sam and Ben, but both went to voicemail. They must be out of range. Nolan's standing on a chair, waving a cob of corn on a stick, and telling anyone who even looks at him that they better find his Barbara Ann. I tried to help him down, and he kicked my hand away." She shook out her right hand, which thankfully didn't look any worse for wear. "I don't suppose you know who Barbara Ann is other than an old Beach Boys tune."

"I think I might," Delaney said. "But that doesn't mean he's going to know who I am. Or that he'll listen to anything I have to say."

Pearl held the door open as Delaney stepped through. "Until Sam or Ben gets here, you're our best shot."

Delaney swallowed. Since she knew the restaurant was to the left, she looked toward the right. She heard him before she saw him, much like the morning when she'd met him.

"Where *is* she?" he snarled. "Where the hell is my Barbara Ann?"

She hoped—like it had worked with Sam—that if Nolan saw a familiar face, it might bring him back into the moment. She wasn't sure, though, how familiar she'd be, having only met the man three times. She crossed her fingers that having spent two full days together had given her a fighting chance.

She knew dogs. And cats. Intuition for what they needed was a no-brainer. But this was a human she was dealing with now—a human with a disease that was attacking his brain, which meant even the most rational approach might go awry.

She crept toward the open entryway to the common room. It was empty except for what looked like a couple of inn staff who'd stayed behind while most everyone else was probably out watching the fireworks. The two young men circled the chair Nolan stood on as if they were coordinating an assault. No wonder he was brandishing his corn on a stick.

"Hey!" Delaney said, shooing them away. "Whatever you're doing, it's not helping."

She stepped in front of one of the men and looked imploringly up at Sam's father.

"Mr. Callahan?" She took a step forward, and he flinched, his chair wobbling.

Shoot. What good was finding Sam's father if she caused him to fall off his chair and injure himself? She guessed she'd be two for three with the Callahan men then, one with an almost broken nose and another probably with something worse. All she had to do was find a way to cause Ben bodily harm, and she'd pull off quite the hat trick.

His brows knit together. "How do you know my name? And where is Barbara Ann?"

Delaney backed up, pulled a chair out from another table, and sat down. She held her hands up indicating she wasn't on the offensive.

"I'm a friend of your son's," she said. "A friend of Sam's. Are you talking about Barbara Ann, Sam's horse?"

Nolan Callahan scoffed. "My son doesn't have his own horse, you idiot. He learned to ride on the ones we board. Barbara Ann is my *wife*, and someone better tell me where the hell she is right *now*."

The chair he was on wobbled again, and she could see one of the legs looked as if it was about to go.

Delaney's heart thundered in her chest as the man's voice crescendoed. She was the wrong person for this job. Up until a week ago, she was a stranger to this man. She was in over her head, but it wasn't going to stop her from trying. Not this time.

She stood slowly and reached out a hand for him.

"That chair's in bad shape, Mr. Callahan. If you'll just come down, we can send for Sam and Ben."

The chair shook again, and even though she knew she couldn't catch him, she reached for him anyway, just as he decided to jump down.

"Oh, thank goodness," Delaney said, instinctively resting a gentle hand on Nolan's forearm.

"Don't *touch* me!" he roared, violently shaking his arm free and accidentally backhanding her across the face.

"Dad!" Sam's voice boomed from behind her.

Nolan looked at Delaney, stricken. "I didn't mean to," he said. "I swear I didn't."

He was a child pleading with his parent, only the roles were reversed now.

"Are you okay?" Sam asked her, his tone caring but his eyes distant.

She nodded, hand to her cheek, still in shock.

He stepped in front of her then and turned back to his father. "Mom moved to Tahoe, Dad, remember?"

Ben jogged into the room as well.

"Ben and I run a ranch now. We let you name one of the horses." He shook his head. "Gotta say it's a little weird having a horse named after my mother, but you insisted. And people don't take kindly to name-calling or hitting. I know it's disorienting when you get lost, but if you want people to help you..."

His voice was gentle, but Sam trailed off, and Delaney knew that he must have had a similar conversation with his father before. She also guessed he was realizing the futility of the argument, of asking a man who didn't have control of his own memory to remember.

Sam moved closer to his father, but Ben hung in the doorway, frozen where he stood. Delaney took a step closer to Sam and reached for his hand, but he shook it free.

"You've done enough," he snapped.

She forgave him for how he behaved when they realized Nolan was missing. But they'd found him. Nolan was going to be okay. Delaney knew Sam was under intense stress, but the words and his tone hurt. She thought Sam was finally letting her in. All she'd wanted to do was show him he had someone in his corner, and he'd shrugged her off as if this was her doing and not something beyond anyone's control.

"I don't know what's happening, Sam," his father said. "Why do you and Benny look so damned old? And where the hell are we? This isn't Oak Bluff."

Sam shook his head and held a hand out for his father. Thankfully, Nolan took it. "I think we pushed things too far this time, Dad. Let me take you home."

Ben, still standing in the doorway, cleared his throat. "I can give Delaney a lift back to the ranch."

"The hell you will," Sam said softly, turning to his younger brother. "It's about time you got involved in this. It's not enough to just pay the bills. He's our father. And the more we know about the progression—you can't ignore it. Not anymore."

Ben's shoulders slumped, and suddenly the over-confident player facade fell away, and Delaney saw what Sam never tried to hide—the weight on his shoulders of caring for his father and likely wondering if someone would need to do the same for him someday.

"What do you want to do about getting the guests back to the ranch?"

"Colt's on it," Sam said. "A lot of them said they wanted to walk back, so he'll only have to make one trip."

"And Delaney?" Ben added.

"I'm right here," she said.

"I can drive you," Pearl told her. "As soon as the fireworks are over."

"Thank you," Delaney said. At least someone was acknowledging her presence.

"Come on, Dad," Ben said. "Revolver's parked down the street."

Nolan Callahan let out a breath. "How did my truck get

here when I don't remember driving?" He waved the hand that was still holding the cob of corn. "I think I just need to sleep this one off, boys. One of those days, you know?"

Revolver was Sam's father's truck? How much did she still not know about the man who'd been in her bed and she in his?

The younger son led his father out of the common room and toward the inn's entrance. Delaney heard the older man mumble something about the corn he was holding, and asking if it was okay to eat it.

"Sure thing," Ben said. "It's the best grilled corn in town."

Sam pressed the heels of his hands to his eyes. Either where she'd hit him no longer hurt or he was simply numb to the pain by now, because he said nothing other than emitting a long, exhausted sigh.

"I'm sorry, Pearl," he finally said.

Pearl held out her arms, and Sam let her pull him into a warm, understanding hug.

"On his good days, he knows how lucky he is to have you," she said, then stepped back to look at him. "You're a good man, Sam. Now that brother of yours..." She shook her head ruefully. "You make sure he doesn't break my granddaughter's heart."

Sam laughed. "From what I've heard, Charlotte can definitely hold her own. I wouldn't worry too much."

Finally, Sam turned to Delaney. She couldn't put her finger on it, but something was missing in his eyes, something that was there every other time he'd looked at her today. It was as if a candle had been snuffed out.

"Thanks for finding him. I'll see you back at the ranch." That was all he said before he brushed past her out of the room and seconds later out of the inn's front door.

After a few beats, Pearl held her hand out to Delaney. "Come on, sweetheart. Let's get you some ice for that cheek and go watch the rest of those fireworks."

They stopped in the kitchen, where Pearl grabbed a soft ice pack from the freezer and handed it to Delaney. Then Pearl led her out to the front porch, where they stood at the railing and looked out over the darkened main street of town. Seconds later, green sparks lit up the sky as the next firework soared into the air in the distance.

Delaney pressed the pack to her cheek and let out a shaky breath as she waited for the pop and crackle to dissipate before breaking the silence between them.

"Look," she said. "I know you don't approve of me being here or making Sam's life any messier than it is, so if there's some sort of talk coming my way, just let me have it so I can stop anticipating."

Pearl laughed. "Oh, honey. You think you have everyone all figured out, don't you?"

Delaney shook her head adamantly. "Not even a little. Remember who I was married to the first time I came to Meadow Valley? I don't have *anyone* figured out, least of all Sam Callahan or anyone else in this town."

Pearl placed a hand over Delaney's where it rested on the porch railing. "You're right. I didn't think you coming back was a good idea, and that was no fault of yours. But Wade Harper brought some not-too-nice folks into our town when you two came here. Once you left and he sold the property, things went back to the way they were supposed to be. I'm not saying any of that was your doing, but you have to understand that we look after our own here. And seeing you after thinking Wade and his antics were behind us, well, it got my spine to tingling. And I don't like when that happens. Then I hear you've been introducing yourself as Spence, and I wonder what you're hiding. I guess old habits die hard."

Delaney got it. It was the same way her own spine had tingled when she heard Wade's voice on the other end of the phone line last weekend. She was struck with a sudden pang of guilt for how she'd just spoken to Pearl.

"It was for Ben and Colt. The Spence thing. Sam didn't want them putting two and two together about who I was until after the festival. Didn't want them worrying about why I was here."

Their conversation paused each time a new color streaked through the sky. She expected the third degree from Pearl about what really brought her back to town, which was why she didn't understand what Pearl said next.

"I've never seen that man smile so much as when you're around."

Delaney's brows drew together. "Wade? He only smiled because I was his next meal ticket, not because he actually loved me. He was damned good at playing his part, though."

Pearl gave her hand a squeeze. "I'm talking about Sam. That man has the weight of the world on his shoulders, and you somehow lifted much of it off in a matter of days."

Delaney scoffed. "I also got him stung by a wasp, almost broke his nose, and threatened to steal half his land."

Pearl's eyes widened.

"Not steal," Delaney corrected. "Only take back what was mine when Wade illegally sold it out from under me."

She wasn't sure why she was admitting everything to this woman. There was simply something about her that Delaney trusted—that made her feel safe.

"Oh, honey," Pearl said. "That man really did a number on you." And then the other woman did for Delaney what she'd done for Sam—pulled her into a hug so warm, so reassuring, that Delaney half believed this night could still end on a good note. "And I know Sam didn't handle himself with you the best way he could tonight, but don't give up on him yet."

Delaney forced a smile as the woman released her from the temporary safety of what she would hereafter refer to as a Pearl hug. "He really is a good man, isn't he?" she asked, even though she knew the answer to the question.

"The best," Pearl said. "And if you're willing to put your heart on the line for a future as uncertain as his, then I'd say they broke the mold when they made you too."

That was when it finally clicked. In all her whirlwind feelings for Sam Callahan, Delaney never once feared what it would mean if Sam's path were to follow his father's. She'd wanted him to get tested for his own peace of mind. So he could maybe lessen some of the weight he was carrying. But never once did she think he'd be any less worth fighting for if she knew that test was positive.

The fireworks finale cut their conversation short, but that was okay. Pearl had renewed Delaney's hope. To-night was tough, but they'd gotten through it. They'd get through more. Together.

"Stay for a quick cup of tea, and then I'll bring you home?" Pearl asked.

"That sounds perfect," she said.

Delaney sure liked the sound of that word. *Home.*

Pearl dropped Delaney in front of the registration cabin, otherwise known as the secret entrance to Sam's apartment. The building was still unlocked, which she took as a good sign. Sam had asked her to spend the night, and he'd left the main door open for her. She took a deep breath and blew it out. He'd had one hell of a night. Make that one hell of a week. She could cut him some slack for being curt with her while trying to talk his father down from yet another chair.

She passed the registration desk and made her way down the small hallway to the right but stopped short when she heard voices coming from Sam's place, the door not completely closed.

"After all your lectures to me about what I do and don't do for the ranch, you've been shacking up with someone who wants to steal half of it away from us? I can't believe you waited until now to tell us."

Delaney's breath caught in her throat. The voice was unmistakably Ben's. Sam told them—without any warning or any discussion with her. What about what she'd said about dealing with Wade and leaving the ranch alone?

"Look," Sam said. "That's part of the reason I've been keeping her close by. I figured after a few days of showing her around the place, of her seeing how important it is to all three of us, she'd change her mind. We bought the property well under market value, and we've definitely done enough in the past couple of years to increase what the property is worth. If we take out a loan against equity, we could offer her half of what we paid for the land, and she can take that money and go anywhere—do anything she wants with it."

She could barely breathe. A week wasn't much, but she'd thought it was *something*. But Sam had only been keeping her close to get what he wanted from her. And here she was, ready to walk through that door and do exactly that. This wasn't how it was supposed to go down.

She couldn't listen anymore. There was no way she was letting another man *keep her around* for his own gain.

"I don't know," another voice said, and she recognized it as Colt's. "Business is shaky as it is. We're only in our first six months. If this goes belly-up . . ."

"It's not going to," Sam said. "And if we give Delaney what she came here for, she'll be able—"

Delaney pushed the door all the way open and strode into the apartment with her head held high. She just hoped none of them could see her shaking.

Colt and Ben were sitting at the table, and Sam seemed to have been pacing right in front of them. But they all froze when she stormed in—all except for Scout and Butch. Scout scurried toward her, tail wagging and tongue hanging out of her mouth as she waited for a scratch behind the ears that didn't come. Butch scampered off the table and stopped at her feet, rubbing his head on her ankle. It pained Delaney to ignore the only people—or, at least, living things—whose affection was without ulterior motive.

"You don't have to worry about paying me off," she said, her voice cool and even. "I get it. You want me gone. I'll grab the deed in the morning and go."

"Delaney, I—you saw what happened tonight. This is the only—damn it, I'm trying to help you!" He ran a hand through his hair as she watched him try—and fail miserably—to explain why he'd just lied to Ben and Colt, why he'd all but told her he loved her only to run her out of town, but she was done listening to excuses for why someone betrayed her trust. The only person she could count on was herself, and she was finally ready to accept that.

"I don't *need* help," she said. "Why don't you tell them the truth?" She turned to the other two men. "I only want the deed to prove that Wade committed fraud and hopefully get back at least some of what he owes me. The ranch is safe." She cleared her throat. She wasn't going to last much longer holding everything in. "Thank you all for your hospitality." She dropped down and scooped Butch into her arms. "And I'm taking my cat!"

Then she spun on her heel and strode back the way she came, cat in tow and her pace increasing along with the thunderous beat of her heart. She heard paws scrabbling on tile behind her but didn't dare turn back or slow her steps until she'd made it to the guest house, her hand shaking as she reached in her bag for her key card to open the outside door.

In the distance she heard a dog barking, but the sound grew nearer by the second until Scout skidded to a halt next to her before she made it through the door.

"Scout!" she cried. "What did you do?"

The dog panted and wagged her tail, and Delaney couldn't help but laugh. She crouched down and scratched behind both of the canine's ears. "Did you run all the way here for this?" she asked as Scout gave a small howl of approval. Then her heart sank when she realized the impact of her bold, don't-look-back exit was about to be diminished since Sam was likely only a few paces behind his runaway pooch.

She pulled her phone out of her bag and shot off a quick text to hopefully cut him off at the pass.

Scout's with me. She's safe. I'll leave her with Jessie at the front desk, and you can pick her up there.

Sam's reply was instantaneous.

I was hoping we could talk.

She shook her head, even though he couldn't see her.

No need. My car's fixed. I'll be out of your hair by late morning. Good-bye, Sam.

She turned off her notifications and headed inside with her two companions.

Jessie, Delaney learned, was a local firefighter who moonlighted at the ranch for the overnight shift whenever she was off duty. It gave Sam, Ben, and Colt a few nights off a week from dealing with issues like replacing lost key cards at ungodly hours, and it also meant that now Delaney could "return" Scout without having to face Sam again.

Jessie greeted Delaney with a smile. "Hope you enjoyed the fireworks," she said. "We could see most of them from here. Looked like a great finale."

Delaney forced a smile. "It was." She glanced down at the dog. "You think Scout could hang here with you for a bit? Sam should be here any minute to get her."

Jessie smiled. "Sure thing. Hope you have a great rest of your stay."

Delaney nodded. Then she and Butch made a beeline for the stairwell, making sure she was out of sight before Sam came through the door.

When she was finally alone in her room, she dropped the cat on the bed and let out a long, shuddering breath. She'd have to get him some food and litter and—she needed to gather her thoughts first.

"You are not going to cry over a man who did wrong by you. *Again*." Delaney said out loud. God, her life was like a sad country song where in the chorus she exacted her revenge by keying a car or poisoning some black-eyed peas. Except she wasn't the vengeful type.

She let out a bitter laugh. All she wanted was for Wade to give her what was rightfully hers so she could find a new town, make friends with a new veterinarian, and start her dream all over again.

Actually, right now, she really wanted a long, hot shower. So she peeled off her clothes, left them in a pile on the floor, and padded into the bathroom where she and Sam had—

"Nope." She cut herself off from thinking things she shouldn't think and turned on the water, letting the room fill with steam. Then she turned on her nineties female artist playlist, cranked up the volume, and stepped under the warm spray to the musical stylings of No Doubt.

She washed away as much as she could of the past week, reminding herself that she was fine on her own when she got here, and she'd be fine on her own when she left with the forged deed in her hand.

She wasn't sure how long she was in the shower, but when Sarah McLachlan's "I Will Remember You," the song she couldn't listen to without the ASPCA commercial playing in her head, piped through her smartphone's speaker, she decided enough was enough.

She turned off the water and stepped onto the rug with renewed purpose—well, as much renewed purpose as she could when she was soaking wet, naked, and heartbroken. But when she was dry and it was morning and Millie was chugging along, she'd be one step closer to getting her life back on track once more.

She turned off the music, then wrapped one towel around her head and another around her body. When she threw open the door, she gasped to find Scout sitting outside it, waiting for her.

For a few seconds her traitorous heart leapt as she remembered her request that next time Sam sneaked into her room, he wouldn't sneak back out. But nothing he had to say mattered, not when it couldn't erase what she'd overheard outside his apartment door.

But when she looked past Scout to scan the rest of the room, her hope quickly turned to dread. Because there was Wade Harper, his long body stretched down the length of her bed, his hands behind his head where it rested on the headboard. He was the perfect picture of nonchalance despite the cat on the nightstand who let loose a low, guttural growl.

"Evening, sunshine. You know, you really should make sure your door is *all* the way shut before you make yourself vulnerable to intruders." He winked. "It's a good thing I showed up when I did."

"How did you even know I was here?" she asked.

He shrugged. "Far as I know, you don't know anyone in LA, and I know how much you hate big cities. Figured if you went missing right around the time that Meadow Valley became interesting to me again that you might have figured out a thing or two." He patted the bed next to him. "Come on sweetheart. Have a seat. We've got a lot of catching up to do."

CHAPTER NINETEEN

S am would take it all back if he could. He'd reacted
out of fear, and now he'd have to live with hurting
Delaney when that was the one thing he wanted to avoid.
At least he wouldn't be backhanding her across the face
in twenty to thirty years.

Maybe he should have waited, let the dust settle after
what transpired at Pearl's. But Sam was in love with Delaney. His own mother left before they even knew Nolan
was sick. If Sam's test results ended up being positive,
how could he ask Delaney to sign up for that life now that
she'd seen how bad it could get?

He shook his head as he trudged toward the guest
cabin. He and Delaney were better off cutting their losses
while there was only a week of their lives to lose. He'd
explain. Apologize. Smooth things over the best he could.
Then he'd pray for time to heal what he'd broken in
both of them.

His phone buzzed in his pocket—a text from Delaney
asking him to pick Scout up at the front desk.

She wasn't going to make it easy for him, not that he deserved easy.

He paced for a good twenty minutes outside the guest quarters, maybe longer, trying to figure out what the heck to say. Being scared to hurt her was one thing. Knowing what to do now that he had was downright terrifying.

Another text came through.

Can Scout stay here with me and Butch for the night? I need some time to think, and she's good company.

I'll bring her by in the morning on my way into town.

Sam let out a long breath.

Scout had grown attached to Delaney in a matter of days. They'd both fallen in love. And Butch Catsidy? It took him only a second. That was why all of this was so damned hard. But he could give her this, especially if it meant they'd get a chance to clear the air in the morning.

He texted her back.

Sure. And Delaney... I never wanted to hurt you.

He waited for a reply, watching with his heart in his throat as those three dots indicated she was crafting a response, one he hoped she'd send.

But one never came.

He trudged back to his place and through the front door, where he kicked off his boots. Then he headed straight to the bathroom, removing articles of clothing on the way, not caring where they fell, until he was wearing nothing but his boxer briefs—a sort of reverse surprise for Delaney that she'd never see—standing in front of his bathroom mirror, toothbrush raised and ready to begin.

He stared at the dark circles under his eyes, and those weren't even counting the mottled purple bruising where she'd surprised him with an unexpected right hook.

You sure are one hell of a mess, Callahan.

Yet the rest of the week following his time in the ring with Delaney Harper had felt anything but messy. They'd felt light, even normal, if ever his life could have a sense of normalcy.

He brushed his teeth and tried to ignore the growing ache in his chest, then crawled into bed without Scout and without the woman he'd wanted in his bed tonight.

Sleep on it. That was what he had to do. And somehow he'd figure out how to make things right before Delaney left Meadow Valley, possibly for good.

He wasn't sure how long he'd been sleeping when he bolted upright, his brow beaded with sweat.

Something felt off. Sam wasn't a guy who believed in hunches, but right now he had a hunch that something wasn't right.

He unplugged his phone and glanced at the time on the lock screen. It was almost four in the morning. His hunch told him he needed to see Delaney. Now.

So he scrambled to find a pair of jeans and a T-shirt and found his boots where he'd left them at the door.

He'd just knock on her door and make sure everything was all right. She'd think he was crazy, but at least he'd know this feeling in his gut was probably something left over from a dream. Or maybe it was his subconscious telling him he needed to see her one more time, that waiting until morning wasn't going to work for him.

He used his master key to enter the building. Jessie was dozing at the front desk but startled awake as soon as he burst through the door.

"Sam!" she yelped. "Is everything okay?"

"Delaney," he said. "Have you seen her? Is she okay?"

Jessie looked at him, puzzled. "She and Scout went for a walk with her visitor hours ago. I'm sure she's in her room asleep by now."

Though if Jessie herself had been sleeping, she couldn't be sure.

"Wait," Sam said, her words finally registering. "Her visitor?"

Jessie smiled and nodded. "Said it was an old friend. Tall guy, lanky, about her age."

Wade.

Sam thanked Jessie and headed straight for the stairs and the second floor. When he reached her room, he paused for a brief moment before muttering, "Screw it," and pounding on the door.

"Delaney?" he called. "It's Sam. I need to talk to you. It's kind of an emergency. I know you're pissed at me, but if you don't open the door, I'll have to use my key."

Silence. And the worst was that he wasn't surprised she didn't answer or when his stomach sank, confirming his feeling of dread.

He slipped his key in the card reader and threw open the door, sure he'd find an empty room. Instead he found Butch yawning and stretching on a bed pillow, the bed itself still neatly made. No Delaney. No Scout. But her phone was on the nightstand and her bag was on the floor.

He'd never rifled through a woman's purse before but guessed this was a worthy enough occasion.

"Damn it," he said when he found her EpiPen inside. She promised she'd never leave the room without it again. So where the heck were she and Scout an hour before dawn?

"Okay," Delaney finally said when she, Scout, and Wade walked past the same tree with the white flowers—again. At least, in the beam of Wade's flashlight, it looked like the same tree. Oh no. What if there were *two* trees that looked exactly the same?

She groaned. "I'm ready to admit we're lost. Are *you* ready to call for help?"

As soon as she'd found him in her room, she wanted him anywhere but. Not that she expected Sam to come banging on her door—although she may have wished it—but if he did, she didn't want him finding her in the room with another man, let alone Wade Harper. So she'd suggested a walk and had ended up on the trail she thought she knew.

Spoiler alert: She didn't know it.

They'd been walking and talking for hours. Sometimes she'd yelled and he winced. Other times she'd cried, and he winced some more. She'd let him have it—everything she'd been holding in since the day she left him in the ER and never looked back.

"Sunshine," he finally said, and all three of them came to a stop. "While I *am* enjoying listening to your laundry list of ways I've done you wrong, we're not lost. *You* are."

She stopped and stared at him the best she could with no illumination other than his flashlight.

"What do you mean *I* am? You're with me, aren't you? Unless you've been letting me walk in circles since who knows when, we're in this thing together, much as I hate to admit it."

He shone the light under his chin so his face was fully lit, then tapped his index finger on his nose.

"*No*," she said, teeth gritted and blood running cold. "It was *my* idea to go outside. My idea to take Scout for a walk."

She squeezed her eyes shut and went over the events of the evening, from Sam breaking her heart to Wade—for all intents and purposes—breaking into her room.

She'd come out of the shower, shooed him out of the room while she got dressed, and then sat with him for a spell on a bench outside the guest quarters' main entrance, where she'd proceeded to unleash her fury—until Scout needed to pee.

"Why don't we take that sweet girl for a walk? Can't imagine she likes being cooped up in that one little room now, does she?" Wade had suggested.

"Son of a gun," she said, coming back to the moment. "This was why you came?" She started backing away from him, and Scout began to growl, like she knew as well as Delaney did that something was up. "To get me lost in the woods?"

Wade took a step closer, and Delaney swung at him with an uppercut, only grazing his chin.

He held up his hands and chuckled. "I'm not going to hurt you, sunshine. But good to know you'd be a worthy adversary." Then he had the audacity to bow. "I have always had a way with you, though. Happy to see I haven't lost my touch."

Her fists opened and closed at her sides. How had she let him manipulate her again? "Let me guess. After selling *our* land without my legal permission, you still need money."

"I don't need money," he protested. "Okay, I might need money, but you hit the nail on the head, sweetheart. I may have tiptoed around the law."

She scoffed and crossed her arms. The late-night/early morning autumn chill struck her right down to the bone, and her teeth started chattering.

"Th-that's an understatement. So what? You're worried about paying a fine? Wh-why don't you just pay me, and the law won't be an issue?"

He shook his head. "See, that's the thing. I don't have the money to pay you, and if you get your hands on that deed, I'm down for forgery, filing the forgery . . . Did you know that could get me up to three years?"

Her throat grew tight. "I don't understand. If you're not going to hurt me, then what are we doing out here?"

Wade smiled, and her stomach churned. "According to the state of California, the statute of limitations on contesting a quitclaim deed is five years. I figured if you were here—which you *are*—then you caught me." He held his hands up in mock surrender. "Guilty. But I also know you have a soft spot for my sweet side, so I figured once we spent some quality time together, you'd see that I had no choice and just lay off the whole deed thing."

"Quality time? Is that your spin on it?" she asked. Then she glanced around their surroundings, realizing how lost she truly felt. But maybe Wade wasn't lost at all. "Did you—" Delaney's breath caught in her throat. "Did you kidnap me? What's your plan, Wade? Tie me up for three years so you can run out the clock? Because I'm all out of soft spots for you."

"Actually, you came willingly," he reminded her.

Her stomach sank. "So you're going to keep us lost in the woods until I agree *not* to contest the deed?" No matter what she did, Wade was somehow a step ahead of her. Even if she made it to the courthouse once the festival was done, she'd bet what little was left of her savings that Wade would find a way to intervene. And Sam—God, if she'd never come here, she never would have met him or fallen for him or gotten her heart steamrolled just when she thought it was her turn for a happily ever after.

"Come on, Scout," she said, patting her side. "We're going to find our way out of here. I'll make sure Jessie gets you back to Sam, and then Butch and I..."

They'd leave. It wasn't like Sam was running after her and saying he loved her and made a mistake.

Scout perked up and started pacing, ready for the adventure ahead.

"You forgetting something, sunshine?" He nodded at the flashlight in his hand. "Where are you going to go without this?"

At some point the sky had melted from black to gray, which meant she could see clearly. It also meant she might figure out the trail. Other than Scout, she had nothing and no one else to get her out of this situation.

"I can see just fine, thank you very much. So unless you're going to call us a middle-of-the-woods Uber or something, I'm going to find my way back to the ranch."

Wade shrugged. "My Uber rating stinks. And I think we're far enough off the beaten path that you'll just keep circling your way back to me." He winked at her. "You always do. And soon you'll see that you don't really want me to do time for this. We'll come to an agreement, and then—"

Nope. No more. Enough was enough.

"Come on, Scout," she said, interrupting what would be his last attempt to charm her. "Let's go for a walk, girl."

It was getting lighter every few minutes, which made it easier to navigate her path. They *were* on the path to the swimming hole. She remembered it now. They'd just gotten turned around—several times.

She also remembered the wasp sting Sam took for her that first day she came to town. He hadn't even known her, and yet he'd sacrificed his own personal safety for hers. That was something, right? It hadn't all been pretend.

She stepped lightly over rocks and twigs, squinting at each tree to try to make out nests hidden in the nooks where branch met trunk. But when Scout ran ahead of her, Delaney ran too. And while nests in trees were easy enough to avoid, she wasn't thinking about a possible nest on the ground, one that might have been knocked down by a rodent or a bird.

At first, when she stepped on it, she thought it was some sort of hollow rock. But then her eyes registered movement on the ground around her foot. It was nearly dawn, which meant she could see the black and yellow stripes just in time for the first stinger to embed itself in the skin above her ankle.

Wade probably thought he was the luckiest man in the world—getting lost in the woods with the only person who had the power to make him answer for all he'd done. Looked like he no longer had to sweet-talk her into backing off after all.

CHAPTER TWENTY

After a late bonfire, Ben and Colt stayed on the property in a couple of empty guest rooms. After all, they had plenty. Their rooms were directly across the hall from each other, so Sam pounded on one and then the other, realizing he was likely to wake guests along with his brother and friend.

Not surprisingly, Colt answered his door first, but Sam was confused to find him alert and dressed in a T-shirt and sweats, no sign that the man had just rolled out of bed.

"What are you doing up?" Sam asked, forgetting for a second why he was there.

Colt shrugged. "Meditating. Always do it right before the sun comes up. Centers me into my day."

"Okay, that was not the answer I was expecting." Sam shook his head. "I need your help. Ben's too. Where is he?" He pounded on his brother's door again, this time more frantic.

"Open up, Ben! This is an emergency!" he called through the slab of wood separating them.

Other doors in the hall creaked open, and Sam waved them off. "Sorry, folks. Just a, uh, family situation. Go back to sleep. Breakfast isn't for another few hours."

The awakened guests rubbed their eyes and happily turned back toward their rooms.

He pounded on his brother's door some more. "Come on, Ben! If you don't get your ass out here—"

The door flew open to reveal Ben Callahan, his dark hair standing on end, not awake enough to even open his eyes, and 100 percent naked.

Colt gave his friend the slow clap. "And the winner for morning wood is..."

"Cover yourself up!" Sam snapped. "You're in the guest house, not your damned living room."

Ben blinked his bleary eyes open, and they widened as soon as he took note of his surroundings.

He laughed and held up a finger, signaling for the other two to wait, then reached behind the door. He came back holding what was very clearly a pair of women's panties over his exposed erection.

"I don't have time to ask if you've got Charlotte in there, and to be honest, I'd rather not know."

"It's Charlotte!" a woman's voice yelled from inside Ben's room. "Tell my gran I'm a grown-up and can have sex with whoever I want!" Her tone was playful, singsongy. But Sam had zero time for playful.

"I just hung up with Pearl a few minutes ago. Asked her what she knows about Wade Harper and how dangerous he is. And she said—"

"Whoa, whoa, whoa, Callahan," Colt said. "Slow down a minute. Wade Harper? Does he know she's here for the property?"

Sam's jaw was tight. His hands balled into fists, but

that wasn't going to do him any good now. "*He's* here. At least, I think he is. I know Delaney tried contacting him before heading to Meadow Valley. Now I can't find her. *Or* Scout. And Jessie mentioned some guy visiting Delaney in her room. Something's not right."

He'd have dealt with Delaney skipping town and leaving him in the dust after the way he treated her. But going for a walk without her phone or EpiPen? Something was wrong, and he'd never forgive himself if anything happened to her.

He pulled Delaney's phone out of his back pocket. It had been unlocked, and he'd totally violated her privacy and checked her texts and messages. But it had all been in an effort to figure out if she was in danger.

"I knew she'd been in contact with him. She told me so herself, but listen to this," he said to Ben and Colt, then played them a voicemail Wade had left for Delaney, one she hadn't told Sam about. "I don't think it's a coincidence he checked up on her the first time she stepped foot back in Meadow Valley since they got divorced."

"Isn't it possible," Ben started, "that she was simply so pissed at you that she skipped town?"

Sam brandished her phone in his face. "Without her phone? Or the cat? Without any of her things? And with my damned *dog*?"

Ben scratched the back of his neck. "I guess my theory doesn't hold up."

Sam pulled something else out of his other pocket, a yellow tube. "And she doesn't have *this*." He didn't want to imagine what would happen if she needed the EpiPen and it wasn't with her.

Colt gripped Sam's shoulder and gave him a firm

squeeze. "Tell us what Pearl said and what you need us to do."

Sam blew out a shaky breath. "She said she never heard of him laying a hand on anyone who didn't lay a hand on him first. But the people he consorts with...If he's here, he might not be alone. You want to know why Delaney's so good in the boxing ring? It's because Wade scared her enough to make her think she needed to protect herself."

"So where are we going?" Ben asked.

"I called the sheriff's office. They've got a car on the streets, and Deputy Garcia is coming with me. We need to hit the trails."

Both of the other men nodded.

"I'll take the new one since I know it best," Sam said. "You two take the others."

He glanced through Colt's open door. "Sun's coming up, so I'm heading out."

"We're on it," Colt said.

"I'll—get dressed," Ben added, but his face grew serious. "We're gonna find them, okay?"

"Yeah," Sam said. "We will." He had to believe his own words because the alternative...There was no alternative.

He left his brother and Colt and strode toward the stairwell, his strides growing longer and his pace growing faster until he was somehow outside the building and breaking into a sprint, nearly trampling his police backup.

"Hey, hey, hey, Callahan!" Deputy Daniela Garcia called after him. "A little warning that the chase is on next time?"

In a black T-shirt, jeans, and tennis shoes—her shoulder-length dark hair pulled into a ponytail—she could have been a local or a ranch guest out for an early morning run. Only the holster at her hips, her radio clipped on one side and her gun on the other, gave her away.

She caught up to Sam in mere seconds. She was a trail marathon runner, and he was glad to have her on his side, but this was one trail she didn't yet know.

"Sorry, Dani," Sam said, only slowing when they made it to the trailhead. But he wasn't wasting another second.

She nodded and held a finger to her lips, then motioned for him to lead the way.

Show me where you and Scout went, Vegas. And tell me we're not too late.

Delaney limped on an ankle swollen not from any typical injury but from the immediate reaction to not one but two stings. She knew it was only a matter of minutes before the venom's effect would be more than skin deep.

She called for Wade, but her voice cracked, and she couldn't seem to get enough air to create the intended volume. Scout ran back and forth in front of her, as if she were guiding Delaney back to where Wade would be waiting with a smug grin, ready to say, *I told you so.* But then the dog stopped and whimpered, pawing at her snout.

"Oh no," Delaney said softly, noticing the red welts on Scout's face. Everything had happened so fast, yet it had felt like slow motion—Delaney stepping on the hive or nest or whatever it was, the first sting and the one after that as she tried not to panic while slowly moving away, and then Scout sensing her distress, nipping at the angry insects who survived being trampled.

Scout got stung, too, and from the looks of things, she was possibly experiencing an allergic reaction as well.

"Wade," she said again when he came into view. She heard the high-pitched whistle of air when she inhaled. So she'd already made it to wheezing.

"What took you two so long? I thought you'd circle back in a matter of seconds..." His words trailed off when he got a good look at her. "Delaney. What the heck happened?"

She could barely stand on her injured foot anymore, and she wavered, trying to keep her balance as her vision began to blur.

"Wasps. Please, stop messing around and call for help. If I don't get a shot of epinephrine in the next few minutes—"

Scout howled and buried her snout in her paws.

Wade looked from her to the dog and back to Delaney, wide-eyed, but he didn't move.

"Snap out of it," she said. "I know you didn't mean for this to happen, but this isn't about the deed or money anymore, so just make the right choice for once."

She could see the swirl of thoughts going through his head—the realization that it was a losing battle whichever way he sliced it. If he called for help, he was as good as turning himself in. If he didn't, she'd die. Come to think of it, maybe *he* was the one who was swirling, because Delaney could see two of him now.

She cried out as she took one laboring step to get close enough, and remembered how when she'd twisted her ankle in the boxing ring, Sam had laid down his defenses and put himself at risk to help her. Even now, though, Wade Harper was too much of a damned coward to do that.

"Give me your phone, *Wade*."

He pulled his phone from his pocket, staring at the screen and then at her.

Then he swiped up, pressed a few buttons, and placed the phone to his ear.

"We're lost on a trail on the outskirts of the Meadow Valley Ranch," he said to whoever was on the other line. "I'm with a woman and a dog who've both been stung by wasps and are having allergic reactions. The woman will go into anaphylactic shock if she doesn't get a shot of epinephrine soon."

That was the last thing she heard before everything sounded like she was underwater. Then she felt the weight lifted off her injured foot, and she exhaled a shallow breath before closing her eyes. She was just going to take a tiny rest.

"Dispatch said a trail," a female voice said. "Wait... I think I see them." The voice was getting closer. "They're over here!"

"She's not breathing," Wade said. "Oh my God, she's not breathing."

"Damn it, Vegas. You promised you'd never leave without this again."

Sam? How did Sam learn to talk underwater?

A sharp sting pierced the skin of her thigh, and she guessed it was a final wasp who'd come to finish the job her friends had started.

"This is it," she mumbled. "Bring on the white light."

"It's working. Get him out of here and call the firehouse. Have my brother run Scout over to Dr. Eli Murphy's place. He'll see her, even at this hour. She's been stung before but not multiple times at once. I'd rather play it safe."

"Nice work, Callahan. Glad I didn't have to handle the injection. Needles scare the heck out of me," the strange woman's voice said.

"Says the badass who just cuffed the bad guy. I think we're good here. I'll carry her the rest of the way if I have to." Someone stroked her hair. "Can you take another breath, Vegas?"

His voice was clearer now, and she guessed that maybe he wasn't some sort of fish person who could speak underwater. She breathed in deeper this time, the whistling wheeze all but gone. Her fingers tingled, and she felt dirt beneath them. She blinked a few times, then looked straight up into Sam Callahan's brown eyes.

"You found me," she said softly. "And—not a bad guy. At least, not tonight. We went for a walk and got lost. Wade just wanted to stay lost until I did what he wanted. Couldn't sweet-talk," she mumbled. "And then wasps."

His brows drew together. At least, she thought they had. But that might have also been her double vision still righting itself.

Delaney realized she was lying with her head in Sam's lap, and she pushed herself up to a sitting position.

She glanced around frantically, but there was no sign of Wade. No sign of Scout.

"Scout," she said. "She got stung. Because of me. I should have walked her straight back to your place when she followed me, but—"

"Scout's fine. Ben will get her checked out. I know there's a lot I need to say right now, but from the looks of the swelling on that ankle, we need to get you to a doctor. Can you stand?"

She nodded. Her foot still hurt, but the swelling was already half of what it was before.

She limped her way back to the semicleared path. An ambulance sat waiting at the edge of the property. She smiled when she saw the familiar face of Carter Bowen where he stood by the vehicle's open back doors.

"Good morning, Delaney," he said. "Can I give you a lift?"

She laughed nervously. "Haven't been in one of these since I was a kid, the first time I got stung."

"You riding with her?" Carter asked Sam.

She opened her mouth to tell him it wasn't necessary, that he should go to the vet and check on Scout, but she never got the chance.

"Of course I am," he said.

Carter helped her into the vehicle and onto the stretcher, where he checked her vitals before strapping her in for the ride.

Sam climbed in after and sat on the bench facing her.

He came for her. And was staying. Despite the horrible things she overheard him saying to Ben and Colt, she knew the past week hadn't been a lie, even if something had changed irrevocably for Sam last night. He cared about her as much as she cared about him. She was sure of that now. But she was just as sure that if he couldn't believe in a future where he deserved more than going it alone until the other shoe dropped, then his future would never include her, and she would have to live with that. The good news was that she would live. She'd just be doing it with a lot more heartache than when she'd arrived here a week ago.

"Thanks for saving my life again," she said with a soft smile.

"Thanks for not dying, Vegas."

He rested a hand over hers, and even though it wasn't a bone-melting kiss, it was somehow everything she'd ever wanted, even though she knew they were still on their way to good-bye. Delaney understood now why Sam did what he did the night before.

She couldn't be in a place where she'd likely see him every day yet not be able to be with him. It would be the worst kind of pain, for both of them.

No wasp sting or near-death experience could measure up to how much it would hurt when she left Meadow Valley for good.

CHAPTER TWENTY-ONE

Once at the hospital, Sam waited in a plastic chair outside the curtain of Delaney's exam room while Delaney gave her statement to Deputy Garcia. He was more than exhausted. The past several hours drained his last reserves of physical and emotional resolve. He was simply spent—every last part of him.

"She gonna be okay?"

He glanced up to see his brother standing there, his hair still rumpled from sleep or lack thereof, and dark circles under his eyes that matched his own.

Sam nodded and stood. "They gave her another dose of epinephrine after listening to her lungs. Finally gave her her walking papers a few minutes ago." He scratched his stubbled jaw. "How's Scout? Did you drop her back at home? How long have we been here?" He'd been in and out of the room with Delaney all morning, but she'd insisted on giving her statement to Deputy Garcia alone.

"Scout's fine. The vet gave her some Benadryl for the

itching, and she's home passed out on your bed. As for question number three? Two hours," Ben said.

"Feels like a week." It was only nine in the morning, but he'd been going full throttle since four.

"You look like hell," Ben said with a laugh.

"You take a look in the mirror lately?" Sam raised a brow.

Both men had been hiding from an uncertain future— Sam in his way, and Ben in his.

"I lost it last night," Sam said. "Dad hurt her, and I couldn't protect her. What if that's me someday?" He cleared his throat. "I was going to get tested. I know we decided not to and to just live our lives, which is why I wanted to tell you. Now I don't know if I could handle the truth if it's not the truth I want." He shrugged, even though the weight of that implication threatened to pummel him to the ground.

Ben nodded soberly. "I had my blood drawn six months ago."

Sam's eyes widened.

"I was afraid to tell you because you were so hell-bent on this pact we made and on not burdening ourselves with something we can't control, but I can't do what you do. I can't tuck it all away. I know you think all I do is avoid the tough stuff, and maybe I do with Dad, but that's only because it hits too close to home."

In that moment, everything fell into place—Ben shirking his ranch duties more and more and visiting their father less and less. Okay, fine, he'd always been the guy to choose fun over responsibility, but lately, since they'd opened the ranch's doors for business, something had shifted in Ben's behavior.

"Your test came back positive," Sam said. It wasn't a question.

Ben nodded. "It's still a goddamn crapshoot. The doc said that even with the gene mutation, some people go on to live long, healthy lives with no symptoms. More *do* end up exhibiting signs, though. Some in their late forties like Dad. Some not for decades more. So I'm changing my diet, taking a lot of supplements— and maybe blowing off a little too much steam every now and then."

Sam's throat tightened. He had no words of encouragement. There was nothing he could say that would change what the doctor had already told Ben. So he did the only thing he could think of, something he hadn't done in years.

He pulled his brother into a hug. And Ben surprised the hell out of him by hugging him back.

"We're going to figure this out," Sam said, not that he had any clue how. "But in the meantime, you gotta keep it in your pants around Pearl's granddaughter. That woman loves you like her own, but she'll kill you with her bare hands if you hurt her flesh and blood."

Ben laughed and pulled away. "She's heading back east. I know you find this hard to believe, but I'm pretty sure she only wanted me for a fling anyway. Love me and leave me. Use me and abuse me. Can't blame her, what with my dashing good looks and huge—"

"All right, all right," Sam said. "Enough stroking your own—ego."

Ben grinned. "Just calling it like it is, bro."

All this time he'd thought he was protecting his little brother by shielding him from whatever the truth about his future was. But Ben had actually been protecting *him*—from the burden of knowing what was too painful to know, from not being able to solve a problem that had no solution.

The examining room curtain opened, and Deputy Garcia stepped out first.

"Callahan," she said, nodding at Sam. "Callahan." She did the same for Ben. "Wade told us a lot about a deed, the sale of the land to you all. I don't think this was a kidnapping, just a couple of people getting lost. But this Wade Harper thing goes deeper than tonight."

Both men nodded.

"Sam, I'm going to need a quick statement from you, but you can come by the station later today or tomorrow if that works okay."

He nodded and shook the deputy's hand. "Thank you for all your help today."

"Anytime, Sam. Let me know when you and your crew clear out that trail. I'd love to give it a run when it's open for business."

Sam smiled. "You'll be the first one I call."

She looked both men up and down, then shook her head. "Get some sleep, boys."

She pushed through the double doors that led to the lobby, and Ben let out a low whistle.

"I think I want to take up trail running," he said.

Sam backhanded him on the shoulder. "I can see this diagnosis of yours has been very sobering."

Ben shrugged. "Who knows how many good years I have left? Might as well make the most of them."

A throat cleared, and both men's attention turned back toward the exam room curtain.

Delaney waved. "Sorry to interrupt. But it, um, looks like I'm free to go. You really didn't have to wait."

"This is my cue to exit," Ben said, bowing dramatically and backing toward the door.

Delaney laughed, and her cheeks flushed. Sam looked her up and down. Her hair was a mess, and he was pretty sure he could still see a leaf or two buried in her matted strawberry-blond waves. Dried mud caked her shoes and was splattered up her legs. Circles rimmed her eyes to rival Ben's and possibly Sam's own.

"What?" she asked, patting a hand over her hair. "I'm a disaster. I know."

"You're beautiful," he said.

"Sam. We aren't—I mean, we can't..." She crossed her arms. "Besides, I'm supposed to be mad at you." She didn't sound mad at all. "You aren't allowed to compliment me when I'm angry, especially when I know I look like some woodland creature who may or may not have smaller woodland creatures living in her hair."

He understood. That she would even speak to him after last night was a miracle in and of itself. Still, no matter what happened next, he needed her to know it was real, that *they* were real.

"About that," he said. "Can I—kiss you? Will that mess with your plans to throttle me?"

"*Sam*," she said again, the playfulness gone from her tone.

"It's okay," he said. "I shouldn't have asked."

"Yes," she said softly. "Yes, you can kiss me."

He skimmed his fingers over the hair at her temples and brushed his thumb over a scratch on her cheek. He cradled her face in his hand and dipped his head, brushing his lips softly against hers. It had been less than twenty-four hours since they'd done this, but it felt like weeks. She tasted so good, and it felt so right to hold her. Yet the second he got scared, he pushed her as far away as possible.

"Scout!" Delaney blurted.

He laughed, thankful for the levity, then leaned back, his brows drawn together. "Um...I may not be an expert at this, but I'm pretty sure when you kiss someone, you're not supposed to call out their dog's name."

She smacked him lightly on the shoulder. "Is she okay? I'm so sorry she got messed up in this, that any of you did. I promised myself I'd keep her safe, and if she—"

"She's *fine*," Sam assured her. "Snout's a little itchy, but she'll be back to sniffing out any rodents trying to get onto the property in no time." He laughed. This was good. They were talking. And kissing. This was progress, he hoped. He just wasn't sure what came next. "That's how she got her name, you know. The shelter who found her said she was keener than a bloodhound."

"She's a lucky girl." Delaney smiled. "Now about that kiss..."

Sam didn't need to be asked twice. He drew her close and tilted his head toward hers.

The kiss was soft and sweet. He didn't want to linger too long, not when he had so much to say.

He held out his right hand, and she linked her fingers with his, like it was the most natural thing to do. And if he weren't so damned terrified, he'd be doing it every day from here on out. But he didn't know how to let go of the fear, which meant the best gift he could give her was letting *her* go instead.

"I need to show you something," he said.

He led her through the ER lobby and out into the blaring, late-morning sun. The small parking lot was fairly empty, so when she gasped, he knew she'd found her surprise.

"Millie!" she exclaimed, then ran toward the old car like it was a shiny new bike sitting under a Christmas tree.

Once she'd decided to stay in town whether her car was fixed or not, they hadn't pushed Boone to get it done sooner rather than later. Just by the end of the festival. But today was the day. She wasn't stranded anymore.

Sam pulled the key fob out of his pocket and unlocked the door just in time for her to throw it open. When he caught up with her, she was sitting on the driver's seat hugging the steering wheel.

"Wow," he said. "You two go way back, huh?"

She nodded and held out her hand. "Key, please."

He obliged. As the engine roared to life, he rounded the rear of the vehicle and let himself into the passenger side.

"Boone and Colt brought it by about an hour ago. Figured you'd be happy about it, but I didn't realize how much."

Cold air blew out from the vents, and she let out a contented sigh. "Millie's my proof," she said. "Bought her all by myself and kept her going all these years. She's my reminder that no matter how many wrong turns I might make, I can still get to where I want to be without anyone else having to rescue me." She winced. "Unless I forget my EpiPen."

But she was right. She could stand on her own two feet, and he loved that about her. She was resilient. She'd bounce back after their whirlwind of a week, and the thought gave him comfort.

She pressed a palm to his cheek, and he held his breath.

"I didn't know about Revolver before last night," she

said. "That he was your dad's. He liked the Beatles, huh? That is a great album." She exhaled a shaky breath. "After what Wade pulled last night—and this morning, I guess—I realized that he is never going to change, not for me or anyone else. It has to be what *he* wants."

"I know," Sam said. He also knew she was talking about more than Wade.

"It really hit me while I was in the exam room," she continued. "All the pieces of your life that weren't entirely yours—the horse named after your mom, a truck that belonged to your dad, and that beautiful framed photograph on your bookshelf of a family before it splintered off into separate parts." She looked away and let out a nervous laugh. "Okay, so I *was* snooping that day. But it doesn't change the fact that you're holding on to pieces of a past that is long gone." She paused. "I know your future is uncertain—more so than for other people. Having to watch your dad go through this and realizing it could be you someday? I can't imagine how scary that is. But I also know that what you did last night—pushing me away—was because you think asking someone else to help you shoulder the burden of that fear is asking too much. But you never even gave me a say. You just made up your mind what was best for me."

Sam's chest tightened. "My father *hit* you," he said, finally addressing the elephant in the room. He couldn't stop seeing it in his head, couldn't stop imagining it was him and not his dad. "I know I need to cope with what might happen to me. But if the test results are positive, that means coping with *me* being the one to hurt you like that someday."

"He didn't *mean* to do it." She shook her head and wiped away a tear before it fell. "I love you,

Sam. Whether you get tested or not. Whether the test is positive or not. If you need to cope, I want to cope with you. But until you forgive yourself for what hasn't even happened yet—until you understand that you are worthy of being loved no matter what—there's no chance for us."

He couldn't imagine hearing any better words falling from her lips. *I love you.* Yet it felt like his chest was caving in.

"I love you too," he said after a long silence. "But I don't know how to do what you're asking of me."

She pressed her lips together and nodded. "Then it's for the best, right? Relationships that start under intense circumstances never work out anyway, and I don't think it gets more intense than us."

He laughed at his romantic life being summed up by a line from an action movie. Yet nothing about the situation was funny at all because Delaney Harper was really leaving.

He kissed her anyway. There was nothing he could say to fix this, not when she could see something in him he couldn't see for himself. So he tangled his fingers in her hair and kissed her good-bye. He took one final taste of her lips and tried to tell her without his fumbling words that he would be the man she wanted if he could. And when she took his hand and pressed his palm over her heart, he let himself believe that for the span of this kiss, in a tiny little car that seemed to defy the odds, he was exactly that.

"I can come back and help you pack up," he said, his throat tight.

She shook her head. "I don't think I could handle saying good-bye to you again," she said. "I know it goes against the reason I came here in the first place, but maybe just this once we should take the easy way out, let this be it."

He nodded once, then exited the vehicle, wishing that if he closed the door she'd turn the car off, come after him, and tell him that she'd wait until he figured himself out. But it wasn't a fair wish. He knew that. Delaney knew it, too, which was why she pulled away and didn't look back.

After she'd gone, Sam drove to see the only person who might understand what he was going through—who'd loved and lost like he had to an even stronger degree. He wasn't supposed to show up until later that afternoon, but suddenly it seemed the only person he could talk to was his father.

When he walked into the game room of the memory care facility, Nolan Callahan was thumbing over a stack of board games trying to pick which one to play, and his partner—sitting at the table his father stood on more than a week ago when he and Delaney had first met—was an older woman with chin-length wavy brown hair, a few stubborn grays woven through. She wore a simple blue sweater, jeans, and her telltale riding boots.

The original Barbara Ann.

"Mom?" he said.

She looked up and smiled. "Well, Nolan," she said, still facing her son. "I guess the cat's out of the bag."

Nolan Callahan spun toward his son, beaming. "You're just in time." He held up a box. "Cards Against Humanity."

"*Dad*," he said. "*No.*"

His mother laughed. "Not while Sam's here, at least."

"Why wasn't I invited to the family reunion?"

Sam turned to find Ben standing behind him. It was the first time all four of them were in the same room since—well, since who knew how long.

"I'm as shocked as you are," Sam said to his brother. "I was just stopping by to check on Dad."

"Same here," Ben said.

Together the two brothers approached the table, both with the same careful steps they'd use to avoid spooking an animal.

Nolan waved them off. "Sit down already. It's just your mother, for crying out loud." He picked up another game box. "How about Yahtzee? It's good practice for casino night."

Sam and Ben kissed their mother on respective cheeks and sat.

"Okay, someone better explain what's going on because I don't think I can handle any Yahtzee until this all makes sense," Sam finally said, and he crossed his arms over his chest.

"Yeah," Ben added. "I'm with big bro. How long has this been going on?"

Their mother blew out a breath, and her eyes grew wet.

"I messed up," she said, a tear streaking her left cheek.

Nolan collapsed into the empty chair and dropped Yahtzee on the table. Then he wrapped an arm around their mother's shoulders and gave her a soft squeeze.

"So did I, darlin'," he said, then kissed the top of her head. "But that's all in the past now. Let's worry about the future." Nolan beamed when he looked at his sons. "There's something I never thought I'd say."

Sam shook his head. "But Ted. And Tahoe. And . . . Ted." He couldn't even formulate a complete sentence.

Their mother nodded. "Ted's a good man. But he's not the right man. We separated last year. When I moved out, the first thing I did was drive out to see your father."

Sam felt as though he'd been leveled with a right hook all over again. His mom left her husband for his dad, after all that had happened?

"Dad, you were telling the truth? When you said Mom would be sad to miss the Orionids? You've been seeing each other regularly?"

"Why didn't anyone here tell Sam about you having other visitors?" Ben asked. "Why didn't *you* tell anyone, Dad?"

Nolan waved them off, but his face grew serious. "Look, I know how much you boys do for me, how much you sacrifice. It's hard for me to put into words what that means. Your mother and I, we didn't want you to worry. We didn't want to say anything until she found a place up here and had a chance to figure out how and what to tell you." He laughed. "I don't think there's a manual for this."

"I guess now would be a good time." Sam's mother pulled a tissue from her purse and dabbed under each eye. "I never forgave myself for leaving when things got tough."

"You didn't know what you were up against," Nolan interrupted. "None of us did. But we know now."

Nolan sounded like himself, like the man he was a decade ago. He sounded like their father again.

Their mom nodded. "I always figured if *I'd* been so angry with myself, then you boys would likely never forgive me. But I've missed you so much—all three of you. I hope you'll let me try again."

Sam had endured enough heartache to last him a

lifetime. He didn't have the energy to withhold forgiveness, not when he was more his mother's son than he'd ever realized.

Delaney would have stayed, would have loved him no matter what. But because he couldn't run away, he'd convinced her to run instead. He didn't want to be that guy anymore. Delaney learned to face her fears head-on, and it was time Sam did the same.

He could still get tested, and if those fears were realized, then they'd have time to prepare. He and Delaney didn't have to be his parents, not if she could forgive him.

He reached for his mother's hand and gave it a firm squeeze. "Welcome home, Mom."

CHAPTER TWENTY-TWO

One week later

Delaney enjoyed the three days a week she worked as a tech in a local veterinarian's office. If not for the couple of slot machines in the waiting room—animal themed, at least—and the fact that Vegas was Vegas and not a small ranching town in Northern California, she could almost make herself believe that she had everything she wanted.

Today, though, she sat in the back office of her family's motel paying a few invoices and cleaning out her inbox.

"Junk mail, junk mail, junk mail," she said to herself as she highlighted a whole column of messages she was too lazy to open and click Unsubscribe. But then she saw it, the email she'd been hoping to receive since she left Meadow Valley last week. It was from her aunt Debra, and the subject line simply read No court!

She clicked open the message, her finger shaking as it tapped the mouse pad.

"Beth!" she called, hoping there weren't any patrons up front. "Beth, get your ass back here!"

She threw a hand over her mouth.

Oops.

There was a reason she was meant to work with animals instead of humans. None of that pesky language etiquette to get in the way.

"What's wrong?" Beth asked. "If you're calling me in here for something related to a living thing with four, eight, or more legs, you've got the wrong girl."

Delaney laughed and shook her head.

"Wade's pleading guilty to the forgery. He's going to prison for six months." She winced. "I didn't mean to sound excited about the second part."

Beth rolled her eyes. "He got off easy," she said.

Delaney worried her bottom lip between her teeth. "When he secures legal employment—somewhere down the line—he's mandated to pay some of his salary to me each month until he makes financial restitution."

Beth's brows rose. "I'm impressed. Wade Harper is finally doing something right."

Delaney nodded. "Which means no court date for the whole sort-of-being-kidnapped incident or to prove the forgery—and no having to go back to Meadow Valley." Her throat tightened as she spoke the last two words. "I can finally close the book on all things Wade Harper and Meadow Valley."

Beth crossed her arms. "You said Meadow Valley twice in the span of about four seconds."

"I did *not*," she said defensively.

"Lanes. You find a way to mention Meadow Valley at least once a day. If I didn't know any better, I'd say you're disappointed you don't *have* to go back. But you know, if you *wanted* to go back..."

Delaney turned her focus back to her laptop, pretending she was typing something important when really she was just seeing how quickly she could type the alphabet without looking at the screen.

"I already tried that, remember? Fell in love, got my heart broken, lost my land again." Well, she never actually got it back. But still. Potato, potahto.

She pointed to the map on the wall behind Beth. "Every day, I throw a new dart, see where it lands, and do my research. Soon I'm going to find the perfect place to open my rescue shelter."

Beth spun and strode toward the map, inspecting it, running her fingers over it.

"Funny," she said, "but it looks like there are an awful lot of holes up here in Northern California. You sure you're not throwing the dart in the same place every time?"

Delaney blew out a breath. So what if she was? She *tried* to aim at the Midwest, the Northeast. But the dart kept going west.

"Hey," her sister said. "It's okay if a lifetime in the desert isn't for you. I don't want to be a Vegas showgirl forever, you know. In fact, as soon as I get the guts to tell Mom and Dad—and come up with some sort of a plan— I'm heading to New York. Don't suppose you'd want to head out with me? I bet there are plenty of stray animals who'd love you to take them in."

For the first time since Delaney could remember, her always bold, take-no-prisoners little sister sounded scared.

Delaney smiled. "You know I'd do anything for you— except that. You're the city girl, not me. But when you're in your first show as the newest member of the Rockettes,

I'll be in the front row at Radio City Music Hall." She got up from her chair and hugged her sister tight. "I know it's terrifying, but if chasing a dream was easy, everyone would do it. Good thing you're the bravest girl I know."

Beth laughed. "That's great advice. Wonder if that applies to anyone else in this room."

She was saved by the bell—the front desk bell.

"Whose idea was it again for me to take Monday mornings so Mom and Dad could sleep in?" her sister asked as she headed back up front.

"I *am* brave," Delaney mumbled, collapsing back into her chair. "And I chased my dream. *Twice.*" To the very same place, and where had it left her?

She stared at the map on the wall, squinting at the cluster of tiny holes all in the same part of one particular state.

Sam wasn't part of the dream she'd been chasing, but maybe dreams could change. Where once it had been a place and a purpose, what if it also included a person? And a dog?

A meow came from under her desk, and Butch Catsidy leapt into her lap.

"And a *cat*," she said.

She picked her phone up off the desk.

"Damn it, Sam," she said out loud. She loved him, no matter what. No matter how scared he was. Yet she'd left.

Maybe he needed to hear it again. Maybe she needed to make a recording of it and play it on loop until he believed her. Maybe—maybe she should tell him.

"Screw it," she said, talking to herself again. "If dreams were easy..."

She typed in Sam's name and then the three most honest words she could muster.

I love you. No. Matter. What.

Message delivered.

"Lanes!" Beth called from up front. She poked her head back into the office door. "There's a guest who wants to talk to the marketing manager. I'm guessing that's you since no one officially has that title."

Delaney's brow furrowed. She didn't talk to the guests. She worked behind the scenes.

She groaned. "Let me guess. The sheets on the beds don't look as white as the ones in the brochure, and they want to know why they're not getting the Bellagio for seventy-five bucks a night?"

Beth shrugged. "Probably. Maybe you should stop taking such good pictures of the rooms."

"Or maybe Mom and Dad should stop buying bargain-basement cleaning products and get a bleach that actually whitens whites." Ugh. She sounded like a damned commercial. But this was the fourth complaint this week she'd had to deal with. Her parents really needed to hire a customer service person because her people skills were waning by the second. Plus, she wasn't dressed for anything more formal than solo office work today.

She brushed her hands off on her jeans and tried to hand iron the wrinkles from her old Pima Medical Institute scrub top and stormed up to the front counter. "If our sheets aren't good enough for you, then pack your own next time."

Sam Callahan—dressed in a fleece pullover and jeans,

a backpack slung over his shoulder—stared back at her from the other side of the counter.

"I wasn't aware I had to bring my own sheets," he said, the ghost of a smile playing at his lips.

It had been a whole week since she'd seen or spoken to him, and their first words to each other since she'd left Meadow Valley were about *sheets*?

Beth nudged her shoulder. Delaney had forgotten she was there.

"I'm going to go find something to do in the office. Maybe throw some darts at a map."

Delaney nodded absently. She stared at him for several seconds, her brows knit together. She loved him, and he was here. Sam was *here*. For her. And she could hardly breathe.

"Did I conjure you?" she asked. She had the sudden urge to reach across the counter and touch his face to confirm that he was really there. Vegas was the desert, after all. People saw mirages when they were dehydrated, and she and Beth did have a few margaritas last night.

She shook her head, and Sam let out a nervous sounding laugh.

"You okay, Vegas?"

She answered his question with one of her own. "Why are you here, Sam?"

I love you. I was scared. I'm sorry. I brought you some of Luis's tacos. All of those answers would be fine by her.

"I finished a project yesterday. It's just a sign right now, but it has potential. Before I publish the photo on our website, I wanted to get an expert opinion on whether or not you think this will improve business, seeing as how your auction and brochure ideas were a big hit." He scrubbed a hand over his clean-shaven jaw.

"That's great," Delaney said, but she was still confused. "You don't have any marketing consultants closer to Meadow Valley than me?"

He shook his head. "Or maybe I do. I don't know. Look, I'm really bad at this."

"Bad at what?" Why was he here? Had he gotten her text and happened to be in the neighborhood? Did he know she'd fallen in love with him the whole time they'd been apart when she'd only figured it out seconds ago? Was she going to hear anything he said if her brain didn't put a leash on the tornado of questions she kept asking herself?

Delaney squeezed her eyes shut and blew out a breath. When she opened them, he was still there.

Not a mirage.

"Sorry," she said with measured calm. "You were saying something about being bad at whatever *this* is."

He lifted the backpack off his shoulder and set it on the ground.

"I didn't know 'no matter what' existed before you," he said. "I panicked. I was so scared about the what-if of hurting you that I never stopped to think...'What if I didn't.' Because here's the thing, Vegas. I love you even if you make me watch Keanu Reeves movies all day long. I love you even if you turned a certified dog lover into a cat man. I love you if you eat all the tacos or if you save some for me. I love you if you're just as scared for the future as I am, and I love you for believing the future is possible anyway." He cleared his throat. "I love you if you come home to Meadow Valley—or if you've finally washed your hands of the place. No matter what."

Her chest squeezed, and the tightness in her throat made it hard to breathe. Not the oh-my-God-I'm-in-anaphylactic-shock hard to breathe, but the kind where she was so close to having everything she never knew she wanted yet it was still out of reach.

Tears fell from both eyes at once.

"You okay, Vegas?" he asked again.

She shook her head, then nodded. She didn't know what the hell she was. But she knew one thing for certain. *This* was the part of the dream she'd been missing—someone to share it with who put her needs right up there at the top of the list with his own.

"I'd have wanted whatever time I had to get to know you and be with you and—and fall even more in love with you," she admitted.

"There might be days where I don't remember falling in love with a woman who could charm the hell out of both my father and my dog, who has an unassuming right hook, and who can muck out a stall in half the time it takes one of my stable hands to do it. But to make up for it, I can promise you that every day for the past week, that's *all* I've been able to think about."

Her heart hammered against her chest.

He called Meadow Valley home. *Her* home. Yet she was still frozen where she stood, terrified to believe it was real.

"Oh. My. God. *Kiss* him already, Lanes. Or *I* will!"

She looked over her shoulder to find Beth standing in the office doorway, staring at the scene before her as though it were the next Netflix rom-com.

Delaney laughed and brushed another tear from under her eye. She pushed through the waist-high swinging half door that acted as a barrier between motel personnel and guests so that she was standing face-to-face with the man she'd thought about every minute of every day since she left Meadow Valley last week.

"If you forgot me in twenty years, we'd still have *twenty* years. And if you'd asked me what I wanted, I'd tell you that I'd have taken those twenty years. And then after that I'd remember for both of us. I'd tell you about a selfless man who towed my car and gave me a place to stay and that no matter how hard he fought it, also gave me his heart."

Sam raised a brow. "Maybe I did all that because I was afraid of that unassuming right hook."

She narrowed her eyes. "And because you really needed my marketing expertise?"

"Oh," he said. "Right. Let's see if my phone found a network. Hit a bunch of dead zones on the way here."

She bit her lip as she saw the phone's screen light up. But there was no notification of an unanswered text. It went straight to the internet, which was already set to the Meadow Valley Ranch page.

"Here's the unpublished tab. Let me know what you think."

She stared at a sunlit photo of the sign he'd affixed above the far side of the stable. MEADOW VALLEY RESCUE. And on top of the page it read *Coming soon...rescue animal shelter. Guest volunteers wanted.*

"I get if it's too much too soon," he said when she kept staring at the screen, unable to speak. "I should also mention, though, that some of the town residents put together a little crowdfunding campaign to get you started and to help compensate Dr. Murphy for the volunteer hours he's still hoping to provide once you get your first residents."

She'd chased a dream, and Sam Callahan was giving her the world. "Some town residents?" she asked. "That was your idea?"

He shrugged. "It's not a means of buying you out or compensating for land that, deed or no deed, we all know is rightfully yours," he said. "So if you think you might want to get in from the ground up, we start renovations next month."

She dropped his phone on the counter and wrapped her arms around his neck. "You better kiss me already, cowboy, or you'll have my sister to answer to."

He rested his forehead against hers. "Is that a yes?" he asked. "Because it's technically still ranch property, so you'll have to earn your keep."

She pulled him to her, their lips colliding with a week of longing and stubbornness and fear, finally getting it right.

"I love you, Vegas," he said, his lips still pressed against hers. "Just so we're clear."

"Yeah, well, I love you right back." She kissed him again, breathed him in, and thanked the stars he was anything but a mirage.

"One more thing," he said.

"What's that?"

"I love you. *No. Matter. What.*"

She tilted her head back. "You got my text?"

He nodded. "Right when your sister went to get you. I already had my I-love-you speech prepared, though. I wasn't plagiarizing."

She laughed.

"But I'm glad it was there," he added. "It's the only reason I knew I didn't have a right hook coming my way. Not that I didn't deserve it."

She shrugged. "There's always tomorrow."

"And the day after that," he added.

And whatever the future held, as long as it was theirs.

Sam woke early and started the coffee. Scout paced the kitchen floor as he scrambled up some eggs and fried the bacon.

He laughed. His women sure loved their bacon.

When Delaney emerged, bleary eyed, wearing nothing but one of his T-shirts—God, he loved when she did that—he ran into the living room with a steaming mug to distract her before she caught a glimpse out the window.

"Today's the big day, huh?" she asked, brushing her lips against his as he handed her the coffee.

"Yep," he said.

"And you're sure you want me there?"

He knew she'd understand if he said no. He had his blood drawn the week she was gone. Today he found out if he had inherited the gene mutation that caused his father's disease. He had no idea how he'd react to either result, but he knew that it must have been hell for Ben to go through it alone, to not have someone in his corner no matter what the future held. Sam had somehow hit the jackpot and had his very own someone right here, right now, with her.

"Always," he said. "Especially for the tough stuff, like today."

She smiled that heart-stopping first smile of the day, the one that was only and always for him. A daily gift he didn't think he'd ever be able to repay—except for today.

He kissed her forehead and set his hands on her hips.

"Turn around, Vegas. I got you something."

Her brow furrowed, but she did as he asked.

She gasped as his arms slid around her waist, his hands clasping against her stomach.

"It's *snowing*," she said, a tremor in her voice.

The landscape outside his back door was a blanket of white—something Scout would take care of soon enough.

"It's cold as hell, too," he said. "Thirty-four degrees. Are you sure this is what you wanted?" He kissed her neck.

She leaned into him, breathing in deep and letting out a contented sigh.

"Always. No matter what."

DON'T MISS THE NEXT
BOOK IN A.J. PINE'S
MEADOW VALLEY
SERIES!

MAKE MINE A COWBOY

Available Summer 2020

ABOUT THE AUTHOR

A librarian for teens by day and a romance writer by night, A.J. Pine can't seem to escape the world of fiction, and she wouldn't have it any other way. When she finds that twenty-fifth hour in the day, she might indulge in a tiny bit of TV when she nourishes her undying love of vampires, superheroes, and a certain high-functioning sociopathic detective. She hails from the far-off galaxy of the Chicago suburbs.

You can learn more at:
AJPine.com
Twitter @AJ_Pine
Facebook.com/AJPineAuthor

KEEP READING FOR A
SPECIAL BONUS NOVEL
FROM *NEW YORK TIMES*
BESTSELLING AUTHOR
CAROLYN BROWN:
*TOUGHEST COWBOY
IN TEXAS*

The last time Lila Harris was in Happy, Texas, she
was actively earning her reputation as the resident wild
child. Now, a little older and wiser, she's back to run her
mother's café for the summer. Except something about
this town has her itching to get a little reckless and rowdy,
especially when she sees her old partner in crime, Brody
Dawson. Their chemistry is just as hot as ever. But he's
still the town's golden boy—and she's still the wrong
kind of girl.

Brody hasn't had much time lately for anything other
than running the biggest ranch in the county. All that
responsibility has him longing for the carefree days of
high school—and Lila. She may have grown up, but he
still sees that spark of mischief in her eyes. Now he's
dreaming about late-night skinny-dipping and wondering how he can possibly resist the one woman he can
never forget.

Chapter One

Order up!" Molly yelled from the kitchen.

Lila picked up a basket filled to the brim with hot French fries just as the door to the Happy Café opened. The hot western sun silhouetted the cowboy in the doorway, but she'd recognize Brody Dawson anywhere—in the darkest night or the brightest day.

The energy in the café sparkled with electricity and her chest tightened. She gripped the red plastic basket to keep from dropping it and slowly inhaled, willing herself to take a step toward the table where a couple of old ranchers waited for their order.

"Well, well," Brody drawled. He closed the door behind him and slowly scanned her from the toes of her boots to her black ponytail. "The wild child has returned."

"But not for long, so don't go getting your hopes up," she smarted off right back at him.

In a few long strides he slid into a booth and laid

his hat on the space beside him. He filled out the butt of his jeans even better than he had when they were in high school and his chest was an acre wide. Lord, why couldn't he have developed a beer gut and two chins?

She carried the order to the other end of the café and set it down between Paul McKay and Fred Williams, two ranchers she'd known her whole growing-up years.

"I'd forgotten that they called you the wild child, Lila." Paul grinned.

"People change," she said. "Anything else?"

Fred squirted streams of ketchup across the fries. "Nah, we're good for now. Might need some more tea before we go. You should wait on poor old Brody. He looks like he's spittin' dust."

"Yeah. I'm dying over here," Brody called from across the small dining room. "How about a glass of half sweet tea and half Molly's fresh lemonade?"

"Anything else, Your Highness?" Lila asked as she turned to face him and made her way to his table.

His sexy grin and that twinkle in his baby-blue eyes made every hormone in her body beg for attention. But then she reminded herself that she didn't have to impress Brody Dawson. She was not that girl anymore. Oh, but to kiss those lips one more time just to see if they still made her knees go weak. *No! No! No!* Yet her fingertips went straight to her lips to see if the memory made them as warm as they felt.

"Whatcha got?" His drawl broke through the haze surrounding her.

She quickly dropped her hand. "What?"

"You asked if I wanted anything else." He wiggled his eyebrows. "So whatcha offering?"

She reached across his booth to pick up a one-page menu stuck between the saltshaker and napkin holder. Her arm brushed against his chest and more sparks danced around the café. Hoping that he couldn't hear the breathlessness in her voice, she straightened to her full height and started reading. "We have chicken fried steak, grilled pork chops, breakfast served all day, burgers of all kinds, and today's lunch special is meat loaf and mashed potatoes. I think there's a little more left if you're interested. I really thought you might have learned to read down there at Texas A and M."

He laid a rough, calloused hand on her arm. Pure electricity shot through her body.

"Are you still as wild as ever?" he whispered seductively.

"Oh, honey, you can't even imagine what all you've missed out on in the past twelve years." The chemistry between them hadn't changed a bit—at least not for her. She pulled her arm back and looked down at the menu. "Want me to go on or have you heard something that appeals to you?"

He raked his fingers through his thick, dark hair. It needed a cut, but then maybe he wore it a little longer these days. "Just something to drink for now," he said.

She turned away from him and headed back to the drink station. With shaking hands, she poured the tea and lemonade, stirred, and carried it to his booth. When she set it down in front of him, he motioned toward the other side of the table.

"Sit with me."

"You're a few years late with that invitation," she told him.

"Ah, come on, Lila," he said.

Throw a plaid shirt over that dirty white T-shirt and he'd still be the boy who had broken her heart all those years ago. But she'd cried her tears and burned the bridges between her and Brody, so bygones be damned.

He nodded toward the other side of the booth. "You're really going to hold a grudge and not sit with me for five minutes?"

"I really am," she said.

"Hey, Lila, we could use some more tea over here," Paul called out.

The years hadn't changed Paul and Fred much. Fred was the shorter of the two and Lila had never seen him in anything but bibbed overalls and faded T-shirts. A rim of gray kinky hair circled his round head. He could put on a thousand-dollar tailor-made suit and in five minutes he'd look like he'd slept in it. With a thick head of salt-and-pepper hair, Paul was his opposite. Always in freshly ironed jeans and shirts, he was tall, lanky, and every inch a cowboy, right down to his well-worn but polished boots.

She carried a full pitcher to their booth and refilled both glasses.

Paul whispered out the side of his mouth, "Brody lost his grandpa and his daddy the same summer you and your mama left town. So he didn't go to college after all. Don't be too rough on him. He carries a lot of responsibility on those shoulders of his."

Fred laid a hand on her arm. "Don't listen to Paul. That boy needs someone to give him hell. I was enjoyin' y'all's fight, so put on the gloves and get back at it."

"I swear on a stack of Bibles, I don't know why I'm even your friend." Paul sent a dirty look across the table.

"Ain't nobody else in Happy who knows you like I do. Hell, I bet I know you better'n your wife does." Fred's wrinkles deepened when he smiled.

Paul turned his attention toward Lila. "I hear that you're a teacher now."

"That's right." She headed toward the counter.

"So why are you here if you're a teacher?" Brody asked from the other end of the diner.

"To get my horns trimmed. I was getting too wild," she said sarcastically.

"Well, darlin', I can't help you with that." He grinned.

"Why?" She took one pitcher of tea and one of lemonade to his booth to refill his glass and pulled over a chair to sit down at the end of the table.

He leaned toward her and whispered, "I liked you as the wild child too much to shave an inch off your horns. God, we had some good times, didn't we?"

"And now we're thirty, not crazy kids anymore," she said.

"Too bad. Being a grown-up isn't nearly all it's cracked up to be."

"No, it's not but we do have to grow up. How's your granny?"

"Alive, kicking and giving out advice like candy at Halloween. Things in Happy don't change much," he answered. "How long are you going to be here?"

"Probably through the summer. Maybe less. Mama decided to put the café up for sale instead of leasing it. So if someone comes along and buys it, then I'm out of here."

He picked up his hat and stood up. "There's not many businesses left in Happy. I sure hope it doesn't close for good."

When she rose to her feet, they were so close that one step would have put her in the position to tiptoe and kiss him smack on the lips. Brody was right when he said not much changed in Happy, Texas. The minute she crossed the county line, she had the urge to do something wild and now she wanted to give in and wrap her arms around Brody.

She'd had a crush on him from the time they were in kindergarten. Truth be told, she'd liked him from before that—one of her first memories was standing on the church pew and staring at Brody sitting right behind her and her parents. He'd been a pretty little boy, had grown into a handsome young man, and now was one damn fine sexy cowboy.

"Hey." He grinned. "Remember when you decided that riding a bull wasn't all that tough? Took four of us—me and Jace and a couple of other guys to lasso that big old bruiser out on the ranch. I can still see you settling down onto his back as you held on to one of his horns with your right hand and waved your left one in the air. You stayed on for the full eight seconds and when the ride was over, you whipped off a straw hat with a glittery headband and bowed while we all hooted and hollered for you."

"Of course I remember that night and lots more, but what comes to mind the most often is the night before Mama and I left Happy the next day," she said with a long sigh, remembering the feelings she'd had that day.

He took a deep breath and settled his hat on his head. "You married?"

"Nope."

"Are all the men crazy wherever you've been livin'?" he asked.

"I didn't give them an IQ test before I robbed banks with them."

"Once a smartass," he chuckled.

"Smart—whatever," she shot back. "Are you married?"

"Never have been and don't intend to be anytime soon." His phone buzzed and he took it from his pocket. "Looks like Jace needs help out on the ranch." He tipped his hat toward her and stopped beside Paul and Fred's table. "Gracie know you're having that big load of taters right here at supper time, Paul?"

Paul shook his head. "No, she does not and don't you dare tell her, neither."

Brody chuckled. "Cross my heart. I've got to get back to the ranch anyhow."

Lila couldn't help admiring his long legs as he strode across the café.

"See, Lila, everyone in Happy doesn't know everything." Brody ducked to get through the door without removing his hat.

"Don't bet Hope Springs on that," she called out.

She whipped a white rag from the hip pocket of her jeans and wiped down the table where he'd been, spending extra time on it so she could watch him cross the parking lot. His distinctive swagger hadn't changed a bit and even from that distance she could see every ripple in his abs through that sweat-stained T-shirt. Her heart raced so hard that she was winded when she tucked the cloth back into her pocket.

Well, crap! So much for time, distance, and a broken heart erasing all the old feelings for that cowboy.

Brody left a trail of gravel dust in his wake, but then that was the story of her past. Always trying to impress him—always hoping that someday he'd go against his family and the whole town of Happy to ask her to go out—just the two of them. They'd sit side by side. His arm would be around her and he'd look deep into her eyes without caring that she was the girl with the worst reputation in Happy, Texas.

"His granny Hope turned the ranch over to him and Jace this past spring," Fred said. "Then Kasey and her three kids came to live on the ranch with them, and Hope moved out into the foreman's house. You remember Cooter Green, the foreman they had at Hope Springs?"

Lila nodded. "He had a couple of kids about my age. Melanie and Lisa, right?"

"Yep," Paul said. "They got married and moved out to Arizona. So Cooter retired and went out there to be with them."

"Last spring Hope turned the business over to the boys and then talked their sister into coming back to help out. So all three of the Dawson kids are living out there," Fred said. "Hey, we're out of fries. Would you get us another basketful and refill these tea glasses one more time?"

"Where's Adam? Didn't he and Kasey get married after high school?" Lila pinned an order on the spinner.

"He got killed in one of them secret missions overseas. I heard they couldn't tell Kasey nothing about it. Had the funeral here but the casket stayed closed," Fred answered.

Molly peeked out through the serving window and tucked a strand of short gray hair back behind her ear. With a round face, gray eyes set in a bed of wrinkles, penciled black eyebrows that made her look as if she were perpetually surprised, Molly hadn't changed much in the twelve years since Lila and her mother had left town. Not just in looks, either. Her attitude was the same too—she didn't take guff off anyone. The whole town would miss her sass when the café sold and she retired.

Molly crooked her finger at Lila. "You come on back here. I got something to say."

Lila glanced at the parking lot. No more customers were on their way inside, so she pushed through the door into the kitchen. What she got was a wooden spoon shaking her way, Molly's dark brows drawn down in a frown and her mouth set in a hard line.

"I heard what Fred and Paul was sayin'."

"And?" Lila asked.

Molly put four big handfuls of potatoes into the deep fryer. "Brody did step up and take on responsibility. He's turned into a pretty fine man when it comes to ranchin' and all, but that don't mean his attitude about bein' better than you has changed."

She'd heard it all many times before. She wondered if Brody had made it home yet and was hearing the exact same words. Without much effort, she could imagine Valerie Dawson threatening him with a wooden spoon as well.

"He's always thought he was a cut above you, girl. I'm not tellin' you nothing new. He broke your heart right before you left here and he'll do it again," Molly growled.

"That was a long time ago. So he didn't go to college like he planned? What's he done at the ranch?" She should be heeding Molly's warning, maybe even dropping down on her knees and thanking her, instead of defending the boy who had broken his date with her on the last night she was in town. For the first time ever, he was going to take her out to dinner and a movie. But he hadn't shown up and she'd cried until her eyes were swollen.

Another shake of the spoon and then Molly went back to fixing two meat loaf dinners. "I told your mama I'd watch out for you and that I'd see to it you didn't fall back into those wicked ways that got you that nickname. When you leave at the end of the summer, the only nickname you'll have is Lila. Why your mama named you Delilah after that wicked woman in the Bible is a mystery to me."

Lila threw an arm around Molly's shoulders and gave her a quick hug. Molly and Georgia had both worked for her mother from the time Daisy started the Happy Café. Then they leased it from her when Daisy and Lila moved to Pennsylvania to help Daisy's sister open a café there. Now, Georgia had retired and moved to Florida. Even with her sharp tongue, Molly had always been Lila's favorite and she was glad that she got to work with her again.

"It was my great-grandmother's middle name. Bessie Delilah was her full name. Do I look like a Bessie to you?" Lila giggled.

Molly shrugged her arm away but her expression had gone from sour to sweet. "Better that than Delilah. You might have been a preacher or a missionary with a name like Bessie. Now get these fries on out there to Fred and Paul before they get cold. Ain't nothin' worse than greasy, limp fries 'cept cold gravy."

"Miss Molly, I've changed from that wild child I used to be and I've been takin' care of myself for a long time." Basket in hand, Lila headed out of the kitchen.

"Yep, but that wasn't in Happy. Person comes back here, they turn into the same person who left."

Lila would never admit it, but Molly was right—the moment she hit the city limits sign in Happy the evening before, she'd had the urge to go out to Henry's barn, drink warm beer, and get into some kind of trouble.

*   *   *

Brody sang along with the radio the whole way back to Hope Springs. Seeing Lila again brought back so many memories. Nothing had been the same after she'd left town. Happy, Texas, didn't have a movie theater or a bowling alley or even a Dairy Queen, so they'd had to drive all the way to Tulia or Amarillo to have fun. Or they would stay in town and Lila would come up with some kind of crazy stunt that sent their adrenaline into high gear.

Like surfing in the back of my old pickup truck. It's a wonder we weren't all killed but the adrenaline rush was crazy wild. He chuckled as he remembered the two of them planting their feet on skateboards in the bed of the truck and then giving Jace the thumbs-up to take off. No big ocean waves could have been as exhilarating as riding on skateboards while Jace drove eighty miles an hour down a dirt road.

Blake Shelton's "Boys 'Round Here" came on the radio and he turned up the volume. He rolled down the window, letting the hot air blow past him as he pushed the gas pedal to the floor.

Seventy miles an hour, the dust kicking up behind the truck just like the song said. At seventy-five, he checked the rearview and imagined that Lila was back there wearing a pair of cutoff denim shorts, cowboy boots, and a tank top that hugged her body like a glove. Her jet-black ponytail was flying out behind her, and that tall, well-toned curvy body kept balance on the imaginary skateboard every bit as well as it had back then.

At eighty, he tapped the brakes enough to make a sliding right-hand turn from the highway to the lane back to the ranch house. The house was a blur when he blew past it and the speedometer said he was going ninety miles an hour when he braked and came to a long greasy stop in front of the barn doors. Gravel pinged against the sheet metal and dust settled on everything inside his truck's crew cab. He sucked in a lungful of it but it did nothing to slow down his racing heart, thumping hard enough to bust a rib. Gripping the steering wheel so tightly that his forearms ached, he checked the rearview mirror. The vision of Lila was gone, leaving only a cloud of dust in its wake.

You're not eighteen, Brody Dawson. The voice in his head even had the same tone and inflection as his mother's did. *You're a responsible rancher, not a kid who drives like a maniac with the music blaring loud enough they can hear it in Amarillo.*

Blame it on Lila. She brought out the wild side in me *back before I had to handle all the ranchin' business,* he argued, and felt a sudden rush of shame because he hadn't stood up for her in those days. Then he had time and opportunities; now he barely had time for a glass of tea with all the sticky situations of Hope Springs falling on his shoulders.

His phone pinged with another text: *Sundance is in a mud bog out on the north forty. Need help. Bring rope. Where the hell are you?*

Just as he was about to get moving, his grandmother stepped out of the barn and made her way to his truck, shielding her green eyes against the hot afternoon sun. Gray haired and barely tall enough to reach Brody's shoulder, she might look like a sweet little grandmother to strangers, but looks were definitely deceiving when it came to Hope Dalley. She had a backbone of steel and nobody messed with her.

"Did someone die? I heard you driving like a bat set loose from the bowels of hell. I bet you wore a year's worth of rubber off them tires the way you skidded to a stop."

"Everything is fine, but Sundance is in a mud lolly, so I've got to get some rope and go help Jace," Brody said.

"Damned old bull. He got bad blood from his father when it comes to breakin' out of pens, but he's a damn fine breeder so we have to deal with his ornery ways," Hope said. "I'll go with you and help."

"We can get it done, Granny. What are you doin' out here in this hot sun anyway?"

"Bossin' the boys about how to stack the hay. I can't just sit around in an air-conditioned house and do nothin'. I'd die of boredom," she said.

"Long as you're supervisin' and not stackin', that's fine, but I'd rather see you in the house with Kasey and the kids," he said.

"I'm not ready to be put out to pasture yet, boy. Kasey don't need my help. She has the toughest job on the ranch, taking care of those three kids as well as all the household stuff and the book work. That's a hell of a lot more exhausting and tougher than stacking hay. And she's doin' a fine job of it. Now go take care of that blasted bull." She waved him away.

Fun and excitement were over. It was time to man up and not expect to relive the glory days when Lila had lived in Happy and everything had been fun and exciting.

*   *   *

When it rained, the pond on their north forty would hold water for a few days and then slowly evaporate, leaving a muddy mess. Sundance, their prize breeding bull, loved water, but this time he'd waded out into nothing but mud.

He was bawling like a baby and thrashing around when Brody parked the truck. "How long has he been there?" he asked his brother, Jace, who was covered head to toe in mud.

"Too damn long. He's so stressed that we'll have to keep him in the barn for a week. We got cows to breed and he won't be worth a damn until he's settled down."

"Since you're already a mess, how about I lasso him and pull, and you keep pushing," Brody suggested.

Brody grabbed a rope from the back of his truck and landed it around the bull's neck on the first swing. "Got him. Now push!"

Jace put his shoulder into the bull's hindquarter.

Brody felt every muscle in his body knot as he tightened the rope. "Son of a bitch weighs a ton."

Jace pushed but the bull barely moved. "Two tons from the feel of it. He's moving a little bit. Pull harder!"

Brody wrapped the rope around his gloved hand another time and hauled back, leaning so far that Sundance wasn't even in the picture. All he could see was sky and big fluffy clouds that reminded him of lying in the grass with Lila beside him on a Sunday afternoon many years ago. She said that one big white cloud was the shape of a bull's horns and he'd said it looked more like two snow cones stuck together.

One minute he was smiling at the memory and the next he was flat on his back with no wind in his lungs and that crazy bull was pulling him along like a rag doll. He quickly untangled the rope from his hand and let go, sucked in enough air to get some relief, and threw a hand over his eyes to shade them from the blistering hot sun.

Sundance kept moving until he was under the shade of a big oak tree and then he threw back his head and bawled. Jace flopped down on the ground beside Brody and groaned. "If he wasn't such a damn good bull, I'd shoot that sumbitch right between the eyes and turn him into steaks and hamburgers."

"Meat would be too tough and rangy to eat—the old bastard," Brody said. "He can stay in the barn a few days to get settled down and by then we'll get a fence built so he doesn't wander back here again."

"My poor body feels like it's eighty years old after all that pushin'," Jace gasped.

Brody groaned as he sat up. "I'll take care of gettin' him back to the barn. You can go on to the house and get cleaned up."

"Thanks." Jace rolled onto his feet. "I'll help get him tied to the truck. He's so tired that he shouldn't give you too much trouble."

"You just best be out of the shower when I get there," Brody warned.

"Will do. Hey, I heard that you stopped at the café for lemonade. Lila changed any?"

Brody stood up slowly. "Who told you that?"

Jace took the first steps toward the oak tree where Sundance was grazing. "Gracie called the café lookin' for Paul, and Molly told her that you were flirting with Lila."

"I was *not* flirting," Brody protested.

"Yeah, right." Jace laughed. "Remember wind surfing and sneakin' into old Henry Thomas's barn on Saturday nights? You always flirted with Lila. I bet all that old stuff about Henry disappearing right before they left town will shoot to the surface now that she's back. Did she say anything about him?"

Brody fell into step beside Jace. "The great Happy, Texas, mystery of Henry Thomas's disappearance didn't come up. I wonder why folks are even still talking about that. It wasn't like he was anyone's best friend. He stayed out on the ranch most of the time and didn't even go to church with his mother."

Jace poked him on the shoulder. "I know but Lila and her mother left and that same week, Henry disappeared. It was all folks talked about for years, and every so often, the gossip starts again. Man, it never was the same here after Lila left. She was so much fun. What's she been doin' since she left?"

"Actually, we didn't talk about much of anything."

"Too damn bad." Jace grabbed the rope around Sundance's massive neck and tied him to the back of Brody's truck. "If he gives you any trouble, he's going to be dog food in the morning. We've got his son, Cassidy, that we can always start using as our prime breeder," Jace said. "See you at home, brother."

Brody kept a watch on Sundance from his side mirror as he drove from the pasture toward the barn. He had to stop thinking about Lila, but it wouldn't be easy. Seeing her standing there in those tight jeans with the waitress apron slung around her well-rounded hips brought back feelings that he thought he'd finally gotten over. Her full lips begged to be kissed and those big brown eyes full of mischief all the time made him feel alive, like he had back in the days when they were meeting in secret out in Henry's old barn—and in her bedroom late at night. That afternoon the perfect woman was right there within arm's reach and there wasn't a damn thing he could do about it. He inhaled deeply and let it out slowly, regret washing over him about that last night she'd been in Happy.

But Brody was not that crazy kid anymore. He was a ranch owner with responsibilities. She was a teacher, for God's sake, so she'd changed too.

"Lord, I've missed those days...and her," he muttered.

Chapter Two

Brody inched along at a snail's pace so the tired critter didn't have to do anything but a slow walk. It had been a long day already but Brody would have to wash the bull down, then feed and water him before he could go to the house and stand under a cold shower himself. But he was glad for the time alone so he could collect his thoughts and give himself a severe lecture about Lila.

The business of sorting things out was a lot easier said than done. It was impossible to shake that picture of her big brown eyes going soft when they were so close to-gether in the café. He jumped and hit the gas when his phone vibrated in his hip pocket. He quickly removed his foot from the pedal and gently tapped the brakes to stop. Checking the side mirror, he could see that Sundance was all right.

He worked the phone out of his dirty jeans pocket, checked the ID, and tossed it onto the seat. After five rings it stopped but only for a few seconds before starting again. He slapped the steering wheel and answered the damn phone. If he didn't, she'd try a half dozen times and then she'd call Kasey to get into the ranch truck to check on him.

Turning the ranch over to him hadn't meant that she'd let go of the reins completely—not by a long shot.

"Hello, Granny."

"Where are you now?"

"I'm taking Sundance to the barn to clean him up," Brody answered.

"Why didn't you tell me Lila Harris was back in town?" she demanded. "I heard you've been at the café flirtin' with her."

Brody rolled his blue eyes toward the sky and then quickly blinked when the bright sun nearly blinded him. "I was not flirting. I was just making conversation. With all I've got on my plate, when would I have time to flirt with anyone? I barely have time to sleep."

"That girl is a bad influence, Brody. I hope that café sells real quick and she goes back to whatever rock she crawled out from under. You'd do well to stay away from her," Hope said.

"Doin' a little judgin' there, are you, Granny? Reckon you'd better go to church twice this next week."

"No, simply statin' facts." Her tone raised an octave or two. "And don't you sass me."

"Did your gossip sources tell you that she's a teacher now and she's only here for the summer?" Brody asked.

Hope's quick intake of breath told him that she was not pleased. "Are you takin' up for the likes of her? I thought you'd turned out to be a better man than that."

"I'm statin' facts. And I'm almost to the barn with this critter, so I'd better say good-bye. See you at supper?"

"Yes, you will and we will talk more about this, so don't think the conversation is over."

Without a good-bye, the phone went dark and he tossed it back onto the seat. He parked the truck in front of the horse barn and got out. When he tugged on the rope to get Sundance started toward the barn doors, the bull balked. He yanked again and Sundance promptly sat down, threw back his head, and glared at him.

"So you don't want to stay in the barn. I wouldn't either. It's hotter in there than it is out here," Brody said. "How about we put you in the corral for a couple or three days until you get over nearly going into a full-fledged stroke?"

Sundance lowered his massive head and took a step. Brody got back in the truck and moved around the barn to the attached corral. This time when he undid the rope, Sundance followed him like a puppy on a leash into the corral.

"I'll get the water hose goin' and get you cleaned off and cooled down. Then we'll fill the tank and bust open a bale of hay for you," Brody said as he shut the gate and locked it. He whipped off his cowboy hat, pulled out a bandana, and wiped the sweat from his brow. When he'd finished, he settled his hat toward the back of his head and stuffed the bandana back in his hip pocket.

Normally, old Sundance had a little mean streak in him but that day he didn't even flinch when Brody hosed him down. "It don't take much of that wallowin' in the mud to wear a guy out, does it? You never knew Lila Harris before she left, but she's a force like you are. Full of spit and vinegar, and God help anyone who ever gets in her way. But underneath all that bluster, she's got a soft heart of the purest gold. I was such a fool not to stick up for her and tell everyone in town to go straight to hell. I damn sure should have kept my word the last night she was in town, Sundance." He dropped the hose into the watering trough to fill it.

He stared at the water for a long time, lost in the thoughts of what he'd do if he could have a second chance with Lila. Finally he shook his head and exhaled loudly. No use wishin' for what couldn't happen. Nowadays he flat out didn't have time for women—not even Lila. He had a ranch to run and too many people who depended on him for any kind of romance.

While the trough filled, Brody went inside the barn and hefted a bag of feed onto his shoulders. Carrying it out to the corral, he shook his head toward Sundance. "You got it easy, old guy. You just breed the cows and then forget them. But me, I've never been able to get Lila out of my mind. Her coming back to Happy is most likely my punishment for being a cocky little shit who didn't know the best thing in the world when she was standing right in front of him."

He dumped the feed while Sundance drank his fill of water. The bull snorted and moved to the feed trough.

"That's all you got to say? Some therapist you are," Brody said as he looped the hose into a circle and hung it on the rack on the back side of the barn. "You think about what I told you and next time I come out here I expect more than a snotty old snort."

*   *   *

"Got him in the barn?" Jace yelled from the porch.

Brody was too tired to hop over the fence, so he went through the gate. "He sat flat down and refused to move. Evidently he didn't like the idea of the barn, so I put him in the corral, washed him down, and fed him. I hope one of those beers is for me."

Jace held out a can, but Brody got sidetracked when Kasey's two older kids, five-year-old Rustin and three-year-old Emma, ran across the yard to wrap their arms around his legs. Rustin was all Dawson with his dark hair and blue eyes, but Emma was the image of her red-haired mother, down to the spunky attitude.

"Uncle Brody, where have you been? Uncle Jace got here a long time ago." Emma was small for her age and her deep, gravelly voice sure did not match her looks and size.

He picked her up and swung her around. "That crazy Sundance got stuck in a mud hole and we had to get him out."

She squirmed. "Put me down. You stink. Did you get in the muddle puddle with Sundance?"

"Yes, I did." He set her on the lawn and she ran off in pursuit of a big yellow butterfly. So much like her mother, Emma had stolen his heart from the first time he'd held her in his arms. Someday he wanted two or three daughters and that many sons—when he found a woman to share his life with.

Rustin tilted his head back and stared into Brody's face. "Someday, I'm going to be a cowboy like you and Uncle Jace and I'm going to stink too."

Brody ruffled the little boy's dark hair and smiled. "Don't get into too big of a hurry, buddy. Be a little kid as long as you can. This adult stuff isn't easy."

"Okay, Uncle Brody, but when I'm a cowboy, I'm going to be good help." He took off toward the jungle gym in the corner of the yard.

Brody sat down on the top step and took the beer from Jace's hand. "Look at those kids. All that energy at the end of the day makes me jealous."

"We were like that when we were their age." Jace finished off his beer and crumpled the can in one hand. "Guess our next job is to fix the fence near the springs so Sundance can't get out. Wonder why he don't wade in the water there?"

"It would freeze his balls off." Brody tipped up the can and swallowed several times before he set it back down.

"Just a heads-up that Granny is in the house with Kasey, and she's not happy," Jace said flatly.

"I got a phone call, so I'm not surprised. Who'd have thought that Lila comin' back to Happy would cause this much crap?" Brody held a mouthful of the icy liquid a couple of seconds before he swallowed.

Jace went on. "Granny is on the warpath. She says it's my job to keep you away from the café and Lila. That a leopard does not change its spots and Lila is going to lead you straight to hell."

Brody grabbed the can and finished off the last two swallows of beer. "What makes Granny think you or anyone else can keep me away from Lila or that she's going to hell?"

Jace's gray eyes twinkled. "She'll get over it. To tell the truth, for some fun like we all had in high school, I'd go with you, not try to keep you away from her. We could always depend on her to come up with something crazy."

The door swung open and Kasey stepped out on the

porch with her third child, Silas, slung on her hip. She slipped between them and set Silas on the lawn. The little blond-haired fellow toddled out to the yard and promptly fell on his butt. Brody was instantly on his feet and hurried over to help him.

"Steady now, Silas," Brody said. "You ain't quite ready to run just yet. One step at a time."

Silas gave him a big grin and toddled off in the direction of the other kids. Brody slumped down on the step, resting his back against a porch post. "He sure does look like Adam."

"I know." Kasey choked up.

Brody patted her on the shoulder. "Sorry."

"Hey," she said, "we can't stop talking about him. Memories are all I have, even if they do make me sad. Silas is like Adam and I love that."

A little bit of anger still ate at Brody when he thought about Adam being killed during a military mission. There were evil people in the world who deserved to die— Adam didn't. He'd had a wife and two kids and Kasey had been pregnant with Silas. Sometimes fate was a bitch.

"So I hear Lila is back in town." She suddenly stood up. "Emma Grace, don't you dare hit your brother with that stick."

"He hit me," Emma said.

"Did not!" Rustin declared. "I was just spinnin' around and she got in the way."

"Then you stop spinnin' around." Kasey sighed as she sat back down. "Heads-up, Brody. Granny is making biscuits and cussin'. I'm supposed to watch you like a hawk circling the sky lookin' for breakfast—her exact words. She says Mama is goin' to pitch a hissy if you get involved with that girl again." Most Dawson women were tall and thin, but Kasey was short and curvy and the only one in the family in three generations with curly red hair.

"Again?" Brody asked.

"Hey, the whole family knew you were sneakin' around with her when y'all were in high school but they thought you'd get over it," Kasey said.

"I can't believe they didn't say anything." Brody shook his head slowly in disbelief.

"Mama figured if she said anything you'd set your heels like Daddy did."

Jace opened another beer. "And back then everyone figured you'd go to college and find someone else, that it was just a passing thing."

"We'll never know what it was." Brody frowned. "I've got to get a shower before supper."

"Well, I'm supposed to watch you so..."

Silas stumbled and fell again. Brody was on his feet the moment the little guy's hands hit the grass. "Easy, cowboy." He picked the toddler up and righted him. The moment he let go, Silas raised his hands in an attempt to catch a bright orange butterfly.

Brody returned to the porch and eased down on the porch step. "Does that mean you're going to stand outside the bathroom door while I shower, sis?"

"Hell no! But get ready for some opposition—not from me. God knows I liked Lila. I admired her. But Granny and Mama?" Kasey wiped her brow in a dramatic gesture.

"Later tonight, I'll get out the binoculars and follow him, Kasey. We can take turns and write down in a little book all about where he's been. Let's see—seven-thirty p.m., went to check on Sundance. Eight-thirty p.m., came back to the house and had a beer," Jace teased.

Brody shot a dirty look toward him. "You going to the Silver Spur with me to keep me out of trouble? Because that's where I'm going after supper, and if Lila happens to be there, I intend to dance with her," Brody said.

Kasey raised her hand. "I'd go with you if they'd let me bring three kids with me. I heard that you stopped in at the café and talked to her. Is she still as pretty as she was in high school?"

"Oh yeah," Brody sighed.

"Well, you'd better not let Granny see you with that look on your face at just the mention of her name," Kasey said.

"Granny, nothing. Wait until Mama hears that Lila is in town." Jace rolled his eyes.

"Sweet Lord! I remember those nights when you didn't come home until thirty seconds before curfew. Mama would rant and rave about you probably being somewhere with Lila Harris," Kasey said.

"He probably was and I was most likely with him." Jace grinned.

Brody ran a hand down his face. "This is worse than being in junior high all over again."

"Ain't that the truth," Kasey said. "I feel your pain, brother. I'll run interference for you as often as I can. Sometimes life throws stuff at us that's pretty damn hard to endure."

Brody patted her on the shoulder. She'd been strong at Adam's funeral, but day after day without him had to be lonely as hell. "I'm going to take a shower soon as I can force my old bones to stand up."

"Old my butt," Kasey laughed. "You've got a long way to go before you can claim senior citizen's rights. Back to the Lila thing. You'll have to suffer the wrath of Mama and Granny if you don't stay away from the café. They're in cahoots to get you and Jace both married and settled, and believe me Lila Harris is not in the picture they're painting for either of you. They want a sweet little ranchin' woman who will pop a kid out once a year and who attends church at least twice a week and it wouldn't hurt if she had wings and a shiny halo."

Jace's gray eyes popped wide open. "Hey, now! That's not even funny. I'm not ready for a wife or kids. Right now I just want to be your kids' favorite uncle. Thinkin' of marriage gives me hives," Jace said. "Granny ain't out kickin' the bushes for a wife for me, is she?"

"She was actin' strange," Kasey answered.

"How so?" Jace asked.

"Well, first she was cussin' about Lila. Then next thing I knew, she was askin' about Henry Thomas."

"Really? Why?" Brody rushed out to remove a handful of petunia blossoms from Silas's hand. "They might be pretty, buddy, but they'd taste awful." He turned him around and showed him a blue jay in the tree. "If you can catch that bird, you can eat every bit of him."

"Brody!" Kasey fussed.

"Well, he can." Brody grinned. "Now what about Henry?"

"Granny got a faraway look on her face and next thing I know she's wipin' away tears on her apron tail. Then she went back to cussin' about Lila was the cause of every bad thing that ever happened in Happy. Hell's bells! I think she even blamed her for all the businesses on Main Street closing down," she said.

"It was a tough time everywhere, but none of it was Lila's fault," Jace said seriously. "We lost Gramps and Daddy. Henry disappeared and Lila left town. In her mind, it's all rolled into one big ball. Blaming Lila for all of it would be easy."

"Seems like Lila's coming back to town sure stirred up a lot of old memories," Brody said.

"I can't imagine why Henry's disappearance was such a big deal. He told his sister he was leaving. His mama had died, so he wasn't needed on the ranch next door. I guess it's the not knowing where he went or what happened to him that worries the gossipin' folks." Kasey lowered her voice. "And we all know that Granny and her church buddies keep the rumor mill going."

"Oh, yes, we do and the gossip vines have been about to dry up lately. This should make them happy. Maybe you ought to flirt with Lila just to give 'em something to talk about." Jace nudged Brody in the ribs with his elbow.

Brody put a hand on his shoulder and shoved him. "Why don't you help me out and do something crazy so they'll have something to talk about?"

"Wouldn't take the spotlight off you for anything." Jace popped him on the shoulder in a friendly brotherly slap. "Hey, Kasey, what's for supper? If our old-man brother will go take his shower, we might get to eat before it gets cold."

"Barbecued chicken and rice. I made two chocolate pies for dessert and it'll be ready in"—Kasey checked her watch—"fifteen minutes."

Brody's head bobbed once. "That'll give me enough time for a fast shower. Emma told me that I stink."

"She's an outspoken one. Reminds me of another little red-haired girl named Kasey," Jace said.

His sister's and brother's voices faded as Brody headed inside. When he and his siblings had all moved into the house a couple of months before, Kasey took the south wing for her and the children and Jace and Brody each chose a room on the north side. Granny Hope still had a bedroom in that side of the house, but she'd moved her furniture out to the house that the foreman had vacated when he moved away. Located about a quarter mile behind the house, it was where she spent a lot of her time these days.

Brody stripped out of his clothes in his bedroom and padded barefoot to the bathroom. Letting the cool water beat down on his back, he remembered a time when he and Lila had sat under the falls at Hope Springs. The water had flowed down on her dark hair, plastering it to her naked back, and they'd made wild, passionate teenage love right there in the cold water.

He sighed and put away the memories, and after he'd dried off, he remembered to splash on a little cologne so that Emma would be happy with him. He dressed in fresh jeans and a snowy white T-shirt and made it to the table just as Kasey and Jace put the last of the food out.

Slinging an arm around his grandmother's shoulders, he leaned down and kissed her on the forehead. "I hope you made plenty of biscuits. Ain't none better than yours."

"Not even Molly's down at the Happy Café?" She walked away from him.

"Can't compare." He smiled. Usually a hug, a kiss, and a compliment worked, but the frown on her face said that it was going to take a while for her to cool down.

"You smell good now," Emma said.

"Well, thank you." Brody dropped a kiss on her red curls. "I wouldn't want to be all stinky when I read to you tonight."

Emma sighed dramatically. "It's not your turn. It's Uncle Jace's turn to read me the bedtime story."

Good Lord, had he lost his touch with all the female population?

"And mine tomorrow night," Kasey laughed. "Looks like you got all cleaned up for nothing."

"If I can't read to the princess, then I'll read to the boys," Brody said.

"No, it's my turn to do that." Hope set the hot biscuits on the table and motioned for them all to take their places.

Brody slid into the chair to Hope's right. "Then I'll just go on to the Silver Spur."

"You can say grace, Brody," Hope declared as she sat down at the head seat. Sure, she'd given the running of the ranch over to Brody and Jace but there were some things she didn't relinquish and the head chair was one of them.

Jace thanked God for the food, family, and life and then said, "Amen."

"I like it when Uncle Brody says the blessin'." Rustin handed his plate to his mother. "He don't have to talk forever like Uncle Jace."

"Your uncle Brody needs to talk to Jesus more and get God's opinion on women and bars," Hope fussed. "I'm not callin' names but he knows exactly who I'm referring to. When it comes time for him to settle down, he needs a good churchgoin' woman who knows how to run a ranch and can cook and—"

"And has angel wings and a halo?" Brody quickly finished for her.

Her green eyes squinted into slits and her mouth puckered so tight that it brought on a new set of wrinkles. "Someday I'm going to enjoy saying that I told you so. Don't come runnin' to me whinin' like a baby when you make the wrong choice, because I ain't goin' to feel a bit sorry for you. Are you goin' out with him, Jace?"

Jace put a chicken leg and a thigh on his plate and passed the platter to Brody. "No, ma'am. I got other plans tonight but they don't have anything to do with one of them angel women, Granny."

"I like angels," Emma said.

"I like cowboys. If cowboys go to bars, then I want to go." Rustin bit into a biscuit.

"Me too." Emma nodded. "Can I wear my boots, Mama?"

"Girls can't go to bars, right, Granny?" Rustin frowned at his sister.

Kasey shook a finger toward the kids. "Neither of you is going to a bar. When you're thirty, you can go with your uncle Brody to the Silver Spur and not before. Now hand me your plate, Emma."

"Thirty?" Brody asked.

Kasey's finger turned toward him. "When you have a daughter, you can decide when your little girl can go to a honky-tonk."

"Forty," Jace said quickly. "And only then if I go with her."

"Amen!" Brody agreed.

"Well, you'd better get to lookin' for someone who can live with your sorry asses because if your daughter is forty, then y'all will be sixty-eight and seventy. And that's sayin' you can find a woman in the next year." Hope slathered a biscuit with butter and laid it on the side of her plate.

"Granny said a bad word," Rustin singsonged.

"And when you're twenty-one you can say that word." Kasey finished helping him with his plate. "For now, you concentrate on eating a good supper and then you can have chocolate pie."

"And ice cream?" Emma asked.

"If you promise to never set foot in a nasty old bar," Hope said with another sidelong glance toward Brody.

"Okay." Emma grinned.

"I'll just have pie if that's the way it is," Brody said. "Or maybe I'll go by the café before it closes and have a banana split."

"I can buy that place and burn it down to keep you out of it," Hope said. "Don't test me, Brody Dawson. Besides, you've got a work load too heavy to be gallivantin' to town every day."

"Oh, Granny, we all know that inside that tough exterior is a heart full of love and sweetness." Brody reached over and laid a hand on her shoulder. "We all love you."

"To the moon and back," Emma said quickly.

"I love you the purplest." Rustin nodded.

"What?" Jace asked.

"It's a book that I read to him last week about a mother who loves her kids in colors," Brody explained. "I think we all love Granny Hope the purplest."

"Oh, hush, all of you." Hope smiled. "Eat your supper before it gets cold."

Chapter Three

Jace had thought that he might go to the bar with Brody that night, but then Paul called. He and the guys were getting together at Fred's house for a poker game and needed a couple more guys to sit in. It didn't take much to talk Brody into going with him rather than going to the bar that Friday night.

But family came first and Jace had to read the kids their bedtime stories. That gave Brody a whole hour after supper with nothing to do but think of Lila.

He paced back and forth across the porch, checked the time over and over, and finally forced himself to sit down on the steps to wait. Patience was not written in the bright stars and the moon that night. Pretty soon he was back on his feet and walking around to the back side of the house. Maybe a walk to Hope Springs, the watering hole at the back of the ranch, would clear his mind. He headed that way and then heard a coyote howling over toward the adjoining ranch, the Texas Star—Henry Thomas's old place. If the varmint was thinking of attacking one of his calves, he'd put it running.

When Brody reached the barbed-wire fence separating the two ranches, the coyote had found a friend because he could hear two distinct coyote voices. Brody leaned on a post for a moment and wondered where Henry had gone when he left the place. He had a sister who lived somewhere over in the eastern part of the state and now leased out the whole section of land to Paul McKay, but the house hadn't been lived in since Henry left more than a decade ago.

He set his hand firmly on the top of the wood post and jumped over it. Paul was his friend and Kasey's father-in-law. He wouldn't mind if the Dawsons walked across his land to the old hay barn where the kids used to hang out. It was only about a quarter mile from the fence and with Brody's long strides, he got there in a few minutes.

Sitting down on a bale of hay, he let his eyes adapt to the semidarkness in the big, old weathered barn. He'd kissed Lila while she was sitting in the seat of the old green John Deere tractor parked right over there. He could visualize her perched on the seat. She wore cutoff jeans so short that the pockets hung down below the frayed out bottoms, and her long legs looked as if they went on forever. Barefoot, a gleam in her eye as the sun set, and those bright red lips begging to be kissed. Later, she'd told him that it was her first kiss ever.

The last time he'd kissed her was at the barn door just before they went their separate ways on a starlit night just over a dozen years ago. That was the night he'd asked her on a real date—their first date—dinner and a movie in Amarillo. He'd promised that he'd pick her up at six-thirty. The thought of living in a big place terrified her. Huntingdon, Pennsylvania, was by no means a big city, but compared to Happy, population less than seven hundred, the place seemed huge with almost eight thousand people. He didn't tell his brother or his family that he was going out with Lila—didn't see any use in starting a war right there in Happy.

A huge white cat startled him when it jumped into his lap and headbutted him until he started petting her long fur. In a few minutes she jumped down and disappeared into the hay, leaving him alone.

He'd left Lila alone that night. He just couldn't face the tears he knew would be coming—combined with the fit his parents and Granny would pitch when they found out he'd gone on a real date with the notorious Lila Harris. So when his buddies invited him to the Silver Spur, he'd taken the chicken's way out.

With fake IDs they'd had a few beers and danced with a lot of girls. He'd been a jerk and was absolutely miserable all night. Nothing, not illegal beers or other girls, would ease the pain of what he'd done to his best friend and secret girlfriend. He'd tossed and turned until morning and rushed to the café to see her before she and her mother left town. He'd known that he'd screwed up really badly and was prepared to tell her that not seeing her again forever was worse than seeing her cry. That he was hurting every bit as much as she was and to beg her to call him when she got to Pennsylvania.

He'd gotten there just as they were getting into the van. He tapped on the window but she wouldn't roll it down. Instead she'd looked straight ahead while tears rolled down her cheeks and left wet circles on her T-shirt. He'd never forgotten her mother's words that morning before she got into the vehicle and drove away.

"I've told her for years that you were just toying with her, that you'd always feel like you were better than her and that she was in for heartache. You finally proved me right, Brody."

It wasn't going to be easy to shake the memories or the yearning he still felt for Lila.

He checked the time and started toward the fence at a slower pace. When he had his hand on the post, ready to jump, he heard something in the distance that sounded like a motorcycle, but he didn't know anyone in Happy who owned one. He glanced over his shoulder and saw nothing.

"Most likely an old truck about to bite the dust," he muttered as he lengthened his stride. Jace said they were leaving at eight and he had only fifteen minutes. They usually played in the tack room at Henry's old barn but sometimes Fred insisted they come to his house. Brody had to admit that the snacks were usually better at Fred's place than they were when they met at the barn.

*   *   *

Lila finished unpacking, took a shower, and quickly found she was too restless to stay in the small apartment her mother had built behind the café.

It was at least an hour until dusk and she'd been inside all day. Swiping her keys from the hook by the front door, she went out to the garage and revved up her motorcycle.

Feet still on the ground, she tucked her black hair

under the helmet, popped the face mask down, and then walked the bike backward out of the garage, leaving the door open. The sun was sinking slowly out where land and sky met in the flat land of the Texas panhandle when she roared out to the cemetery. She went straight to her father's tombstone, dismounted, and was busy pulling weeds when her phone rang.

"Hi, Mama," she said.

"How'd the first day go?" Daisy asked.

"It went fine. And fast. I'm sitting in front of Daddy's grave right now. Decided I needed some fresh air, so I rode my bike out here," she said.

"What are you doing in the cemetery at dark?" Daisy asked.

"Texas is an hour behind Pennsylvania, remember? It's not even eight o'clock yet, so I can still see without turning on the bike's lights."

"I worry about you on that thing. I wish you'd sell it," Daisy said. "Just last week I read about a girl who was killed because she hit a pothole and went flying through the air. I know what those roads are like in Happy and—"

"Mama, quit worryin'," Lila interrupted. "I'm careful and I wear a helmet." She changed the subject. "Would you believe that everyone is trying to figure out what happened to Henry Thomas? You'd think they'd be talking about Molly and Georgia, right?"

"Molly is still there and no one believes she'll really leave. Georgia was last week's topic when she retired and moved," Daisy said.

"But she worked here and leased this place for more than a dozen years," Lila said. "And there's very little talk about the café bein' for sale. But nearly everyone who comes in mentions Henry. What was so great about him anyway? I don't hardly even remember him except that he came in the café a few times and always ordered jalapeños on his burgers. I wonder if they even realized that you and I left."

"We didn't just fall off the face of the earth like Henry did. That makes him their go-to topic when all the other gossip has gotten old like Georgia leaving Happy and moving to Florida. I'm surprised that you aren't the center of the rumors right now," Daisy said. "Comin' into town with a Harley. Flirting with Brody Dawson."

"I'm not flirting with him and tonight is the first time I've taken the bike out," Lila protested.

"Okay, okay, have it your way. Has anyone even asked about buyin' the café?"

"Not yet. Word will get out that the place is for sale and I did put a sign in the window. We may have to go with a Realtor." She braced her back on the tombstone.

"We might have to do that. I need to get back there for a visit," Daisy said. "I haven't been to your daddy's grave in all these years and..." There was a long pause. "Sometimes I wish I'd never left."

"Why?" Lila asked.

"Your aunt Tina and I aren't getting any younger and I don't want to spend my elderly years in this cold climate," Daisy said. "And yet I'm not so sure I want to live in Happy again, either. I guess as long as the café was mine, I kept a connection to your dad, even though he never did know I'd bought the old building and put in an apartment and a café. I don't know, I'm rambling."

"I understand. I'm undecided about going back to

Florida. I might start looking around at other places," Lila said.

"I thought you were happier there than you'd been in Memphis or in Little Rock."

Lila shut her eyes tightly but all she could see was Brody in that tight, sweaty T-shirt. Her therapist said that she kept moving to hunt for happiness but she had to find it inside herself first. Maybe it wasn't Brody that drew her back to Happy but the whole big picture where she had to prove to everyone that she was no longer that wild kid who was constantly in trouble. When she did that, she could move on.

"Lila?" Daisy raised her voice.

"I was thinkin'," she said quickly. "I was happy in Memphis and in Little Rock and I do love teaching in Panama City Beach. Maybe I've just got a travelin' bug that begins to bite me after a couple of years."

"Or maybe Happy is the only place that feels like home for both of us."

"I kind of doubt that, but who knows? We'll see what happens this summer. I'm off for a little country ride and then I'm going home to read a boring book until I fall asleep," Lila said.

"Promise me you will be careful on that thing. I hated it when your daddy rode one and even more when he put you in front of him and took you all over the county," Daisy said.

"I promise." She took a long, deep breath. "Good night, Mama."

As Lila hung up, she caught a movement in her peripheral vision. A black cat with a white blaze on his face was sitting on top of a tombstone and staring right at her.

"Here, kitty, kitty," she called to him.

He didn't budge. She held out her hand and called out to him again. Finally, she got up slowly and started walking that way. "You're a pretty boy. Where do you live?"

When she was close enough, she reached out to pet him but like a lightning streak he jumped down and in seconds he'd disappeared, knocking over a fresh wreath of daisies in his hurry. She straightened the flowers, made sure the metal tripod was secure in the ground, and then noticed the name on the tombstone—Weston Dalley. Birth and death dates recorded right there. Brody's grandpa had died June 1, twelve years ago. On the other side of the granite tombstone was Hope Dalley, birthday engraved but no death date.

"I know how much you loved him, Brody. I'm so sorry that you lost him." She went back to her father's grave and laid a hand on his tombstone. "I miss you, Daddy. I miss those afternoons when you took me for a ride down through the canyon, so this ride is for you."

Helmet on and a kiss blown toward the skies in hopes that her father would know that she was thinking of him, she headed off to the east. Her idea was that she would ride through the canyon, but when she got to the lane leading back to Henry's ranch, she slowed to a crawl and turned. The white picket fence around the yard shined in the moonlight. The long, low house felt empty even from that distance, but then it probably hadn't been lived in for years. Molly said that Henry's sister left it as it was in hopes that he'd come home someday.

The old barn drew her in. Heeding her mother's warnings, she drove slowly, keeping her eyes open for potholes. Scraggly weeds grew between fresh tire tracks left by trucks. She parked the bike close to the side door, which squeaked when she opened it just as it had done years ago.

Sitting on a bale of hay, she imagined a big green tractor between her and the door. That's where she'd gotten her first kiss and it had been from Brody. It had plumb set her insides on fire and every one after that had had the same effect.

A big, white cat made its way from the stacked hay toward her, rubbing around her legs and purring until she picked it up and held it close to her chest. Two cats in one night—one wary of her, the other wanting to be loved. Was this one of her mother's omens? And if so, should she pay attention to the cemetery cat or the one that liked her?

She inhaled deeply and let it out slowly. She sniffed again and then one more time. The cat smelled just like Stetson, the cologne that Brody used to wear back in high school. She glanced around the barn but didn't see anyone—most likely another kid used the same kind of cologne and had been out here earlier waiting for his girlfriend.

The cat hopped down and disappeared into the dark shadows, leaving Lila alone. She brushed the white hair from her dark T-shirt and jeans and inhaled again. The smell still lingered, so someone had been there. It couldn't have been Brody, because at thirty, he'd be taking his women to something a little more upscale than an old barn.

Chapter Four

So where have you been?" Jace asked.

"Out for a walk. Don't have many free evenings when nothing is hollerin' at me to come take care of it," Brody answered.

"Amen to that, brother. We've worked on these two ranches our whole lives but owning one is a lot different. It's a twenty-four-seven job." Jace started toward his truck.

Brody followed him. "You're sure enough testifyin' but I'm grateful to Granny for this. If we worked our whole lives and saved every penny, we couldn't buy something like Hope Springs."

"Or Prairie Rose." Jace nodded. "Fred and the guys are already itchin' to take our money. How much you got to lose?"

"Not more'n ten dollars but at a cap of a quarter we shouldn't lose too much," Brody chuckled.

Fred met them at the door and ushered them into the dining room. They took their places around the table and Paul shuffled. "So what do you think about Lila bein' back in town? Y'all goin' to get things started where you left off?"

"Lord almighty, this boy has so much on his platter that he ain't got time for women," Fred said. "He's got a ranch to run, kids to help his sister raise, and a granny to take care of."

"He's always got time for women, especially Lila." Paul winked dramatically.

"What makes Lila so special?" Jace asked as he arranged his cards.

Brody sorted through the hand he'd been dealt and bit his tongue to keep from giving them a list half a mile long.

"I'm not sure but there's sparks all over the place whenever she's around him." Paul nodded toward Brody.

"We here to talk women or play poker?" Fred asked.

"At our age we can do both. That woman on the television says it's multitasking." Paul reached for a cookie from a full platter in the middle of the table. "How'd you get your wife to let you have all these when all the other women are takin' stuff to my house for that social thing them women do every month?"

"I didn't ask," Fred answered. "I just emptied the cookie jar into a plastic bag and hid them until she was gone. Got some cold beers and soda pop in the 'fridge when y'all get thirsty. And there's a bag of pretzels if you want something salty."

Brody laid a card down and held up a finger. Paul slid one across to him.

"You gettin' serious about playin' or just wantin' us to hush about Lila?" Fred asked.

Brody nodded. "Maybe a little of both."

"If I were in your boots, I'd damn sure move in a hurry." Paul threw away three cards and motioned for more. "Young cowboys around here are going to come sniffin' around that café real soon when they hear that somethin' that pretty is workin' there."

"Why don't you hush? You're worse than an old woman at meddlin' in people's business," Fred fussed at him.

"Have some pretzels and beer and don't tell me what to do," Paul shot back.

Jace chuckled. "You reckon when we get old, we're goin' to be like these two, Brody? And I thought there was a couple more guys who would be here."

"Old!" Fred gasped. "We're like fine wine. We get better and see things clearer with age. Y'all young whippersnappers would do good if you were half as smart as us when you get to be sixty."

"Just us four. The others all had stuff to do," Paul said.

Brody looked at his terrible hand and thought of the hand life had dealt him. Grandfather and father both passing away the same summer that Lila had left. Going straight to work on the ranches rather than going to college like he'd planned. Now like Fred said, helping Kasey raise three kids, helping Jace organize and run Hope Springs. He loved the work but sometimes the weight of it all was pretty damn heavy. But a picture of Lila flashing through his mind brought a ray of light the likes of which he hadn't even realized was possible.

Still, after that last night and twelve years' worth of

water under the bridge, there was probably no way she'd ever want to start anything new with him. He'd blown his chance and the bridge had burned, leaving them on opposite sides of a deep gully.

"Brody!" Paul raised his voice.

He laid all his cards but one on the table, keeping the queen of hearts. "Guess I need a wheelbarrow full," he said.

Paul slid several cards across the table. "Not too lucky tonight, are you?"

"It can change," Brody said.

"Never too late to change or to start over," Fred said.

"You gettin' all philosophical on us, Fred?" Jace threw down two cards.

"Just callin' it like I see it." He shoved a quarter out to the middle of the table.

"I'll see your two bits and raise you four," Paul said.

Brody's hand had improved enough that he wouldn't lose too heavily on the first go-round. His mind kept wandering back to Lila. He'd rather be sitting in the hayloft with her than playing poker with Fred, Paul, and Jace but he didn't have that option. He glanced down at the queen of hearts and smiled.

"He must be about to take all our money," Paul said.

"Nah, he's thinkin' about a woman. Poker don't put a grin like that on a man's face," Fred argued.

Jace pushed three quarters out to the middle of the table. "I'll raise your four bits and add two more to it."

Brody laid his cards on the table. "Y'all got me. I'm out."

"Can't believe a Dawson has a bad luck streak," Paul said.

"We're playin' poker, not talkin' women, remember?" Jace teased.

Brody punched him on the arm. "You're as much an old woman as these two are."

Fred laid out a full house and raked in the quarters. "I'll have enough to buy a hamburger at the Happy Café if my luck holds out."

A vision of Lila in those tight jeans flashed through Brody's mind and he bit back a groan.

*   *   *

Lila hadn't awakened that Saturday morning with dancing on her mind, but when the café closed, she'd turned on the radio and danced through the top five country songs with the mop as a partner. She hadn't been out to an old country bar in years but the music brought back memories of the time when she and Brody managed to get into the Silver Spur with fake IDs. They'd drank beer and danced until thirty minutes before curfew, then drove like bats set loose from Hades to get home in time.

She was dressed in skinny jeans, boots, and a sleeveless Western shirt after she'd applied makeup and curled her hair. She'd worked hard for the past years to subdue that wild inner child, but tonight she was turning it loose and letting it come out to play. She listened to a Blake Shelton CD on the way to the Silver Spur and wiggled her shoulders to the beat. The words to his song would be her theme song for the night. She'd leave when the place shut down or when they ran completely out of cold beer.

The parking lot was pretty full when she arrived. That

meant that she would have plenty of guys to dance with. Lila held her breath as she walked through the fog of cigarette smoke and ignored the whistles of several cowboys who'd already drank too much. She had her money out to pay the cover charge but the bouncer waved her on in.

"Ladies' night every first Saturday. Free cover charge and beers are two dollars until ten o'clock. Enjoy," he said.

"Thank you." She shoved the money back into her small purse and went straight toward the bar.

The dance floor was full of line dancers and the sound of their boots hitting the wooden floor was music to her ears. She hiked a hip on a bar stool and ordered a beer.

A tall, blond cowboy with pretty blue eyes claimed the place beside her within seconds. "How about I buy you a drink? I'm Rick, short for Derrick, and you're Angel, right?"

"No, I'm Lila, short for Delilah, which is about as far from Angel as you can get. But that's a pretty good pickup line, Rick," she answered. "I've already got a drink ordered but thank you."

The line dancers made a beeline for the bar as the next song started. When the first guitar strands of "If You're Gonna Play in Texas" began, Rick held out his hand and she put hers in it. He led her to the middle of the floor and wrapped his arms around her. She was grateful that they were the same height and his nose wasn't resting between her breasts. He was smooth on the dance floor and dancing with him was fun.

The band's singer stepped up to the mic. "We have a request for 'Sideways' by Darryl Worley. This isn't the Rendezvous Club like he sings about but it's definitely time to get a little sideways in the Silver Spur for most of you folks and there's plenty of fiddle in this one."

The blond cowboy was pretty smooth on his feet and Lila was enjoying the dance until a petite redhead tapped her on the shoulder. "Mind if I have a turn at this cowboy?"

Lila stepped back and someone grabbed her hand, spun her around in a swing dance, and then brought her back to his chest. Her heart knocked against her chest so hard that she thought it would fly out of her chest when she looked into those cerulean blue Dawson eyes.

"Brody?" Of course it was Brody. No one else created such turmoil in her body, soul, and mind.

"Lila." He smiled.

"I thought you were too busy for a night out or maybe I should say two nights since you played poker with Fred and Paul last night. I sure didn't expect to see you here tonight."

"How'd you know that I was at Fred's playin' poker?" he asked.

"Rumors are nourished and fed at the café." She grinned. "Paul and Fred came in for their usual afternoon snack and gossip session. I don't know how they get anything done on their ranches."

"They've each got a good foreman and lots of hired help. And I probably shouldn't take two nights off in a row but I heard that you might be here tonight."

"Oh, really?" She raised both dark brows.

"The café isn't the only place that gossip flourishes." He smiled. "Molly was fussin' about you and it got back to Kasey."

She should walk away and not look back but she was

enjoying being close to him too much to do that. "I don't imagine your granny and your mama will appreciate that," she finally said.

"Right now I'm not real concerned about what anybody thinks." He drew her closer and buried his face in her hair.

Every nerve in her body was aware that she was in his arms and all her hormones kicked into double time, begging her to drag him out to the truck and fog the windows. When the song ended, another line dance started. He kept her hand in his and led her back to the bar, where they claimed the last couple of stools at the very end. He held up two fingers and pointed to the Coors bottle the guy beside him held. The bartender nodded and brought two ice-cold longnecks to them.

"Talk to me," he said.

"About?"

"You. Why didn't you call me after you moved?" he said.

"My heart was shattered, Brody. Why did you stand me up that night?" She couldn't tell him that she'd called the ranch but when his mother answered, she'd hung up.

"I didn't want to see you cry again, so when the guys asked me to go with them, I went. And..." He paused, leaving a big empty space hanging over their heads.

"You didn't want to be seen in public with me without a crowd around us, right?"

He nodded. "I'm sorry. I wish I could go back and redo that night, Lila. But there was another reason."

"And that is?"

"I didn't want you to see me cry," he said. "I really do wish I could get a redo."

"Sometimes it's too late to do what you should have been doing all along, Brody."

It had taken a lot of therapy for her to realize that Brody had been a complete jerk. That the way he treated her wasn't her fault and that she had been worthy of a decent relationship even if they were just teenagers.

"I tried to sweet-talk a phone number out of Molly and Georgia both. I still can't believe that she retired and moved so far away. She and Molly were an institution at the café. I knew they'd have some way to get in touch with your mom but they wouldn't budge. Then I sent a letter to you, thinking they would forward it to your new address but it came back stamped with 'refused' in big red letters."

"Mama was tired of watching me get hurt. She knew we'd been sneaking around and that I was...that I'd had a big crush on you for years." She couldn't make herself say that she'd been in love with him. "Then when you finally asked me out for real, you stood me up. If a letter had come, she would have burned it." She lowered her voice. "And your folks thought I was a bad influence on you and everyone else. I just wanted you to like me, Brody, but that ship has sailed and I burned the bridge between me and you. It's too late for us."

"Then we'll have to build a new ship and a new bridge." He ran a rough hand down her cheekbone. "You're still as beautiful as I remember and it's never too late." He parroted Fred's words from the night before. Or was it Paul who'd said that? Either way, it was good advice.

Sitting so close that his arm grazed hers when he took a drink of his beer, looking like sex on a stick, smelling exactly like that white cat in Henry's barn—the wild child inside her wanted to come out and play so badly. But she wasn't that girl who'd fall all over herself for a little attention from Brody Dawson. When she'd started college at Penn State, she'd become the girl who studied hard, got good grades, and graduated with honors. According to her therapist, she'd been out to show everyone that she'd amount to something.

Brody opened his mouth to say something but a young woman who was probably right out of high school pushed her way between them and motioned toward the bartender. Evidently he knew what she drank because he grabbed two mugs and began to fill them with beer. While she waited, she turned her face toward Brody and flashed a brilliant smile. "Hey, there. Want to dance?"

"Not tonight. I'm with this lady right here."

"This old gal"—she eyed Lila up and down—"is way below your league."

"No, thanks," he said. "And don't talk about my... my..."

"Your mother?" the woman giggled.

Lila would bet that her ID was fake and she wasn't a day over eighteen. The joke about her age wasn't what lit a fire under her anger—it was that nasty little remark about her being way below his league.

"I'm not his mother, darlin'," Lila said.

"Sister, mother, friend, neighbor. It don't matter." She worked a quarter from her skintight jeans and laid it on the counter in front of Lila. "Here you go. Go call the senior citizens' van to take you home."

"What did you just say to me?" Lila's temper flared

as she tucked a leg behind the woman's knee and gave a slight kick. The girl crumpled to the floor in a heap.

"You bitch," she said as she tried to regain her footing.

Lila hopped off the stool and pulled her up. Then she leaned in close to her ear and whispered, "If you want to play with the big dogs, you'd best get your rabies shots."

"I was just teasin' and havin' a little fun. My friends dared me to get him to dance with me," she whimpered.

"Be careful who you insult next time you want to have a little fun," Lila said.

"God, I've missed you," Brody laughed as the girl limped away. "She thought she was tough."

"She's just a kid out with her friends." Lila could remember acting just like that more than once, but it hadn't been her girlfriends she'd wanted to impress—it'd been Brody Dawson.

"I guess we've all been young and stupid. Did you ever think about all the good times we had before you moved away? Want another beer?"

She shook her head and put a hand over the top of the beer so the bartender could see. "Sure I thought of you. I taught in a high school in Memphis where I was the junior class sponsor. That meant I had to attend the prom as a chaperone. I thought of you that night and how handsome you looked in your tux when you escorted Gloria Tanner into the room. Hmmm." She tapped her chin with a finger.

"I told you back then that I wanted to take you but...," Brody stammered.

"It's water under that bridge that I burned down." She slung her purse over her shoulder and slid off the bar stool.

"Don't go. I'm sorry, Lila, for everything," Brody said.

"When I come back home, I'm still the wild child and you're Brody Dawson, the most popular cowboy in Happy, Texas," she said. "You were the quarterback of the football team, the high-point shooter in all the basketball games, class president, and voted most likely to succeed. If they'd had a tough cowboy title, you would have won it too."

"We are the cowboys," he reminded her. "Do you remember everything about everyone?"

"Of course. I remember dancing with you one time right here when we snuck in with fake IDs. You didn't mind holding me close in a bar but you wouldn't even sit with me in church. What does that tell you?" She wanted to dance with him again so badly that she could feel his arms around her, but wild horses or a Texas tornado couldn't drag her back out onto the floor.

"Stay until I finish my beer and I'll walk you out to your truck. I'm about ready to call it a night too. Just five more minutes, please?"

She fought with herself for a moment before she sat back down on the stool.

"So you're a teacher now?" he said.

"Yup. High school English."

He took a long draw from the bottle. "Where do you teach?"

"Taught in Memphis and, believe me, in the neighborhood where I taught, the fourteen-year-old girls were as tough as nails. Then I taught in an inner-city school in Little Rock that was even rougher and the past two years I've been in an upscale place in Panama City, Florida."

"I can't imagine you in a classroom," he said.

"Where did you imagine I'd be in twelve years? Living in a run-down trailer park with six or seven kids and a drunk for a husband?"

"No, you were too smart for that. I just figured you'd be a lawyer or maybe the mayor of Philadelphia or something really big and important. Not that a teacher isn't a fine job. So you never got married, right?"

"Your beer is done. To answer the question, though—I told you in the café I wasn't married."

"Yes, you did but that's not what I'm askin'. You aren't married now but have you been at some time?"

She shook her head. "My therapist says I have commitment issues."

It was the truth and Brody was the one who'd caused those issues.

"You?" she asked.

"Nope, my sister says the same thing about me and commitment. She's probably right."

Lila slid off the stool. "How's Kasey? Adam's death must have hit her hard."

"She's trying to move on but it's not easy. Three great kids help but she misses Adam a lot." Brody threw a few bills on the bar and followed her.

"Tell her hi for me. See you around." Outside, she inhaled the clean night air and wished that she could get him out of her mind and heart as swiftly as leaving a bar full of the smell of sweat and beer.

"You're two different people. One is the smart teacher. The other one is the girl who left and they're fightin' with each other," he said.

"You got it. And the winner takes all." She walked faster. He matched his long strides with hers. "Which is?"

"The prize." She stopped abruptly. "Don't feel like you have to walk me to my vehicle. I'm a big girl and I've been takin' care of myself for years."

"You've always been able to take care of yourself, Lila, but I want to walk with you." His hand went to her lower back.

The intense heat would probably leave a print on her back that would look like a bright red tattoo for days, but she didn't argue or shrug it away.

When they reached her bright red truck, he whistled under his teeth. "Nice vehicle."

She dug around in her purse and found the keys. "I left the motorcycle at home."

"Oh, really?" His expression said that he didn't believe her.

"Yep, I didn't want to arrive with helmet head."

"Are you serious?"

"Why would you be so surprised? I am, after all, the resident bad child of Happy, Texas. I'm surprised there's not a picture of me beside the city limits sign warning everyone to steer clear of Lila Harris. If you rub shoulders with her, you get an instant ticket to hell. Do not pass go. Do not collect two hundred dollars. Just get on your poker and get ready for the ride."

"Motorcycles are dangerous. You shouldn't—"

She laid a finger over his lips. "I stayed on a bull for eight seconds and climbed to the top of the water tower. You didn't fuss at me about those things because, wait, you were right there with me. Well, darlin', buy a Harley and we'll terrorize Happy before we have to use that quarter and call for the senior citizens' bus. Good night, Brody."

With a hand on each side, he pinned her against the truck door. She put both hands on his chest with intentions of pushing him away, but she made the mistake of looking into his eyes. Lashes slowly closed to rest on his cheekbones and she barely had time to moisten her lips before she was swept away by a scorching hot kiss.

She should push him back but instead, her arms went around his neck and she touched his bottom lip with her tongue. He groaned and opened his mouth, deepening the kiss into fiery hot passion. She would have been there until daylight, but he finally stepped back, picked up her hand, and kissed her palm twice.

"One kiss for the Lila I remember, the other for the woman she's become. Both are very special." Then he turned and disappeared into the darkness.

With weak knees, she hit the button to unlock her bright red truck and crawled into the driver's seat, leaned her head back, and sighed. Her whole body tingled and every single frayed hormone was crying out to call him and tell him to meet her at the springs. But instead she started the engine and drove south toward Happy at five miles under the speed limit.

She pulled into the garage and got on her cycle, rode it out to Henry's ranch, and parked it at the barbed-wire fence separating Hope Springs from Texas Star. Jumping a fence was like riding a bicycle—once done, it was second nature to do it again, even after a dozen years. She put a hand on a wooden post and gave a hop, cleared the top strand, and came down on Brody's property.

Hot! Damn hot! If hell is seven times hotter than this, the devil might already be cooling off in Hope Springs, she thought as she made her way from the fence to the cold spring that bubbled down over a tiny little waterfall into a pool. The water came from an underground spring that flowed all year and no matter how hot the weather was the water was never warm.

She jogged a quarter mile back to the springs, where she jerked her boots and socks off and waded out into the icy water until it reached her knees, not caring if her jeans got wet. That didn't help the place where his hand had been on her back. It was still too warm, so she went back to the grassy shore, shucked out of every stitch of clothing, and dove into the icy water.

"Oh. My. God!" She gasped when she surfaced. "I forgot how cold this is even in the summer. Are you happy, my inner wild child? I'm a thirty-year-old woman out here trespassing and skinny-dippin'."

Somewhere down deep inside her soul she heard a very loud, *Hell, yeah, I am.*

Chapter Five

On Sunday morning, Lila awoke to the sound of rattling pots and pans in the kitchen. She covered her head with a pillow. "This is summer. I'm not supposed to be working. June, July, and August are the number one reason people go into the teaching field. This place makes me crazy. I'm talking to myself. I need a pet." She threw the pillow at the wall.

Molly was rolling out dough for morning biscuits by the time Lila showered and made it to the kitchen. She frowned and shook the wooden rolling pin at her. "You won't ever live down that wild kid reputation by going to the bars. You *will* be in Sunday night church services this evening. You can sit with me. We can't go to morning services what with having to run this business but God will be there tonight as well as this morning."

"You aren't my boss," Lila said.

"Oh, yes, I am, especially on the Sundays after I hear that you were seen talkin' to Brody Dawson at the Silver Spur of all places. You don't need to be hangin' around with him. Your mama told me that he plumb broke your heart the night before y'all left town," Molly said.

"Maybe he's different now that he's grown up."

"Why are you takin' up for him?" Molly stopped what she was doing and cocked her head to one side.

"I don't know but—"

"No buts." Molly shook her head. "If things are right, then there are no buts."

"Don't stomp a hole in that soapbox." Lila filled both coffeemakers.

"Don't sass me. I can still walk out that door, and if I do, you'll have to close down this place. Then it won't ever sell. Nobody will buy a café that's been shut down for months," Molly declared.

Lila threw up her hands defensively. "Yes, ma'am. I won't sass you again, Miss Molly."

"That's better. Now let's get to work."

* * *

Brody only caught a sentence here and there of the Sunday morning sermon. With Emma on one side of him and Rustin on the other, he spent the time switching between handing Rustin crayons so that he could work in his cowboy coloring book and peeling off stickers for Emma to plaster in her book.

His heart went out to Kasey, who was sitting on the other side of Emma. Adam should be the one helping with the two older children and making Kasey smile every evening when he came home from work. Only when she looked at her kids did her eyes light up—the rest of the time she was still struggling with her loss.

He wondered what it would be like if things had worked out between him and Lila right out of high school, and then he'd lost her to an accident that no one could even talk about. His chest tightened and the pain was so sudden that it brought tears to his eyes. If nothing more than a thought could bring on that much hurt, his poor little sister was doing good to crawl out of bed every morning.

He glanced over his shoulder to see if Lila might be back there somewhere, then reminded himself that she was at the café. If she attended Sunday services at all, it would be that evening. If the family wasn't gathering at his mother's for dinner, he would have gone to the café just to be sure that Lila was okay. But he'd promised Emma that he would sit beside her, and a man was only as good as his word, whether it was to a three-year-old girl or a ninety-year-old cowboy.

Guess you learned that lesson the hard way, didn't you? that irritating voice in his head said. *If you'd kept your word, maybe you and Lila would have stayed in touch all these years.*

Yes, I did. He nodded. *And after the misery I've lived with for years over that, I've tried to never go back on my word again.*

There were few parking spots left at the café when he drove past it after church. He tapped the brakes and slowed down, but all he could see in the windows were people sitting at tables and in booths. He could picture Lila practically jogging between customers as she took orders, served them, and kept everyone's drinks filled. Her black ponytail would be flipping from side to side. She'd be smiling at Fred and Paul's banter. And those tight jeans would stretch over her butt, and her T-shirt would hug her breasts.

When he got to his mother's house, he untucked his shirt, more to cover the bulge behind his zipper than for comfort. He removed his hat at the front door and hung it on a hook beside Jace's on a hall tree in the foyer. He could hear three distinct women's voices in the kitchen—his mother, Valerie; Granny Hope; and his sister, Kasey. Jace was in the living room surrounded by three kids all begging him to go outside with them. Brody slipped down the hallway to his old bedroom and slumped down in a rocking chair.

"Hey." Kasey poked her head in the door a few minutes later. "Dinner is on the table. Rustin said he thought he saw you coming this way. Everything okay?"

Brody shook his head. "No, but there's no one to blame but me."

"Want to talk about it?"

He pushed out of the rocking chair and draped an arm around her shoulders. "Short version. I really hurt Lila the night before she left town. We had a date, a real one where I was going to take her to dinner and to the movies."

Kasey whistled through her teeth. "Did Granny and Mama know about it?"

He shook his head. "Nobody did but me and Lila. I stood her up and when I tried to apologize the next day, right as she was leaving, she wouldn't talk to me."

Kasey stepped back and popped him on the bicep. "I

wouldn't have talked to you either. I might have shot you. You liked her a lot. Why would you do that?"

He grabbed his arm and winced. "Damn, Kasey, that smarted. To answer your question, I couldn't bear to see her cry."

"That's not a good reason or even a good excuse," Kasey said. "She was probably floating on cloud nine and then you didn't show up. God, Brody, that's terrible."

"I blew it with her and now all these years later..." He hung his head and let the sentence hang.

"Maybe she'll forgive you if you show her that you really care," Kasey said as she started walking again. "But just between me and you, I wouldn't."

Emma patted the chair beside her when they reached the dining room. "Right here, Uncle Brody."

Jace said grace and then it got loud. Plates, platters, and bowls were passed. Brody cut Emma's meat into small pieces while he listened to her talk about butterflies and kittens.

"So what's on your agenda for the rest of the afternoon, Brody?" his mother asked.

"I'm going out to check on Sundance, to make sure that he hasn't broken through the fence again. I was gone two nights and that wild critter is like a kid. He has to have constant supervision. Then I'm going to Sunday night services," he said.

The room went uncomfortably quiet for several seconds; then Rustin slapped a hand on either side of his face. "Why would you do that? Church is boring."

"Rustin!" Kasey gasped.

"It is." Emma nodded.

"Is it because Lila might be at church tonight?" Valerie

passed the green beans to him, and he sent them on to Jace without taking any.

"You got to eat your beans or you don't get any cake, and Nana made a pecan pie too." Rustin tucked his chin down on his chest and looked across the table at Brody.

Brody motioned to Jace and the bowl came back to him. "I sure wouldn't want to miss out on Mama's pie."

"You didn't answer me," Valerie said.

"Could be," he said. "But if she's not, I know how to knock on her door."

Hope rolled her eyes and Valerie shot a dirty look his way.

Brody fixed his eyes on the green beans. He wasn't arguing or fighting with either one of them but his mind was made up. He was going to church and hopefully Lila would be there.

"Guess I'm going to church tonight," Hope said.

"Me too." Kasey nodded.

"I wouldn't miss this for all the dirt in Texas." Jace grinned.

"What's going on here?" Brody asked.

"We want to see if the clouds part. You haven't been to Sunday night services since your grandpa died. You usually only go on Sunday morning," Hope answered.

"He didn't go to Sunday morning," Brody said defensively. "So I waited and went with him to night services. Besides, I always liked to hear him sing."

"Well, if y'all are going, then I am too," Valerie said.

Brody shoveled green beans into his mouth. They might get more than they bargained for, but hey, it was their decision.

*   *   *

The buzz in the packed café at lunch that day was that the old grocery store out on the edge of town had burned to the ground that morning while church was going on. A tornado had ripped off the back part of the roof ten years ago and the building had gone to ruin since then.

"Where were you this morning about ten o'clock?" Fred whispered when Lila set his plate of chicken and dumplings on the table.

"Right here helping Molly make those dumplings," Lila answered with a smile.

"Does seem strange," Fred's wife said. "We ain't had trouble since you left and you come back and it starts all over again. Maybe you don't have to do anything at all. Could be that trouble follows you around like a puppy dog."

"Well, I'll be gone at the end of summer and nothing bad will ever happen in Happy from that day forth. Maybe if you find a buyer for this café, I'll be gone even sooner. Y'all enjoy your dinner and holler if you need anything," Lila said.

"Order up!" Molly yelled from the kitchen.

When Lila reached for the plate on the shelf, Molly turned around from the stove and smiled. "Blamin' you for this mornin's fire, are they?"

"How'd you know?"

"I figured it would happen when I heard the fire engine going and heard that the old grocery store burned to the ground. The volunteer firemen have been tryin' to get the owner to let them burn it for years."

"Why didn't he?" she asked.

"Have no idea, but it's good riddance to bad rubbish. That thing was an eyesore. I wouldn't be surprised if the owner set the fire himself. When the store went belly-up, he moved off to San Antonio. The property has been for sale so long that the Realtor's sign has faded until you can't see who to call for information." Molly went back to filling orders. "Don't let them rile you. Tell 'em all to go straight to hell ridin' on a rusty poker."

"That's bad for business."

"Where else they goin' to eat without driving fifteen to thirty minutes?" Molly laughed.

The café cleared out a little by one-thirty, but there were still a few sipping glass after glass of sweet tea or coffee and discussing the fire. At two-thirty, Molly started cleaning the kitchen and putting the last of the dirty dishes in the two commercial-sized dishwashers. There was no one in the place at three when Lila locked the doors and started sweeping the floors.

Molly waved from the door into the kitchen. "I'm going home for my Sunday afternoon nap. I'll pick you up right here at six-thirty for evening services. I like to get there a little early and visit with my friends before the singin' starts at seven."

Lila leaned on the broom. "I'm not going to church."

"Yes, you are. Churchgoin' women do not set fires," Molly declared. "See you at six-thirty. And wear a dress."

"Okay," Lila sighed. "But I'll drive myself and be there at a quarter to seven."

"Promise? It won't hurt you and you'll see a lot of your old friends."

And all those old friends probably think I burned down

a building just for kicks. The only thing I ever set fire to was a tire Jace Dawson got out of the ranch trash pile. And it was in the middle of Main Street where it couldn't hurt a thing. It stirred up smoke and a big stink, but it didn't destroy property.

"I'll be there. Have a good nap," Lila said.

She got everything ready to open again the next morning and carried a tall glass of water with a slice of lemon in it to a table. She kicked off her boots, sat down, and propped her feet on a chair. Tomorrow she intended to drag out her sneakers with a nice thick, cushy sole. Running the café was a seven, six, six job—seven days a week from six in the morning until six in the evening, except Sunday when they closed at three.

Her eyes grew heavy, so she picked up her water in one hand and the boots in the other and padded through the kitchen. She made sure all the doors were locked before she went to the apartment and stretched out on the sofa.

A ping on her cell phone awoke her two hours later. She checked the text, saw that it was from Molly reminding her about church, and shut her eyes for another few minutes. Then she realized that she had twenty minutes to get dressed and get to the church or she might be running the café single-handed tomorrow. She sat up so fast that the room did a couple of fast spins.

She jerked her shirt over her head and was yanking her jeans down as she rushed to her bedroom. No time for a shower. She applied fresh deodorant and shook her hair out of the ponytail, slipped into a cute little knee-length orange sundress, and cussed loud enough to blister the paint when she had to search for both sandals in the bin of shoes she hadn't unpacked yet. In the garage, she eyed the motorcycle but the rumor mill would have a feast with the story of her riding to church with her skirt blown up, showing off a pair of red bikini underbritches.

She did take a moment when she reached the church to flip down the visor mirror of her truck and apply bright red lipstick and a touch of mascara and run a brush through her hair. Then she rushed into the church and located Molly, who frowned, tapped her watch, and gave her a you-were-testing-my-patience look before she pointed at the third pew from the front. Now wasn't that just the big old red cherry on top of a hot caramel sundae? Lila would have been much happier claiming a corner on the backseat where she could escape quickly after the last prayer.

"I overslept and had to rush," she whispered.

"Next time set an alarm. Them fancy phones y'all carry can do everything, including telling you bedtime stories, so there's never an excuse to be late for anything," Molly said out of the corner of her mouth.

The preacher took his place behind the pulpit and cleared his throat, and silence filled the little church. "I'm glad to see Lila Harris with us tonight and to hear that she's helping out at the Happy Café. Now, if you'll all open your hymn books to page three hundred, we'll sing together before the sermon."

The hymn ended and the preacher made a few comments about hell being seven times hotter than the Texas heat wave. That brought out a few chuckles, and Lila was sure if she turned around, she'd see more than one person using those cardboard fans to ward off such fire and brimstone.

"And now I will ask Brody Dawson to give the benediction," the preacher said.

Lila's heart stopped, then raced ahead, beating twice as hard as it ever had. From his voice, it was plain that he was only a couple of pews behind her, but she couldn't hear a word he said for the pounding in her ears. Her cheeks turned fire-engine red as she remembered the kiss from the night before.

Any second the skies were going to go dark and lightning was going to split through the roof and zap her dead for thinking about the heat she'd felt when Brody kissed her. She glanced out the window to see nothing but big, fluffy white clouds and the sun slowly sinking toward the horizon. Evidently God had given her a pass since she hadn't been in a church since she left Happy and he was just glad to see her sitting in a pew.

She heard Molly loudly say, "Amen!" so she knew when to raise her head and open her eyes.

Molly smiled as she stood to her feet. "Didn't hurt too bad, did it?"

"What?" Lila asked.

Molly bumped shoulders with her. "Coming to church."

"Hey, Lila," a feminine voice said at her elbow. "You haven't changed a bit."

"Kasey? It's great to see you, and, darlin', you look the same as you did in junior high school. Are these your kids?" She smiled.

"Yep, these three belong to me. This is Rustin." Kasey pointed toward a little dark-haired boy with blue eyes. "This is Emma, and this critter here on my hip is Silas."

"You've got a beautiful family. Emma is the image of

you at that age. Bring the kids to the café sometime and I'll treat them to an ice cream sundae and we'll catch up."

"Yes!" Rustin pumped his fist in the air. "Can we go tomorrow, Mama?"

"Maybe later in the week. Tomorrow all three of you're spending the day with your nana." She winked at Lila. "That's Adam's mother. You remember Gracie McKay, right? And we will take you up on that offer, Lila. Maybe later in the week?"

"Any day that's good for you. I look forward to it," she answered.

"Does the invitation extend to me too?" Brody's warm breath tickled her neck as he stepped out into the center aisle.

"Only kids under twelve get free ice cream. You might not be older than that mentally but your size gives away your age." Lila hoped that her voice didn't sound as high and squeaky to everyone else as it did in her own ears.

Kasey giggled and nudged Brody on the shoulder. "You've met your match, brother. You've got to pay for your ice cream."

"Is that right, Lila?" His eyes bored into hers.

Neither of them blinked for several seconds and then she smiled. "Yes, it is right. Free ice cream comes at a great price. You'd have to rob a bank to get that much money."

Suddenly, a tiny little hand slipped into hers and she looked down to see Emma smiling at her. "I like ice cream," the little girl said. "And you're pretty. Can I be your friend?"

"I would like that very much and you're very pretty

too." Lila ignored all the people around her and stooped to Emma's level. "What is your favorite kind of ice cream?"

"Strawberry," Emma said seriously.

"Then I'll be sure that we have lots of that kind when you come to visit me sometime this week."

Emma nodded. "And will you read me a story?"

"That's what good friends do, isn't it?" Lila answered. "But I don't have any books that I can read to you, so maybe you'd better bring your favorite one with you that day."

"'I will bring ABC. C is for camel. C. C. C,'" Emma quoted.

"Dr. Seuss?" Lila glanced over toward Kasey.

"Her favorite, but...," Kasey said.

Lila stood back up. "I would love to read to the kids. Please pack a couple of books to bring along. Most any evening is good for me. Just give me a call."

"Thank you." Kasey smiled.

Lila shook hands with the preacher and was ten feet away from her truck when she realized that Brody was parked next to her. Standing there, with his arms crossed over his chest, wearing a white pearl-snap shirt and creased jeans, he flat out took her breath away. By the time she reached her truck, he'd dropped his arms to his side and opened her door.

"You look very pretty tonight," he said.

"Thanks."

"I'll see you sometime tomorrow at the café if I can sneak away for a few minutes or if I have to come into town to the feed store."

"For real or will you change your mind?"

"Not this time, darlin'," he said as he shut the door.

Lila sat in the hot truck, sweat rolling down into her bra, heart pounding and her thoughts running around in circles for a long time before she finally switched on the air-conditioning. Being angry at him when he was hundreds of miles away and when he wasn't standing so close that she could have touched him was a whole different ball game.

Chapter Six

Lila danced around the café with the broom to Gretchen Wilson's "Redneck Woman." The singer asked for a big hell, yeah, from the redneck girls like her and the broom turned into a microphone. From then on, Lila lip-synced the rest of the song and then hit the replay button on her phone so she could get the message out there to the whole empty café.

The beat was still pounding in her ears as she two-stepped the broom back to the kitchen, where she kept it in one hand and loaded a tray with ice cream toppings with the other. In a few minutes, Kasey and the kids were coming for an ice cream party and she'd looked forward to the evening all week.

She carried the tray to the dining room and set it on a table that she'd covered with a red and white checkered cloth. She wanted it to be a real party for the kids and for Kasey.

It had been a crazy week. On Monday, Brody had come into the café, had a glass of lemonade, and didn't even get to drink it before he got a call from the ranch about fencing. On Wednesday he dropped by again but didn't even get to sit down before Jace phoned saying that they needed six more rolls of barbed wire, so he turned around and left. On Thursday a florist brought a single red rose with a pretty white ribbon around it. The note said: *Welcome home. Brody.* Molly was fit to be tied when she put the rose in a pint jar.

"I'm tellin' you that you're on the road to heartache," Molly fussed.

"All over a single rose?" Lila asked.

"Just that much will bring Hope and Valerie out gunnin' for you," Molly had said.

"I'm not a kid anymore. I'll take them on," she'd answered.

He didn't come around at all on Friday but Kasey had called that morning to see if she and the kids could come to the café for ice cream about six-thirty that evening. Lila had been so excited all day, just thinking about reading to the kids. She went back to the kitchen and placed five crystal boat dishes on a tray. The last time they'd been used was probably for her sixteenth birthday but they'd only needed two that night—one for her and one for her mother. She heard doors slamming and hurried back to the kitchen to bring out four flavors of ice cream. She hummed all the way back into the dining room.

The door flew open and Emma's short little legs were a blur as she ran across the floor to meet her, but Rustin stood back close to Brody's side. Lila stopped so fast that the cartons of ice cream started to slide and it took some fancy footwork to keep them steady. Even blinking a dozen times didn't magically turn Brody into Kasey.

"Hey, Lila. Kasey got one of her migraines about thirty minutes ago." He lowered his voice. "I can't stand to see Emma disappointed. So I hope you don't mind getting me instead?"

For the first time in many years, Lila was totally speechless. He looked like he was afraid she was going to kick him out of the café. And she wanted to set the tray on the table, hug him, and assure him that it was fine.

"Thank you for bringing them and of course it's all right. I couldn't disappoint that precious child either." Her voice finally came out hollow and slightly breathless. "Emma says her favorite is strawberry. What's yours, Rustin?"

"Chocolate." He crawled up in a chair, pulled a napkin free of the dispenser, and tucked it into the neck of his T-shirt. "We already had our baths and Mama said not to get all messy."

Rustin's dark hair still had a few droplets of water hanging on it. Emma's braids were damp and Silas's blond curls kinked all over his head. She could never deny the kids, or herself either for that matter, the party—even if Brody was there.

"I bet Silas likes chocolate with whipped cream on top, right?" Lila reached for the baby and he didn't even hesitate before holding out his little arms.

"He loves anything chocolate." Brody's arm brushed across hers in the transfer. The tension, sparks, and heat were so steamy that it was a pure miracle the ice cream didn't melt.

"I'll get a booster for Emma and a high chair for Silas," Brody said.

"Bananas!" Emma peered over the top of the table.

"Whipped cream and cherries. Yummy." Rustin rubbed his tummy. "This is the bestest party ever."

Emma poked a finger in his shoulder. "Lila is my friend, not yours."

"I'll be everyone's friend." Lila settled Silas into the high chair that Brody brought from the far end of the café.

"Everyone's? Does that include the ones that are too old for free ice cream?" Brody set the booster in a chair and then helped Emma into it.

"Depends on lots of things," she answered.

"I don't need a booster anymore," Rustin said. "I'm a big kid and someday I'm going to stink just like Uncle Brody."

Lila locked eyes with Brody. The toughest cowboy in the whole state of Texas was blushing.

"Sometimes Uncle Brody stinks," Emma whispered, and her little nose twitched. "You don't stink. You smell good, like Mama's perfume when she's gettin' all pretty. Uncle Brody took a bath, so he don't stink no more, either."

"Man, she talks plain," Lila said.

"Since the day she said her first word. She has to keep pace with Rustin." Brody chuckled. "But she's right. You do smell really good. And this cowboy refuses to let us feed him anymore." He pulled a bib from his hip pocket and fastened it around the baby's neck. "Can I help with anything, Miss Lila?"

"I'll scoop and you can put on the toppings," she answered. "Let's start with Silas."

The baby pointed to the container of chocolate as soon as she opened it.

"He's gotten real definite in what he likes and doesn't. Anything that has orange flavor isn't his thing," Brody said.

"Must run in the family." She dipped out a big round scoop of ice cream and put it in one of the fancy dishes.

Their eyes met over the table.

"I still don't," he whispered. "Surprised that you remembered that detail."

"Like I told you." She tapped her forehead with a forefinger. "I remember everything."

"Banana?" she asked.

The baby nodded several times.

"Whipped cream?"

He shook his head.

"Guess he really does know what he likes."

"Uncle Brody don't like whipped cream neither and he don't eat the white stuff on chocolate pie," Rustin said. "Mama says that Silas is just like him but I don't think he'll stink as bad as I will when I'm a cowboy. I get to haul hay when I'm ten and I'd like a banana and whipped cream and two cherries on top and some of that chocolate syrup."

"And I just want plain old strawberry. And a banana to eat all by itself," Emma said. "These dishes sure are fancy."

"My mama used them for special times." Lila filled the dishes and slid them across the table for Brody to do the rest.

"So tonight is special?" Brody asked.

"Anytime I can spend an hour with three kids falls into that category. What can I get for you?" she asked.

"I thought free ice cream was only for kids under twelve," he drawled.

"Rules change when the place is officially closed." If someone had told her a month ago that she'd be spending a Friday evening with Brody and three kids in her café, she'd have thought they were certifiably insane.

"Double dip of vanilla with caramel topping and a layer of nuts over that," he said. "Next to pumpkin pie, this is my favorite dessert."

She dug down deep into the container and heaped each scoop.

"What are you having?" he asked as he poured caramel on the top of his ice cream.

"One of each," she answered as she fixed her sundae. "With whipped cream and nuts and a cherry for each flavor."

Rustin grabbed his forehead. "Too much. Too cold."

Lila felt the same way. Too much Brody but not too cold. Much too hot. She rushed over to the counter and filled a pitcher with tap water, and took it back to the table with a stack of unbreakable glasses.

Filling a glass half full, she handed it to the child. "Drink this and it will get better real quick."

He tipped it up and swallowed several times before he set it down. "That's magic water." He grinned.

"I want magic," Emma declared.

"She can't let Rustin get a step ahead of her," Brody said in a low voice.

His whisper was every bit as sexy as his deep Texas

drawl. If a doctor could invent a pill to take care of that crazy infatuation called first love, he could sell it for a fortune and retire with enough money to buy a remote island.

Lila poured water into a glass and gave it to Emma. Brody reached into the diaper bag and brought out a sippy cup and handed it to her. She was careful not to touch his fingertips but that didn't keep the electricity between them from sparking. When was that doctor going to get busy and create those pills?

* * *

Brody kicked back in a booth where he could see Lila reading the second book to the kids. She was even more adorable sitting on the floor covered in kids than she'd been with that dollop of chocolate stuck to her lip a few minutes before. He'd wanted to lick it away with a kiss but—there always seemed to be a lot of buts in his roller coaster of relationships with Lila.

Rustin sat on one side, and Emma and Silas had both managed to crawl into her lap. Were all the men in the states where she'd lived total idiots?

His phone vibrated in his back pocket. His sister's picture appeared on the screen and he hit the button to answer. "We're on the second story, so we'll be home soon. Are you feeling better?"

"Are the kids behaving? Better yet, are you?" Kasey asked.

"We're all having a great time. They'll be full of sugar and want to tell you about it as soon as we get home," he said.

"Good. I'm going to lie right here on the sofa until you get here."

"Need anything?"

"Not a thing," Kasey said. "Tell Lila thank you."

He stole long glances at Lila. Those could be their three kids in her lap if he'd done the right thing that last night like he should have.

Silas crawled out of Lila's lap and toddled over to where Brody was sitting and raised his arms. Brody got out of the booth and took the little guy into his arms. Someday he was going to have a house full of kids just like these three. Kids who would snuggle down into his chest like this and a wife who was willing to sit on the floor and read to them like Lila did.

"I think it's getting close to bedtime for this little guy. We should be going. Rustin and Emma?"

"Thank you." Rustin threw his arms around Lila's neck. "I like it that you can be my friend too. When I'm a big cowboy, I'm going to dance with you."

"I'm going to remind you of that when you're a big cowboy." Lila grinned.

Brody was jealous of his nephew for putting that twinkle in her eyes. Granny Hope said that you can't fool kids or dogs. But Brody Dawson was living proof that idiot cowboys were a different matter.

Emma yawned. "Me and you can paint fingernails and chase butterflies."

"I'd like that." Lila hugged her. "Maybe next time your mama will feel better and can come with y'all."

Emma laid her head on Lila's shoulder. "You will sit by me at the rodeo."

"We've taken enough of Miss Lila's time, kids."

Brody offered his free hand to help Lila get to her feet.

To his surprise, she didn't shake her head but put her hand in his. "Thank you for bringing them. It's been a lovely evening."

Rustin craned his neck back to look up at her. "It's not a rodeo. It's a bull riding and Uncle Brody and Uncle Jace are going to ride in it. I'm goin' to win the sheep ridin'."

"I bet you will," Lila said. "Do you have sheep out on Hope Springs?"

"No, but Uncle Brody and Uncle Jace made me a ridin' thing that they pull the ropes and it tries to buck me off. I'll be ready," Rustin answered.

Brody threw the diaper bag over his shoulder and headed for the door. "Well, we have to get out of here or your mama will send all the hired hands out to look for us."

"So you're ridin'? When?" Lila asked.

"Tomorrow night but it's not a big thing. Just a bunch of us local guys havin' some fun and the admission fees all go to a family between here and Tulia who lost their home in a fire last week."

"And you clearly don't want me sittin' with Emma," she said.

"I don't care where you sit," he said. "If you do want to go, it's five dollars at the gate and there will be a few vendors selling stuff."

Lila took a step forward into his space. "Still don't want to be seen in public with me, do you?"

"I won't even be in the stands. I'll either be riding or helping out with the chutes," he argued. "And I'd say that the rose I sent would let everyone know that I didn't care what they thought."

"Thank you for the rose, but, Brody, this isn't my home. I'm just passing through for a few weeks to help my mama sell this place." She caught his gaze and refused to blink.

"You're very welcome, and..."

"No ifs, ands, or buts. That's the way it is," she said.

"I see. Well, thanks for having us." His tone turned cold.

Emma tugged the leg of Brody's jeans. "Are you fighting with my friend?"

"No, darlin'." Lila stooped down to her level. "We are havin' a big-people discussion, not a fight. You enjoy the rodeo and maybe in a couple of years you'll be in the mutton ride."

Emma puffed out her chest. "I will ride a bull."

"And I bet you'll be really good at it, Emma." Lila stood up. "Y'all sleep tight and have sweet dreams."

"Thanks for the ice cream." Brody hurried the kids out to the van and got them situated.

"I love Lila," Emma said.

"Me too. I'm goin' to dance with her," Rustin said. "You won't care, will you, Uncle Brody?"

"Why would you ask that?"

"Because Uncle Jace says you got to ask a cowboy for his okay before you dance with his woman," Rustin answered.

Brody looked back over the seat. "What makes you think that she's my woman?"

"If she ain't, then what's wrong with you?" Rustin threw up his hands in exasperation. "We love her and Mama says she's a good person."

"You're five years old, boy, not fifteen," Brody chuckled.

Rustin crossed his arms over his chest. "Well, do I have to ask if I can dance with her or not?"

"When you get to be a big cowboy, we'll talk about it then," Brody told him.

"Shhh, Silas is sleepin'." Emma shushed them.

He was about to start the engine when he heard a tap on the window. Turning, he saw that Lila was standing there in the shadows, looking like an angel. He hit the button to roll down the window.

"I wanted to thank you for that beautiful rose. I didn't thank you properly. I would have called but I don't have your number," she said.

"Are red roses still your favorite?" He removed an ink pen from the visor and reached for her hand.

Without a moment's hesitation, she stuck it out and he wrote his number down on her palm. "Call me anytime, night or day."

"Yes, red roses are my favorite. Probably always will be. Well, I'd better get back inside. I enjoyed the kids this evening. Thanks for bringing them." She turned around and went back to the café.

"I'll buy her roses," Rustin said.

"Me too," Emma said. "I'll buy more than you will."

"Will not!"

"Will too."

"That's enough or you'll both wake Silas." He started the engine and Vince Gill's voice came on the radio singing "Feels Like Love." Brody could relate to every single word, especially when the lyrics said that it felt like love wanted a second chance.

Kasey met them at the door when they got home. Her

eyes were still bleary and her face said that the pain wasn't completely gone but she had a smile on her face. "Did y'all have a good time?"

"Lila is goin' to be my girlfriend when I grow up," Rustin said.

"She's my friend and you can't have her," Emma declared.

"And you?" Kasey asked, glancing at her brother.

"It was good ice cream but I like your pumpkin pie better," he said. "How's the headache now?"

"Functional now that I had a couple of hours to lie down with an ice pack. Thanks for taking them. Would you please put Silas in his crib for me?"

Brody carried Silas to the bedroom and gently laid him in the crib. He removed the boy's sandals and handed them to Kasey.

"I bet he doesn't even wake up when I change his diaper and clothing," Kasey said.

"I'll do that while you get the other kids into bed."

"She rattles you, don't she?" Kasey whispered.

"Little bit," Brody said.

"Lila is going to sit with me at the rodeo," Emma said from the doorway.

"Well, that sounds like fun. Let's get you into bed and you can tell me which two books Lila read to you." Kasey took her hand and led her across the hallway.

Rustin had toothpaste on his lips when he came from the bathroom. He peeled out of his clothes and tossed them on a chair. "Mama says I have to wear a T-shirt to sleep but Uncle Jace sleeps naked. Do you have to wear a shirt, too, or do you get to sleep without no clothes?"

Brody chuckled. "We'll talk about that later on too."

Rustin sighed. "I got a lot of growin' to do."

"Yes, you do." Brody finished with Silas and tucked Rustin into bed. "But don't get in too big of a hurry, son. Once you're a big man, you can't go back and be a little one again."

"But bein' a big one looks like so much more fun." Rustin yawned.

"Not all the time." Brody kissed him on the forehead. "Good night, little cowboy."

"Night, Uncle Brody."

Back in the kitchen, he found Kasey with a cup of coffee in her hands.

"You sure you're all right? You don't usually drink caffeine this late."

"It helps with the headache. I don't get them often anymore but today is the anniversary of the first time that Adam kissed me. I guess I thought too much about losing him."

He opened his arms. "I'm so sorry that you have to go through this, sis."

She set the cup on the cabinet and walked into his embrace. "It helps to be here at home with y'all. The kids have grandparents and relatives. It's just that letting go is so hard. Now, what's this about Lila sitting with us at the bull riding?"

He raked both hands through his hair. "I sent her a rose this week, but she made it clear she's not sticking around Happy for the long haul. Why start something that will just cause both of us to get hurt again?"

"Do you have any idea what I'd give to have Adam sitting beside me at that bull riding? I'd use every bit of my strength to talk him into getting out of the army and staying in Happy and going into the ranchin' business with his dad. I'd do anything to keep him with me, even live in a tent under a pecan tree with no indoor plumbing. You've got an opportunity here, brother, that might not come your way again." She laid her head on his shoulder and sobbed.

His heart broke for her and at the same time for Lila. He couldn't bear to see her hurt again, and if she went to sit with Emma...well, it could be a damn disaster. Little Emma was already going to be sad when Lila left. Getting even closer to the woman would make it tougher.

Who are you preachin' at? Emma or yourself? that aggravating voice in his head asked.

Kasey took a few steps back and carried her coffee to the table. "The whole time I was growing up, Lila was my idol because she was such a daredevil. I didn't want to be like her. I wanted to be her. And for your information, that crap about her burning down the old grocery store is just that—a load of crap. The fire department said someone probably threw a cigarette out because they could see a trail from the road to the building."

"I didn't think that she burned down anything. I'm going out for a ride to clear my mind."

"Get over her, Brody, or man up and do something about the way you feel." Kasey swiped a kitchen towel across her eyes.

His brow furrowed so tight that a pain shot through his head. "I got over Lila Harris years ago."

"Yeah, right," Kasey said. "Like I got over losing Adam."

"I'm not having this conversation with you, sis." He

snapped his mouth shut and left her in the kitchen with a cup of coffee and a headache.

*   *   *

Brody peeled the T-shirt over his head and grabbed his last clean pearl-snapped one from the closet. In no time he was back in his truck, heading north to the Silver Spur and hoping that it was jumping with noise and excitement—anything to take his mind off the picture in his mind of Lila sitting on the floor reading to three little kids.

Two miles out of town he took his foot off the gas and tapped the brakes. He pulled off to the side of the road and sat there for several minutes before he turned around and went back home. He drove straight to the corral where Sundance was kept and sat down on the ground, bracing his back against a fence post. The bull eyed him from across the corral but stayed his distance.

"I've messed up again, old boy," Brody said. "It was all goin' good until the kids mentioned the bull riding. I've been going by every day so that she can see I'm keeping my word when I tell her that I'll see her tomorrow. Lila is so different from other women that I think fate or God or destiny is hitting me in the head with a two-by-four and yet I keep thinking about my responsibility for this ranch. I have to make it grow. I have to leave it bigger than it was when it was put in my hands. Lila doesn't need a man who is already married to a ranch. I work most days from daylight to past dark. She deserves someone better than that."

Sundance bawled once at the moon and stuck his head into the water trough.

"That all you got to say? Well, this ranch pays for your comforts, so you can listen to me," Brody said. "I don't like this feeling, so I'm going home. Thanks for the therapy session."

The bull snorted and turned his back on Brody.

Chapter Seven

Lila stopped by the rodeo's concession stand and bought a big dill pickle, an order of nachos, and a bottle of root beer. The bottle went into her purse and the pickle in the side of the cardboard container with the nachos. That way she could make it to the top of the stands without dropping anything. She was halfway when she saw the Dawson family all sitting with the grand matriarch, Hope Dalley, down at the other end of the rough wooden bleachers. She kept going until she was at the very top and sat down on the end of the empty row.

Dust boiled in the arena as the first cowboy lasted all of three seconds on a big bruiser of a bull. The clowns in all their bright, outlandish costumes hurried out to lure the bull away from him so the cowboy could get up, take a bow to the folks in the stand, and swagger back to the chutes.

A chip covered with cheese and jalapeños was halfway to her mouth when she saw Brody's tall figure disappear down into the chute. The chip fell from her hands, splattering on the toes of her boots, but she didn't even look down. Her breath caught in her chest, tightening it into a dull ache.

When she decided to attend the bull riding, the last thing she expected was such an explosion of emotions rattling around in her heart and soul.

"Devil Dog is a tough bull to ride, and Daniel has only been riding six months, so let's give him another big hand." The announcer's booming voice filled the place. "Better luck next time, Daniel. You've got the makings of a fine bull rider. And now coming out of chute two is Brody Dawson riding Barbed Wire, a young bull destined for great things. Brody is no stranger to riding bulls. He's been doing it since he was in high school. He is the co-owner now of Hope Springs Ranch right here in Happy, Texas. He's testing the rope and getting his hat set just right and..." The announcer paused and all noise stopped. Then he yelled, "The chute is open!"

Yelling and whistling began the minute that the bull came out with both hind feet in the air. Barbed Wire twisted around until his head was practically touching his tail and then he whipped back around, almost putting his big wide horns on the ground. Two seconds down, six to go when Lila clasped her hands together so tightly that they hurt.

Brody kept one hand in the air but his straw hat flew off after the first two seconds and the bull stomped it into the dirt. Four seconds, halfway through the ride. Lila wanted to shut her eyes but she couldn't.

Six seconds into the ride, Brody went flying over the top of Barbed Wire's head and landed on his side. She jumped to her feet so fast that the rest of her nachos went flying everywhere. *Please, God, let him get up.*

He quickly scrambled to his feet and she plopped down with a thud. Then she realized that the bull was right behind him. She was back on her feet, mouth open but no words came out. The noise in the stands sounded as if it were a mile away. The bull got closer and closer. Lila's racing pulse thumped in her ears, blotting out the whoops and hollers from the crowd cheering him on. Then Brody slapped one hand down on the top fence rail and cleared it in a graceful jump. She let out the pent-up air in her lungs in a long whoosh.

One of the clowns grabbed Brody's hat and made a big show of popping it back into some kind of shape. Another one stole it from him and ran toward the fence. On the way the third one snatched it and took it straight to Brody, who settled it on his head and took a bow to his screaming fans.

With her heart doing double time and the only one in the whole stands still on her feet, she lost sight of him as he rounded the arena and headed toward the chutes. The announcer was introducing the next rider when she finally slumped back down into her seat. The next rider came out and it was an exciting eight seconds, but it didn't produce nearly the adrenaline rush of Brody's ride.

*   *   *

When Brody reached the chutes, Jace handed him a cold beer. He rubbed it across his forehead before he washed the dirt from between his teeth with a long swallow. "That Barbed Wire is one mean hunk of bull."

"But he could help a rider rack up the points. He's pure evil," Jace said.

"So when is it your turn?" Brody asked.

"Last one on the docket. They're saving the best until last," Jace teased. "Lila is in the stands."

"When did she get here?" Brody located his family. There was Emma in her pink cowboy hat and Rustin pointing at the clowns but no Lila. His eyes swept the stands a section at a time until he located her at the very top.

"She saw you ride, if that's what you're askin'." Jace grinned. "Now she knows you aren't perfect."

"She's known that for years," Brody said.

"Yeah, right." Jace air slapped Brody on the arm. "All I've heard since this morning from Rustin and Emma is Lila's name. I heard about the ice cream and the reading but mostly they talked about how they wished she lived on the ranch with them."

"She was really good with the kids last night." Brody nodded.

Jace nodded. "I'd better warn you. Granny was not happy about you taking the kids to the café. She didn't mind if Kasey did, but not you."

"I'm thirty years old and both Granny and Mama can mind their own business and let me take care of mine," Brody growled.

"I hear you and so do they, but they don't believe it like I do. Granny told Kasey that the two of you were going to have a long talk," Jace told him.

"Please tell me you're kiddin'," Brody moaned.

"Wish I was but she said she was coming to our house tonight right after the riding. You might want to offer to do a second ride so you'll have an excuse to soak the soreness out of your muscles until she gets bored and goes on to her house," Jace said.

"I'll give you a hundred dollars for your ride. You can say that you decided to get into your clown gear and help the guys out," Brody said.

Jace laughed. "If you got hurt, she'd sit beside your hospital bed all night. You've always been her favorite."

Brody swiped sweat from his forehead with his palm. "I'd thought about going to sit with the family after my ride, but I think I'll stay down here and help with the chutes. And I'm not her favorite. I was just the firstborn, so she's had a little longer to smother me."

"No gripe from me. I'll let you be the favorite because you have to endure the consequences. And you're welcome for the warning, brother."

Brody clamped a hand on his brother's shoulder. "Thanks."

Jace handed him a second can of beer. "Anytime. We learned a long time ago when it comes to Granny's meddling that we have to stick together."

Brody found an old metal folding chair behind a chute and popped it open. He sat down and propped his boots on the rails of the chute where Barbed Wire was still penned up.

"Don't you snort around at me. You won that battle, but this isn't the last time we'll cross paths this summer, and next time I'll win." Brody raised his can toward the bull.

He could see Lila at the top of the stands all alone.

She was sipping on either a bottle of pop or a beer. When she finished, she got to her feet and started down toward the concession stand. A couple of cowboys stopped her, their body language saying clearly that they were hitting on her and hers leaving no doubt that they'd been refused. She waited in line at the concession and exchanged a few words with a couple of women, using her hands as she talked to them like she'd done back in high school. He remembered telling her once that if he tied her hands behind her back she wouldn't be able to say a word.

She bought something at the concession stand and then headed off toward the gate. He pushed out of the chair and leaned on a rail so he could watch her disappear into the darkness.

*   *   *

Lila set the nachos on the passenger seat in her truck beside two cans of cat food. She'd thought she'd pass plumb out when Brody hit the dirt, but the next two riders, though exciting, didn't affect her like those six seconds had when she'd watched Brody try to hang on to the rope. When her heart finally slowed down, it was time to go on the mission that she'd planned after the bull ride. One would involve being a Good Samaritan and giving a black and white cat a good home. The other would mean she was blowing the bottom out of that commandment about stealing because she wasn't going home without a cat.

She drove to the cemetery and parked in front of her father's grave. "Daddy, I want something to talk to and to cuddle with me while I watch television at night. If you've got any connections with a cat whisperer up there—" She tilted her head back to get a better view of the full moon and stars. "You might tell that homeless critter to show his face or else I'm going out to Henry's old barn and I'm stealing that big white cat. You going to keep me on the straight and narrow or let me fall back into my wild ways?"

She got out of the truck, pulled the tab from the top of the can, set it on the ground, and propped a hip on her father's tombstone. Eating a few of the nachos while she waited, she saw the black and white cat slink out from behind a floral wreath not far away. He sniffed the air and warily made his way to the cat food. Careful not to make a fast move and scare him off, she set the nachos to the side and, speaking in a calm voice, took a step toward the cat.

When she was two feet away, he took one more bite and was nothing more than a blur as he took off into the darkness. She slapped her thigh. "I tried to do it the right way, so I don't think I should be punished for stealing. Besides, Paul might not even know that cat is in his barn. I might be doing him a favor."

Carrying her food back to the truck, she frowned at the stars. She started the engine and drove straight to Henry's old barn. She parked the truck and made her way across the floor—nachos and cat food in a wooden crate in her arms.

"I'm here to get a cat and I'm not leaving without one," she muttered as she sat down on a hay bale, opened the can of food, and dumped it into an old pie pan she'd brought from the café.

She chewed on nachos as she waited. The white cat came out first but it wasn't long before she was surrounded by four kittens. Two black ones, a white one, and a yellow one with four white feet. Lila captured one of the black ones by the scruff of the neck. It clawed and growled, slinging its paws all the way to the crate. In the commotion, the mama cat and two of the other kittens skittered off to hide behind a bale of hay. But the fearless white kitten kept right on eating.

"And you will keep Mr. Feisty here from whining because he has no one to play with." She scooped it up and put it in the crate with the black one and they howled out their anger together. "You'll have a good home and lots of food and I'll pet you every single day. Hawks won't swoop down and carry you away, so stop your belly-achin'."

The big mama cat came back out after a bit and rubbed around her legs. "Good thing those babies came out with you. I'd feel terrible if I took you away from them when they were too young. Are you thanking me for giving them a good home? Well, you're welcome. Now I have something to talk to other than a broom, so thank you, mama cat, for letting me adopt two of your babies."

She put her nacho trash on the top of the crate, and carried the whole thing to the truck, where she set it on the passenger seat. She had driven down to Tulia right after work and bought litter, a pan to put it in, and a dozen cans of cat food. The kittens were going to love their new home once they got used to it. And she'd be willing to bet that Paul would be glad to get rid of the kittens. But to be on the safe side and not get into trouble with that business of thou shalt not steal, she would ask him the next time he came into the café.

Her phone rang as she turned the key to start the engine and she dug around in her purse until she found it. "Hello, Mama. I wasn't expecting a call from you tonight."

"You're in Texas and for the first time in years, I'm homesick. Where are you right now?"

"Out at Henry Thomas's old barn stealing kittens. Paul McKay leases this place and I don't reckon he'll mind. He probably doesn't even know how many there are," she answered.

Daisy gasped. "I was afraid when you crossed the Texas border you'd get crazy."

"It's just kittens. I didn't set fire to anything or borrow a tractor or..."

"Delilah Harris." Daisy's voice went all whispery like it did when Lila was in trouble.

"Would you rather I adopted two children?"

"I definitely would not!" Daisy's voice jacked up an octave. "It's an omen that I got homesick today. Fate is telling me that you need me. I should take the café off the market and move back to Texas."

"I'm doing all right now that I've got something to talk to that breathes and even meows once in a while," Lila said. "Hey, I even went to church last Sunday and Molly says I have to go tomorrow. She's keeping me pretty straight and very busy. So be sure you want to make a drastic move before you talk to Aunt Tina. And remember, Mama, it's hotter'n hell in Texas in the summertime."

"You can't tell me anything about the panhandle of Texas that I don't already know. But it's either sweatin' in

Texas or suffering through butt-deep snow here in Pennsylvania. I can get cool with air-conditioning in Texas."

"But that danged old northern cold can cut right to the bone, can't it?" Lila said.

"Promise me you won't steal anything else."

"I promise, but I'm not giving my word about skinny-dippin' out at Hope Springs."

"Sweet angels in heaven!" Daisy shrieked. "I was right. Texas brings out that wild streak in you."

"Yep, the minute I crossed the line I got the urge to steal something, go skinny-dippin', and make out with Brody Dawson in Henry Thomas's old barn. Blame it on Texas," she laughed.

"I'm not having this conversation with you. Tell me about those cats."

"One is pure white with a little yellow spot on its head and the other is black as sin. Want to help me name them?"

"I do not," Daisy said emphatically. "I'm not going to contribute to your crime spree."

Lila laughed harder that time. "If they throw me in jail for thievery, will you bail me out?"

"No, but I will feed the kittens for you until you serve your time. I'll be glad when you're back in Florida this fall. Now good night," Daisy said.

"Good night, Mama."

*   *   *

Granny Hope showed up in the kitchen before Brody took the first bite of the chocolate cake he'd put on his plate. She cut out a slab of cake that came close to being too big for the dessert plate and brought the gallon jug of milk with her to the table.

"We need to talk," she said to Brody.

"About?"

"You already know but I'll say it out loud. Lila Harris."

"You talk and I'll listen," he said.

"Have you ever heard the history of Hope Springs?"

"I can recite it to you."

She lowered her chin and looked at him from under arched gray eyebrows. "Don't be a smartass. It don't hurt you to hear a little of this again. You know that I was the fourth-generation owner of Hope Springs. I've been pleased with the way you're doin' things since I turned the place over to you. You and Jace are doin' a great job."

He nodded as respectfully as possible and bit back a yawn.

Hope stopped long enough to take a few bites of cake and drink half a glass of milk. "Since you know the story about my great-grandparents helping get this area settled, I'll skip that part. At the same time Hope Springs was coming into its own as a reputable ranch, the Dawsons were doing really well with their ranches on down the road toward the canyon."

Brody poured another glass of milk. A history lesson was better than a scolding, but so far she had not mentioned Lila, so that might still be on the agenda.

"The rest of what I'm going to say is in confidence. That means it doesn't go any farther than this kitchen. Agree?"

He nodded. She had his full attention.

"The ranch had a reputation to uphold by then. So as the only heir, I had a lot to learn and a tremendous amount of responsibility upon my shoulders. It was a big place by then and I couldn't let my folks down."

Brody had never seen his grandmother flustered. She took the bull by the horns, spit in its face, and dared it to come after her. But that night her eyes kept shifting from one corner of the kitchen to the other.

"It's not easy letting go of the control. I was so tired of making decisions that I thought it would be good to step back and turn it all over to you boys. But I was wrong. I miss the work and all of it," she said.

Scenarios played through Brody's mind at warp speed. In the foremost one his grandmother was about to change her mind about the ranch.

"I feel like a duck in a desert. No water in sight and I can't swim in sand."

He patted her arm. "Sometimes I feel like that, too, and that's when I call you and ask for your advice. You're always going to be needed, Granny. We're all taking baby steps in this whole transfer and we're glad that you decided to stay in Cooter's place so you're nearby. I'm not sure Kasey could handle the load without you to help."

"Thank you, darlin' boy, but that's not the point I'm trying to make. I'm not sure that I can put it into words, and I'm past seventy years old. Your grandpa has been gone a dozen years and without work from daylight to past dark, I'm lonely."

"Granny, do you have a boyfriend?" Brody whispered.

"Good God, no!" she gasped. "I'm tryin' to put my feelin's into words and explain to you how I felt tonight at that bull riding. But in order to do it, I have to say some things I've never told anyone."

"I'm listening." He covered both her hands with his and squeezed gently.

"I was twenty years old the year that Dad hired a new foreman. He came from over near Clovis, New Mexico, and his name was Weston Dalley."

"Grandpa, right?" Brody asked.

"That's right. Wes was twenty-five, a good man and a fine manager. My dad loved him like the son he'd never had." Her eyes misted slightly.

"And so did you evidently," Brody said.

She took a deep breath and let it out slowly. "I did love your grandpa. Don't ever doubt that for a minute. But..." She paused.

"But?" Gramps had been Brody's idol. He didn't want there to be a *but* anywhere in his life or in his relationship with Granny.

"But he was not my first love." She met his gaze and her eyes floated in tears. "Wes was a good man."

She didn't have to convince Brody of that. Wes Dalley was well respected in the whole area and he loved his entire family. In Brody's eyes he was more than just a good man—he could walk on water.

"I've never told anyone this before and I expect you to keep it to yourself."

Brody swallowed hard and nodded in agreement.

"I had an argument with the man I loved. Over Wes. In a fit of anger, this other guy joined the service and I turned to Wes for comfort. We were married six months later, and Daddy built the north wing onto the house for us to live in. Mama had come down with her illness by then and someone needed to be here all the time. We had your mother that next year."

"And the first love?" he asked.

"He spent more than twenty years in the service, came back to Happy to take care of his parents, and then left when they died," she said. "The point of this whole story is to tell you that I had a responsibility to the ranch. My first love hated ranching. He was a dreamer with no roots. I did the right thing by marrying your grandfather."

"Do I hear another *but*?" Brody asked.

Her eyes met his. "I always wondered what my life would have been like with him, and there was a little part of my heart that Wes never had because of him. Now remember that when I go on to the rest of my story."

"Lila?" Brody yawned.

Hope inhaled deeply and let it out in a gush. "Always in a hurry. It comes from all that instant gratification you kids have with technology. I knew when you were born I was going to leave Hope Springs to you when you were old enough to take the reins."

"What about Jace? Right now you've given it to both of us."

"But when he gets ready to settle down or if Valerie decides to step down from runnin' the ranch, he will inherit Prairie Rose and this one will be yours alone. Lila Harris is your first love, right?"

"Can I answer? You told me to be quiet."

"Just nod."

He did.

"I saw her at the bull riding tonight. She sat at the top of the stands all alone. I watched her actions without her even knowing it. Emma talks about her all the time and Rustin thinks she flat out hung the moon. I hear that Silas went right to her when y'all went for ice cream last night."

He nodded again.

"I stand by my reasoning back when you and Lila were teenagers. She was wild and I could see that you would mess up your life if you got involved with her at eighteen."

"And?" Brody asked.

"I could feel what she was experiencing tonight. Neither Wes nor my first love rode bulls but when you came out of the chute, I was experiencing that rush that I used to get when I was sneaking off to see—" She stopped before she said his name.

"Sneaking?" Brody's eyes widened.

"Dad didn't think he was good enough for me. Like I said, he was a dreamer, not a rancher, and I had a lot of responsibility toward Hope Springs. Back to what I was trying to say—she had eyes for no one else tonight and almost fainted when the bull was chasing you. She left before the rides were finished. I know that feeling that she had, and I expect your heart reacts the same way when you're around her, right?"

Another nod.

"Then it's time to see if there's enough left for another chance or to get over her," Hope said.

"Was it worth losing your first love for this place?" Brody asked.

"At this point in life, I can say yes, it was," she answered. "If I'd done what my heart wanted instead of what my mind knew was the right course, you wouldn't be sitting here having this conversation with me."

A long, heavy pause hung over the room like dust at the rodeo arena.

"You're thirty years old and so is Lila. You have a chance that I never had. You cannot re-create the past. It's gone and done with. Decisions made. Consequences paid. But if you see something in that woman, then you have the opportunity to see if there is a future there," she said.

Brody almost fell out of his chair. "You aren't against me seeing her?"

"You're a grown man and you had a lot of responsibility laid on your shoulders when your grandpa and daddy both died that summer. I'm proud of you, Brody."

"You didn't answer my question," he said.

Hope inhaled and pulled her hands free. "Always in a hurry. That's your decision. Lila is a responsible woman with a pretty good head on her shoulders from what I've found out since she came back to Happy. I knew that wild girl but I don't know the woman Lila. Take my advice and either get her out of your system while she is here or else do something about the attraction. It's time for you to have a child so Hope Springs can live on through another generation. This summer needs to tell the story of who the mother of that child will be."

"Again, Jace?" he asked.

"I told you. He will inherit your folks' place when Valerie steps down like I did, probably in the next couple of years at the most, and he will sign Hope Springs over to you and move back down the road to Prairie Rose," Hope said. "And that is the confidential part."

"And Kasey?"

"We'll cross that bridge when the time comes. Now it's well past my bedtime and you need to get a shower. You've got dirt in your hair and behind your ears."

"Yes, ma'am." He grinned.

She covered a yawn with her hand. "Good talk, as you kids say today."

"It was and thank you, Granny," he said.

"But," she whispered, "let Jace think I gave you a hard time. It keeps up my image."

"You got it. I'll take care of the cleanup here and see you in the morning," he said.

"Bright and early. Ranchin' starts with daylight and ends when there's not enough light to see anymore."

"Amen." Brody rose to his feet and kissed his grandmother on the forehead. "Sweet dreams."

Hope stopped at the door and turned around. "Your mama has never forgiven Lila's mama for trying to get between her and Mitch Dawson when they were in high school, so you might not get off so easy with her. But that's not my business so you're on your own there."

Chapter Eight

Lila hated the church social, where everyone who had ever preached at the church, had ever attended, or who had even lived in Happy was invited back for a reunion of sorts. More than once in her younger years she'd faked sickness in an attempt to get out of going but it never worked. Molly insisted that they were going to close the café just like always and go to morning services and then to the social.

"No buts about it," Molly said seriously as they prepared for the breakfast run that morning. "Your mama started the tradition when she managed this place and we ain't changed it."

"I'm not going. I've got two kittens I have to take care of today. They're in new surroundings and I need to spend time with them," Lila said.

"You'll be home all evening to do that." Molly slid another pan of chicken and dressing into the oven to warm.

"You can tell them cats bedtime stories and rock them to sleep."

"Okay," Lila sighed. "I'll rush back to my apartment and get a shower right after we close."

"Good! Glad that the spiritual light finally showed through into your soul." Molly slapped a thick slice of ham on the grill for the next breakfast order.

Molly was a tyrant. Lila loved her and appreciated her staying on at the café until she could get the place sold, but good grief, Molly was the same to her as Hope was to Brody. They both had a grandmother figure who was doing their dead level best to make their lives miserable.

"If I didn't love you like my own kid, I wouldn't tell you what to do. You can ride with me."

*   *   *

It was less than a mile to the church and Molly parked as close to the back door as she could so she could unload the food. The kitchen was empty but four tables were laden with covered dishes. Space had been left at the end of the first table for Molly's four large pans. When they were situated to suit her, she pointed toward the door leading from there to the sanctuary.

"You go on in and get settled. I'll be there soon as I make a stop in the restroom."

Lila nodded and headed toward the sound of "I'll Fly Away." Well, now, that was a fitting song to hear since she would have rather been appreciating the handiwork of God while riding her bike down in the canyon rather than in a packed church that morning. Flying away to anywhere sounded better than sitting on a hard oak pew.

She found the song in the hymnal and sang the last verse along with everyone else. The choir director stepped aside and the preacher took his place behind the pulpit. Feet shuffled, folks whispered to children to settle down, a few old men cleared their throats, and a couple of Amens floated out over the church.

The preacher had just read the scripture when Molly took her place beside Lila. "Good timin'. I won't miss the sermon." Molly set her purse and Lila's on the floor. "I brought your purse. You left it in the kitchen."

"Thank you," she whispered.

The preacher said something about sin being in many forms and then hesitated. It was during that pregnant pause that the phone in her purse started playing an old tune, "Heaven's Just a Sin Away." She'd turned the volume as high as it would go earlier that day because she expected a call from her mother. In the quiet church, it sounded like it was coming from a concert stage.

Some folks tried to part the back of her hair with dirty looks; others giggled. She blushed scarlet and grabbed her purse, plopped it down on the seat between her and Molly, and started digging for the phone. It stopped before she could get a grip on it and she set the purse on the floor again.

"Like I said..." The preacher's booming voice reached to the back of the room. But then Lila's phone started again, as if trying to help him prove the point. She grabbed the purse and, thinking she had both handles, jumped up to get out of the building. Blushing crimson, she stepped out into the center aisle, hit the lopsided purse on the edge of the pew, and sent everything in it flying everywhere. She dropped to her knees and started gathering it all up, snatching the phone first, but it slipped from her hands and skittered under the pew right beside her.

Valerie Dawson's high heel hit the thing and sent it back another pew. Lila was ready to crawl in that direction when Brody left his seat, knelt in front of her, and helped her get everything put back in place. Her face burned like fire with embarrassment when Rustin crawled out from under a pew and handed the phone to Brody. It had stopped ringing but every eye in the entire congregation was on them. Some would even have kinks in their necks tomorrow from trying to see around other folks. The buzz of whispers filled the place as Brody handed it to her.

"As I was saying," the preacher cleared his throat, "sin comes in many forms."

"Guess he don't recognize your music or he'd know you were agreeing with him," Brody whispered as he extended a hand to help her and made sure she was seated before he returned to his own pew.

The preacher went into a long-winded explanation about sin and Lila sent a text to her mother: *Church. Annual social.*

She immediately got one back: *OMG! So sorry!*

"Why in the world do you have that song on your phone?" Molly said out the side of her mouth.

"Mama always liked it," she answered.

"Well, thank God she didn't call during benediction," Molly said.

Lila should have set her foot down and refused to go to church that morning. This whole thing was one big omen telling her that she did not belong here. She'd smooth things over with Brody to ease the anxiety in her heart and then she wasn't doing one thing but working and talking to her cats. No more church, not even if Molly did quit.

The little church was so full there wasn't room to cuss a cat without getting a mouthful of hair. Paul McKay's wife, Gracie, a short, round woman with a bouffant hairdo and enough perfume to douse down the whole church, was on the other side of Molly and then there was her husband and another couple beyond that.

Lila felt someone staring at her, so she took a quick look over her shoulder and right into Brody's sexy blue eyes. He winked slyly and she started to whip around but caught Valerie Dawson glaring at her. After the morning she'd had, she wasn't going to let that woman intimidate her, so she slowly slid one eyelid shut. Valerie's jerky body language said that she was totally offended.

Tall, dark haired, and slim built, Valerie had always had a no-nonsense way about her that reminded Lila of those old tintype photographs—the ones where the woman looks like she could cut steel with her eyes and would shoot first and ask questions later. Lila straightened her back and smiled. Valerie's cold eyes piercing her head like a bullet didn't matter. She'd lived through the embarrassment and Brody had helped her right out in public, even though they hadn't parted on good terms. And now that she'd had time to settle down, she thought the whole episode was humorous. She couldn't wait to tell her mother about it.

The sermon seemed to last an eternity. She bit back a sigh when the preacher finally asked Paul to deliver the benediction. There was a little more room on the pew when he stood to his feet, bowed his head, and gave thanks for everything from the beautiful day to the folks who'd come from afar to attend the social. Lila began to think that the whole congregation was going to die of starvation before Paul wound down and said, "Amen."

But finally he got around to thanking God for the food they were about to eat in the kitchen and for the hands that had prepared it and said the magic word that made everyone in the church pop to their feet.

"Hey." Gracie McKay reached out a hand toward Lila the second they were standing. "So is it true? You going to sell the café since Georgia retired? We are going to miss Molly so much in the Ladies' Circle here at the church," Gracie said.

"Yes, ma'am, the Happy Café is for sale. If you know anyone who might be interested, just give them the phone number." Lila nodded.

"Well, good luck, darlin'. Much as we love havin' a café in town, folks around here ain't got two pennies to rub together and those who ain't from here don't want to be," Gracie said.

"Ain't it the truth," Molly agreed. "Let's sneak out the back door and go straight to the kitchen. That way we don't have to stand in line. I'll shake the preacher's hand before we leave."

Lila followed the two older women out of the sanctuary and down a short hallway to the kitchen. When they arrived, the place was already bustling with women taking covers off the dishes and getting things ready for the dinner.

Molly grabbed her arm and led her to the far end of the tables. "You can help Valerie cut cakes and pies and get them ready to serve."

God hates me for sure. She should have listened to

the sermon and she dang sure should not have winked at Valerie Dawson. This was her punishment for both infractions right there in the church.

"I'd rather help with the chicken and dressing and roast," Lila said.

"Nonsense!" Molly protested. "Gracie and I have taken care of this job for years. You go on and help out with desserts." Molly lowered her voice to a whisper. "Face your enemies head-on. Don't run from them."

"She's not my enemy," Lila protested.

"Yeah, right."

Gracie nudged Lila on the arm as she passed by her. "You know what they say about the social?"

"What?" Lila asked.

"That if you ever help serve at one, you'll be serving at them until you die," she answered.

Lila sighed and went to the other end of the food line.

Valerie handed her a knife. "You can cut the pecan pies. Make them into six slices each," she said with ice dripping from her tone.

Was the woman certifiably goofy, handing her a knife? Evidently she did not value her life one bit.

She leaned in close to Lila and whispered, "I don't like this any better than you do but we will be civil while we are in church. Understood?"

"Mrs. Dawson, this is such a treat to get to work with you. I haven't got to see you since I've been back in town," Lila said in a voice made of pure sugar. "We can use this time to catch up. So how are things on Prairie Rose? I was so sorry to hear about Mitch's passing."

"Sarcasm will get you nowhere with me," Valerie said from the corner of a pasted-on smile.

"And threatening me won't get you anywhere," Lila said.

"I hear that you aren't stickin' around after the summer?"

"One never knows what might happen by the end of August," Lila answered.

Brody pushed through the back door and yelled from across the room, "Miz Molly, I'm here to carry tables out under the shade trees. How many do you think we'll need?"

"Eight," Gracie yelled. "We used ten last year and two weren't used. Old folks like to sit in the cool to eat, so we've already got two extra ready in here."

Brody's biceps strained against his plaid shirt when he had a folding table under each arm but he stopped dead when he saw his mother and Lila side by side.

"Great to see you here, Lila," he said from across the room.

"Thank you," she muttered.

"Guess I'd best get busy or Molly will fire me." He grinned.

"She's pretty tough on the hired help." Lila smiled back as she eyeballed the three exits. One at the back, one at the side, and the last one through the kitchen. Any one of them would provide a good escape as soon as dinner was over.

*   *   *

Jace met Brody midway across the church lawn and relieved him of one of the tables. "What happened with Granny last night?"

"It didn't go like I figured it would."

"Really?" Jace's dark brows shot up.

"Nope. She was pretty calm and she didn't threaten to disown me. She says I'm thirty years old and it's time for me to settle down but whoever I want to do that with is my decision. She did say that Mama would have a different notion because Lila's mother tried to get between Dad and Mama when they were dating. And I'm supposed to tell you that she came down on me real hard so she won't lose face, so that's confidential."

"Small towns!" Jace said. "I love Happy but there's a part of me that wishes it was so big that everyone didn't know everyone else."

"And who they did and where it was." Brody nodded seriously. "Mama and Lila are in there working together."

Jace's eyes widened and he sat down hard on a chair. "How in the devil did that happen?"

Brody shrugged. "I don't think either of them would ask to cut cakes and pies together. Molly probably has something to do with it."

"Holy hell! They both have knives?" Jace asked.

Brody nodded and sat down beside his brother. "There's a chill in the room that ain't got a thing to do with the air-conditioning."

Kasey pushed a baby stroller in between them and slung an arm over each of their shoulders. "Have y'all seen Rustin? If I don't watch him, he'll get a plate full of desserts and nothing else."

Emma came running and tugged on Kasey's hand. "Mama, Rustin is with Grandpa Paul and I'm hungry to death."

Brody stooped down to Emma's level to hug her.

"Then we'd better get on over to the door and get in line if you're that hungry. What are you going to eat today?"

"Chocolate cake and cookies." She beamed. "And so is Rustin."

"And chicken?" Brody stood up.

She frowned and nodded at the same time. "No Russell sprouts. They are nasty."

"I agree." Brody took her hand and started toward the building where the people were starting to line up.

"Mama and Lila were cutting cakes together," Jace whispered to his sister.

"Sweet Jesus!" Kasey looked over her shoulder at Brody.

His wide shoulders raised slightly. "Mama needs to get over it."

"Y'all need to go first." Paul took the stroller from Kasey and led them all to the front of the line. "And don't worry, Kasey. I'll see to it that Rustin eats more than chocolate. Oh, and did Gracie tell you guys?" He handed the stroller back to her. "Y'all are taking care of the bouncy house right after we eat. You might need one more person to help out, though."

"Why's that?" Jace asked.

"Not me." Kasey shook her head. "I've got my hands full with my own brood."

"I'll watch after Rustin," Paul offered. "I bet Valerie will take care of Silas so you can take care of Emma."

"Grandpa, don't make me eat those old nasty green beans that's got white stuff in them." Rustin wrinkled his nose.

"I won't if you'll eat all your fried chicken and potato salad." Paul grinned at Kasey.

"I'll even eat baked beans," Rustin said seriously.

Molly threw open the double doors into the fellowship hall and folks flowed inside, laughing, talking, and getting into a line behind the Dawsons.

"Lila!" Emma yelled so loud that everyone in the place turned around and silence filled the room. "Mama, I want Lila to help me. She won't make me eat Russell sprouts."

Brody's mouth went dry at the sight of her crossing the room. Her hips swayed, swishing that skirt about her legs. Her eyes were all soft and dreamy as she zeroed in on Emma.

"I'd love to help," Lila said, and slipped in between the stroller and Brody. "What does Emma want for dinner?"

"No Brussels sprouts," Brody whispered.

"I understood that much." Lila smiled.

She filled a plate for Emma and let her pick out the table where she wanted to sit and was back around the table by the time Brody reached the dessert end of the tables.

"Pecan pie, right?" she said, and heard someone say her name right behind her.

"What?"

"Brody said that he and Jace need a third person to help with the bouncy house. I just volunteered you." Molly set a pumpkin pie on the dessert table. "She loves kids."

"Thanks, Lila." Brody flashed a smile her way. "And yes, ma'am, I do want a slice of Mama's pecan pie."

Closed inside a bouncy house with Lila—now that's what Brody called a stroke of fate. He felt as if he were floating on air as he carried his plate to the table where Kasey and the rest of the family were sitting.

* * *

Lila cornered Molly as she headed back to the kitchen. "Why did you do that? You fuss every time his name is even mentioned and now you're putting me right with him?"

"If I didn't, folks would think y'all was carryin' on in secret, especially after the looks that was goin' on between the two of you in church this mornin'. This way they'll know there is nothing between you," Molly whispered. "Go on and fix your plate since you're going to help out with the kids." Molly gave her a quick hug. "I told your mama I'd watch out for you and I know what I'm doin'."

Lila had planned to sit in the kitchen when she'd gotten her food but Brody had come back to get a plate of hot rolls for the folks at his table. "We've got an empty chair at our table. Emma would love it if you'd come sit with us."

"No!" Molly hissed at her elbow. "That's going too far."

"I'd be glad to. Save me a seat and I'll be right there," Lila said.

"You're going to be the death of me," Molly groaned.

"Don't die this week. My black dress is a little snug."

She inhaled deeply and made her knees take her across the floor to sit with the Dawson family. Kasey was smiling. Jace and Hope were both leaning forward to look at Valerie.

Emma waved and yelled out, "My friend Lila! Look, Mama. She's goin' to sit with me."

"Hello, Emma," Lila said as she sank into the chair that Brody held for her.

Then he sat down right beside her. "Lila is going to help us in the bouncy house."

"I saved you this seat," Emma said.

"Well, thank you." Lila's knee brushed against Brody's under the table. "So sorry, Brody."

"No problem." He grinned.

Yes, there was a problem. Every time she was around him, that inner wild child begged to be released. She'd started to feel like a person with multiple personalities.

"So, Emma, are you ready to play in the bouncy house?" Lila hoped her cheeks weren't as red as they felt. Or if they were, that everyone at the table thought it was from working near the hot kitchen.

"Yes, and the pool too. My bathing suit is in Silas's bag," Emma answered.

"About twenty minutes in each one and then one of the games inside the church and we're goin' home to get our naps," Kasey said.

Emma stuck out her lower lip. "I want to stay with Lila all day."

"Naps are wonderful." She leaned down close to Emma's ear and whispered, "And I'm going home when you do so I can have a nap too," Lila said.

"Thank you!" Kasey sighed from across the table.

"What else is new? I don't remember bouncy houses and kiddy pools when I was a kid and coming to these things. I don't even remember having anything when I was a teenager," Lila said.

"I know." Kasey shrugged. "They didn't have anything to entertain us when we were kids, did they? All we got was lectures if we whined."

"Uncle Brody." Emma tugged on his arm. "Did I eat enough mean beans?"

Brody scooped up the last spoonful of green beans and ate them for her. "Looks to me like they're all gone."

"Look, Mommy, I made a happy plate." Emma beamed.

"Good job," Kasey said, and turned back to Lila. "Has anyone shown an interest in buying the cafe?"

"Not yet but it's only been on the market a couple of weeks."

"Be a shame if it closed. Not much left of the town as it is," Hope said.

Lila was shocked that Hope was talking to her and daggers were not shooting from her eyes. She ate a small bite of the pecan pie. "Oh. My. Goodness. This is amazing. What's your secret?"

"A little bit of cream cheese between the crust and filling keeps it from getting soggy." Valerie's eyes went to Brody. There was definitely a heavy dose of pride there. "It's Brody's favorite."

"Yes, it is," Brody said. "And Kasey's pumpkin pie comes in second."

Emma tugged on her arm. "Are you going to get in the pool with me?"

Lila's attention went to Emma. "I didn't bring my bathing suit, but I am going to get into the bouncy house with you. I'll sit in the corner and you can bounce all the way to me."

Emma pumped her fist in the air. "Yay!"

"Hey, Brody." Kasey grinned. "I forgot to tell you. Gracie said that we're getting a new pianist at the church. She's moving here from Abilene to teach junior high English at the end of summer and she's already contacted the preacher about transferring her church membership. You should think about asking her out."

He shook his head emphatically. "No thank you."

Valerie's eyes cut across the table like a machete through warm butter. "I know her family very well. They live in Canyon and are in the Angus Association with me. You'll remember her if you think about it. Tara McDowell—she's a good woman."

"Not interested, Mama," Brody said. "Jace can ask her out."

"Don't throw me under the bus," Jace protested.

Valerie turned her gaze on her younger son. "She might be the very thing to settle you down. I'm going to invite her to supper on Friday night and you will be there."

"Can't. I have a date," Jace protested.

"With whom?" Valerie asked.

"You don't know her. I don't bring a woman home unless it's serious."

"You're both too late," Hope said. "I heard that the preacher himself has already been out with her a couple of times."

"Well, you could beat the other guy's time." Lila looked around Emma toward Brody.

"No, I will take the higher road and not interfere with true love. Jace can work on taking her away from the preacher." Brody sighed and then a wide grin spread across his face.

"Is your heart shattered in a thousand pieces too?" Kasey looked down the table toward Jace.

"Humpty Dumpty could never put it together again," Jace joked.

"You're all horrible," Valerie snapped.

"Hey, Paul, I hear you got some kittens out in Henry's barn." Kasey changed the subject before it went into a full-fledged argument. "Emma's wanted one for a long time. Got one I could have?"

"Go get whatever you can catch. Gracie is going to make me take a couple more mama cats out there this afternoon. Someone dumped them on us and they're about to pop. If you can't find one you like right now, there will be more in six weeks," Paul said. "You want one, too, Rustin?"

"No, Grandpa Paul. I want a puppy. It can be an old mutt and I'm askin' Santa for one if I don't get it before Christmas," Rustin answered.

"Gracie already told Lila to go out there and get however many she wanted too. Why don't y'all take that big white mama cat that's in the barn and whatever kittens she didn't already take?" Paul said.

"I want a baby cat, not a mama cat," Emma declared.

"Then that's what you should have." Brody gave her a sideways hug. "Hey, Paul, have you got your hay all cut and in the barn?"

"Yep, got the second cutting done this week. Why?"

"I'd like to hire the kids you had workin' for you. Reckon you could send them over to my place tomorrow?"

"Be glad to." Paul nodded. "They were wonderin' where they could find some more work."

Fred stopped by and laid a hand on Brody's shoulder. "Did that prize heifer of yours ever throw that calf?"

"Not yet but she's been keepin' me awake," Brody answered. "I sure don't want to lose her and didn't mean for her to even get bred this year."

"So that's why you've got dark circles under your eyes. I thought it might be you was worryin' about something else." Fred winked and chuckled. "Let me know when that calf is born. I'd sure like to see the critter. Maybe it'll be one of Sundance's boys and turn out to be good breeder stock."

"Don't know what bull got in with her but the way Sundance can jump a fence, I wouldn't be surprised," Brody said.

"Y'all ready to get that fun house goin' for the young-uns?" Jace finished off the last bite of food on his plate.

"Yes," Emma squealed. "Me and Lila are going to have fun."

"Yes, we are, sweet girl. Kasey, is it all right if I take her with me now?" Lila asked.

"Of course. I'll come get her in about twenty minutes. She'll be ready for the kiddy pool by then."

"Glad you got that job." Fred squeezed Brody's shoulder. "With my arthritis, I'd be moanin' for a week if I had to crawl inside that bouncy house thing."

"We might be groanin' after today," Lila said.

"Oh, so you're goin' to help him?" Fred raised an eyebrow.

"Yes, she is," Emma piped up.

"Okay, let's get the show on the road." Jace led the way outside.

Emma tucked her hand into Lila's and chattered all the way out to the children's area. "Do you like my granny Hope?"

Lila wasn't sure how to answer that question. It was loaded like a double-barreled shotgun. Finally she said, "Of course. She's a lovely lady."

"I like her too. She reads to me like you do and makes the voices." Emma skipped along beside her. That kid was brilliant. The teachers were going to absolutely love working with her when she got to school.

"Here we are." Brody unzipped the house and stepped back to let Lila and Emma in first.

"You've got a bouncy house and the kiddy pools for the little kids. What about the older kids?" Lila crawled inside with Emma right behind her.

"There's Ping-Pong and games going on in the Sunday school rooms," he answered.

"No poker, though," Jace teased.

"You remembered." Lila smiled.

"Oh, yeah," Brody said. "You wiped all us boys out over there under that old lonesome scrub oak tree that summer after our sophomore year."

"I'd just finished the eighth grade and thought I was a better poker player than anyone, especially a girl. By the time we went home that day, I was just glad we weren't playing strip poker," Jace said. "I'd have lost my socks and everything else. As it was, I lost my lunch money for a whole week. Had to eat in the lunch room."

"Poor baby. Did you lose your lunch money too?" she asked Brody.

"I lost a big chunk of my pride." He crawled inside behind Emma and Lila. "Jace, you see to it they take off their shoes and know the rules. No shoving or hitting or spitting or fighting. I'll sit in one of the supervisor's corners and Lila can sit in the other."

Within ten minutes the noise was deafening and Lila couldn't stop laughing at the antics of the kids. Give them something to jump up and down on and they were happy critters. Too bad adults weren't as easily pleased. Half an hour later, Kasey took Emma out of the crowd and in a little more than an hour the rest of the children had had their fill and had one by one run off to play in the kiddy pool or to go inside to one of the rooms where popcorn was being served while an animated movie played.

"Break time," Brody said from his corner. "Let's call it a day and go get something cold to drink. It's hot in this place even with the fan running."

"You don't have to twist my arm."

Lila tried to get to her feet but tumbled right over onto Brody. He wrapped his arms around her but still they wound up tangled together like a basketful of baby kittens. Pushing away from him only made her roll toward him more.

When she finally got a grip on his broad chest and was able to sit up, her first thought was that adult toy stores needed to sell these houses. Then two strong hands gripped her around the waist and drew her toward him like she weighed no more than Emma. One second she was floating; the next she was sitting firmly in Brody's lap.

She started to thank him but his dark lashes fluttered closed and his lips came down on hers. The kiss started off sweet and tender, then the embers turned into a blaze and the heat came close to melting the bouncy house into nothing but a pile of plastic right there on the church parking lot.

Her arms went around his neck and her fingers tangled into his dark hair as she pressed closer and closer to him. The entire world disappeared and they were in a special vacuum created just for them. Desire for more than scalding hot kisses filled her body. Then she realized where she was, who she was with, and what was going on. Thank God they were still zipped inside the bouncy house and no one saw them.

She pulled away quickly.

"You're still that famous wild child." He grinned.

"But it's time for me to be something else," she whispered. "I need a glass of cold water or lemonade. I'll see you inside."

"We should really talk," he said.

"About what? This is Happy, Texas, where nothing ever changes, not even when it wants to," she said as she crawled out of the house.

Chapter Nine

Slow days in the café were much worse than busy ones. Time dragged and the tips for the whole day wouldn't buy an Orange Julius at the mall in Amarillo. But that was Wednesdays—always had been and most likely always would be—especially on rainy days. Molly left six o'clock sharp. It was time to lock up the place and go on back to the cats but Lila was sitting in a booth finishing the last bites of a grilled cheese sandwich when Kasey darted inside out of the drizzling rain.

"Oh my gosh. It's closing time for you, isn't it? I thought I had half an hour, but I guess I lost track of time." Kasey threw back the hood on her shirt and nodded toward the clock on the wall above the cash register.

"No problem. Come on in. What can I get you? The grill and grease are still hot," Lila said.

"I wanted a burger basket and a glass of lemonade but..."

"Have a seat and it'll be right out," Lila said. "Where are the kids?"

"Mama wanted them for the day and she's taken them to Bible school tonight. My brothers drove down to Plainview to talk to a man about the fall cattle sale on the ranch," she said. "First time in weeks that I've had a day to myself."

"What'd you do?" Lila called out as she flipped a patty on the grill and dumped a bunch of fries into the grease.

"Errands that have been piling up. What I wanted to do was spend the whole day at the spa. Adam gave me a gift certificate for my birthday the first year we were married to that fancy place and I've always wanted to go back. Believe me, he got lucky that night." She smiled.

"I can't imagine how tough losing him would be. Everything on the burger?" Lila asked.

"Mustard and no onions. I'm not sure I'll ever get over it. Crazy talking about food and him at the same time," Kasey said. "I can say his name now without crying, so I guess that's progress."

"I can't even imagine the shock," Lila said seriously.

"It's like an earthquake. You know it's possible, even in Texas, but you never expect it to happen in your area. Then it does and it upsets everything in your life. But it doesn't end there. There's the after-tremors that keep shaking things up. I got used to him being away pretty often. I keep thinking that in two days or two weeks, he'll be back and things will be fine, but then reality hits, and it hurts all over again." Kasey's eyes went all misty but she kept the tears back.

Lila could relate to that better than Kasey realized. There was the shock of leaving Happy and settling into a new place. Her mother and aunt started working at the new café they bought and Lila and Daisy moved into the apartment above the business. She'd thought that the loneliness would kill her. Then she went to college and found out that being away from her mother and relatives was even worse.

There were days when she'd walk down the street, see a guy ahead of her and think for a split second that it was Brody Dawson—that he'd come to take her home. Then there were all the nights that she dreamed about him and woke up with a wet pillow from crying. Oh, yes, she could certainly feel what Kasey was saying.

Lila threw the burger together, shook the fries from the basket, and put them into two separate baskets. "You said lemonade, right?"

"I got my own and refilled your tea glass. Hope that's all right," Kasey said.

Lila sat down at a table and propped her feet on an empty chair. "Ever want a second job, I'll hire you as a waitress."

"Don't think I can fit another job into my schedule. Thank you for doing this. Other than church dinners, I can't remember the last time I sat down by myself and had a burger," Kasey said. "Can I ask you a personal question?"

"Shoot," Lila said.

"What was it like when you moved away?"

Lila swallowed hard. Putting emotions into mere words was near impossible. She'd left part of her heart behind in Happy, Texas, and found out that it was impossible to get it back anywhere else.

"Different," Lila finally whispered. "And a little intimidating. I knew who I was in Happy but..." She paused. "It's hard to explain. No one knew me or anything about Happy, Texas. I was just another waitress in my aunt and mama's café and then I was just another student at the college. I felt like a real fish out of water until I reinvented myself."

"I know exactly what you mean." Kasey tucked a strand of red hair behind her ear. "I became a different person. I was an army wife, not Brody and Jace's kid sister. I had responsibilities even before I had a family. New friends with the same lifestyle I had and we all stuck together when our guys were out on a mission. We worried together, shopped together, babysat each other's kids, and then Adam was gone and I had to start adjusting to something different again. I'm sorry for unloading on you like this."

Lila reached across the booth and patted Kasey on the shoulder. "Don't be. I can so relate to what you're saying. I didn't lose a husband but when I got to a different state I was a new person. It took me a while to know that girl. I felt like a shell, a walking, talking person who smiled and did what she was supposed to but had no heart."

"And now we are back and we are the same as when we left. You're in this café and I'm living on a ranch with my brothers. It's like there's two women fighting inside me and I'm not sure which one I want to win," Kasey said.

Lila couldn't have stated it any better than Kasey did. That's exactly what she was fighting against these days. The two attitudes inside her were so very different. But when it all burned down to ashes, it was actually kind of simple. One had a beating heart in her chest and the other one was a walking, talking shell.

"One is the wild child and the other is a responsible schoolteacher," Lila said softly.

"You got it. Only with me, one is still an army wife who organizes lawn picnics and car pools and then there's this kid sister who's trying to be as smart and as tough as her two older brothers. Which one will conquer?"

"You ever hear the story of the old rancher and the coyote?"

Kasey shook her head.

"Coyote had ribs showing and was plainly starving, so the old rancher tossed out some scraps for the poor thing. Coyote came back the next night and the next and the rancher didn't want him there because it was time for spring calves to be born and coyotes can't be trusted. So he asked a friend what he should do."

"And?" Kasey squirted ketchup on her fries.

"Friend said, 'Stop feeding him if you don't want him around.' I expect it's the same with us. With me, if I want to be the respectable schoolteacher, I have to stop feeding the desire to be the wild child."

"But what if we want to be both? I love the ranch and living around family but I'm tired of them all bossing me around like I'm still a teenager," Kasey said.

Lila frowned. "Is that possible?"

"Don't know but I intend to find out. And it'll take some severe putting my foot down with my brothers and my mother," Kasey said.

Was it possible to pick what she wanted from both personalities? She was mentally making a list of what she'd keep and what she'd trash when she realized that Kasey was staring at her.

"Sorry, I got lost in my thoughts," Lila said. "Will you let me know how that turns out?"

"You bet. I owe you that for keeping the café open and cooking for me." Kasey nodded. "I admired you so much when you were in high school. Lord, I wanted to grow up and be just like you."

"Really?"

"Oh, yeah. You had it together."

"Oh, honey, I didn't have jack squat together." Lila shook her head. "Still don't."

Someone in Happy had believed in her after all. Kasey might have been five years younger, but knowing how Kasey felt put something indescribable into Lila's heart.

Kasey stuck her fingers in her ears in a dramatic gesture. "Don't ruin my memory. Let me keep it."

"Sure thing." Lila smiled.

The fingers came out and Kasey finished off her burger. "This has really been the best part of my day. Most of my friends left Happy. Let's be honest, if you're not a rancher or, in your case, own a café, there's not much here to come back to. It's nice to sit and talk to someone who knows the way things are, and yet…"

Lila took Kasey's glass to the fountain for a refill. "And yet what?"

"It's more of a feeling than it is something that can be put into words. I guess I just need to stop overthinking things and stop feeding that particular coyote. Can you put that in a to-go cup? I've got to get to the church or Mother will start calling every thirty seconds. And tally up how much I owe you."

"It's on the house. We'll call it payment for a therapy session," Lila said.

"Thank you," Kasey said. "Sometime we'll have to take a swim in Hope Springs and call it a spa day."

Lila handed her the cup and followed her to the door. "I'd like that."

Kasey stopped at the door and turned around. "You're welcome anytime on the ranch, Lila. Come have a glass of tea with me or, better yet, we'll have a cold beer."

"That is so sweet. I might do that sometime." She flipped the sign around from OPEN to CLOSED, locked up, and turned off the lights. She had an invitation to Hope Springs without breaking the law by jumping the fence where a NO TRESPASSING sign was posted.

She crossed the kitchen and went through the storage room into her apartment. The kittens were playing a cat game of hide and scare each other around the coffee table. She removed her shoes and stretched out on the sofa. The conversation with Kasey had been both wonderful and yet strange at the same time. She was Brody's sister and the two people inside of her were different than Lila's two but the feelings were the same.

"Kind of like y'all are as different as night and day," she muttered at the cats. "Black and white and yet both of you are still kittens."

Would this summer be the turning point in her life? The meeting point of that wild girl and the responsible one? She stared at her surroundings and got to her feet. Pacing from the living room, through the kitchen, and back down the hall, she tried to get a handle on all the emotions.

She grabbed a long-sleeved chambray shirt on her way

past her bedroom and in a few minutes she was roaring out of town on her motorcycle. She turned to the east at the first opportunity and had gone only part of a mile when she saw a white truck in her rearview. It got closer and closer and then started to pass her before she realized that it was Brody. When he was right beside her, she flipped up the face shield and winked at him. Then she sped out ahead of him.

He stayed right behind her all the way to the T in the road, where there was a stop sign. She turned on the left blinker. The highway would take her right down into the Palo Duro Canyon and then up on the other side not far from Claude. From there she'd ride to Amarillo and then south to Happy.

Brody didn't stop at the sign but pulled right out in front of her and skidded to a stop. He jumped out of the truck and swaggered back to where she'd stopped. "You weren't kiddin' about havin' a bike. That's a pretty piece of machinery. But..."

"But what?" She jerked her helmet off and shook out her black hair.

He took two steps forward, bookcased her cheeks with his calloused hands, and then his lips were on hers in a hungry, fierce kiss. She dropped her helmet on the ground and wrapped her arms around his neck. His tongue teased its way past her lips to make love to her mouth. The sun's heat was nothing to the fire in the kiss that came close to melting the paint off his white truck as well as the stop sign.

He took a step back and she almost fell off the bike before she could catch her breath. "I missed you, Lila."

"You missed the wild Lila. You barely know the

responsible Lila." She picked her helmet from the ground and slapped it back on her head. "Now if you'll get out of my way, I'm going to Amarillo."

"Good God! Not down the canyon? You could get killed on those turns and curves."

"If I do, your mama will dance a jig on the church altar. You want to go with me?" She patted the seat behind her.

"No, thank you."

"I watched you ride that mean bull, so I know there's some daredevil left in you. I guess you're too macho to ride behind a woman. I suppose you could ride on the handlebars."

He crossed his arms over his chest. "I'm not sixteen anymore."

"Too bad," she said as she took off in a blur around the truck. She glanced in the rearview mirror to see him slap his thigh with his hat.

*   *   *

Brody got back into his truck and gripped the steering wheel so tightly that his hands ached. That woman had always twisted his insides in knots and time had done nothing to change that. He turned the truck around and drove toward the ranch. He felt like he'd been doing that for years—leaving her and going to the ranch. It didn't feel right but he had no idea how to fix it.

Not even the kids chasing lightning bugs out in the yard put a smile on his face when he parked next to the yard fence, got out, and slammed the truck door. He stomped toward the porch where Jace and Kasey were sitting and went straight into the house without a word. Getting out the bottle of Jack Daniel's from the cabinet, he set his mouth in a firm line, and poured a double shot in a water glass.

Kasey followed right behind him. "What's got your britches in a twist? You don't get that bottle down unless you're mad, sad, or a mixture of both."

He took a sip, letting the smoky flavor sit on his tongue a second before the warmth shot down his throat. It didn't replace or erase Lila's kisses. "Nothing that you'd understand."

"We might understand if you'd explain. Use your words, brother. What's her name? Lila Harris?" Jace joined them with the three kids trailing right behind him.

"Is Lila comin' to see me?" Emma crawled into a kitchen chair. "I want cake and milk."

"You've had enough sweets for one evening. Peanut butter sandwiches are what y'all are havin' for night snacks," Kasey said. "I saw Lila this evening. She kept the café open late and made me a burger and fries. We had a wonderful visit."

Brody tossed back the rest of the shot. "What did you talk about?"

"Your name didn't come up, believe me." Kasey put the bottle back in the cabinet. "We talked girl stuff that guys aren't interested in."

Brody settled Silas into his high chair, then helped Emma get into her booster seat.

Jace headed toward the counter to help make sandwiches. "So, am I right? Lila?"

Brody shrugged. "I'm going for a walk to clear my head."

"If you find Lila, can she read me a bedtime story?" Emma asked.

"Girls!" Rustin rolled his eyes.

"Boys!" Emma huffed.

He could hear Jace's laughter all the way out into the yard but it did not lighten his mood one bit. With no place in mind, his long strides and anger soon took him toward Hope Springs. The sound of bubbling water calmed him before he ever sat down under the drooping branches of a weeping willow tree.

A splash out there in the water took his attention slightly upstream from where he was sitting. There was no doubt that it was Lila even if her back was toward him. Moonlight lit her up, showing jet-black hair flowing over white skin, water rippling around her in big, wide circles.

He blinked twice and then a third time but every time he opened his eyes, she was still there. Then a flicker of white caught his eyes and he realized he was looking at a T-shirt lying not four feet from him. Thrown beside it were jeans and shoes, along with a white bra and a skimpy pair of underpants.

He stretched out his long legs, crossed them at the ankles, and drank in his fill of her. The water covered most of her body, but he didn't need to see her to know what she looked like or even how she'd feel in his arms if he were out there below the rocky water falls with her. Those things had been burned into his mind for years and years.

She finally turned around and sank down farther into the water. "What are you doin' here?"

"Hot night brought on thoughts of cool water," he answered. "I would've brought a bottle of Jack Daniel's if I'd known you were here."

"How long have you been there?"

"Long enough to know that you're skinny-dippin'. I thought you were going to the canyon."

"Changed my mind." She moved to the shallow edge and hurriedly sat down so that she was still covered.

He kicked off his boots and tossed his plaid shirt and white T-shirt over with her clothing before he waded out toward her.

"What changed your mind?" He gasped when the water reached his knees.

"Needed cooling off after that kiss." Lila never beat around the bush or played games. She dealt in black and white, not shades of gray.

"Well, this will for sure cool a person off." He sat down beside her in the shallow edge and quickly ducked his whole body under the water. "I haven't done this since…"

"Since when?" she asked.

Use your words, Jace had said, but when it came to Lila there were no words. Only raw emotions and hot passion, both of which were the lifeline to his heart.

"I think you remember as well as I do. After all, you have the memory of an elephant, right?" With very little motion, he was glued to her side. "I'm just now realizing it was our body heat that kept us from freezing to death."

"Why, Brody Dawson, have you gotten too old for sex in cold water?"

"Probably, but five minutes under that willow tree would cure the problem in a hurry," he answered.

"If that willow tree could talk, it could tell some tales, but we can't go back," she said. "And even if we could, I'm not sure I want to."

"No, but we can go forward," Brody told her.

"I'm not so sure that's a good idea, either," she said. "There would always be the shadow of the past hovering nearby."

He moved his foot slowly down the side of her leg. "That might make for an interesting relationship."

She moved her leg away from him. "What brought you out here anyway?"

"Thinkin' about you and worryin' that you'd get hurt in the canyon. When you left that summer, I'd sit under the willow tree and imagine you like this in the water on hot evenings. I'd go to Henry's barn in the wintertime and wrap up in that old quilt we liked."

"Oh!" she gasped.

"What?"

"I'm going to name my white cat Cora. It just came to me when you said something about that old quilt."

He'd been baring his soul to her. Using his words. And she was thinking about naming a stupid cat? What was wrong with this picture?

"That's a definite change of subject. And what's this about cats?"

"I got two from Henry's old barn. I'm naming the white one Cora from that old movie we saw. *Quigley Down Under*. Remember Crazy Cora?"

Suddenly it all made sense. They'd snuck into Henry's house one time, just the two of them, and put the old movie into the DVD player. She'd wrapped a quilt that had been draped on the back of a rocking chair around both of them. He'd wanted to have sex right there on the sofa but she wouldn't. Said it wasn't right. Borrowing his house to watch a movie and his quilt to stay warm was one thing and a few kisses were okay, but nothing past that.

"The black one is Duke," she said.

"For John Wayne?"

"No, for the character in *The Notebook*. Did you ever see that one?"

"Only movie that ever made me cry," he said.

"I didn't know that tough cowboys ever cried." She stretched.

He sucked in air when part of her breasts showed in the moonlight. Even though the water was cold, he was getting hard. "I believe that Hope Springs might be the fountain of youth. Looking at you in this light—God, Lila, I want you so bad but I want more than a fling."

She leaned over and cupped his chin in her hands. "I'm not even going to answer that, Brody. It's getting late. I should be going. Shut your eyes."

"I've seen you naked, Lila. I'm sitting close enough that I can feel a lot of your bare skin right now." He covered her hand with his and brought it to his lips to kiss each knuckle.

"Tonight you're going to shut your eyes and promise me that you won't open them until I tell you that I'm dressed," she said.

"Whatever you say," he said. "Can I have a good night kiss?"

She leaned over and gave him a quick kiss. "Good night, Brody. Now shut your eyes."

He pulled her closer and tangled his hands in her wet hair, pulling her to his body for a real kiss so hot and passionate that it left them both panting. He pulled away, his eyes still closed. "*Now* you can get dressed."

He waited a few seconds before he opened his eyes. If possible, Lila was even more beautiful than she'd been when she was younger. Shapely legs and a small waist above the curve of rounded hips. She disappeared under the willow tree branches and when she reappeared, she was fully clothed.

"Your turn." She raised her voice. "I'm being a good girl and not taking your clothes with me. I should because you opened your eyes."

"Seems only fittin' that I get a little glimpse of you since you got a full-frontal nude shot of me when I got into the water," he said. "Did you like what you saw?"

"Did you?" she threw back at him.

"Oh, honey," he groaned.

"Liking the way you look was never my problem," she said. "Be seein' you around, I'm sure."

She disappeared into the night and he got out of the water, let the warm night air dry his body before he got dressed, and whistled all the way back to the house.

Chapter Ten

Four days.

She'd had four days to talk to the cats about the skinny-dipping event, to relive every word and feeling that she'd experienced sitting next to Brody with nothing but water between their naked bodies. For the next three days—Thursday, Friday, and Saturday—she'd watched for him every single moment of the day. And that night she'd thought he might be at church but he wasn't.

After services, she'd driven out to the cemetery and laid a wildflower bouquet wrapped with a bright red ribbon in front of her father's tombstone. She removed her sandals, sat cross-legged on the grass, and ran her fingers over the engraving: BILLY HARRIS, 1962–1999.

"Happy Father's Day, Daddy." She wiped a tear from her cheek.

She felt a presence before she got a whiff of Brody's shaving lotion, but before she could turn around he'd sat down beside her. They were as close as they'd been when they were skinny-dipping out at Hope Springs. His bare skin wasn't touching hers but the heat still flowed through his jeans and plaid shirt just as well as if it had been.

Brody took her hand in his and rested it on his knee. "I've missed seeing you, but we've been so busy on the ranch that I couldn't even get away for an hour. Thought I could make it to church tonight but Sundance got out of his pen again. Sometimes I'm ready to let Jace turn him into dog food. I finally got things finished and remembered that it was Father's Day. I didn't bring flowers but I had to come see Dad and Gramps."

"It's been years since I got to visit my dad on his special day," Lila said softly.

"I remember when he died in that oil rig accident. We were in the seventh grade and it was the first time any of us had lost a parent. I didn't know what to say to you." Brody's sincere voice reached deep into her heart, making her forget the angst over the past four days. It had been like that when they were in high school. She was constantly watching for him, disappointed when he wasn't around, and then when he was, everything was all right.

"You hugged me at the dinner they had at the church after the funeral. You didn't say a word but that hug meant the world to me right then," she said. "You must have been totally devastated to lose both your grandpa and your dad the same summer."

"It was the toughest year of my life," Brody said. "You left and then I lost them. Mama wanted me to go on to college that fall, but I couldn't leave her and Granny both with big ranches to take care of. We had a foreman on both Prairie Rose and Hope Springs but..." He shrugged.

Lila waited a few seconds while he collected his thoughts. He swallowed hard several times before he said, "Even more than being tough, it was the loneliness that was horrible. I threw myself into the work and that was that."

Lila nodded. "I did the same with college. Turned my DNA completely around and became more like Mama."

He drew his brows down. "How's that?"

"Mama was the stable one. Daddy was the fun parent. Probably because he was gone a lot of the time and we all wanted everything to be happy when he was home. When we moved, I made a complete switch and went from the fun Lila to a more serious girl. Looking back, it was a form of coping and escapism, I guess."

Brody gently squeezed her hand. "Funny how that works, isn't it?"

"I still miss him." She swallowed hard and a lonely tear found its way down her cheek.

He let go of one hand and gently brushed it away. "I'm sorry if I brought back sad memories."

Her mind flashed back to that day. She had come home from school and found her mother sitting on the sofa crying with her Sunday school friends surrounding her. There was already food everywhere, more than two people could use in a month. She knew before Daisy even stretched out her arms what had happened. She dropped to her knees and put her hands over her ears. If no one said the words, then it wouldn't be true.

He took her hand back in his and made lazy circles on her palm with his thumb. "And right after that, y'all moved to the back of the café. My family was there on the first Sunday to eat dinner and you were helping by serving the drinks. It was the first time I ever really noticed how pretty you are."

"I hated it," she whispered. "It was like we left Daddy behind in that trailer. I knew he was dead but his spirit lived and we didn't move it to the new place with us. He was back there with strangers. I used to sneak out at night and go sit in the backyard and pretend that he came outside to talk to me."

"I'm so sorry," Brody said.

She stared at the tombstone and visualized her father sitting beside her in those old metal lawn chairs in their postage-stamp-sized backyard. Sometimes they didn't talk at all but if she had a problem concerning anything, from snotty girls to pre-algebra, they'd discuss it.

"Then we left him again when Mama made us move. I didn't want to leave Happy. I even offered to not go to college and to help her run the café if she wouldn't make me leave. It took a long time for me to forgive her." Lila's voice sounded hollow even to her own ears. "Her only sister was out there in Pennsylvania and she wanted to get me out of this atmosphere and for me to go to college. She was afraid I'd never get an education if we stayed here. She was probably right."

He dropped her hands, wrapped both arms around her, and pulled her close to his chest. With an ear pressed right next to his heart, she could feel the steady rhythm of the beat—not just hear it, but actually feel him doing his best to ease the pain they both felt in remembering.

"This is always an emotional time of year for me too," Brody whispered hoarsely.

Lila nodded and then repositioned the side of her face

so that she could hear his heart again. "It was a bad summer for both of us, wasn't it?"

"You leaving broke my heart, Lila."

"Sure didn't seem like it at the time." She leaned back and their gazes met in the few inches separating their faces.

"Men don't cry. Cowboys don't cry. Boys don't cry."

"And that has to do with what?"

He gulped a couple of times. "I wanted to be with you that last night but I couldn't bear to see you in tears again. When you told me you were moving away—well, like I said, boys don't cry and I would have carried on like a little girl."

"But I did cry, remember? When Mama said that we were moving in a week, I cried until my face hurt and your shirt was wet." She looked even deeper into his eyes.

He nodded. "So did I when I got home but I couldn't go through it again. So I went out with the guys and was miserable all night. I was going to apologize to you the next day but you wouldn't roll down the window. Not that I blame you one bit."

"I thought I would die just looking at you in the rearview mirror," she said.

He buried his face in her hair. "I sat down behind the café, put my head in my hands, and thought the worst thing ever had happened. Then..." He hesitated again.

She wrapped both arms around his neck and hugged him tightly. If she'd lost her mother and Aunt Tina that summer in addition to leaving Brody behind, she might have truly stopped breathing. How Brody had survived was a mystery.

She had shared things with him that evening that she'd kept closed off from the therapist she'd started seeing last winter in Florida. Raw things that brought about pain and yet, there she was sitting in a cemetery telling Brody about them.

"Have you forgiven and forgotten?" he whispered.

"Who? You or Mama?"

"First, your mother." He inhaled deeply. "I love the smell of your hair."

"Forgiven." She nodded. "She was only doing what she thought was best for me and she let me finish school here with my class. She'd wanted to be near her sister for a long time."

Lila loved Aunt Tina and all her kids and grandkids. Thanksgiving and sometimes Christmas was fun at her house, but Huntingdon, Pennsylvania, would never be home, not like Happy, Texas. Not even if they moved her father's body out there and she could visit him every week.

"And your dad's family?" Brody asked.

"Dad was a foster child from the time he was about two years old. Thrown about from place to place until he was eighteen and then he went to work in the oil fields. He didn't talk about his life but he did say that all those drunk driving tickets he hadn't paid was the best luck he'd ever had."

"How could unpaid tickets be lucky?" Brody asked.

"They put him in front of the judge, who said that he had a choice of six months in jail or he could join the service. He chose the army and got stationed over in Lawton, Oklahoma. A guy invited him to go home with him one weekend and it turned out the fellow was from Tulia. He was dating my aunt Tina and they introduced Dad to my mother. He and Mama married when he got out of the service and he moved here so he could work in the oil wells again. My aunt Tina didn't marry that soldier but she did marry an oil man and moved back east the next year after Mama and Daddy married."

"I can't imagine going through those tough years without my dad. Thinking about losing him even now makes me so sad," Brody said. "I should go and let you have your time alone."

"Stay." She held on to his hand when he started to pull it away.

They sat engulfed in their own memories for a long time before she finally said, "What happened to your grandpa?"

"Heart attack. Doctor said he was gone instantly. Granny ran the ranch until this spring. Then she turned it over to us."

So much had happened between that last night out at Henry's barn and that moment and she wanted to know everything. "Do you ever wish for one more hour with him to ask him important questions?"

"Oh, Lila," Brody sighed. "Him and my dad both. Daddy died in a tractor accident. I couldn't talk fast enough if I had another hour with either of them, especially right now. After he was gone, I threw myself into the ranch work. That's all I know or ever wanted to do anyway. My folks and Granny both had huge places with plenty to do, so I never had to worry about a paycheck."

"Lived with your folks all this time until you moved over to Hope Springs?"

"I moved into the bunkhouse when Grandpa died.

When Jace graduated from college, he moved into it with me," he said.

"So Jace went and you didn't?"

"He's kind of felt guilty about that but Mama and I insisted. And he's really smart when it comes to agriculture business. What did you do after you graduated from college?"

"I took a job in Memphis for a couple of years, then moved over to Little Rock for a while and I've been in Panama City Beach since then."

The therapist told her that she moved so often because she was searching for happiness but until she found peace within herself, happiness would always be a step ahead of her.

Happy, Texas. Maybe she wasn't searching for the elusive euphoric happy but the place that was a tiny town in the panhandle of Texas.

"Come home with me," Brody finally said after several minutes of silence. "It's my night to read bedtime stories to the kids and I don't want to miss it. It's the second Father's Day without Adam and you of all people understand. But I don't want to leave you."

"Not tonight, Brody. You go on and read to those babies. They need you." She pushed away from him. "But for the record, I don't want you to leave either."

He kissed her on the forehead and straightened up. "Good night, Lila."

"Night, Brody," she said.

Was Kasey right? Could Lila really have both sides?

*   *   *

Brody sat in the middle of Rustin's bed with Silas in his lap, Emma hugged up to his left side and Rustin leaning over his shoulder as he read *Bedtime for Dogs*. There were lots of pictures and only a few words on each page but it still took almost half an hour to get through the book. Rustin and Emma had dozens of questions about each page and Silas wanted to point to the dog and jabber about it.

Finally, Kasey rescued him and put Silas into his crib, tucked Rustin in, and led Emma to her bedroom. While she got them settled, Brody went to the kitchen and popped the tops on two beers. He carried them to the living room and set Kasey's on the coffee table.

She plopped down on the other end of the sofa. "Thank you. I need this tonight. Father's Day is tough on me. Even worse than Christmas and his birthday." She took two long swallows before she set it aside. "I miss him so much, Brody."

"It doesn't get any easier, does it?" Losing Lila was one thing but she was still alive and able to come back. Kasey's loss was final, down to standing in front of a closed casket.

"Hasn't yet. After the initial shock wore off, I thought it would get better with the passing of time. It hasn't," she said. "Did you go see Grandpa and Daddy?"

"I did," he answered. "Lila was there at her father's grave. We talked."

It wasn't the first time that they'd held hands and talked for hours but in the past it had been either in the barn, under the willow tree, or in her bedroom. They'd talked about things that teenagers did in those days. Today had been different in so many ways and he'd used his words like Jace said. Not to banter or to tease, but emotionally.

"Argued or talked?" she asked.

"The latter. I can't imagine what you're going through but I know that I missed her horribly when she moved away. I'd finally given up on ever seeing her again when she came back to Happy."

"I knew that you had a crush on her, but I had no idea that you missed her like that," Kasey said. "Does she know?"

He shook his head. "There was chemistry between us back then that is still there but, Kasey—"

"When you get past everything that's keeping you two apart, there will be no more buts. However, you've got to work on all those things. Like talking to her. Like not keeping secrets from Mama. Like not caring what Mama or Granny thinks or anyone else for that matter. You have to let the past go and dwell on the future."

"That's a lot to do in one summer," he said.

"Yes, it is. We can't bring back the water that's already flowed under the bridge, can we? If we could, Adam would still be with me and I'd be in Lawton where folks treated me like I had a brain instead of looking down on me like I'm nothing but your kid sister," she sighed.

"You miss that life, don't you?" Brody asked.

"Yes, I do sometimes. I wasn't the odd Dawson kid with red hair who wasn't as pretty as all the Dawson girl cousins or even as her older brothers. I wasn't the only one who got married right out of high school. I was Kasey McKay who could organize a picnic or take care of the Fourth of July party at the recreation hall for the guys who stayed on base. And I was the woman in charge of ordering all the fireworks for the display," she said.

"And then Adam was gone and you had to move right back here," he said.

"Like Lila." She nodded. "Only she's come back where people remember her as that crazy kid who was always gettin' into trouble, not the teacher with a responsible job. Neither of us knows who we are anymore. Difference is that she gets to leave at the end of summer. I've got nowhere to go and three kids who are better off on this ranch than anywhere else. What can I do? Flip burgers or check out customers at a grocery store?"

Brody slid over next to her and put his arm around her. "Kasey Dawson McKay, this ranch is your army base. Without you, Jace and I would be lost. You're our rock. And as of right now, you can do whatever you want for a ranch picnic and fireworks display on the Fourth of July. Just don't leave us, darlin' sister. We'd be runnin' around like chickens with their heads cut off without you."

"I know you're just sayin' that to make me feel better, but thank you." Kasey smiled, her eyes watery.

"It's the truth. Cross my heart. When someone wanders onto the ranch and steals your heart, we'll have to hire five women to replace you," Brody said. "And I'm not whistlin' Dixie, sister."

"I don't reckon you've got a thing to worry about there. It'd take a big man to sweep me off my feet and he'd have to love my kids. Not many men are willing to take on a ready-made family."

"You never know," Brody said. "If I've learned anything, it's that life has a way of surprising you sometimes."

"Well, whatever comes our way—you, me, Lila—we'll figure it out as we go."

"Of course we will." He grinned. "Want to watch a movie? I'll even let you pick it out."

"And you won't bitch if it's a romance?"

"Not tonight," he answered.

He and Jace both had been protective of their little sister since the day their mama brought her home from the hospital. At three and five, they had no idea what to do with a girl baby but their mama said they had to watch out for her and they'd done their best. Now it was time for them to recognize that she wasn't a kid anymore.

"What if I'm not in the mood for something all sweet and sappy but I want some kickass stuff?" she asked.

"Then I might not snore."

"How about that old *Blue Collar Comedy Tour*? Would you snore through some redneck comedy?" she asked.

"Never. If you'll find it, I'll make some popcorn and pour us a couple of Cokes," he said.

"Laughter might help." She stood up and stretched, then opened the door to the place where the DVDs were stored.

"Hey, did you ever watch this *Lethal Weapon* movie? Granny must have left it behind. It's got Mel Gibson in it and he looks real young," Kasey yelled.

"Nope. Heard of it but never watched it. Want to trade redneck humor for kickass?"

"I think I do. If we don't like it, we can stop it and put in the other one."

Lethal Weapon.

That was Lila in a nutshell. She could destroy a man's heart or protect it, depending on how he treated her.

*   *   *

Lila padded barefoot from the bathroom to the living room of her apartment. Wearing boxer shorts and a tank top, she got comfortable on the sofa and towel dried her long hair and then tossed the wet towel on the coffee table. Duke and Cora took it as an offering and proceeded to use it to climb up on the table to play a game of king of the mountain, knocking each other off the table.

She got bored watching them and flipped through the old DVDs on the shelf below the television. Most of them needed to be tossed in the garbage but one with Mel Gibson and Danny Glover on the front caught her eye.

"*Lethal Weapon Four*. The last one." She put it into the player. "I remember this, Daddy. You and Mama sent me to bed early so you could watch it. I was in the sixth grade and I snuck out of my room and crawled on my hands and knees over to the cabinet. I peeked out around the side and saw some of it before Mama caught me and sent me back to my room."

The cats got tired of playing and flopped down on the edge of the towel they'd pulled from the table. She gathered both of them in her arms and laid them down beside her on the sofa. Her phone rang as the first scene of the movie started, so she hit pause. Duke grumbled in his sleep but he didn't wake when she reached across him for her purse on the end table.

"Hello, Mama," she said.

"Did you go to church tonight?"

"I sure did. Are you checkin' up on my soul?"

"Did you go to the cemetery?"

"Yes, ma'am. Daddy and I had a visit and then Brody Dawson showed up and we had a visit too," she said. "But I imagine that you already knew that and that's why you're calling, right? Who told on me?"

"It doesn't matter who. What matters is that you stay away from him. He's just flat out not the man for you," Daisy fussed. "You're lookin' at another heartbreak. You went inside a shell and didn't come out for years when we moved away all those years ago."

"I thought I kept my feelings hidden pretty good," she said.

"Honey, you don't hide things from a mama. When you have kids, you'll understand that," Daisy said.

"I can handle myself, Mama." She quickly changed the subject. "Guess what I'm fixin' to watch?"

"Depends on where you're going to watch it. Are we talkin' about Henry's old barn or television?"

Lila sighed. "*Lethal Weapon 4*. You remember when you caught me…"

Daisy giggled. "Yes, I do. That wasn't long before your dad died. It was the last movie that we watched together. I'm glad that you went to see him today."

"First Father's Day I've been able to do that since we moved away," Lila said seriously. "I know you miss him, Mama, because I do."

There was a long, pregnant silence and then Daisy said, "Well, I'd best let you get to watchin' the movie that you didn't get to watch almost twenty years ago."

"I wish you were here to watch it with me," Lila said softly.

"Me too, honey. And if that café doesn't sell by the middle of August, we'll watch it together before you go back to Florida. I've decided to move back to Texas if it doesn't have a buyer by the fifteenth of August."

"Seriously, Mama? You'd leave Aunt Tina and all those kids and grandkids?"

"It wouldn't be easy but I'm getting an antsy feelin' since you've been there. Kind of like something is calling me back to my roots."

"The café is going to sell. I just know it will. But I'll take this movie with me when I go and when you come down for Christmas, we'll watch it then, okay?" She would love having her mother right there with her that evening. December seemed so far away. By then nine months would have passed since spring break when she saw Daisy last. Then it had only been a short three-day visit and Daisy and Aunt Tina had worked every day except Sunday while she was there.

"It's a date," Daisy said. "Maybe I'll buy the first three next time I see them on sale and we'll have a marathon one day. Your dad would like that."

"Sounds good to me. Good night, Mama."

"'Night, kiddo."

Lila wasn't five minutes into the movie when she said, "Good grief! Mel's character is every bit as cocky as Brody Dawson used to be. Maybe those fifteen minutes I got of this movie is what made me like the bad boys."

Chapter Eleven

Brody hadn't planned to go with Kasey to Walmart but as she and the kids were leaving, Emma fell off the porch steps and scraped her knee. He couldn't stand to see her cry and the only thing that she said would make it better was if he'd go with them and if she could have a purple bandage on the tiny little cut.

When they all arrived at the store, Kasey situated Silas in the cart and then pointed to the side. "Emma, you hold on right here and don't let go."

Emma crossed her arms over her chest and sucked in a lungful of air. "I want to go see the toys."

"Me too," Rustin said.

"You want to see toys or go for ice cream? We can't do both," Kasey said.

"Ice cream," Rustin said quickly.

"Toys!" Emma pushed him and he fell on his fanny.

Like a feisty little rooster, he popped to his feet, hands

knotted into fists ready to fight until Brody got between them. "Okay, kids. No pushin'. No arguing. Give me half the list and I'll take Emma with me, Kasey."

Kasey divided the list and handed half to him. "After that, you don't deserve to get ice cream or go see the toys either."

"I want to go with Uncle Brody," Rustin declared.

Brody started to put Emma into her seat but she wiggled free of his arms and ran back to her mother.

"I'm not a baby. I'll go with Mama if I have to ride in the basket like Silas."

"Testy today, isn't she?" Brody said.

"Didn't get her nap and everything Rustin does aggravates her today. I remember when you and Jace did the same to me," Kasey said.

"Okay, big girl, you've made your decision. Even if your legs get tired, you don't get to ride in the cart," Brody told her. "But if I look around and you've disappeared, there will be no ice cream or toys and I won't read to you tonight."

"Granny Hope is reading to me tonight." Emma stuck her nose in the air.

"She won't either. Remember what I told you. You got to listen to your uncles and granny but..."

"Mama's word is the law," Emma sighed.

"That's right and both of you better behave." Kasey gave her the mama look. "Now I'm taking Silas to the grocery section."

"No, no, no!" Silas screamed. "Want Memma." He stretched out his hands and tears rolled down his cheeks.

"Take them both and go on. He'll settle down when they're out of sight," Kasey sighed. "It's been a day."

Brody nodded and walked in the other direction. With Rustin telling him all about what kind of ice cream he was going to order and Emma butting in every chance she got to talk about Lila and the ice cream party they'd had with her. Brody made his way to the area where the things on his list were located. He'd put two bottles of tear-free baby shampoo in the cart and was looking for a special kind of kid's toothpaste when someone tapped him on the shoulder.

"There is my friend!" Emma pointed toward the end of the aisle.

"Lila!" Rustin waved.

Brody wondered how in the world perfect little demons could trade their horns in for haloes in a split second. It was pure magic and he'd like nothing better than to put it into a bottle to give to Kasey for her birthday.

*   *   *

"Well, what a treat, gettin' to see my favorite kids tonight." Lila beamed.

She parked her cart beside Brody's and quickly hugged both of the children. "Hello, Brody. I saw Gracie and Paul back at the pharmacy. Guess everyone in Happy is out shopping tonight."

"Yep," Rustin said. "And then we're going for ice cream."

"And you're going with us," Emma declared.

"I'm afraid I've got to get back to my kittens. Duke and Cora will miss me if I stay too long."

"I could go home with you and read those kittens bedtime stories if you'd go with us," Brody said.

"Uncle Brody reads a real good story," Rustin piped up.

"And they have strawberry ice cream," Emma whispered.

"I guess I could but are you sure, Brody? I wouldn't want…"

Kasey parked her cart beside Brody's. "Hey, Lila, good to see you. I just bumped into Mama. If I'd known she was coming, I would have sent my list with her and saved a trip. You about ready, Brody?"

"Soon as we get the toothpaste." Rustin tossed two boxes into the cart. "That's it, Mama, and now can we go for ice cream? At McDonald's so we can play?"

"Lila is going with us," Emma said. "And I don't want McDonald's. I want the ice cream store and then we can go to the park."

"I should probably be getting home," Lila said. "Storm is brewing and dust is already flying out there."

"Nonsense," Kasey said. "Get the rest of your stuff gathered up and we'll wait until you get to the store before we order and then we'll go to the park for half an hour."

"The park sounds like so much fun. Can I push you on the swings, Emma?" Lila asked.

"Yes," Emma said with a tilt of her chin. "And then I'll push you."

"It's a deal." Lila smiled. "I'll get on with the rest of my shopping and meet y'all at—it is the ice cream place right beside the park, right?"

"That's the one," Brody said. "They make a mean banana split."

*   *   *

Lila remembered laundry soap and hairspray but forgot at least five items on her list, which meant she'd be making a trip to Tulia to one of the dollar stores later in the week.

Her brain ran in circles all the way to the small ice cream place. It was not a date. It was only ice cream with a family. If it was a real date, Valerie would have Brody committed and Hope would take the ranch away from him. She parked her truck and sat there for several minutes.

Through the window, she could see Kasey and the older two kids on one side of the booth. Silas was in a high chair at the end, leaving Brody alone across from his sister. That meant she'd be sitting with him but it was still not a date. Grown-ups sat beside each other at all kinds of events without it being anything that folks would gossip about.

Decision made, she hopped out of the truck, grabbed her purse, and slammed the door. The wind was blowing even more now, sending all kinds of dirt swirling through the air. She hurried into the store and was halfway to the booth when Brody stood up. His eyes lit up like they used to when she walked into Henry's old hay barn. He met her in the middle of the store and draped an arm around her shoulders. She wasn't a bit amazed when hot little shivers danced down her spine.

"Thank you for coming. The kids are being little devils today and Emma would have thrown another fit if you hadn't come, plus I wanted you here with me," he said.

"Then I'll do double duty?" She grinned.

"Triple. I've volunteered you to help carry the ice cream back to the booth as the lady gets it ready," he said as they walked past the booth. "I've got the list right here." He showed her a napkin with writing on it. "Kasey says if we'll order and then bring it to the booth, she'll corral the three monkeys."

"We ain't monkeys. We're childrens," Rustin declared loudly.

"I'll be a monkey if they eat ice cream," Emma said.

"They eat bananas, not ice cream, so you can't be a monkey," Rustin argued.

"Girl monkeys eat ice cream. Boys don't," Emma argued.

"Enough!" Kasey said in a tired mother's voice.

"Brody, this might not be such a good idea," Lila said on the way to the counter.

He laid a hand on the small of her back and escorted her across the floor. "What? Me ordering and you totin'? I trust you not to stumble over your feet and waste good ice cream."

"You know what I mean," she said, enjoying every delicious little shiver that his hand created.

He gave the girl behind the counter the order and then drew Lila even closer. "The end—except for your banana split, unless you want to share with me."

"Sharing is fine." She nodded.

Oh, Lord! What had she just agreed to? If anyone saw them eating from the same bowl... She took a deep breath and reminded herself that she was thirty years old and so was Brody.

"You tell her what toppings we want, then." His hand slipped around to rest on her waist.

She was amazed that she could utter a word with all the heat his hand created but she managed to rattle off strawberry, caramel, and chocolate.

When everyone had their order, Kasey put a bib on Silas and Lila slid into the booth with Brody right after her. Then Kasey sat beside him so that she could help all three kids: Silas at the end in a high chair and the other two across the table from them.

Brody was a big man and the booth wasn't one of those huge ones, so their sides were plastered tight together. It was a miracle that the heat between them didn't melt every bit of ice cream in the whole place.

Brody filled a spoon with ice cream and moved it toward Lila's mouth. She had no choice but to open wide. She'd barely gotten her mouth shut when Gracie and Paul McKay entered the store and headed straight toward them.

"Nana!" Emma squealed.

"Hey, kids." Gracie smiled. "Imagine finding all y'all at an ice cream store. I saw your van outside, Kasey. Can we steal the kids for a couple of hours? We'll have them home by bedtime. We'd take them to the park but the dust storm out there now is just the tip of the iceberg. There's a big one going to hit in about an hour. What we're seeing in the sky isn't clouds at all but dirt."

"That would be great. I can get some computer work done this evening without having to stop every five minutes." Kasey nodded. "Drag over a couple of chairs and join us."

Paul was already busy getting two from a nearby table and placing them on either side of Silas's high chair. "We had to run in to get prescriptions at the drugstore. I guess y'all heard about the new church pianist coming in. I'm glad to hear that we'll have another person who can play. That way if Gert needs to be gone, it won't be such a big deal."

"Just don't try to fix her up with me. I'm not interested." Brody grinned.

"She is not my friend," Emma said bluntly.

Rustin pushed her arm. "She can be my friend."

"Mama, he hit me," Emma tattled.

"Did not!"

"Did too."

"Whoa!" Brody said. "Let's eat our ice cream without fighting."

"Emma! You haven't even met her," Kasey scolded.

"She can't be my friend because Lila is." Emma glared at Rustin.

Paul chuckled. "So how'd you get tangled up with this bunch of renegades, Lila?"

"Met 'em in Walmart," she answered.

"Lila is my friend," Emma said seriously.

"And a mighty good one," Gracie told her. "How's your mama? Any way we could talk her into coming back to Happy and running the café rather than selling it?"

"She's been thinkin' about that." Lila wondered how quick it would be all over Happy that she was out with Brody. Maybe she'd better hightail it to Australia with him. Valerie Dawson was a pretty good shot with a rifle, the last she heard.

"Well, tell her to think real hard," Paul said.

Lila smiled and nodded. Daisy had grown pretty fond of the whole family out there, so it wouldn't be easy for her to move back to Texas.

After they'd eaten their ice cream, everyone drove away from the parking lot. Paul and Gracie had shifted Silas's car seat and Emma's and Rustin's boosters to the backseat of Gracie's van and waved as they headed out toward the park. Kasey had driven off in the van on her way back to the ranch. That left Lila and Brody standing beside her truck.

"I thought you drove the van for Kasey," she said.

"No, I like to bring my own vehicle in case I want to go home before they do."

"Thanks for invitin' me. I love bein' around the kids." The wind swept her hair across her face and blew dust into her eyes. "I'd forgotten about sandstorms in this part of the world. We'd better get on out of here before it gets really bad. Thanks again."

"Anytime." He pulled his hat down tighter, opened the door, and took a step closer, shielding her from the wind. "One more thing. Will you be my date for the Hope Springs Fourth of July ranch party?"

"I know I keep saying this but..."

He ran a finger down her cheek. "Yes, it's a good idea. We've got to get over this thing between us or embrace it and we can't do either by running from it. Can't rewrite history or do a thing about it. But it doesn't have to ruin the future."

She laid a palm on his cheek. "It's tough playing second fiddle to a woman who is going to play the church piano. Besides, what is your mama going to say about that?"

He grabbed her hand and kissed the palm. "Darlin', you will never be second fiddle to anyone and Jace can have Tara if he wants her. And I don't really care what Mama or Granny has to say. Just tell me that you'll go with me."

"Pretty good pickup line there and the kiss on the palm is a nice move. Yes, I will go with you and thank you for asking me. I'll wear my runnin' shoes so when your mama brings out her rifle, I'll at least have a fightin' chance," she laughed.

"I'll lock Mama's firearms in a safe place and pick you up at nine that morning. But we'll see each other before then." He brushed a soft kiss across her lips and disappeared around the back of her truck into a fog of sand blowing half of New Mexico into the Texas Panhandle. She started the truck and licked her lips. They tasted like a mixture of chocolate and sand. Not a bad combination; not bad at all.

The passenger door opened and Brody's big frame filled that side of the truck. Without a single word, he leaned over the console and wrapped his arms around her. Their lips met in a scorching hot kiss that made her knees weak. It was a good thing she was sitting and that her truck was not a stick shift because she couldn't have walked and she sure could not have held down the clutch. The weatherman on the radio said something about a fierce sandstorm and then Jennifer Nettles started singing "Unlove You."

He looked deeply into her eyes when the words said that it wouldn't work and would be nothing but hurt but that she couldn't unlove him.

"I can't unlove you either."

"Like it says, we have other lives," she whispered.

"We can change that," he said.

"What are we talking about here?" Lila asked.

Brody kissed her again. "One of those alternate endings to an old story." He got out of the truck and walked away, his head bent against the blowing dust.

Chapter Twelve

Before she pulled out of the parking lot, she found her Jennifer Nettles CD in the console and slipped it into the stereo and listened to that same song over and over all the way home. Lila could have written that song when she was sixteen, but that night every word became a part of her soul as she drove home with dirt swirling around her. She'd parked in the garage and hit the remote to close the door when she noticed a shadow in her side window.

Her door opened suddenly and with a flick of the wrist, Brody unfastened her seat belt. Then he scooped her into his arms like a bride and carried her toward the door into the apartment.

"You sure you want to carry me over the threshold, cowboy?" she whispered.

"Right now I'm not sure of anything except that I want to hold you in my arms and I want more than one kiss," he said.

She reached down and opened the door and his lips closed on hers.

"The same room as when we...," he whispered.

"Yes, the same," she said.

He carried her to the bedroom, shut the door with the heel of his boot, and sat down in an old rocking chair with her in his lap. Light from an almost full moon flowed through the window that he'd crawled in and out of dozens of times all those years ago.

"God, I missed you so much, I thought I'd die some nights." His voice was deeper than usual.

"But was it just rebellion because we weren't supposed to be together?" she asked softly.

Half of his face was in shadows, the other half lit by moonlight coming through the window. The story of their lives right there. One side lived in secret, the other in the light of day. One wild side, one responsible. Tonight she had a passionate desire to feed the hungry wild child.

She slowly ran her hands under his T-shirt. "How are you not married?"

He tugged her shirt out of her jeans and his calloused hands felt like fire on her skin. In a split second her bra was undone and he had free rein of her whole back. "How are you not married?"

"I almost was...once. You?"

"Never, not even almost." He nibbled on her earlobe. "But I want to hear about your near misses."

"Not now," she panted.

Effortlessly, he stood up with her in his arms and moved to the bed. "Is this the same..."

"Oh, yes, the same one where we both lost our virginity." She smiled.

He removed her shoes and socks, kissed her toes, one at a time. "I remember that night very well. You didn't cry."

"Why would I? It was wonderful."

Her jeans went next and then her shirt and underwear, all tossed on the floor. Her breath came in short spurts but she wanted him as naked as she was, so she pushed him backward on the bed.

"My turn." She sat on his knees with her back to him and removed one of his boots, tossed it across the room, and then tugged off his sock. He massaged her back the whole time.

Lord have mercy! He had learned some impressive moves since the last time they were together. She flipped around to undo his zipper and turned loose an erection that took her breath. Tugging his pants down to his ankles and then shoving them off the bed, she decided that a long, slow bout of foreplay was not going to happen. She crawled back up his long frame and held out her hands. He put his in them and she pulled him forward. Effortlessly, he went from lying down to sitting and removed his shirt. It was nothing but a blur as it joined the other clothing thrown haphazardly around the room.

"Dammit!" he swore under his breath.

"What?" she asked.

"I don't have a condom."

"No problem. I'm on the pill." She covered his mouth in a long, hard kiss that left her aching, just like words to the song in her head said. "I want you, Brody," she whispered.

He flipped her over on her back and her long legs

wrapped around his waist as he slipped inside her and they began to rock together. His mouth found hers and the last thing that crossed her mind was that she loved, loved tall men and then there was nothing but a scorching desire to put out the flames in her body... and only Brody Dawson had ever had the power to do that.

He took her right to the edge of release, then slowed down. She tightened her legs and he groaned. "Lila, I can't...," he said hoarsely.

"I know, me neither. One, two..."

"Three!" He managed a smile as they both hit the heights together. When he could breathe again, he rolled to one side, taking her with him and holding her tightly against his side.

"You remembered," she panted.

"So did you." He snuggled his face down into her hair. "One. Two. Three. We go together."

"Yes," she mumbled, and shut her eyes. She was back in Brody's arms, where she belonged. Past and future didn't matter—only the present.

*   *   *

Brody awoke to the sound of someone tiptoeing down the hallway. His first thought was that Jace had come in late, but then he realized that Lila's long leg was thrown over his. The footsteps stopped at her door and a female voice whispered softly, "Lila, darlin', are you awake?"

Every hair on his neck stood straight up. Even after more than a decade, he would recognize Daisy's voice. In a few seconds, she chuckled softly and then he heard the wheels of a suitcase cross the hall. The hinges on that door didn't squeak like Lila's did but there was no mistaking the latch when she closed it.

He rolled out of bed, landed on his hands and knees, and quickly found his clothing, jerking each item on when he located it. The door across the hall opened again and Daisy cussed when she stumbled over a kitten; then her tone changed and he could hear her high-pitched apology to the cat.

He unlocked the window and, holding his breath, slid it open enough to crawl out. God, he felt eighteen years old all over again.

The clock on the dash of his truck said it was five a.m. and the sun was barely peeking over the horizon. He broke every speeding record he'd ever set on the way to Hope Springs and had just sat down on the porch when Jace came out of the house.

"You're awake awfully early. Did you put a pot of coffee on?" Jace asked.

"Not yet. Had the dust storm stopped when you got home?" Brody answered.

"Only lasted about an hour, but that was enough. Kasey got home and then Paul and Gracie came in about ten minutes after her with the kids. They were going to keep them longer but Emma's bandage fell off and she wanted her mama. I got involved in a television movie and didn't go to bed until midnight," Jace answered.

"Reckon we ought to get back inside and get a pot of coffee going. Kasey is an old bear if it's not ready first thing when she gets to the kitchen." Brody stood up, stretched, and rolled his neck to get the kinks out.

Jace frowned. "You were wearing that shirt when you left last evening. Where did you spend the night?"

"A cowboy does not kiss and tell."

"You better not let Mama— Speak of the devil." Jace pointed to the truck coming down the lane.

"Let Mama what?" Brody groaned when he saw Valerie's bright red truck coming toward the house.

"Hey, I'm just sayin' and I don't have to spell it out for you. I can see the way you look at Lila but remember, she leaves at the end of summer. We ain't kids anymore and Mama has never liked her. Family gets complicated."

Brody waved when the truck came to a stop. "I wonder what she's doing here at dawn."

"Have no idea but Granny is in the passenger seat."

Brody quickly crossed the yard and opened the door for his grandmother. "Y'all are sure out early this mornin'."

"I left my cell phone in the kitchen. We're on our way to have breakfast at the café and then we're going to the cemetery to get the family graves in shape before it gets hot this mornin'," Hope said.

"Want me to run inside and find your phone? Why didn't you holler? I'd have brought it to you."

"Didn't know it was missin' until this mornin'. It's really your grandpa's phone. I had mine so I could make calls but I carry his around with me," Hope explained. "He had some pictures of the two of us together on it and sometimes..." Her voice cracked. "Yes, please go get it for me."

"Be right back," Brody said.

"Whoa! Before you leave, I heard that you had ice cream with Lila last night. What's goin' on?" Valerie asked.

"Sure was a demon dirt storm last night." He smiled.

"Don't change the subject. I want answers." Valerie crawled out of the vehicle and got right into his face.

"Answer is that I had ice cream with Lila and Kasey and the kids. Paul and Gracie were there too. I'm not sure what's going on but I've still got a lot of feelings for Lila and I intend to see where they go before she leaves at the end of the summer."

She looked like she could chew up railroad spikes and spit out staples right at him. "I won't have it, Brody."

"It's not your call, Mama. I've invited her to the Fourth of July festival."

Valerie inhaled deeply and let it out slowly. "I don't like it one bit."

"Well, I don't like it that you're being obstinate about something that's in the past," he shot back.

She crossed her arms over her chest just like Emma had done. Females! Didn't matter how old or young they were, they could be a handful.

"You're just like your daddy. He'd argue with a damn stop sign," Valerie said.

"Get back in the truck, Valerie," Hope yelled out the window. "He's not a little boy. He can make his own decisions and live with the consequences."

"Thank you, Granny. Sure you don't have time to come in for a cup?"

"No thanks. I've got my heart set on some of Molly's sausage biscuits this morning," Hope answered. "We'll visit later. And don't forget, the Dawson family reunion is this Saturday."

Brody shook his head. "No, ma'am. I'm lookin' forward to it. Jace and I will be over Thursday evening to help Jack get the barn ready. If y'all need anything between now and then, just yell. And I'm giving you a heads-up, Mama. I intend to ask Lila to be my date for that too."

"Well, crap!" Valerie got back into the vehicle.

Brody jogged to the house and brought out the phone, handed it to Hope, and took a step back. "See y'all later."

Valerie kept her eyes straight ahead and didn't even acknowledge him. Hope gave him a broad wink and a big smile.

"I love you, too, Mama!" Brody yelled as she drove away. Then he crossed the yard and flopped down on the porch beside his brother.

"You totally forgot that this was the week for the family reunion, right? Lila is messin' with your brain. I can't believe that you fought with Mama like that," Jace chuckled. "Jack called this mornin' to remind me about the reunion. Are you really going to ask Lila to be your date?"

"Jack is a good foreman. We'd have never made it without him when Daddy died," Brody said. "And, yes, I'm going to ask Lila."

*   *   *

Lila reached out to wrap her arms around Brody but all she got was an armful of pillow and covers. Her eyes popped open wide and her heart fell to her knees. Same ole, same ole! A booty call and then gone when she awoke. What ever made her think he would change? In the past, it had been necessary. If her mother had caught them sleeping together, her hot temper would have burned down the café. But now they were adults and her mother was in Pennsylvania for God's sake.

Her alarm sounded and she hit the button to turn it off and crawled out of bed. More than a little angry, she headed toward the bathroom, took a quick shower, and then with only a towel around her body, she padded back to her room. Her phone pinged when she was tugging on a pair of jeans, but she ignored it. If it was Brody, she wasn't ready to talk to him. When she was fully dressed and had her long black hair pulled into a ponytail, it pinged again.

Sure enough, there were six messages from Brody. The first one said: *Call me.*

The last one said: *We have to talk. I can explain.*

"There is no explainin'," Lila muttered on the way to the café kitchen. Duke and Cora were sleeping together on the sofa, but she didn't take time to stop and pet them.

She pasted a smile on her face even if she didn't have one in her heart. "Good mornin', Molly!"

"I'm not Molly but good mornin' to you." Her mother pulled a pan of biscuits from the oven, set them on the cabinet, and then opened her arms. "Surprise!"

"Wow." Lila's heart skipped a beat and then raced. Sweet Jesus! Was that what Brody wanted to explain? She walked into her mother's arms and hugged her tightly. "When did you get here and where's Molly?"

"Five minutes until we open the doors and there's already trucks out there in the parking lot, so you get the short version. I wanted to see you, so Molly and I hatched a plan. I'd get into the airport at the same time she did and she'd loan me her vehicle for a week. She's going to Florida for a test to see if she likes it there. I came here for the same reason. We meet again next Monday evening at the airport."

Lila was speechless but finally found enough voice to at least ask, "And what time did you get here?"

"About five this morning. I knocked on your bedroom door but you didn't wake up. Thought I heard you as I headed toward the kitchen to get things going, but it must've been those two kittens runnin' around. Cute little fluff balls, by the way." Daisy stepped away from Lila and stirred a pot full of sausage gravy.

Lila's phone vibrated in her hip pocket. She pulled it out to see another text from Brody: *Have you gone to the kitchen yet?*

Her thumbs moved like lightning: *Yes. No explaining necessary.*

His came back: *Thanks. Call you later.*

She headed toward the dining room to turn on the lights, adjust the thermostat, and open the door for business. *How did you get this number?*

Lights on and she was flipping the sign around when she got the next one: *Stole it after you went to sleep.*

She sent a smiley face and tucked the phone back into her pocket.

The first two people to enter the café were Valerie Dawson and her mother, Hope. Lila hoped neither of them heard her quick intake of air and that they didn't know where Brody had spent last night.

"Good mornin', Lila. We're here for the pancake special that Molly makes on Tuesday mornin's," Hope said.

"What gets you ladies out this early?" she asked as she came to their table with two steaming mugs of coffee.

"We're makin' sure the Dawson graves are cleaned up. The family likes to go to the cemetery while they're here for the reunion." Valerie's tone had a definite chill to it.

"Hey, I saw a black cat out there in the cemetery. Y'all ever seen it?" she asked.

"That would be Chester O'Riley's old cat. He lives in the house right beside the graveyard," Hope said. "I heard that you got a couple of kittens out at Henry's old barn."

Lila nodded. "Cora and Duke. One is black and the other is white. Cute little things."

"Speakin' of Henry's barn, did you or Daisy ever hear anything about where he went when he left Happy?" Hope asked.

It seemed strange that Hope was eager to engage her in conversation when Valerie's whole body language said that she'd rather be talking to the devil than to Lila.

"Mama told me about him leaving town but it went in one ear and out the other. I hadn't thought of him until I came back this summer," Lila said.

"To answer your question, we have no idea where he went or why." Daisy pushed through the swinging doors that separated the kitchen and dining room. "How are y'all doin' this mornin'?"

"Daisy Jo." Valerie shot icy looks toward Daisy.

"Valerie." Daisy nodded. "I haven't been called that since I left Texas."

"Well, you'll always be Daisy Jo to us. That's what your mama called you," Hope said. "I came for pancakes and crispy bacon and a side order of biscuits and gravy. And what are you doing in town? Coming back for good?"

"I don't know yet. Molly is decidin' if she really wants to leave. I'm decidin' if I want to return. It's a test. What do you want, Valerie?"

"For Molly to stay and you to go," Valerie said without a hint of a smile.

"Well, some things never change, but I was talkin' about food," Daisy said.

"I'll have the big country breakfast with three eggs," Valerie answered.

Daisy propped her hands on the table and leaned in until her nose was only inches from Valerie's. "Just for your information, I'm not in the market for a husband, a significant other, a boyfriend, or even someone to date, so if you're seeing someone, he is totally safe."

"That is enough," Hope said. "Good God, y'all are both well past fifty years old and you're actin' like a couple of teenagers. Get over it, Valerie! And, Daisy Jo, you stop bein' bitchy."

"Mama!" Valerie gasped.

"Hope!" Daisy's voice went high and squeaky.

"We'll have those orders right out." Lila looped her arm in Daisy's and led her to the kitchen. "What just happened?"

"She accused me of trying to seduce Mitch Dawson in high school and she's never gotten over it and neither have I."

Lila bit back a giggle. "So that's why she didn't want me and Brody to date. Because you were still mad at his dad."

"Maybe." Daisy poured pancake batter on the grill. "But I didn't want you dating Brody either. I'd rather see you in a convent as married to a Dawson."

"Why?" Lila asked.

"They all think they are only a notch below God and the angels and you'd spend your whole life tryin' to be what they want you to be rather than who you are. We've got a whole week to have this conversation. Take this to them and if Valerie asks, I did not poison her eggs but I might next time."

"Well, you sure flunked this test with flying colors." Lila smiled.

"Or I passed it. I'm not moving back here and it didn't take a week to make me figure it out," Daisy said.

"I'm surprised that you stayed as long as you did with the kind of anger you two have," Lila said.

Daisy shook a spoon at her. "Don't get me started."

"Yes, ma'am." Lila picked up the orders and got the heck out of the kitchen.

Chapter Thirteen

Someday when Lila had daughters, she might understand her mother but that Wednesday evening, she was glad to see Daisy drive off to church and leave her alone. Working with Daisy was a whole different thing than vacationing with her a couple of times a year. Or maybe it was simply that when they were both back in Happy that Daisy reverted to the mother of a teenager rather than treating Lila like she was a grown woman.

"Which is understandable," Lila told Duke and Cora that evening. "This wild streak inside me is hard to keep reined in when I'm here, so I'm not surprised that she thinks she can run my life like she used to."

Cora bit Duke's ear, so he latched on to her tail and the fight was on. Black and white fur all mixed together made Lila laugh but she needed to get outside to clear her head.

A few minutes later she was headed out toward the canyon with intentions of riding through it without getting sidetracked. But when she reached the lane back onto Henry's old place, she slowed down and turned into it. She told herself it was because she wanted to see that big white mama cat, but the voice in her head said that she was lying.

That same niggling voice said that she shouldn't go into the barn when she saw Brody's truck parked in the shadows of a big oak tree, but she didn't listen that time either. She parked beside the barn doors and hung her helmet on the handlebars.

The white cat came out immediately when Lila sat down on a bale of hay and she stroked its pretty fur from head to the tip of its tail. "So are we here alone? Did someone leave that truck and go off with a friend? Too bad you can't talk."

"I'd trade places with that critter." Brody's voice came down from the loft.

"I saw your truck. How long have you been here?"

"I decided to swing by after replacing fence posts all day. Join me."

Without hesitation, she left the cat and started up the ladder toward his voice. He reached down to help her from the top rung into the loft and sent a shot of pure unadulterated fire through her body. She noticed the quilt spread out over the loose hay in the corner.

"I wasn't expectin' anyone, but I have to admit I was hopin' you might feel the vibes of me wanting you to come out here tonight." He kept her hand in his and led her to the quilt. "Sit with me."

She let him pull her down onto the quilt and a soft breeze fluttered her ponytail. She'd been in this same spot more than one time.

"Remember all the times when we used to spend time here?" he asked.

"Oh, yeah," she whispered. "How many other women have been here with you on this same quilt since I left?"

His free hand covered his heart. "I'm hurt that you'd even think I'd let another woman look at our quilt."

She giggled. "This isn't really that same old quilt that you kept in your truck, is it?"

"It really is the same one—our quilt." He nodded. "And, honey, no other woman has even laid eyes on it. This is my secret place where I come when I'm lonely and want to think."

She'd never thought so much about what Brody went through when she left. She'd always figured that he'd gotten over her within a week and moved on to someone else. "What do you think about?"

"Everything," he said. "Important decisions have been made sittin' right here but mostly I think about you, Lila."

"What are you battling with tonight?" she asked.

"It's not the breath you take but the moments that take your breath away," he said. "I've been thinking about that phrase all day. And I realized that just about every breathtaking memory in my life involves you."

She turned toward him and let her soul sink into those blue eyes. His dark lashes fluttered and then rested on high cheekbones. And then his lips found hers in a long, passionate kiss that raised the heat at least ten degrees. His tongue touched her lower lip and she opened her mouth to allow him entrance. That kiss led to more, each one getting hotter than the last.

Just when she was ready to start unsnapping his shirt,

his phone rang loudly, breaking the mood. He ignored the first five rings. Then within a second, it started again.

"Dammit!" he said as he fished it out of his shirt pocket. "This had better be good, Jace."

He listened for a minute and then hung up. "Our prize bull and two heifers are out on the road. I have to go help get them corralled. Will you wait here for me?"

"I could go help," she said.

He hesitated half a second as if he was weighing the idea and then he nodded. "I'd like that but only if you'll come back here with me when we get done."

She planted a kiss on his cheek. "Want to take the cycle?"

"It would scare them half to death. Jace is bringing the old farm truck. They know that sound. We just need to get them roped and tied to the back. I'm sorry we got interrupted."

She patted him on the knee. "Ranchin' is a twenty-four-hour job, Brody. I understand that. Let's go get the cattle off the road."

He held her hand and she kept pace with his long legs as they left the barn. The moonlight silhouetted an old bull and two cows grazing on the grass beside the road. That old adage about the grass always being greener on the other side of the fence flashed through Lila's mind.

"Hey, Lila." Jace grinned.

"Jace." She nodded.

One of the heifers suddenly raised her head and bawled, then trotted off toward town. The other one headed in the other direction. The bull sauntered to the back of the truck as if he understood exactly what he was supposed to do. Jace quickly wrapped a rope around his neck and tied him to the truck.

"I'll turn around the one going toward town," Lila said over her shoulder as she jogged in that direction.

"I'll keep the one headed in the right direction toward the ranch," Brody yelled.

Lila managed to get ahead of the cow and take a stance right in the middle of the road. The heifer lowered her head, eyed Lila, and started to charge but Lila waved both arms and yelled. The cow stopped in her tracks and simply turned around and began to run back the other way with Lila right behind her.

She caught up with Brody near the lane going back to the ranch and found that the problem with the fence was right beside the cattle guard. "It's a wonder only two got out. I see a dozen or more," she said breathlessly.

"Hey." Jace's voice carried through the darkness. "I came back for the truck. I got Sundance in the corral. I can get this fence fixed in no time."

"I'll stay and help," Brody said quickly.

Jace bumped shoulders with him. "I've got this. You want to use the truck to take Lila back to wherever y'all were?"

Lila could see that Brody was battling with the decision—stay and help where he was needed or go with her. "I can walk back to the barn and get my cycle. I know the way."

Brody reached over and took her hand in his. "Thanks, Jace. I'll be home in a little while."

"See you at breakfast. First one to the kitchen gets the coffee going." Jace waved him away.

"Well, that was fun," Lila said. "But honestly, Brody, I can go back alone or else stay and help y'all fix the fence."

"Jace has got it and I want to spend time with you," he said.

"But it's not easy for you to let him, is it? Tough cowboy that you are, you think you've got to take charge of everything," she said.

Brody gently squeezed her hand. "You know me too well."

"Right back atcha, cowboy," she said.

The sky was filled with twinkling stars surrounding a moon with darkness on one side and light on the other. Lila felt as if that was her life that evening. Light flowing around her in the present and darkness where the future was concerned. Maybe, she thought, she should concentrate on the present and not worry about what the future holds.

"You're awfully quiet," Brody said when they turned to go down the lane leading back to the old barn.

"Just enjoying the moment," she said softly.

He stopped, dropped her hand, and tucked his knuckles under her chin. She tiptoed to meet him part of the way when he bent to kiss her. Like always, her knees went weak, her palms resting on his chest became clammy, and her pulse raced.

"I'm enjoying the moment too," he said when the kiss ended. "Would you go to the Dawson family reunion at my folks' ranch with me on Saturday?"

She cocked her head to one side. Had she heard him right?

"Brody, going to the Hope Springs thing for Independence Day is one thing. Everyone in the whole county is invited to that. The Dawson family reunion is personal."

Valerie might really get out the gun if she showed up with Brody, but then if they were going to test the waters of the future, they'd both better stop thinking about her or Hope or even Daisy.

"I'll introduce you to my whole family." He squeezed her hand.

"Are you sure about this?" Lord have mercy! The Dawson family reunion with Valerie and Hope both there—Lila might as well sign her own death warrant and pick out her burial clothes.

"Never more sure about anything in my life, Lila. Please," Brody whispered.

A star shot across what was left of the moon, leaving a trail of brilliance in its wake. Was that her sign? She and Brody had hoped to see a falling star many times when they were teenagers and God saw fit to throw one through the sky that night. It had to be an omen.

"Okay." She nodded.

"Thank you." He leaned over and brushed a soft kiss across her cheek. "I'll knock on your door at six-thirty."

"If you change your mind—" she said.

"I won't." That time he stopped the words with a steamy string of hot kisses.

When she finally drew away, she said, "I would have floated all the way to the clouds if you had invited me to your family reunion when we were in high school."

* * *

"I'm not that kid anymore," Brody said as he took her hand in his again and began to walk the rest of the way to the barn. "I want to go forward, not backward."

"Sounds good to me." She stopped at the bike. "I should be going."

"Come inside for just a little while with me." His heart was about to float right out of his chest and he couldn't bear to let her leave—just another hour, maybe two so that he could hold on to the feeling.

She looped her arm in his and he led the way back inside the barn, and let her go ahead of him on the ladder. When they were in the loft, he pulled her down to rest in his arms as he stretched out on the quilt.

"I was a fool," he said. "You know what they say about not missing the water until the well runs dry."

"What happened after the well went dry?" she asked.

"I tried to get you out of my mind with hard work. So what kind of girl were you after you left?"

"I turned into a quiet nerd in college."

"That's hard to imagine," he chuckled.

"Mama said that no one knew I was Lila Harris, that crazy kid from Happy, Texas, who caused all kinds of trouble. She said I could be anyone I wanted to be, so I became the quiet Dee Harris and molded myself to fit into the character that she was," she said. "I made excellent grades, graduated with honors, and had my pick of teaching jobs."

"And the Harley?" he asked.

"I didn't get it until last year. Every so often that Lila girl would surface and want to go on a ride with her daddy down through the canyon. I bought it so that she'd be quiet and leave Dee alone."

"I can't imagine anyone ever keepin' Lila quiet and I sure don't see you as Dee."

Lila nodded. "Brody, in six weeks, I'm going back to Florida. I don't know if I'll stay there for another year or move to another state, but wherever I am, it'll most likely be far away from this part of the world. Are you sure you want to start something with no future?"

"So you like teaching better than runnin' a café?"

She rolled over and propped up like him, her face just inches from his. "What do you think?"

"There's schools all around us," he said. "Lila, I can't imagine why you'd want to hide yourself in another person. You're beautiful, witty, fun, and we were just kids who did crazy things. We never hurt anyone with our shenanigans."

"And Lila was also the poor girl who lived in the back of her mother's café that no one asked to proms or family reunions or even to a rodeo."

"I'm sorry," he said. "Brody was a fool who didn't listen to his heart but he won't make the same mistake twice. Let's give it the six weeks and see where it goes. What have we got to lose other than time? And when summer is done..."

"We can wave good-bye without tears this time," she said.

If he had a lucky bone left in him, maybe there would be no good-byes. "What are you thinkin' right now?"

"Something that your smart little sister said," she answered.

"And that would be?"

"That we might be able to have both the inner child and the responsible adult if we want," she said.

"So maybe you could be responsible for everyone else and be my wild child?" Her lips called to him. His body ached for her. But that night shouldn't be about sex. He needed to show her that he was willing to court her properly, and that was more than sneaking into and out of her bedroom for a fast roll in the hay.

She flipped over on her back. "This business of being both is confusing. What if I forget who I am at your family reunion?"

He traced the outline of her lips with his forefinger. "Might liven things up."

"You sure?" Her mouth tingled from his touch.

"You're so beautiful," he whispered as he leaned down and kissed her softly.

She wiggled around until her head rested on his chest. "You know what I missed most when we left?"

"Me?"

"Well, there was that, but I missed the smell of hay and hot summer nights."

"I missed you, Lila. Everything about you. Your wet hair hanging down your naked back when we went skinny-dippin'. Your wit and the way you never let me get away with anything," he said. "I missed holding you and not just for the sex. I flat out craved even half an hour with you nearly every evening. No matter how much I tried to lose myself in work, it never eased the pain."

"I think you were the reason I invented Dee Harris. If I changed it all, the heartache of leaving Happy and you wouldn't kill me. If I was someone else, a studious girl with no background or memories, I had no reason to hurt." She yawned.

Lying there with her in his arms and not saying anything else should have been awkward, but all the words in the dictionary were useless. Nothing could begin to describe the peace in his heart and soul. He pulled her closer to his side, not caring that the night was hot or that the only thing they were doing was enjoying being close.

She mumbled something and then her body went limp when she fell asleep.

He smoothed her hair, drew her closer to his side, and closed his eyes, hoping that she believed in second chances.

*   *   *

Lila awoke with a start. She squirmed out of Brody's arms and sat up, wrapping her arms around her knees.

"Good mornin'," Brody yawned. "Did you sleep well in this five-star hotel?"

"Yes, I did. What time is it?"

Thank God it was still dark. Hopefully, still early enough that her mother was still at the church affair or else she'd gone to one of her friends' houses to catch up on the gossip.

"Still night," he said.

"I've got to get home. Mama is drivin' me crazy with advice already. If she thinks I've been with you, she'll never shut up."

"You should ask me for a date," he said.

"What?"

"I asked you to my family events. I'll make my mother face the fact that there is an us—as in Lila and Brody. Maybe you should do the same with yours," he said.

"Good advice. Would you go with me to church on Sunday night? I will come and get you at six-thirty and we'll be there by the time it starts," she said.

"Wow!" He grinned. "That's a pretty big step, going to church. I mean the family reunion is one thing, but a public thing like sitting together in church? You expectin' to share a hymn book too?"

"I don't share a songbook on a first date. I save that for the third date and only then if I really like the guy," she teased.

"Well, then, I suppose I'm free on Sunday night but only if I can take you and Daisy to Tulia for ice cream afterward."

"Why go all that way? We'll just open the café and invite Mama to join us," she said.

"Long as I get to pay for it so it's my treat, that's fine." He draped an arm around her shoulders.

"Then it's a date. I'll tell Mama when I get home," she said. "And when are you telling Valerie to expect me for the family reunion?"

"I already told her I was invitin' you," he drawled.

"Are you kiddin' me?" she gasped.

"Nope. Told her that I'd invited you to the Fourth of July picnic and that I was asking you to be my date for the reunion."

"And?"

"She didn't like it but that's her problem. Mine was convincing you to go with me." He pulled her tighter into his embrace and kissed her on the tip of her nose.

"I really do have to go, Brody." She rolled to her feet and started for the ladder but stopped after a couple of feet. "Want me to help pick the hay off that quilt?"

"No, it's so dry, it'll shake right off. Give me a minute and I'll walk you out to your bike. I still have trouble believing that you ride that thing."

She shimmied down the ladder and waited at the bottom for him. In the darkness she had to use her imagination to really see the way he filled out those snug jeans. Could she really say good-bye to him at the end of the summer with no tears?

He tossed the quilt into the bed of the truck on the way to her bike and took her hand in his. Would even the simplest touch of those big, rough hands ever stop sending delicious hot little shivers through her heart?

She threw a leg over the seat of her bike and settled onto it, but he didn't let go of her hand. He leaned in and captured her mouth in a scorching kiss that made her weak in the knees. She pulled her hand from his and wrapped both her arms around his neck and opened her mouth slightly to allow his tongue entrance. He made such sweet love to her mouth that she wanted to take him back to the hayloft or better yet to the bed of his truck since it was closer.

Then he took a step back. "Text me when you get home."

She nodded as she settled her helmet onto her head. "Betcha I beat you."

"I'm right next door." He grinned.

"I've givin' you a fightin' chance against my Harley."

He took off toward the truck and she left a dust storm for him to follow. When she reached the end of the lane, she leaned into the curve and gave the cycle more gas when she straightened up. Glad that there were no cops out at that time of night, she didn't even look at the speedometer. She braked at the café parking lot, slinging gravel against the old building in a spray.

"So much for sneakin' into the apartment," she giggled as she grabbed her phone and hurriedly sent a text: *I beat you.*

One came back immediately: *Only by a few seconds.*

Her thumbs typed: *You owe me something wonderful.*

She put the phone back in her pocket, removed her helmet, opened the garage door, and pushed the bike inside. Her phone pinged and she grabbed it to read: *Name the time, the place, and the poison and I'll pay up.*

She eased the back door open and took off her boots. She made it to the living room to find her mother standing in the middle of the floor with her hands on her hips.

"God I hate that bike. I bet you were down in that damned canyon, weren't you? Actually, I don't want to know. You're home and safe and I'm going to bed. Kids!"

"Good night, Mama."

"I'm glad I made the decision not to come back here. I'd die of a heart attack in a week worryin' about you. If I'm eighteen hundred miles away, I won't know what you're doing," Daisy fussed. "At least if you were riding too fast in that canyon, you weren't with Brody Dawson."

"See you bright and early, Mama."

"I don't know which is worse. The bike or Brody." Daisy got in the last word as she slammed her bedroom door.

Chapter Fourteen

Lila tied on an apron and tucked an order pad into the pocket before she flipped on the lights and unlocked the doors to the café that Thursday morning. No one was in the parking lot yet so she went back to the kitchen, stuffed a biscuit with crispy bacon, and ate it as she watched Daisy crack eggs into a bowl.

Lila took a deep breath and faced her mother. "I'm going to the Dawson family reunion on Saturday night with Brody," she said.

"Well, that ought to go over like a cockroach in the punch bowl at a church social," she said. "It might be the smartest thing for you."

"Really?" Lila had expected a hundred reasons why she shouldn't go and lots of talk all day about the issue.

"Sure," Daisy said. "It will show you that those people ain't never going to accept you. You'll always be my daughter and Valerie would rather have Lucifer's sister for a daughter-in-law than my kid. Go on and be miserable."

"And you won't say 'I told you so' one time, right?" Lila finished the biscuit and made another one.

"Oh no. I'm going to say that at least fifty times on Sunday. You never would listen when it came to Brody Dawson," Daisy said.

The bell above the door dinged and Lila laid her biscuit to the side. "Well, just be careful you don't say it in front of Brody. I asked him to go to church with me on Sunday and we—as in me and you and him—are coming back here for ice cream afterward."

"Are you nuts?" Daisy whispered.

"Not according to my therapist!"

Lila made her way through the swinging doors into the dining room. "Good mornin', Paul and Gracie. How y'all doin' today?"

"Coffee for us both and the breakfast special," Gracie said. "We're on the way to Amarillo to get some things for Hope and Valerie for the Dawson family reunion and thought we'd splurge and have breakfast out this mornin'."

Lila pinned the order on the merry-go-round in the window and poured two mugs of coffee. "Sugar or cream?"

"No, just black," Gracie said. "We started helping with the reunion when Adam got in the family. Since our family is down to just the two of us, we like having the Dawsons take us in."

"That's sweet of them," Lila said, glad that several more folks were arriving so she'd have an excuse to walk away.

"Order up," Daisy yelled.

From then until after the noon rush, there was someone in the café all the time and Daisy was kept busy. But at two o'clock things slowed down enough that Daisy brought two burger baskets to the front. She pointed at the drink machine and then at the food.

"You know what I drink," she told Lila.

"Sweet tea for both of us." Lila nodded. "No lettuce and extra pickles, please?"

"I raised you, kiddo," Daisy told her. "I know how you eat your burgers."

Lila carried the tea to the booth and sat down across from her mother. Each of them stretched forth their long legs and propped their feet on the other side and sighed at the same time.

"Been a morning." Daisy dipped a French fry in a small container of ketchup.

"Felt more like a weekend than a Thursday." Lila poured ketchup over her fries.

Lila had just bitten off a bite of burger when the bell above the door rang. She looked around to see Brody swagger into the café. Looking like he'd spent the whole morning in the hay fields or maybe building fences, his white T-shirt was smudged with dirt and his hair wet with sweat. His forehead had a definite line between dusty and clean where his hat had been all morning.

She didn't realize she was mentally stripping him out of his clothes until Daisy kicked her under the table. Shifting her gaze from him to her mother, she tucked her chin and shot a mean look across the table.

"Something wrong, Lila?" Brody headed around the counter to the drink machine.

"Not a thing." She smiled. "What can I get you?"

"Y'all keep your seats. I'm just here for a glass of ice tea and I can get it myself," he said.

"Kasey don't make tea at the ranch?" Daisy asked.

"Yep, but I had to come into town to get a load of feed and I'm thirsty," Brody answered. He poured a tall glass from the drink fountain and carried it to the booth where he slid right in beside Lila.

"How you been Miz Daisy?" he asked.

"Busy," Daisy answered tersely.

Under the booth, his hand rested on Lila's knee. She took a big gulp of iced tea but it did nothing to cool her off.

He squeezed gently. "Lila tells me that you'll be here until Monday. You need a ride to the airport?"

"I've got Molly's car. I'll drive myself and she'll be here in time to cook breakfast on Tuesday," she said.

"She hates Florida and can't wait to get home to Texas. Crazy thing is that Georgia doesn't like it so much either and she might be coming back to Happy also. They might buy the café after all."

"Why does Molly hate Florida?" Lila asked.

"Too much sand. Molly says it's in everything from her hair to the corners of her suitcase. It's like it follows her." Daisy almost smiled.

"Well, would you look at that? I wonder what Clancy is doing in Happy, Texas." Daisy beamed.

Lila whipped around so fast to look out the window that it made her light-headed. She dropped the French fry in her hand and gasped at the sight of her ex-boyfriend walking toward the café. "Mama?"

"Hey." Daisy shrugged. "We still talk occasionally."

"Why?" Lila glared at her mother.

"Should I leave?" Brody asked.

She grabbed his free hand and held it on top of the table. "No, stay."

It was Daisy's turn to glare and if looks could kill, Brody would be nothing but a bag of thirsty bones on the floor right then. The bell rang and Clancy entered the café, glanced around, and smiled when Daisy waved him over to the booth.

"Well, hello, Clancy. Can I get you something?" Daisy pulled a chair out for him.

"Got a drink back down the road," he said. "I'm good. Keep your seat, Daisy. Hello, Lila."

"Clancy, meet Brody Dawson." Lila made introductions. "Brody, this is Clancy. He and I are colleagues at the school where I work in Florida."

Brody slid out of the booth and extended a hand. "Pleased to meet you, Clancy. I take it that you're friends with these folks or is it family?"

"More than friends, right, Dee?" He shook with Brody and then sat down. Wearing perfectly creased dress slacks, a pale blue shirt open at the collar, and loafers, he looked exactly like he did every day at school. Not a blond hair was out of place and his cute little mustache was trimmed.

Brody's phone pinged and he checked the message. "That's Jace. The kids we've hired to help us this summer are down to the last fence post, so I'd better get back to the ranch with what I've got loaded on the truck. See you Saturday, Lila." He stood up. "Nice to meet you, Clancy."

"Lookin' forward to it," Lila answered. "Call me later?"

"Of course." Brody dropped a kiss on her forehead and started toward the door.

"So what are you doing in Texas?" Lila asked, but her eyes stayed on Brody as he crossed the floor.

"I came to see you, Dee. Why would he call you Lila?" Clancy asked.

Brody stopped at the fountain and filled a takeout cup with ice and tea. He took his time, throwing a wink over his shoulder toward Lila before he finally laid a five-dollar bill on the counter. He waved at the door and she couldn't keep her eyes or mind off him as he made his way across the parking lot.

"I asked you a question," Clancy said brusquely.

"Because that's what I'm known as in this town. Why would you drive fifteen hundred miles to Texas to see me? If you're going to fire me, you could do that by phone," Lila said.

Clancy chuckled. "Darlin' Dee, I'm not going to fire you. I can't wait for the end of summer when you come on home where you belong."

"Does Belinda know you're here?"

"Blunt." Clancy's grin got bigger. "Like always. Texas didn't change that a bit, did it, Daisy?"

"When she crosses the border into Texas, it gets worse," Daisy said. "I've got to get back to the kitchen. You two have things to discuss. And, Lila, we'll talk later."

"Oh, yes, we will," Lila said, and then turned her attention to Clancy. "What's going on? Did my mother call you?"

For some insane reason, an old song by Vince Gill played through her head—"Which Bridge to Cross (Which Bridge to Burn)." She thought she'd burned the bridge between her and Clancy when they'd broken up last year. If she hadn't at that time, she sure enough had the torch in her hand now and he'd better run because she was about to set fire to the damn thing.

"No, actually I called her last week and she said she was coming to Texas for a week. Then we talked on Monday. I got a flight from Pensacola to Amarillo today just to see you. I've only got about an hour before I have to head back to the airport, but what I wanted to say needed to be said face-to-face," he said seriously.

"I'm listening." She imagined skipping across the bridge like a little girl and pouring gasoline from a red can as she went from one end to the other.

"I missed you." He scooted closer and ran a hand down her arm. It did nothing but irritate her.

"What about Belinda?" Sorry sucker was two-timing his girlfriend of four months. He deserved to get a little gasoline on his expensive shoes, so in the video playing in her mind, she doused them down good.

"Things are going well. We like the same things, love the same old movies, the same books, and we have so much in common. We're both coaches at the school, so we understand what the job means," he said. "But there's this thing between me and you that I need to resolve before I take it to the next step."

"Which is?" Mentally, she flicked a candle lighter and a flame shot out from the end.

"Which is asking her to marry me. Are you listening to a word I'm saying?" He squeezed her arm too tightly.

"Congratulations. I'm happy for both of you." She jerked her arm free and scooted over to the other side of the booth.

"Is that Brody cowboy the reason you called it quits with me?" Clancy raised an eyebrow.

"Could be." She'd seen that look on his face before when he didn't get his way.

He combed back his hair with his fingertips and not a single strand fell over his forehead like Brody's did when he did the same thing. "I really love you, Dee."

"Then why are you marrying Belinda?"

"I won't if you'll give me another chance. We had something good and I can't get you out of my mind and heart. It's not easy for me to sit here and say this when I saw the way you looked at that dirty cowboy," Clancy answered.

"You shouldn't have come to Texas," Lila said.

"Is there hope for us after school starts? If you get that rancher out of your sights, you might see things different. A marriage shouldn't be based on a high school whim," Clancy said.

"There is no hope for you and me," she said.

Flaunting the fact that he had money enough to fly to Texas and back in one day did not impress her one bit.

"Then I wish you the best and I'll go now."

"Thank you and give my best to Belinda," she said.

"A good-bye kiss? It might change your mind." He stood and pushed the chair back in place.

She shook her head. "Not a good idea."

Propping his hands on the booth, he leaned close to her and whispered, "We could have had something really good."

That was as far from the truth as black was from white. What they would have had would have been far from good and would have probably ended in divorce.

"I want something that will take my breath away and if I can't have that, I'll do without," she said.

In an instant, his hands left the table and he was plastered next to her in the booth, her face cupped in his hands and his tongue halfway down her throat. She pushed him away so hard that he slid off the end of the booth and sprawled out on the floor.

"You just made the biggest mistake of your life." Clancy's voice went cold as ice as he got to his feet.

"Or I just made the smartest decision of my whole life. I can't believe that you came all the way to Texas to try to get back together with me when you're living with Belinda." She wiped the feel of his lips away from hers. "She deserves better."

"I care too much about you to see you throw away your life on a worthless, dirty farmer," Clancy said. "You know I could give you a good life, if you would just get over this silly teenage infatuation."

In her vision of the bridge, she wrung every last drop of gasoline from the can and poured it out.

"You sound more like a parent than a boyfriend and that's a little creepy." The imaginary torch she'd held in her hands hit the bridge, sending it into a blaze. "I've got to get back to work. Have a nice flight home."

She made her way out of the booth, sidestepped around him, and headed toward the kitchen. The decision to not go back to Florida for the new teaching year was made in that instant. She would reopen her employment files at the college and teach in central Pennsylvania, as badly as she hated the winters there, before she taught with Clancy as her principal for another year.

"Then this is good-bye?" he asked on his way across the floor.

"Exactly." *Run, Clancy, run. The fire is on the way.*

"Just remember I tried, Daisy," he called out as he slammed the door.

Lila pushed through the swinging doors to the kitchen and popped her hands on her hips. "What were you thinkin'?"

"Keepin' you from a life of misery," Daisy shot back. "What did you tell Clancy? He loves you and he'd do right by you."

"Oh, like he's doing right by his current girlfriend?" Lila said through gritted teeth. "I can't imagine how she'd feel if she knew he was only going to propose to her if I wouldn't take him back."

Daisy's brows drew down into a solid line. "He said that?"

Her mama just got a glimpse into the real world. Not every man out there was like Billy Harris who adored his family and who let them be a part of the decisions.

"Pretty much. You talk about Brody's family feeling like they are above me socially, well Clancy is a thousand times worse." Lila propped a hip on a bar stool. "What'd he tell you?"

"That you had commitment issues, whatever that means. You kids talk a different language than we did at your age," she sighed.

"He's right," Lila said. "I do have trouble giving my heart to someone."

Daisy searched in her purse for her phone. "I'm going to call him and give him a piece of my mind. I'm so sorry that I even talked to him."

Lila took the purse from her hands. "Remember what you've always told me?"

"About what?" Daisy's dark brows drew into a tight line.

"Anyone who stirs in a shit pile..." Lila got tickled.

Daisy finished the old saying. "Has to lick the spoon."

Arms around each other's shoulders, they laughed so hard that tears ran down their cheeks. Finally, Lila wiped her mother's face and then her own with a bar rag.

"Everything works out as it should, Mama. Ignoring him is the best thing we can do. This helped me decide that I'm definitely not going back to Florida, though. I'll take a job wherever I can find it next year," Lila said. "I can't work with him after this."

"Come to central Pennsylvania. I promise I'll...," Daisy started.

Lila crossed the room in a couple of long strides. "You're the mother. If you didn't meddle and worry, I'd call the undertaker."

Daisy wrapped Lila in her arms. "Thanks for not being mad at me. Now get on back out there. I hear truck tires on the gravel."

"And if it's Brody?"

"I don't want to see Clancy again but..."

Lila handed Daisy the towel. "When you were my age, you had a ten-year-old daughter. And your mother didn't run your life."

"She tried," Daisy said, "but I was every bit as stubborn as you. She didn't want me to buy this café or put an apartment behind it."

Lila waved over her shoulder and she went back out to the dining room. "Well, hello, Brody Dawson. Haven't seen you in days."

She could almost hear Daisy's sighs.

"We good?" he asked.

"We are very good." Two bridges had been burned but she was very interested in rebuilding one of them.

Brody had come back to check on her. That meant more than a Sunday date, the Dawson reunion, or the Fourth of July party. Not caring that Paul and Fred were on their way into the café, she walked right up to him and wrapped her arms around him.

"Want to talk about anything?" He drew her close.

"Not a thing. I just want you to hold me for a minute so that I know you're really here," she said.

"I'm here for you always, Lila," he whispered. "As long as you need."

The door opened again and two of Daisy's old friends, Laura and Teresa, rushed inside from the blistering heat with Fred and Paul right behind them.

"Well, hello, Brody," Laura said.

Lila stepped back away from him. "Hello. What can I get y'all?"

"Ladies." Brody nodded toward them and turned back toward Lila. "I'll see you Saturday night, right?"

"I'll be ready." Lila beamed. "Don't work too hard."

He rounded the end of the counter and kissed her on the cheek.

"Does Valerie know about this?" Laura raised a dark brown eyebrow that matched her hair—all but that inch of gray roots shining at the part, anyway.

"Lord, she's going to have a hissy," Teresa whispered. Laura's opposite, she was tall and thin with dyed red hair cropped at chin length and a face so full of wrinkles that it looked like a road map of Dallas.

Drying her hands on her apron, Daisy pushed back the swinging doors and motioned them back into the kitchen.

"Good enough for her, the way she's acted toward me and Lila. Not that I'm for my girl going out with Brody but Valerie don't get to call the shots. Y'all come on in here and we'll make us a batch of sweet potato fries to nibble on while we have a visit."

Lila carried two glasses of sweet tea to Fred and Paul's booth. "A big order of fries?"

"Sounds good, sweetheart," Fred said. "It's my turn to buy, so make the ticket out to me. He's wishy-washy like an old woman. Changes his mind all the time."

"And you're one of them DOC people," Paul shot back at him.

"OCD, obsessive-compulsive disorder. Get it right, old man," Fred said.

"Only someone who had it would know how to spell it," Paul joked. "And does Valerie and Hope know that you and Brody are makin' out in public?"

"Why would you ask that?" Lila asked.

"Because we need to know whether we should warn the volunteer fire department," Fred teased. "Those two women are going to burst into flames when they hear what we just now saw."

Paul lowered his voice and his eyes shifted around the café. "I heard that you might be going to the Dawson family reunion. That true?"

"Might be." Lila patted him on the shoulder.

Lila listened to their banter and yelled the order through the window rather than pinning it up. She'd barely gotten that done when her phone rang. Seeing Brody's picture put a smile on her face.

"Hello," she said.

"Just thought I'd let you know that I did tell my family

that you're my date for the family reunion and for the Fourth of July picnic at Hope Springs. There's no surprises," he said.

"Tell that to Laura and Teresa. I'm not sure they believe their eyes," she laughed. "What do I hear in the background?"

"George Strait and I are enjoying the morning now that Conrad has driven out of Happy," he answered.

"Clancy, not Conrad," she said. "But that doesn't matter. He's gone. And I think that is 'Check Yes or No' playing. Am I right?"

"If I gave you a note with the words 'will you be my girlfriend' and there were two boxes at the bottom with yes by one and no by the other, which would you check?" he asked.

"Well, I checked no when Clancy handed me the note today. I haven't gotten one from you yet, so I don't know. Maybe you'll have to write the note and see which box I check," she answered. "Order is up. Got to go."

"Maybe I will write that note," he said.

*   *   *

Brody let out a whoosh of air that he didn't even know he was holding until he put the phone back in his pocket. It rang immediately and he jerked it out, hoping that he'd hear her say that she'd check yes on that childish note.

"Hey," he said.

"Come on to the springs. Sundance is belly deep in the water and refuses to get out," Jace said.

Brody parked the truck and one of the high school boys he'd hired for the summer came running over.

"Glad to see you with the wire. We strung the last of what we had."

"Got to go get that pesky bull out of Hope Springs. Wouldn't happen to have a rope, would you?"

"Sure thing, Mr. Dawson." He removed his keys and tossed them at Brody. "Take my truck. Rope is behind the seat. The clutch is a little tight so you got to stomp it real good. We'll get this unloaded and keep on workin'."

"Mr. Dawson. If that don't make me feel old," Brody complained as he started the ten-year-old vehicle, jammed it into gear, and took off across the bumpy pasture toward the springs.

Jace was sitting at the edge of the water when he parked the truck. Boots were set off to one side and his jeans were soaked all the way to the waist. "There ain't no coaxin' or cussin' him out of there."

Brody grabbed the rope and headed that way. "How'd he get out of the corral?"

"I have no idea but I'm ready to put him in a steel pen with no gate," Jace groaned. "I might as well go on out there and rope him since I'm already wet."

Brody handed him one end of the rope and kicked off his boots. "I'll go this time. It's so damned hot that I'll enjoy the cold water."

"Kasey called. Who was the citified feller who came to see Lila?" Jace wrapped the rope around his broad palm twice.

"Don't know much other than she put him packin'." Brody waded out into the water and sucked air when the bull kicked backward and drenched him from the neck down. "You sorry sucker. You want to act like a rodeo bull, then I'll ride you out of this water."

Sundance shook his head and bawled.

"Feelin' feisty, are you," Jace laughed.

"Yes, I am." Brody slipped the rope around the bull's neck.

"Hey, I was talkin' to Sundance, not you. He's already mad. Just push and let me get him tied to the truck and he'll come out of there."

"I'm going to teach him a lesson." Brody mounted his back, holding on to the rope with one hand.

Sundance went completely wild. His back feet shot toward the sky and his nose went straight down into the water. He snorted, slung water and bull snot everywhere as his hind legs hit the water with a splash. Twisting his head toward his tail one way and then reversing the process, he tried to shake Brody off.

"Hey, we could use him for rodeo stock," Jace hollered as he removed his phone from his shirt pocket and started recording.

Brody hung on, getting angrier by the minute as he watched Jace film him rather than checking the time to see if he'd managed eight seconds. Then suddenly, the bull's back legs reached for the sun and his head went into the water again. His hide and Brody's jeans were sopping wet, so there was no way Brody could hang on another minute. He slipped into the cold water and his straw hat floated down the stream.

"Guess your family jewels is a bit cold now too," Jace laughed.

"Delete that video," Brody panted.

"Okay," Jace said, and hit a few keys. "Deleted."

"Thank you."

"But I did send it to Lila before I deleted it."

"You..." Brody shook his fist at Jace and ran toward his brother.

Sundance, now rid of the burden on his back, walked out of the water, his head held high as he strutted off toward the pickup truck and stopped at the rear.

Brody had Jace in a headlock when he realized that Sundance was staring at them. "Would you look at that crazy fool? He's waiting for us to tie him to the back of the truck and lead him back to the corral."

Jace wiggled free and plopped down on the grassy bank. "Why shouldn't I send that to Lila?"

"You didn't see that guy, Jace. He was everything that she probably needs in her life. All spruced up." Brody fell down beside him, flopping onto his back. "She deserves better than a crazy old rancher who gets mad and rides a bull out of icy-cold water."

"Maybe so, but she put him goin', didn't she?" Jace lay back beside his brother. "If that bull moves an inch, I swear this is when he goes to the market to be made into bologna."

"That don't mean she can't reconsider. He looked at her like she was...Well, he looked at her like I feel when she's in my sight. Like there's no one else."

"She loved you first and you know what they say about first loves. Let's get this old cuss back to the corral." Jace stood up and offered a hand to his brother.

"Thanks, brother."

"Just helpin' my elders," Jace teased.

"Hey, I'm not old yet." Brody slid into the truck seat.

"You'll always be older than me," Jace said as he headed toward the back of the truck.

Brody grabbed his phone from where he'd tossed it

onto the passenger seat and found a message from Lila: *Call me.*

She answered on the first ring. "What was that all about? I was afraid you'd drowned when you went into the water like that. I swear it was worse than the fear in my heart when you rode at the bull riding and fell off."

"You care!" he chuckled.

"I don't want you dead. And I bet you and that bull both will have to warm up for a long time before..." She paused for a breath.

"Before what?" he asked.

"Call me later when your HDTs are thawed."

"HDTs?" he asked.

"Hangin' down things," she said as she hung up.

The screen went dark and he roared with laughter.

"What's so funny?" Jace asked.

"Nothing." Brody had no intention of sharing the moment. "You going to drive or ride on the tailgate and keep him moving?"

"I'll tailgate and then we're going to the house to get cleaned up. Mama says we're supposed to be over at her place at six to start helping get things ready for the reunion. I'm steering clear of her. She'll be fuming or trying to lay a guilt trip on you. I don't want to hear either one," Jace said. "And for a man who's about to get strung up by his mama, you sure got a happy expression on your face."

"I'm doin' now what I should've done in high school. I just hope it's not too late." Brody got inside the truck and started driving slowly back to the barn.

Chapter Fifteen

The pile of clothing grew on Lila's bed as she tried
on outfit after outfit. Who would have thought that she'd
have so much trouble picking out an outfit for a family reunion? Jeans and a shirt should do fine but thinking about
a first official date with Brody had her insides twisted
into a knot. She was checking her reflection in the mirror
when Daisy pushed her way into the room. She handed
a cup of chamomile tea to Lila and then sat down in the
rocking chair.

"Thought that might calm your nerves," Daisy said.
"This is not a date with the governor. It's just Brody
Dawson."

Lila set the cup on the dresser. "Thanks, Mama, but I'd
be less nervous if it was the governor. Does this look all
right? Is it too short?"

The bright red sundress left her shoulders bare. The
waist fit snug and the skirt lay in gentle folds, stopping

at the top of her knees. She'd shaved her legs, put a few curls in her long, black hair, and applied a minimum of makeup.

She was every bit as nervous as she had been when she dressed for her first date with Brody twelve years ago. Her mother had brought her a cup of tea that night, too, and then held her while she wept when he didn't show up. She glared at the tea, refusing to take a sip for fear it would jinx the whole night.

"You look beautiful. But, honey, I'm sure the almighty Dawsons wouldn't take too well to you comin' to their affair in your bare feet, so you better find a pair of shoes to match that dress. Or, you could just blow this silly notion off and go to dinner with Laura, Teresa, and me," Daisy said.

Lila slipped her feet into a pair of leather sandals and groaned. "Molly was right—I really should have gotten my hair trimmed and my nails done. My toes look horrible and I don't even have time to do them myself now."

"Wear cowboy boots. Those fancy ones I bought you for Christmas a couple of years ago. They've got that red inlay in the front," Daisy suggested.

"Oooh, good idea." Lila pulled the boots from the closet and shoved her feet down in them.

"Now that completes the outfit," Daisy said. "Wipe off that light colored lipstick and put on clear red. It's on my dresser."

Lila checked the mirror. Daisy was right. The outfit called for red lipstick.

"I hate to see your heart broken again, but I guess you've always had to learn your lessons the hard way," Daisy said. "It's tough on a mama to see her kid hurting."

"Sometimes the only way to get past the pain is to wade through it to the other side." Lila raised her voice as she crossed the hall. "Right now I'm standing right in the middle of the river, not knowing what to do. Behind me is the past. Ahead is the future and the water is rising."

"That sounds like something your father would have said," Daisy said. "Now you're ready. I hear his truck driving up. I'm going to play the mama card even if you aren't a teenager. You will not go rushing out there to meet him and if he honks rather than coming to the door like a real date should, then I'm going to shoot the tires out of his truck."

"That's a step up." Lila extended a hand and pulled her mother to her feet. "You would have shot him, not the tires, when I was younger."

Daisy led the way down the hall to the living room. "The mama of a grown daughter can only do so much."

The phone rang at the same time that Brody knocked on the door. "You answer that and I'll get the door," Daisy ordered.

Lila grabbed the phone and said, "Happy Café. Lila speaking." Lila held up a finger to give her a moment. "Yes, ma'am, we are interested in selling the café. You heard right and I'll be glad to see you tomorrow morning at ten-thirty. Bye now."

She turned to find Brody standing in the middle of the floor. He held a bouquet of wildflowers tied with a bright red ribbon in one hand and a black cowboy hat in the other. The top button of his blue and white plaid shirt was left undone, showing a tuft of dark hair. Her eyes had trouble moving away from the belt buckle engraved with a bull rider.

"You look amazing." He stuck the flowers out toward her. "I picked these for you."

"Did I hear that you were meeting someone about the café?" Daisy asked.

"Yes. They're coming tomorrow morning." Lila smiled. "Thank you so much for these, Brody. Give me a minute to put them in some water."

"I'll do it for you and they'll be on the dresser in your room when you get home this evening. I'll shut the door to keep the cats out." Daisy took them from him.

"Thank you, Mama," Lila said, but her eyes didn't leave Brody's. "They are beautiful."

"Not as beautiful as you are. Does she have a curfew, Miz Daisy?" Brody asked.

"Only if I do," Daisy said.

Lila hugged Daisy and whispered, "Wish me luck."

"Never, not with that guy," Daisy told her.

"Ready?" Brody asked.

"As I'll ever be. Excited but nervous."

He settled his hat on his head and held the door open for her. "You have a good time, Miz Daisy."

"I'm sure I will," she said.

When they were near the truck, he put both hands on her shoulders and turned her around. His gaze started at her toes and traveled slowly to her hair and then back to settle on her lips. "You take my breath away, Lila. You're stunning."

"You clean up pretty good, cowboy, but I got to admit, I kind of like a little dirt on your shirt."

His lips landed on hers for a brief, sweet kiss as he helped her into the truck. "I like you in your tight jeans and tops, too, but, darlin', you look like something out of a movie in that outfit."

She flipped the visor mirror down and checked her lipstick as he rounded the hood of the truck and took his place behind the wheel.

"Brody, I'm really stressed about this." She put the mirror back up and fastened her seat belt.

He drove to the highway and turned right. "Would you have been if we were still in high school and I'd asked you to our reunion?"

"Of course, but I bluffed my way through things better in those days," she answered.

"I've got a confession. I felt like a kid tonight when I knocked on your door. My hands were sweaty and I almost threw the flowers behind the garage. I should have thought to go to Amarillo and get you roses. You deserve something more than wildflowers picked from our back pasture." He parked the car at the end of a long row of other vehicles in the pasture beside the ranch's sale barn. "Ready?"

She shook her head.

"Hey, any woman who would be willin' to climb on a bull that refuses to get out of Hope Springs and ride the critter with me isn't afraid of anything." He grinned.

She hit the button to undo the seat belt and threw open the door.

"Whoa, darlin'," he said. "You see all those cowboys around the barn door? They need to see me bein' a gentleman or I'll have to beat them off with a stick all evening."

She sat still until he made it around the truck and held out his hand. Putting hers into his turned the whole world around. The jitters in her stomach settled. Her heart stopped racing.

"Is that your cousin Toby with Jace?" she asked.

"It sure is, but he's married now so I don't have to worry about him." With an arm slung around her shoulders, Brody led her toward the barn.

She tried to take it all in with a glance but it was impossible. A group of cowboys had gathered around Toby and Jace, and they were all staring at her. Kids were running around everywhere, but she didn't see Emma or Rustin. Country music was playing. The aroma of smoked brisket filled the air.

"A band?" she asked.

"Just a local group. It's not Blake Shelton," Brody said. "But I'm askin' right now for every dance."

"Yes," she said without hesitation.

"Lila Harris?" Toby smiled. "Is that you?"

Toby was a Dawson—tall, sexy, great angles to his face and gorgeous eyes. But in Lila's eyes, he fell far short of Brody when it came to looks and charm.

"It is really me," she said. "You haven't changed a bit, Toby Dawson. And I hear that you're married."

"I am," he said. "You'll have to meet my Lizzy. We're expecting our first baby in a few months."

"Congratulations! And Blake?"

"He and Allie are here somewhere. They have a little girl already." Toby nudged Brody on the shoulder. "You'd best keep her close, Brody. We still got lots of cousins who'd just love to steal this one from you."

"Don't I know it!" Brody nodded. "We'll see y'all later, I'm sure."

"Lila?" Hope was suddenly right there in front of them when they walked inside the barn. Her eyes started at Lila's red lipstick, then traveled to her boots and back up again.

"Doesn't she look beautiful tonight?" Brody flashed a smile.

"She's always been a pretty girl. I do like those boots and I'm a sucker for red lipstick," Hope said. "Girls today ain't got a bit of style with all them browns and pinks on their lips."

"Thank you." Lila nodded.

"You should wear more red." Hope looped her arm through Lila's. "Brody, you go on and visit with your cousins a little bit before Jace says grace and we're turned loose on the food. I'm going to take Lila around and show her everything."

Rustin appeared out of nowhere and tugged at Hope's hand. "Granny, I'm hungry. When are we going to eat?" Then his eyes grew big and he yelled, "Emma, Lila is here!"

Emma squealed and she ran across the barn toward them.

Lila dropped down to a squat and hugged both kids at the same time. "This looks like a great party. What's your favorite thing on the food table?"

"The baked beans," Emma said.

"Chocolate pie but you got to eat everything on your plate before you get any," Rustin said seriously.

"You're not my boss, Rustin, but you can dance with me." Emma pulled him out to the dance floor.

Hope wrapped her hand around Lila's upper arm. "They're cute kids. We'd like to have a dozen more on Hope Springs."

Lila was stunned speechless. Hope might be telling her that she wanted her to produce twelve little Dawson kids or else she was being nice to lure her to her death in a dark corner of the barn. Lila wasn't ready for either one of those options right then.

"Hey, Valerie, look who I found," Hope called out to her daughter, who was in the midst of several women.

Valerie's quick glance said that she'd rather be home with a migraine than attending a reunion with Lila.

"We'll be around to introduce you later." Hope waved as she kept walking toward the stairs leading to the buyer's balcony. "Now it's your turn to hold my arm. My knees ain't what they used to be."

Lila took the steps slowly and waited for Hope to get a firm stand on every one before she moved on. Was the old gal going to push her over the top railing to her death or did she have a gun hiding between the bleacher seats?

"I used to sneak up here with my boyfriend," Hope said when they reached the top. Three layers of wooden benches ran the length of the balcony. During the fall livestock sale, the buyers could have a bird's-eye view of the cattle being offered.

Without thinking, Lila glanced to the top bench on the far end—the one where she and Brody always had a making-out sesssion.

Hope giggled. "That was our favorite spot, too, but we'll sit right here on the bottom seat because my legs need to rest."

Lila waited for Hope to get comfortable before she removed her hand from her arm. Then she sat down beside her and looked down at a barn full of people. There was Valerie still visiting with a group of women that Lila didn't know.

From the way Kasey was motioning with her hands, she was giving the caterers their last orders before they took all the lids off the food dishes. Kids were running every which way and the band was playing one country music song after another.

Then she spotted Brody talking to Jace and Toby. He kept scanning the barn and finally as if a sixth sense got a hold on him, he looked up. She waved and he grinned—she had no doubt that they were sharing the same memory. Her cheeks filled with high color but she couldn't take her eyes off him.

"Looking down from here puts a new perspective on things. Getting away from the forest so you can see the trees. Henry was my neighbor, you know. We grew up right across a barbed-wire fence from each other. Even graduated from high school together."

Lila shook her head. "I guess I did know that but it never dawned on me that y'all were the same age."

Hope sighed and blinked a few times. "We were very different."

Lila sucked in a lungful of air when she realized why Hope was talking and why they were sitting in the balcony. Henry Thomas had been her boyfriend at one time. Holy crap!

"Do you love my grandson, or are you going to break his heart to pay him back for the way he treated you?" Hope changed the subject so abruptly that her question shocked Lila.

"I'm not that kind of person."

"Okay, then do you love him?"

"I've been terrified of you in the past, Miz Hope. I respect you in the present but that is something I'm not going to discuss with you. It's between me and Brody," Lila answered.

Hope giggled. "Yep, I knew I was right. You've grown into a responsible woman who would do good on Hope Springs. Now if you can stand up to Valerie like that, you'll be fine."

"Yes, ma'am." Lila let the air out of her lungs slowly.

"Hey, what're y'all doin'?" Brody asked as he cleared the top step.

"We're visitin' away from all that gawd-awful noise. That stuff ain't country music. Why don't they play some Hank Williams or some Ray Price," Hope fussed. "You can help me get back down the stairs. I bet it's time for Jace to say the blessin' on the food, ain't it?"

"Kasey says in fifteen minutes. I've got time for one dance with Lila before then," he answered, and raised an eyebrow at Lila.

She hoped that her smile told him that everything was all right.

Hope headed off in Valerie's direction when they reached the bottom of the steps and Brody pulled Lila onto the wooden dance floor. He twirled her around a couple of times, then brought her back to his chest. He sang along with the band when the lyrics talked about them getting a little wild on Saturday night and then she went to church on Sunday in ribbons and pearls.

"Ain't this the truth?" he said.

"I don't own any pearls and never did wear ribbons in my hair but we did get a little wild on Saturday nights," she answered breathlessly. The whole world had always disappeared when she danced with Brody, whether it was at the Silver Spur to a live band or in an old hay barn to the music of a truck radio turned up as loud as it would go.

Barely taking a breath, the singer went right into Sammy Kershaw's "Don't Go Near the Water." Lila swished her red skirt a few times and then Brody grabbed her hand.

She caught Valerie glaring from the sidelines but she didn't care. She wasn't going to take Brody to the springs after dark for a night of hot, passionate sex under the willow trees and then a time of skinny-dipping to cool off, so the woman could back off.

Jace hopped up on the bandstand and rang a cow bell to get everyone's attention. When the noise settled, he picked up the microphone. "Welcome to the Dawson family reunion. Looks like we all took that verse in the Good Book about going forth and multiplyin' very literally."

Laughter rang out and he gave it time to settle down before he went on. "Rustin, that would be Kasey's son, has been tellin' me for nearly an hour that he's starving and his sister, Emma, says that she is hungry to death. So without any more comments, I'm going to say grace and y'all can hit the food tables. As usual, Prairie Rose is catering the meat and the drinks but we thank all the rest of you for bringing a covered dish to go with it. Now if you'll bow your heads."

Brody whipped off his cowboy hat with all the other men in the barn and laid it over his heart but he kept Lila's hand in his left one. Jace said a brief prayer and then folks began to form a line in front of the tables.

"If I remember right, you eat when you're stressed. Hungry?" He kissed Lila on the forehead.

"Starving," she answered.

"Then we'll eat and then I want my older aunts who

aren't from Happy to see that I am with you. Maybe they'll stop trying to fix me up with every woman in their church or at their school or— You understand."

"Oh, yeah, I do," she said. "You brought me here so all your relatives would stop trying to get you married off?"

"I brought you to the reunion because I want to spend the evening with the most beautiful woman in Texas. The other is a little bonus," he said. "What did Granny want to talk to you about or is that confidential?"

"Did you know that she and Henry Thomas dated?"

He looked as stunned as if she'd hit him between the eyes with a shovel. "Did she say that?"

"Not in so many words but I figured it out."

"We had a conversation a few days ago and that does make sense. But Henry?" He frowned.

"About as likely a match as Brody and Lila, right?" she asked.

"Oh, honey, we make a beautiful match." He grinned.

"Brody!" Hope waved from a table where she'd claimed a seat. "You kids bring your plates and sit here beside me."

Brody nodded. "The queen bee has summoned us. You don't mind, do you? We can go skinny dippin' afterwards."

"In your dreams, cowboy," she said. "This is a real date. We will stay in plain sight all evening and you will take me home and come straight back here."

"Then they'll all think you're respectable, right?" he asked.

"What do *you* think? You're really the only one that matters to me."

"I feel like my world has stopped spinning and it's

tilted right on its axis again. I like you the way you are and anyone who doesn't can go to hell." He handed her a plate. "I told you everything would be okay."

"I'll be respectable but I insist on a good night kiss." She grinned. "I've waited too many years for this date to be left at the door with no kiss."

"Yes, ma'am. Eat hearty so you'll have the energy to dance all evening. I've waited too long for this night to waste a single minute of it. And before you say a word, yes, it's my fault that it didn't happen sooner."

She loaded her plate and waited at the end of the table for Brody and they crossed the barn together. Forget about hiding in the shadows. Everyone in the whole place could see her. She felt like turning around and running when Hope motioned to the chair right beside her. Brody set his plate down and pulled out a chair for her before he took his place on her right.

"Where is your mama this evening? You should have brought her with you," Hope asked.

"She's out with Laura and Teresa."

"Just between me and you"—Hope leaned over and whispered—"I'd rather be with them. This is too many people for me at one time. I can BS my way through it for Valerie's sake but I like smaller groups."

"A little BS and a lot of 'ain't that nice' gets us through," Lila said.

Hope laughed loudly, drawing a lot of attention to the table, and then she leaned around Lila to speak to Brody. "Darlin', would you go get me a couple of hot rolls? I forgot to put any on my plate and Gracie makes the best yeast bread in the state."

"Sure thing, Granny. You need anything, Lila?"

"Maybe another glass of tea," she answered.

When he was halfway across the barn, Hope leaned over to whisper softly, "And now everyone in the place knows that we're talkin' and playin' nice. But, sweetheart, know this, if you hurt my grandson or break his heart, you'll answer to me, and that's not BS. You treat him right and you've got a friend in me for life, but if you don't, well, I can be a real bitch."

"Tell him the same thing and you won't have a thing to worry about," Lila said.

Hope patted her on the shoulder. "Glad we had this talk and the one in the balcony. You've got brass as well as class."

Brody returned and took his seat; then he leaned over and whispered, "What was she sayin' when I left? Your face went all serious and I was afraid you were going to leave."

"Just girl talk," Lila said. "This is excellent potato salad, Miz Hope. Which one of the relatives made it?"

"I did," Hope said. "Brody loves bacon, so I fry a couple of pounds good and crispy to add to the mixture."

"I'd love to have the recipe," Lila said.

"I'll write it off and send it with Brody tomorrow night when y'all have your second date," Hope said.

"You think we're going to have a second date?"

"You've invited him to church tomorrow and that's a date in my books. Brody, did you hear that Henry's sister isn't going to renew Paul's lease this fall? She says that she's got other plans for the ranch. Wonder if Henry might be ready to come back home?"

"First I've heard of it," Brody said.

"If she's interested in selling that ranch, we'll sure

make her a good offer. It would be a nice addition to Hope Springs. I'll call her in the next week or so," Hope said.

Jace sat down on the other side of Hope and soon they were deep in a discussion about the possibility of buying the Texas Star.

Brody draped an arm across the back of Lila's chair and asked, "You remember the night before the fall sale when we snuck away and went to the buyer's balcony?"

"That was the closest we got to gettin' caught. I thought for sure your dad would..."

"I never got dressed so fast in my life except the other night when your mama snuck in the apartment. If she'd opened that bedroom door..."

Kasey startled both of them when she leaned down between them and whispered, "Granny is being really nice tonight. What did you put in her tea, Brody?"

Both of his hands shot up defensively. "I'm innocent. I didn't spike her tea. How you doin', sis?"

"This is my first family reunion without Adam. It's kind of strange. We used to sneak off to the buyer's loft and make out." Her smile didn't erase the pain in her eyes. "Even after we were married and had kids."

"I wonder how many kids we'd disturb if we flipped on the lights in the balcony," Brody said.

"Don't do it. Let them have the thrill that we had," Kasey said. "It's good to see you, Lila."

"Hey." Jace touched Lila on the arm. "I wanted to come on over and ask you to save me a dance later this evening."

"Her dances are taken," Brody said quickly.

"Hey, now!" Lila spoke up. "I've got an extra one right now if you want to dance, Jace."

He held out a hand. "Yes, ma'am."

The band was playing the very song that had been playing in her mind when Clancy was in the café— "Which Bridge to Cross (Which Bridge to Burn)."

"Sounds like maybe this is special for you tonight," Jace said as he drew her close for a two-step. "Brody was worried."

"Truth is I burned the bridge between me and Brody years ago. The one I burned with Clancy is still smoldering but it's gone. I don't care about that one but I wouldn't mind rebuilding the one with Brody," she said.

"I've got nails if y'all run out and if there's anything I can do to help, you just call me. I like seein' him as happy as he is right now," Jace said.

"Thank you. Reckon you've got any pull with your mama?"

"Now that's something you and Brody got to do on your own. She's my mama and I love her but she can be a handful. Granny used to be even worse but she is mellowing since she retired," Jace chuckled.

*   *   *

Brody leaned forward and put his hands on the table so he could watch them. Not because he was afraid his brother would try to steal his woman, but Brody enjoyed just seeing Lila move around the floor. The song was so appropriate for the night. He didn't have a single bridge to burn. But Lila had two before her and it scared the hell out of him when he thought of her going back to Florida and being around Clancy.

He had eyes for only her, moving so gracefully. Jace

said something and her body language said that she was very serious when she answered him. Then she smiled and nodded when he made another comment. Brody wanted to cut in and ask her what they were talking about, but he just watched from a distance. The next one and all those after belonged to him.

The song ended and Jace brought her back to the table. "I told her to make sure that you need to resole your boots when tonight is over since you're being selfish. She dances like a dream. No wonder you always kept her to yourself in high school."

Lila patted him on the shoulder. "Thank you, Jace."

"You're very welcome," he said. "Hey, you ever think about all those crazy things we did when we were kids?"

"Happy memories." She smiled.

"Yep, they are. Can I get y'all a beer?"

"Love one," Lila said.

"Just leave them right here on the table," Brody said. "We're about to hit the dance floor if this gorgeous woman will let me step on her toes again."

"Will do." Jace disappeared toward the bar.

Brody led her out to the middle of the floor. "We'll dance a couple of times and then go back to the table and drink those beers while they're still cold. And then I'm going to kiss you."

"Oh, so you've got the whole evening planned, do you? Are you trying to prove that you're brave enough to bring the wild girl to a family reunion in spite of what everyone might think?"

"Nope. I'm trying to prove to you that I mean business this time and I don't care what anyone or anything thinks of our relationship," he said.

"So this is a relationship?" she asked.

She'd expected the clouds to part the day that Brody said something like that. But not even the crowd on the dance floor parted. The only way that anyone would even know what he'd said would be by the way her heart had tossed in an extra few beats. And no one could even see that happening.

He sank his face into her hair. "It's whatever you want it to be. I'll take what I can get."

She looped her arms around his neck and his slid down to her lower back when the singer started Tracy Byrd's song "Holdin' Heaven."

"It's the truth. I really am holdin' heaven in my arms."

"You know why, don't you?" She looked into his eyes.

"Because you're in my arms?"

"No, sir, if you're holding heaven in your arms, then I'm an angel, and honey, I traded my halo and wings for horns back when we had sex the first time," she laughed.

"Then I should have a set of long horns right along with you," he laughed.

He didn't wait until they were at the bar to kiss her. His dark lashes closed slowly and then his lips were on hers in a kiss so hot that it would have melted the devil's pitchfork. She leaned into it, not caring if she was at his family reunion and everyone was watching them. This night had been a long time coming and she deserved her Cinderella evening.

*   *   *

They were the only ones on the dance floor when the band closed out the evening at eleven-thirty with a request from Brody. "Bless the Broken Road," by Rascal Flatts, a slow country waltz, brought Brody and Lila together in the middle of the floor.

"This was playing that year when you left," he whispered. "But it didn't have the meaning that it does today."

"Do you think that God did bless the road that led me back home to Happy?"

"I do," he said.

She laid her head on his chest and listened to the steady beat of his heart.

Home.

She'd called Happy home.

Her pretty red dress didn't turn into rags at the stroke of midnight. His truck didn't instantly become a pumpkin. But when he kissed her at the door, she felt as if she had truly had her Cinderella night.

"Good night, Lila," he whispered hoarsely, desire in his voice.

"Good night, Brody." Her whole body wanted more.

"I really don't want to let you go," he said.

She leaned into his arms, her face resting on his chest. She could have stood there until dawn simply enjoying that steady heartbeat. "We both know this night has to end at the door. But there's always tomorrow."

He brought her palms to his lips and kissed each one. The warmth of his breath, the feel of his lips on the tender part of her skin, and the slight scruff on his face against her fingertips made her wish that all time would freeze— that they could stay right there in that scene forever.

"Until tomorrow." He dropped her hands and walked to his truck.

She watched until even the sound of the vehicle had

faded, leaving nothing behind but a lonesome old owl and a coyote vying for attention off in the distance. She opened the door and made it to the living room before she melted into a chair and kicked off her boots.

"Only a few minutes late," Daisy said from the sofa where Duke and Cora both rested in her lap. "Lipstick is gone and you've got a faraway look in your eyes. Valerie must have been at least halfway decent."

"It was magic, Mama, and I held my own with Valerie Dawson."

"Good for you!" Daisy pumped a fist in the air.

Lila could hardly believe that her mother had made that gesture.

"Don't look so surprised. Tina has grandkids and that's what my favorite one of the bunch does when things are good," she said.

"You want grandkids?" Lila asked.

"When you're ready but I'd really like for their name to be something other than Dawson," Daisy said. "But if it happens to be, then by golly, I'll be the favorite because Valerie won't have anything to do with them. That's the only good thing about it, though."

Lila's phone pinged in her purse and she took it out to find a message: *H.O.L.Y.*

"And that would be?" Daisy asked.

"A text from Brody."

"More magic?"

"Just the title of a song."

"I worry about you," Daisy said. "Even if it was magic, I still worry that you're trying to re-create the fun times of when you were a kid. Now you're grown, Lila. It's time to say good-bye to the past."

"Tonight I did just that, Mama. I don't want to go back but I do want to enjoy the present and look forward to the future. I don't give a damn if Valerie Dawson hates me or if Hope threatens me," Lila said.

"What did Hope say?" Daisy's eyes flashed anger.

"Just that I'd better not break Brody's heart."

"What about all the times he broke yours? Where was she with all her threats back then? Did she tell him to ask you to the prom or not to stand you up that last night?"

Lila kicked off her boots. "Tonight was wonderful. I want to think about that."

"So what does that text mean?" Daisy asked.

"Did you stop listening to country music when you moved away from Happy?" Lila asked.

"You know I've always loved jazz. Etta James and Sam Cooke. I can handle those beer drinkin' songs but they aren't my favorite."

Lila found the song on her phone, turned the volume as high as it would go, and set it on the coffee table. She leaned back in the chair and watched her mother's face as she listened to lyrics that said he was high on loving her.

"That's pretty damned romantic," Daisy said.

"It is, isn't it?" Lila said. "I'm going to get a shower and go to bed. Folks will be flocking in here tomorrow morning lookin' for gossip about the family reunion."

"On a church mornin'?" Daisy frowned.

"Oh, yeah, and then there will be even more at noon, so I hope you fixed lots of chicken and dressin' today." She stooped to get her boots and stopped long enough to pet her kittens on the way down the short hallway to the bathroom.

"So"—Lila turned around—"did you have a good time this evening?"

"Always enjoy spending time with old friends, but I'm gettin' too old for this late night crap. I'd rather spend the evening watchin' an old movie with a shot of whiskey in my hand," Daisy said. "I'll see you in the morning and, honey, I figured that we'd be swamped tomorrow so I did fix plenty."

"Love you." Lila yawned.

"Right back atcha, kiddo. Always have and always will," Daisy said.

*   *   *

The church was packed that morning with every pew full but Brody would have gladly let Lila sit in his lap if she could have left the café. He didn't even have to close his eyes to visualize her in that cute little dress that she'd worn the night before.

"Good mornin' and thank you to the Dawson family for draggin' all their relatives to church this mornin'," the preacher said.

A few giggles erupted and then there was silence.

"I'd like to talk to y'all about family this mornin'," the preacher said, and read a few verses from the Bible in front of him on the oak pulpit.

Brody could agree that family was a good thing but that morning he couldn't get his mind off Lila and the way she'd fit into his arms the evening before, the way she'd leaned into the good night kiss, the way she'd drank a beer with him at the bar without even glancing at all his single Dawson cousins. And especially the fact that she'd shaken her head when more than one of those cousins asked her to dance.

He folded his arms over his chest and attempted to listen to the thirty-minute sermon that lasted every bit of six hours. He nodded off twice and Hope had to poke him to wake him. Finally, the preacher asked Jace to deliver the benediction.

Jace kept it short and when he finished, the whole congregation said a hearty "Amen."

"What is wrong with you?" Hope frowned as they stood to their feet with the rest of the crowd. "You didn't hear a word the preacher said."

"I was daydreaming about Lila," he answered honestly.

"Dammit!" Valerie whispered under her breath.

"In church, Mama?" Brody scolded.

"Don't take that tone with me and believe me when I say I'm not ready to fold yet." Valerie shook her finger at him. "I haven't changed my mind about that woman. She's going to leave at the end of summer and you'll be left with a broken heart. There are other women around here who are a lot more suitable for you and for Hope Springs."

Brody slung an arm around his mother's shoulders. "Mama, I love you, but I'm going to keep seeing Lila, so get used to it. I'm going to the café for dinner today."

*   *   *

The truck felt like an oven when he settled into his seat. Only a little more than twelve hours ago, Lila had been sitting there in the passenger seat. And then there was that kiss—that wonderful, amazing good night kiss. He started the engine, switched on the A/C and drove straight to the café.

His step was lighter than it had been in a long time when he pushed the door open into the café. Every seat was full and every booth crowded, so he stood in the doorway for several minutes trying to decide whether to stay or go on home.

"Hey," Lila said as she passed by him. "You stayin' or goin'?"

"Jace is holding down the ranch for me so I'm stayin'," he answered.

"If you'll man the drink machine until this rush is over, we'll have dinner together in the kitchen, my treat. Mama made chicken and dressin'," she said.

He unbuttoned the cuffs of his shirtsleeves and rolled them up. "You got a deal."

She kissed him on the cheek. "You're a lifesaver."

A low buzz of whispers started with Valerie's and Hope's names floating around as folks hurriedly got out their phones to call and text the newest gossip.

Chapter Sixteen

It was hard for Lila to believe that she'd been back in Happy less than four weeks that Sunday evening as she flipped through hangers in her closet. The calendar said that it was June 25, which meant she should give notice in Florida and get her résumés in soon for other jobs. The best ones had probably already been taken.

She finally chose a cute little sleeveless dress with twenty-seven buttons up the front and since it had red trim, she decided to wear her boots again. They'd brought her good luck the night before and on a whim, she applied her mother's red lipstick. She really intended to drive her truck out to Hope Springs to get Brody for their church date but the Lila who'd kissed him in front of a packed café took one look at her Harley and changed her mind.

She got her dad's beat-up old helmet from behind the seat in her truck and tucked it into a saddlebag. "I hope you don't mind, Daddy. I don't do this lightly and no one else has ever gotten to wear this but...well, I think you'd understand."

Not a cloud floated in the summer sky that evening. The sun was sinking toward the tops of the trees, putting a glare in her rearview mirror. She had second thoughts about her decision to ride the bike as she turned into the lane for Hope Springs and rode across the cattle guard, but it was too late to turn around.

Brody was sitting on the porch with Kasey and Jace when she parked outside the yard fence. He stood to his feet and shook the legs of his jeans down over his boot tops, settled his hat on his head, and crossed the yard.

"You goin' to let me drive that thing?" he asked.

She removed her helmet and shook out her hair. "If you leave your hat at home and wear a helmet."

He slung his cowboy hat toward the porch. Jace caught it like a Frisbee and laid it on the top step.

"You kids don't stay out too late now," he teased.

Emma ran to the fence and crawled up on the bottom rail. "Lila! Can I go with you?"

"You have to wear boots and a helmet. Mine are too big for you but when you get big enough, you can ride with me," Lila said.

"Rustin, did you hear that? I'm goin' to ride bulls and get me a motorcycle like Lila has when I get big."

"Helmet is in the saddlebag," Lila said.

Brody pulled it out and cocked his head to one side. "Is this what I think it is? Does this big B in the lightning streaks stand for Billy?"

"It does," she said with a serious nod and moved back so that he could straddle the cycle.

"I'll wear it with pride." He jerked it down over his head and they exchanged a meaningful look. "It's been a few years since I've been on one of these things," he said.

"Gas is a little sensitive." She flipped her hair up under the helmet as she settled it on her head.

He turned it around, revved it a couple of times, then popped the clutch and the front wheels shot off the ground several inches. She wrapped her arms around his waist. She doubted that riding a bull behind him would be any more exhilarating than a bike ride with him.

Her skirt whipped around her thighs as he opened it up on the straight stretch of highway from the ranch to town. When he parked it at the church and removed the helmet, his eyes were twinkling. Nothing could ever take away their need for adventure but could a relationship survive two people like Lila and Brody? Or would it burn itself out, leaving nothing behind but a pile of ashes and two broken hearts?

"That was amazing. Now I can see why you were so mad when your mama sold your dad's cycle and didn't give it to you." He put the helmet back in the saddle-bag.

"She was a smart woman. We'd have gotten into all kinds of trouble if we'd had a motorcycle. We probably wouldn't be alive today, as crazy as we were then. I'm just glad that she let me keep his helmet."

He popped down the kickstand and dismounted. "Ain't that the truth? Shall we go inside and get saved and sanctified?"

"You're expectin' a lot out of one single preachin'." She took off the helmet and fluffed out her hair with her fingers.

"Do you know how sexy you are when you do that?"

"Really?" She tilted her head to one side.

"Oh, honey!" He groaned. "Let's skip church and take this bike out to the barn or better yet to the springs," he said.

"Can't. Mama is saving us a place," she said.

He slipped his hands around her waist and swept her off the cycle as if she were one of those tiny women who weighed only slightly more than a feather pillow. When he set her on the ground, he cupped her chin in his hand. The soft, sweet kiss left her wanting more and seriously considering his offer.

"Didn't you hear me? I said we are sitting with Mama," she said breathlessly when he clasped her hand in his and started toward the church.

"You think I'm not tough enough to sit on the same pew with your mother?" He opened the door for her and stood to the side but he didn't let go of her hand.

"She's pretty mean."

"Since you held your own last night with my mama, I'll do my best not to crawl under the pew and cower in fear," he teased.

Several heads turned when they went inside the church but after the news of a kiss that morning right out in public, holding hands didn't seem like such a big deal. Daisy was sitting near the middle on a pew all by herself. She nodded at them when Brody stood to one side to let Lila enter ahead of him before he took the spot at the end.

"You aren't late," Daisy whispered.

"Neither are you," Lila said.

"Please tell me I did not hear a motorcycle out there in the parking lot."

Lila shook her head. "Can't tell lies in church, Mama."

"And you wore a dress. The whole town probably knows what color your underpants are," Daisy fussed.

"White. Bikini with lace around the top. Since it was Sunday I left the red thongs in the drawer," she said.

"Great God!" Daisy gasped.

"Yes, ma'am, he is." Lila smiled.

"It's Happy, Texas. I swear to Jesus, it makes people crazy."

Lila nudged her. "There's a song that says that you're always seventeen in your hometown."

"Well, whoever sings it is a genius," Daisy whispered.

Lila sang with the congregation and made an effort to focus on the preacher's Sunday night sermon about how everyone should be thinking of how fast time flies. He snapped his fingers and said that it wouldn't be long before it was time for each and every one of them to leave this earthly world.

"Ever had sex on a Harley?" Brody whispered.

His breath sent shivers down her backbone. "No, but I'll give it a try if you're willing."

"Oh, yeah!"

Daisy elbowed her on the upper arm and she straightened up. She wasn't the only one who was the same in her hometown. So was her mother.

As soon as church services were over, Lila leaned over and said, "Mama, it's only two hours until you have to leave. Let's sneak out the side door. We'll meet you at the café."

"Let me tell Laura good-bye and I'll be right behind you," she said.

*   *   *

Brody parked the cycle in the garage and got off, and they both removed their helmets at the same time. Lila hung them on the handlebars and moistened her lips with the tip of her tongue. His mouth closed over hers and the only thing that mattered was that he was with her right then at that moment. He was a big, tough cowboy but in the hot garage, his heart and soul melted.

If he could live right there for the rest of his life, he would have been a happy cowboy. Just let him have Lila to come home to every evening after a long day of ranching or even fighting with Sunday and the world would be all right.

The kiss ended and he held her close to his chest for another moment. "It's been an amazing weekend. I've loved every minute of it. I can't even begin to think of you leaving at the end of summer."

"I agree," she said, and took a step back when the sounds of a car engine approached. "That would be Mama turning into the parking lot."

"I think your mama might know that we have already kissed each other more than once," he said.

"Surely not," she teased as she crossed the garage floor and unlocked the door. "Well, look who's here to meet us. Here, you can hold Cora. She's a sweetheart." She picked up both kittens and handed him the white one.

"Hey, I figured y'all would already have the ice cream ready for sundaes." Daisy followed them into the apartment, and crossed the living area and into the café kitchen. "I'm having a triple dip and then I'll sleep all the way to the Harrisburg airport."

"You going to work tomorrow or are you going to rest a day or two?" Lila asked as she hugged Duke to her chest.

"Put those cats back out in the apartment. If we got a surprise inspection and they found cat hair in this place, we'd get a citation and we ain't never had one," Daisy said.

"I'll take them back." Brody picked up Cora by the scruff of her neck and carried both of them across the utility room.

"So," he said when he returned. "Are you ready to go back to Pennsylvania?"

"I'm ready to be back in my routine even if I'm not ready to tell Lila good-bye. I hate that part even worse than she does," Daisy answered. "I'm not on the schedule until eleven for the noon rush, so I'll sneak in a few more hours of rest before I have to go in."

"Did you get back with that lady who called to reschedule?" Lila asked.

Daisy nodded. "I did but Molly asked me to wait a week before I make arrangements for you to talk to her. She and Georgia are thinkin' about buyin' me out. I hope they do."

Lila put her kitten on the sofa and led the way into the café. "I can't imagine why they wouldn't like Florida. It's a perfect retirement place."

"It's not Happy," Brody said. "They were born here and they know everyone in the place. The café has been the hub of all the gossip and news since you first put it in, Daisy, and they miss their place in the fun."

"You're probably right." Lila got out the ice cream.

Daisy split three bananas and laid them in the fancy

glass boats. "I was born here and was in the middle of that hub for years and I still miss it. Someday, maybe when I retire, I'll come back home. But that's a long way off and who knows what'll happen between now and then. Well, that's everything except the cherries for the top," Daisy said. "We might as well make this a classic banana split to celebrate, right?"

"Yes, ma'am." Lila bent to get the jar of maraschino cherries from the bottom rack in the refrigerator. The tail of her dress slid above her knees, showing a lot of those sexy legs. Brody got a visual of them wrapped around him and the pressure started to build behind his zipper. He quickly turned around and made himself think about ice cream.

"Crazy, ain't it? If Molly and Georgia decide to buy the place, they'll be coming home from pretty close to the same place in Florida that you'll be returning to," Daisy said.

Lila set the cherries on the table. "I'm not going back. If Clancy won't let me out of the contract, I'll take a year's sabbatical. Maybe I'll work on my master's degree."

"Oh?" Brody's heart threw in an extra beat.

"If he lets me out of the contract, I might try Montana or Wyoming next, or maybe I'll go back to Conway. I kind of liked it over there." She scooped out a perfect round of ice cream.

"Why Wyoming?" Daisy asked. "I'd think you'd get tired of taking those tests every time you move."

An empty feeling, as if someone had ripped his soul out and threw it in the trash, hit Brody in the chest. He'd been living in the present, but soon he and Lila would have to face the next step. And he'd have to figure out how to live without the hope of seeing her every day.

"Why don't you teach around here? You haven't tried Texas yet." He took the scoop from her. "Here, let me do that."

"Seventeen," Daisy said.

"What's that mean?" Brody deftly put three mounds of ice cream on each banana.

"The song," Lila answered.

"You mean that one by Cross Canadian Ragweed?" Brody asked.

"That's it," Lila said. "It says that you'll always be seventeen when you go home again."

"I'm not," Brody said.

Daisy topped off her banana split with a layer of whipped cream and then carefully carried it out to the dining room. "No, but Happy has seen you mature from a reckless teenager to a responsible adult. Folks saw her leave and then when she comes back, she is that same girl because there was nothing in between."

He handed Lila the chocolate syrup. "How's that a reason not to teach in Texas?"

"Not all of Texas, just Happy. No one will look at her like a responsible adult. They'll whisper behind her back and remember the stupid things that she did."

She passed the chocolate back to him and finished her toppings. "Mama's right, you know."

His phone rang. "Excuse me, this is Jace. I have to take it."

He stepped away from the table but locked gazes with Lila while he talked. "You can take care of that, Jace. I'll be home after a while."

When he slipped the phone back into his shirt pocket, she raised an eyebrow. "If you're needed at the ranch..."

"We've got a cow that's calving out of season. Jace knows how to pull a calf and Granny is there to help if he needs it. Let's go join Daisy." He smiled.

"So if they let you out of the contract, you'll move again? Want me to take a long weekend and fly down to help?" Daisy asked when they'd sat down across the table from her.

"I'd love it," Lila answered. "I'll let you know tomorrow or the next day. I'm going to call Clancy. I don't think he'll have a problem with it after his visit here."

"I'll be glad to take a few days off and help you," Brody said quickly. She might have put Clancy going but the man could swoop in with a lot of promises and smooth talk and convince her to stay in Florida. Then he'd have a whole year to win her back. As badly as Brody hated to be away from her, anywhere was better than Florida.

"I'll take all the help I can get but first I have to find another job." Lila ran a hand from his knee to his thigh under the table.

He shoveled ice cream in his mouth to cool him down and to keep from moaning. He'd miss her touch, the way her hair smelled and everything about her when she was gone. Skype was a good thing but it would never take the place of having her right there beside him sending desire through his body with nothing but her touch on his leg.

Chapter Seventeen

A flash of lightning shot out of the dark clouds as Brody drove the motorcycle out of town that Sunday evening after their ice cream date. To the north, Lila could see stars and a sliver of a moon. But to the southwest where the storms usually originated, the sky was black with only an occasional burst of light. She counted when the next streak zigzagged as if trying to reach for the treetops. Ten seconds. That meant the storm was ten miles out. Depending on whether it was traveling slowly or with the speed of a bullet, it could hit in a few minutes or take half an hour.

The first drops of cold rain hit when they were halfway between the café and the ranch. Then the hail started pinging off her helmet and stinging her back when it hit with the force of the high wind pushing it. Brody turned into Henry's old ranch and drove straight to the barn.

She hopped off the back of the bike as soon as he stopped and slung the barn door open wide enough that he could drive inside. By the time he'd parked, she had her helmet off and was wringing water from her dress tail.

"That's some cold rain and biting hail." She shivered.

He quickly hung his helmet on the handlebars and gathered her into his arms. "I know where we can wait out the storm."

"Tack room?" she said.

"Oh, yeah."

With his arm still around her, he headed that way. Not watching where she was going, she stumbled over the white mama cat and had to do some fancy footwork to keep from falling and pulling Brody down with her.

"Poor old thing must crave company," Lila said. "You should take her home with you. Kasey's kids would love her and she wouldn't be lonely."

"Why don't you take her home? She could snuggle up next to you at night and keep you warm," he said.

"That's your job." Lila groped around for the string that would turn on the light. Finally her fingers found the same old wooden thread spool at the end of a length of jute twine and she gave it a tug. "Well, would you look at this," she said.

There was a small electric heater in the corner, a tiny air conditioner in the window, and a futon on one wall with a quilt tossed over the back.

"Paul turned it into a poker place a few years ago. Said he needed a room for the boys on the nights when the girls gather at his house for those church meetings every month," Brody said.

"I don't remember anything in here but lots of musty old saddles and a couple of horse blankets." She wrapped her arms around herself trying to get warm.

He hugged her close to his own chilly, wet body. "Hail produced a cold rain. You're shiverin', Lila. Let's get you out of those wet clothes."

Brody slowly removed her dress and draped it on the back of a chair. His warm hands on her chilled skin as he unfastened her bra and removed it made her shiver even worse but it had nothing to do with the weather. He gently hooked a thumb under the edge of the elastic on her bikini underwear and strung warm kisses from her belly button to her toes as he pulled them down to her ankles.

Then he stood up, grabbed a quilt, and whipped it around her body. "As warm as it is in here, your things will be dry by the time the storm passes."

She adjusted the quilt like a sari and undid the snaps on his shirt one at a time as she started undressing him. Running her fingers through the soft black hair on his chest, she tiptoed and kissed him on the chin. Then she quickly undid his belt buckle and pulled his jeans off, admiring all the hard muscles from his broad shoulders down his ripped abdomen and the V that led down below his flat belly. Then she took his hand and led him to the futon. In a blur the quilt left her body and she sat down, pulling him down with her. She moved into his lap and covered them both.

His fingertips grazed her jawline, tilting her chin for the perfect angle so that his mouth could cover hers, and she leaned into the kiss. The tip of his tongue touched her lower lip, asking permission. She opened slightly and he eased inside as the hail and rain made beautiful music on the barn's old tin roof.

His work-roughened hands lightly skimmed from her shoulders, ever so slowly down her bare arms. When they reached her fingers, he made slow circles on the tender part of her palms as he deepened the kiss. Her body on fire, she pressed closer to him, her breasts against his chest.

Then his hands were on her back, massaging and working kinks out from her shoulders all the way to her butt and then down the backs of her legs. The kisses got hotter and hotter until she couldn't bear it anymore. She wiggled a few times and guided him into her but he controlled the movement with a long, slow gliding motion.

"My God, Brody," she panted.

"Good?" he asked as he maneuvered her onto her back and laced his fingers in hers, holding her hands above her head. "There is no one else on the earth right now but me and you."

"*Good* isn't even close," she said.

Talking stopped and they moved together until she was frantic with need. He slowed down and let her cool down just enough to catch her breath, then started building the speed again until she squealed his name and dug her fingernails into his back.

The heat as she tumbled into steaming hot desire into complete and utter satisfaction was more than she'd ever experienced, even with Brody. He rolled to one side but the futon was so narrow that they were still plastered together. She kicked the quilt off to one side and slung a leg over his body to keep him from falling off on the rough wooden floor.

"That was amazing," he whispered.

"I know." She stifled a yawn. "Don't you love the sound of rain on a tin roof?"

"Mmmm," he said as his blue eyes fluttered shut.

* * *

Brody awoke to her soft breathing. The rain had stopped and he could see stars shining in the window above the air conditioner. As hot as it was and as much as he would have loved to have had cool air, he didn't want to wake Lila. That would mean they'd have to go home and he didn't want to ever let go of her.

"Hey." She opened her eyes slowly. "What time is it?"

"Have no idea. Phones are on the table over there," he said. "Let's lock the door and live here forever."

She snuggled down deeper into his arms. "Sounds like a plan to me, but I bet Molly would send out the National Guard if I wasn't in the kitchen by opening time. It'll be strange not havin' Mama there."

"So that means our date is over?" Brody asked. "I think it better be. I'll get dressed and walk home. You can take the bike." He sat up and rolled the kinks out of his neck. "I love sleeping with you. I love the way you fit in my arms."

"Me too." She left the futon and went straight for her clothing.

"Seems a shame to cover something that beautiful." He grinned.

"Right back at you," she told him. "I'll take you home, Brody. You don't have to walk." She checked the time on her phone and gasped. "Holy smoke! It's four o'clock."

"Be best if that loud bike don't go roarin' down the lane at this time of mornin', don't you think," he said.

*   *   *

She made it home by four-thirty and went straight to the shower. When she came out with a towel around her head and one around her body, two kittens were sitting on the floor staring at her.

Duke meowed.

Cora laid back her ears.

"Young lady, you don't get to give me those kind of looks either," Lila said. "It was worth losing a little sleep over. Besides I liked sleeping with him. Not as much as I like the sex but having someone to snuggle with is nice."

Duke meowed again.

"See, there, Duke agrees with me. He likes having you to sleep with." She bent forward and dried her hair.

At five o'clock she heard pots and pans rattling in the kitchen. She dried her hair and dressed in jeans and a T-shirt, laced her shoes, and fed the kittens. Duke put his paw on Cora's head and tried to push her back but she wasn't having any part of that.

Lila left them tumbling around on the floor and went straight to the kitchen where she wrapped Molly in a fierce hug. "I'm so glad to see you."

Molly stepped back and narrowed her eyes. "I leave and everything goes down the toilet."

"Mama left this place clean as a pin. What's your problem?"

"Nothing to do with my kitchen. I told you to stay away from Brody Dawson."

"Ah." Lila grinned. "I missed you, too, Molly."

"Who said I missed you or anything about this place. I just hated the sand more than I do..." She fussed. "I'm lyin'. I didn't like the sand or the beach or anything about that place and I found out real quick that I love Happy, Texas, and do not want to leave it. And Georgia agrees with me."

"So where are you going when you go on another vacation?" Lila opened a drawer and took out a clean apron.

"Maybe to the mountains or maybe I've been broke from suckin' eggs and I'll stay where I'm happy from now on and that's right here where I know everyone and they all like my cookin'," she said. "I hear that Hope is coming around to being civil to you but that Valerie isn't. That right?"

Lila tied an apron around her waist and tucked an order pad into her pocket. "That's about it."

"Valerie means well. I can remember when Hope was a lot like her. She sure didn't like Mitch Dawson there at first and Mitch's mama wasn't very happy with the marriage either. It's the way of mothers—always interfering, but they do it out of love." Molly flopped a bowl full of biscuit dough on the counter and started rolling it out.

Lila laughed. "How do you know all that when you've only been home a few hours?"

"I keep my ears open. Speakin' of that, I heard your motorcycle comin' past my place about the time I was havin' my first cup of coffee and gettin' ready for work this mornin'. I expect you were out at Hope Springs all night," Molly said. "He's goin' to break your heart, girl. You know the old sayin' that goes 'Fool me once, shame on you. Fool me twice, it's my own blamed fault'?"

Lila glanced at the clock. "Time to open the doors and I don't think that's the way that sayin' goes."

"Close enough," Molly said. "It's goin' to be your own fault."

"Note taken," Lila said.

"Smarty pants," Molly huffed. "Turn on the lights and let's get this week started."

"So is Georgia comin' home too?" Lila poured herself a cup of coffee and carried it with her.

"Soon as she can get here. She had all her belongin's moved down there. Thank goodness her house hasn't sold and she hadn't signed on the dotted line to buy one down there. Do you know what it costs to buy a place in that state?"

"Not much more than here unless you want beach-front," Lila said.

"Do you own a house?" Molly asked.

She'd thought about buying a little cottage on the beach and had decided she might give it more serious thought if she stuck around for five years.

"Oh, no, I rent a garage apartment and it's furnished. I could put all my belongings in the back of my truck. I can't afford the taxes on a place in that area—not on a teacher's salary."

"Well, thank God for that. When are you comin' home to Happy, then?" Molly asked. "If me and Georgia buy this café, we'll hire you as a waitress. You probably make as much in tips as you do teachin' and Lord knows, you don't have nearly the hassle. Teachin' a teenager anything is like nailin' Jell-O to the smokehouse door."

"You got that right, Molly, but what on earth gave you the impression I would ever come back here permanently?"

Molly grinned and pointed. "That right there."

Lila whipped around to see the first customer of the day getting out of his truck in the parking lot. In the dim morning light he was nothing but a silhouette settling an old Stetson on his head but that swagger left no doubt that it was Brody, and the feeling deep inside Lila left no doubt that Molly was right.

Chapter Eighteen

Good mornin'!" Lila said cheerfully when Paul and Fred entered the café that Tuesday morning. "Y'all boys ready for a cup of coffee?"

"Oh, yeah, and we'll have two of Molly's big country breakfasts with all the trimmin's," Paul said. "I'm buyin' this world traveler breakfast this mornin'. Our wives are at the church with the Ladies' Circle so there ain't no food at home."

Fred chuckled. "It's an excuse for Mary Belle to tell them all about the cruise and I'm glad I ain't there."

Lila filled two mugs with coffee and took it to the guys. "So two big breakfasts? Anything else?"

"That should do it," Fred said. "I got tired of all that fancy food on the ship after the first week. It was pretty good there at first but all them choices kind of bewildered me. I'm ready for some of Molly's cookin'. You ever been on a cruise, Lila?"

She shook her head. "Not yet but it's on my bucket list."

"It's all right. Mary Belle liked it better than I did and she'd go again. I told her if we made it to our seventy-fifth I'd consider another one but only if it lasted one week and not two," Fred said.

"You and Brody could go on one," Paul whispered. "All cooped up like that would tell you if you were really meant for each other."

The blush was instant with two red spots filling her cheeks and burning like wildfire. "I'd better get that order in. Holler if you need any more coffee before it gets ready."

"What's happened since I've been gone?" Fred asked. "Brody and Lila? Really?"

"Hey, I can hear you," Lila said.

Paul, with his salt-and-pepper hair, leaned forward until he was practically touching Fred's snowy white mop and lowered his voice. Lila couldn't hear a word they said but whoever made the comment about old women being the biggest gossips in the world was dead wrong. Old guys could outdo them any day of the week.

Her phone rang and she pulled it out of her hip pocket. "Hello, Mama. Breakfast rush over?"

"Just about but there's still a few stragglers. I tried to call last night but it went to voice mail. Georgia is coming in early and I told her she could use the apartment. Got a problem with that?" Daisy asked.

"They're buyin' the place, so I guess I shouldn't have," Lila answered.

"That's not what I asked."

"No, Mama, not a problem at all," Lila said.

"What's wrong with you this morning? I hear something in your voice."

"Nothing—just dreading the move and hoping that the school board in Conway, Arkansas, offers me a contract. They gave me every hope but things could go wrong."

Hope—the word brought visions of Hope Springs and Brody to her mind. She dreaded telling him good-bye, even if it wasn't final. Just thinking about it brought tears to her eyes.

"And if they do, it's not too late to go somewhere else. I heard on the radio yesterday that Oklahoma, Kansas, and Texas still have jobs open everywhere. There was a number to call but I didn't write it down," Daisy told her. "I'd just as soon you lived far away from Happy so this thing you and Brody have started again would die in its sleep, but I'm glad you aren't going back to Florida this fall. That Clancy sure snowed me."

"So you think we couldn't survive a long-distance relationship?" Lila asked.

"Most people can't. I've got customers. Talk to you later. Hug my grandkittens for me."

She was gone before Lila could say another word.

"Order up!" Molly called out as she slid two platters of food onto the serving window ledge.

"I didn't even put the order on the roller," Lila said.

"I heard them," Molly said. "And they've gone to talkin' about that cruise and cows now. Talk of you and Brody didn't last long."

"You've got ears like a bat," Lila laughed.

Molly shook a wooden spoon toward her. "And Georgia's are even better, so you'll have to be even more careful when she gets home. You might need to meet Brody out at his bunkhouse."

"Molly!" Lila blushed.

"Just callin' it like I see it." She shrugged.

When things had quieted down in the café, Lila poured herself another cup of coffee and took it to the back booth. She sat down on one side and stretched out her long legs to prop her feet on the other side. Her phone had pinged half a dozen times that morning but there was no way she could check messages in their busy hours.

The first one was from Brody and put a brand-new blush on her face. The second one was from Clancy saying that he would be glad to let her out of her contract. Third, fourth, and fifth were from Brody asking her to call him as soon as possible.

She hit the speed dial for Brody and he answered on the first ring. "Hello, gorgeous. I sure hated to leave before daylight. I wanted to watch you wake up."

"Me too. What are you doing right now?" she asked.

"Jace and I are finishing a corral for this pesky bull and tryin' to get a fence built that he can't get through and then we've got cows to tag and two pastures that need to be plowed. Ranch work is like wipin' your butt on a wagon wheel—there's no end to it. At least that's what Grandpa always used to say. But if I get done by dark, would you like to ride down to Tulia for an ice cream? I could be there at nine."

"I'll be ready."

*   *   *

Brody whistled all the way from Hope Springs to the café that evening. He knocked on the back door and she opened it immediately. One step and she was in his arms, his lips were on hers, and their hearts were both racing. Then she stooped to pet the cats that were right at her feet.

"Are you okay, Lila? Is something wrong?"

"Georgia is stayin' in the apartment until her stuff arrives on Monday. I hope she likes cats."

"If she don't, they can stay in the bunkhouse until you get ready to go to Florida," he said. "And, darlin', you look beautiful tonight in that red dress."

"Thank you," she said.

"Don't worry, darlin'. We can spend time away from here when Georgia moves in." He kissed her pretty red lips again and they left the apartment together.

He opened the passenger door on his truck for her. "I reckon I should've brought along my pistol to keep some handsome cowboy from stealin' you away from me."

"Then I should have brought my pepper spray to keep the women from trying to take you away from me. Reckon we should call in our pizza so we don't have to fight off the crowd?" she teased.

He started the engine and backed the truck out enough to turn around and start south to Tulia. "I know I've said it before but I'm really going to miss you when you have to leave. I can't imagine how Kasey gets through the days, knowing that she'll never see Adam again."

"Think she'll ever get a second chance at love?" Lila asked.

"I hope so but it'll have to be a really special man. It'll have to be something like what we have got."

"What we have is special, but is there going to be an

us after I'm gone? Do you really want a long-distance relationship?" Lila asked.

He laid a hand on her shoulder. "More than anything in this world."

"But is it an us like we were in high school or is it something more? Have we simply gone back to wild sex and the way we were or is this something lasting and real?"

"What do you want it to be?" he asked.

"I'm askin' you." She turned so that her eyes met his.

Men, especially Dawsons, didn't normally do all that analyzing their feelings crap. They took things as they were and moved accordingly.

"I've loved every minute of this summer with you, Lila, and it's not like we are still in high school. Admit it. We've been to church together, to my family reunion, and out on dates. That much has changed but..."

"There it is," she said.

"What?" he asked.

"In a real relationship there are no buts," she told him softly, and looked away. "Let's not ruin the evening with an argument. I'm lookin' forward to an evening with you, one that doesn't have a single *but* in it."

What's wrong with you? the voice in his head screamed loudly. *She's an amazing woman and you're in love with her, so why don't you man up and tell her so.*

Because I want it to be more than words. I want it to come from so deep in my heart that she doesn't doubt it for a minute because I never want to hurt her again like I did last time. I love her too much for that.

"It's not so far from here to Conway. We can do weekend trips a couple of times a month," she said.

"And you'll have two weeks at Christmas and spring break." What he wanted to say was that he wasn't sure he could live without her for two weeks at a time. And the way Clancy looked down on Lila, like he was the king and she was one of his servants, aggravated the hell out of him.

"Do you want a big wedding if you get married?" he asked, and then wondered if he'd said the words out loud and where they'd come from.

Her head snapped around and her brown eyes were huge. "Where did that come from?"

He grinned. "A picture of you in a big white dress flashed through my mind."

"All those times you could have—and probably should have—proposed and you choose now? Why?" she asked.

"Who says I proposed? And when should I have asked you to marry me?" he asked.

"Well, there was the time when we lost our virginity."

"We were both too damn young to think about marriage," he said.

"Yes, but you should have at least told me that we were headed that way in the future."

"You didn't propose to me, either," he said. "What about all the other times?"

She laid a hand on his thigh. "The morning Mama and I left."

"We still weren't even old enough to get married without parental consent. Can you imagine your mama and mine signing those papers? Besides, you wouldn't roll down the window. And…"

She held up a finger to hush him up. "But you should have offered."

*   *   *

He wrapped his hand around her fingers and kissed them, the heat from his lips warming her from the depths of her heart. He kept her hand in his, holding it on the console separating them. "And if I had proposed tonight?"

"I would say no." Lila hoped that she would be able to tell him no. Her mind knew that they needed more time— her body, not so much.

"Why?" His voice came out in a raspy whisper that made her wonder if he might be testing the waters instead of teasing.

"Because you'd only be sayin' it to keep me from leavin' and because if you were askin' for all the right reasons, I still would not. We need to see if we can survive a long-distance relationship before we talk about a commitment like that. So let's have a good time while we can."

"Lila, are we okay?"

"I think so," she said.

"Think or know?" He kissed the tip of her nose first and then moved on down to her lips. There was no thinking or knowing when his lips were on hers. If he'd have proposed even in a teasing manner right then, she would have said yes and followed him to the courthouse as soon as it opened the next morning.

"The jury is still out," she panted when the kiss ended and grabbed for the door handle.

Chapter Nineteen

Lila awoke on Wednesday morning to find Duke and Cora sharing the same pillow with her. Duke's little paws rested in her hair on the left side while Cora purred into her ear on the right side. She carefully moved them over to the other side of the bed and headed for the bathroom for a morning shower.

The cats were sitting side by side when she started across the living room floor. She'd only been in Happy for a month. How could so much have happened? When she first arrived, all she could think about was selling the café and getting out of the town. Now she dreaded telling Molly, Fred and Paul, Kasey and her kids—but most of all Brody—good-bye. Knowing that Georgia was coming home and she really wasn't needed at the café was like a big awkward elephant sitting on her chest. Her heart hurt and she had trouble breathing.

"I've been lookin' at this all wrong," she said out loud.

All she had to do was load her cats, pack her clothes, and get in the truck and drive away. That way she didn't really have to tell anyone good-bye. Maybe that's why she moved so often.

She was struggling with the idea of simply going after work one evening when she opened the door into the café kitchen.

"Well, good mornin'. What's the matter with you? You look like you're about to cry." Molly narrowed her eyes at her.

"Nothing's wrong," Lila answered.

"Don't give me that crap. You look like you lost your best friend. Did you and Brody have a fight?"

Lila put on a clean apron and shook her head. "No, ma'am. Things are good between us."

"Is it because Georgia is coming home? I told you that we really want you to stay on here. You can choose your hours and live in the apartment, free of charge as long as you like."

Lila layered a sausage patty, a slice of cheese, and a scoop of scrambled eggs inside a biscuit. "I appreciate that. I've got to take a few days after July Fourth and get moved out of my apartment in Florida. I've got an interview in Conway, Arkansas."

"That's good, isn't it? Closer to here if you and Brody do stay together."

"I'm not sure what's a good thing right now. My world is kind of crazy."

Molly shook a knife at her. "I told you that gettin' mixed up with Brody was not a good thing."

Was that knife an omen? Should she simply leave? It wouldn't be like the last time because she and Brody had the foundation of a relationship. There would be phone calls, texts, and Skype. But there wouldn't be those painful last-minute tears. Plus, if she got back to Florida and cleared out her apartment by the first of July, she wouldn't have to pay another month's rent.

She'd weighed the pros and cons until closing time at the café and decided that leaving that night made sense. She wanted to hug Molly and tell her that she wouldn't be there the next morning but she couldn't make herself do it. She did take time to write her a note before she packed everything into the truck and got the cats into the old wooden crate.

"We'll stop at the first store we come to and I'll get you a proper carrier and a new toy to keep you entertained on the ride. If you don't whine, I'll even buy you some cat treats." Talking out loud helped take the sting out of driving away from the café.

She couldn't leave town without talking to her father first. Stopping at the cemetery, she got out of the truck and sat down in front of his tombstone. "I never did tell you good-bye. Not even at your funeral and I can't do it tonight. Remember when you would leave and I'd beg you not to go away? We'd touch each other on the forehead and we'd say 'see ya later.'" She traced his name with her forefinger. "I love that cowboy so much. Am I doing the right thing, Daddy?"

No answers came floating down from the big white puffy clouds above her. The sun didn't stand still in the sky. Her phone pinged a couple of times but she ignored it.

"Evidently you're tellin' me to figure this one out on my own, aren't you?" she finally said as she rose to her feet. "See ya later, Daddy. I promise I won't wait twelve years to come back this time."

The kittens had decided to claw at the crate and whine about being cooped up. "Y'all might as well settle down. We'll be driving most of the night and I expect you to stay awake and talk me out of making a U-turn anywhere between here and the Louisiana border. I didn't bring you to listen to you fuss at me the whole way."

Duke meowed pitifully.

Cora glared at her.

She stopped at the edge of town and pulled off to the side of the road. In five minutes she could be back at the apartment. Tears rolled down her cheeks. If leaving without even saying the words out loud created this kind of pain, she didn't want to even think about seeing Brody waving in her rearview mirror like she remembered from the last time she left Happy.

She pulled back out onto the highway and flipped on the radio. Every single song had a message to her heart but she kept going until she got through Tulia. Then she saw the flares and hit her brakes hard. She counted four cars ahead of her truck but the traffic was lining up behind her pretty fast. A semi blocked both lanes of traffic but it didn't obliterate the flashing lights of half a dozen police cars, along with a couple of ambulances not far ahead of the traffic jam.

"Okay, guys, is this an omen? And if it is, what's it tellin' me? To turn around and go back to Happy or is it telling me that there will be obstacles in the way of this long-distance relationship?"

Not a single meow came from the backseat.

"Some help you are," she fussed.

It took thirty-two minutes to get the semi pulled out of the way and the ambulances going back south with their sirens blaring. For the next half hour the traffic was horrible and it was nearly midnight when she stopped to buy the things she'd promised the cats, along with a bag of chocolate donuts, a couple of apples, and two bottles of cold Dr Pepper. That much caffeine and sugar should keep her awake for several more hours.

She set the new carrier with a fluffy throw in the bottom, along with a little bowl of treats and a new toy on the passenger seat. She managed to get a kitten in each hand and relocate them. They nosed around, ate a few of the little treats, sniffed the toy, and went back to sleep.

She smiled for the first time since they'd left Happy. She'd bought some ribbon and a leash so they could get out and run around later but right then she needed to get more miles in before she stopped for a rest. She turned on her phone before she started the engine. Six messages and four missed calls from Brody. One call from Molly and two from her mother.

She hit the button to call her mother first.

"Where are you?" Daisy answered. "Molly went back to the café to get some sugar and found the note you left. What were you thinkin'?"

"I'm on my way home. I'll stop in Shreveport or sooner if my eyes get heavy. What was I thinkin'? That I couldn't bear another good-bye," Lila answered.

"What about Brody? Did you kiss him good-bye?"

"No." Her voice cracked.

"That's good enough for him."

"Why would you say that? He came back that morning we left to apologize but I didn't want to hear it," she said.

"You're taking up for the man who broke your heart?"

"I guess I am, Mama."

"You love that cowboy, don't you?" Daisy sighed.

"Always have. Probably always will. Can we talk about this later when just the sound of his name won't make me tear up?" She wiped away a fresh batch of tears.

"Turn around and go back, Lila."

Had she heard Daisy right? Surely she wasn't throwing in the towel and admitting defeat where Brody Dawson was concerned.

"I can't. Something in my gut says that we need this time apart to see what happens and where this is going. If it is meant to be, I'll know it. If not, I'll survive on the memories," she said.

"I know this is hard for you and hearing the pain in your voice is making me cry with you," Daisy said. "I wish I'd stayed in Texas all those years ago. I may have ruined your life."

"You did the best you could with what you had to work with that day, so don't have any regrets. You were only thinkin' of me when you left, not yourself. I'll text after a while. Bye now. I'm going to get back on the road. I'll text you when I check into a hotel. I love you, Mama."

"Call Molly. She's worried sick that she offended you," Daisy said.

"I will. I promise." She hit the END button before Daisy could say anything else.

Molly answered on the first ring. "I'm sorry for whatever I did."

"It wasn't anything you said or did. You've been great, Molly, and I've loved working with you but I couldn't endure a bunch of tears and good-byes."

"When are you comin' back?"

"Don't know that I am," Lila said.

"Oh, yes, you are. It's just a matter of time," Molly said.

"We'll see. Thanks for everything. I need to get back on the road."

"Don't drive when you get sleepy. Get a hotel room."

"I promise I'll be careful," Lila said. "Tell Georgia hello for me."

"Hmmmph," Molly snorted. "You can tell her yourself when you come home."

She waited another hour to send a text to Brody: *Too late to call. We'll talk tomorrow morning.*

Seconds later the phone rang.

"I thought we were good." His voice sounded raspy.

"We were. We are. But you said it when you told me you were lost and your heart hurt when I left the first time. Imagine how hard it would be to go through that again."

"I am going through it again," he said.

"So am I but I have to get moved out of my apartment and we need some time apart."

"How long is some time?"

"I don't know. I just couldn't say good-bye, Brody."

There was a long silence before he said, "I understand. Does that mean you're coming home to Happy for the rest of the summer after you get this job in Arkansas?"

"It means I'm leaving Florida. I'm not sure where I'm going. I'm at a rest stop right now and I need to get back on the road."

"Be careful, darlin', and call me every couple of hours so I know you're okay," he said.

"I'm a big girl, Brody. I've been traveling alone for years. I'll text you when I get to a stopping point. If you're awake, you can call me."

"Lila, I don't like this."

"Neither do I, Brody."

She hit the outskirts of Shreveport at four in the morning. She'd thought she'd feel a tremendous sense of relief when she crossed the line from Texas into Louisiana. The inner wild child would disappear and she'd be another person.

It didn't happen.

Her eyes felt like they'd been worked over with eighty-grit sandpaper but she couldn't rationalize paying out money at that time of night for a hotel. Checkout in most of them was noon and only a few would let her take the cats in without a hefty deposit. Three or four hours' sleep, maybe just until the sun rose, would get her on into Panama City Beach by bedtime.

She saw a sign for a roadside rest at the next exit. She whipped over into the right lane and slowed down. The place was empty except for a van with a family who looked as if they'd been traveling longer than she had. A little red-haired girl must've slept through the night because she was running circles around a picnic table where her daddy slept on top of it.

The child reminded Lila of Emma but her mama wasn't a thing like Kasey. The dark-haired lady was sitting on a quilt next to the picnic bench with a second little girl in her lap. The lady watched the little girl run off energy and smiled as Lila passed by them on her way to the ladies' room.

Someday Lila would have a family like that. It

wouldn't matter if she and her husband were too strapped for money or time to get a hotel room on their travels. The important thing would be if they had each other. The family had left when she went back outside.

The kittens were quiet, so she rolled down the windows a few inches, threw the seat back as far as it would go, and shut her eyes. She wiggled around until she was semicomfortable, tucked her hands under her cheek, and was sound asleep in seconds. The sun pouring in the window and Duke howling awoke her four hours later.

"Okay, guys, let's try out this new thing." She put collars on each of them and tied a ribbon to each before she took them outside and tied the other end to the leg of the picnic bench. She expected both of them to fight against the collars but they were too fascinated with the grass, a butterfly, and the new things to fuss. Duke was the first one to scratch out a hole in the loose dirt under the bench; then Cora followed his lead.

"Good kitty cats," Lila praised them.

She kept them in sight and went back to the truck to get the new water dish and food bowl. When they'd finished eating and romping, she took them back to their carrier and removed the collars and ribbon leashes. They were not happy but they didn't have a choice. It was still a long way to Florida and she didn't want them getting lost amongst the luggage.

She rolled the kinks from her neck and fastened her seat belt. The second Dr Pepper she'd bought was warm but it washed down half a dozen donuts. She wouldn't need food again until noon. She was on the road again, trying to put the disappointment she'd heard in Brody's voice out of her mind without much luck. By supper time she'd be back in her apartment but right then she wished she was helping with the breakfast rush at the Happy Café.

I miss you, Brody. It's only been a few hours but I miss you so much. Why does love have to be so hard?

Chapter Twenty

On Thursday morning, Brody awoke to the same empty feeling he'd taken to bed with him on Wednesday night. There had been hurt the first time Lila left Happy, but this time it went beyond simple pain and he had no idea how to make it go away. He put a pot of coffee on, made a peanut butter and jelly sandwich, and carried it with him to the corral where Sundance was penned up.

He sat down on the other side of the fence and ate two bites of the sandwich before he tossed it to the side for the ants or the squirrels. Whichever got there first was welcome to it.

"I'm back, old friend," he told the bull.

Sundance made his way over to the fence and tried to poke his head through the railings.

"Grass ain't a bit greener on this side," Brody said. "She's gone and I don't know what to do or say to make her come home for good. I feel like half my heart is gone.

Hell no! That's not right. She took the whole thing with her when she left. I hate good-byes, too, but if she'd have talked to me, we might have avoided ever havin' another one. Movers could have taken care of her stuff and she had a job at the café."

The big Angus bull hung his head over the top rail.

"Nothing we can do now. I sent a text an hour ago and she hasn't responded yet. What if she doesn't? What if she gets down there and Clancy convinces her to stay? I don't know why I'm talkin' to you. You don't have any answers and every time you get a chance, you break out of the corral and get into trouble."

Brody chuckled. "I guess that's why—we're a lot alike. We don't like being penned up and we know what we like. Well, thanks for the visit. I don't know what I'm going to do, but I'm not going to figure it out here."

He started back to the house and checked his phone but there were no messages or missed calls. He didn't want to talk to Jace or Kasey, so he detoured and walked over to Henry's old barn. He heard Blake Shelton's voice singing from his first album before he even peeked inside the door to see Paul loading feed.

"Hey." Paul waved and reached inside the truck to turn down the music.

"I like it loud but Gracie won't let me play it like that when she's in the truck." He grinned. "I heard Lila left last night without tellin' nobody, not even you. Thought maybe Henry might reappear."

"Why would you think that?" Brody asked.

"Just a feelin' I had. I know that they left and then he disappeared but since it all happened in a few weeks, I've wondered if they were connected in some way. Guess I was wrong. There ain't no one at the house. I go through and check it every month or so just to be sure there ain't been no vandalism."

Brody grabbed a pair of gloves from a hook beside the door and hoisted a bag of feed onto his shoulders. "I'll help you get this unloaded since I'm here."

"How're you takin' it?" Paul asked. "Looked like y'all was gettin' pretty serious."

"I wish she would've stayed."

"Maybe the stars wasn't lined up right," Paul said.

They finished loading the feed and Paul removed a glove and stuck out his hand. "Thanks for the help and remember that old thing they say about lettin' something you love go."

"If it comes back, then it's real. If it don't, it wasn't?" Brody asked.

"Something like that. I remember once when Kasey and Adam were havin' a big fight. Can't remember what it was about but Gracie told him to love her enough that she'd come back. What'd y'all fight about?"

"We didn't. She hates good-byes," Brody said.

"I can sure relate to that. Telling Adam good-bye every time he left made me come out here to this barn and cry like a baby. Mamas are pretty smart when it comes to things like this. Speaking of, you talked to yours?"

Brody shook his head slowly. "Oh, no!"

"You might be surprised how smart she is about these things, son. Thanks again for the help. There's that white cat again. I sure wish someone would take her home with them. She's a sweet-natured old gal but Gracie ain't one much for cats. You think about talkin' to Valerie or Hope." Paul got into the vehicle and drove away.

Brody worked his phone from his hip pocket and had his finger ready to call his mother but he couldn't. He jogged back to the ranch, got into his truck and drove over to her place. He knocked on the back door and then pushed on inside.

Valerie was braising a roast and scarcely even glanced his way. "Good mornin', son. Coffee is in the pot. What brings you out this early?"

"Lila's gone."

"I heard." Valerie finished the job and slid the roast into the oven. "The only thing that surprises me is that you're here talking to me about it."

He removed the phone from his pocket and found the song that had come to his mind when Paul made that comment about mamas. "I want you to listen to this and then we'll talk." He laid it on the countertop and turned up the volume.

"So Much Like My Dad" started playing and tears ran down his unshaven cheeks. George Strait sang the words better than he could express them. His mother had always said that he was just like Mitch Dawson. By the time the song was nearing the finish, Valerie was wiping both her tears and Brody's away with a dish towel.

"Like it says, if I'm like Dad, then there must've been times when you wanted to get in the car and leave this place too. So please, Mama, she's gone and I need to know what it was that Dad said to make you stay, because I don't think I can live without her," Brody said.

Valerie poured two cups of coffee and set them on the table. "It's normal for people in a relationship to have arguments and times of doubt, son, but I don't know that I can help you."

Brody had a hard time swallowing all his tough pride around the lump in his throat. "How did he do it, Mama? I know it's personal, but I need to know if I'm so much like him."

Valerie motioned for him to sit down at the table. "He said the three magic words. *I love you.* That's what always made me stay with him. Have you told her that?"

"Not seriously," he said.

"As much as I've fought you being with her, I'm going to give you a piece of advice. You're both adults and if you love her, then go to Florida and tell her so. Not here in Happy where you're both still battling against being those two kids that you used to be, but in a different place where you're adults. Jace and Kasey can hold down the ranch for a few days."

He shook his head. "I can't go anywhere right now. The middle of summer is our busiest time for repairing fences, plowing and planting for winter pasture, and... well, you know, Mama. You've been runnin' this ranch for years, so I don't have to tell you how hard it would be to leave for several days right now."

"Do you love her or the ranch more? Or is this a pride thing?"

"Granny Hope expects me to be responsible when it comes to the ranch." He raked his fingers through his hair.

"You didn't answer me," Valerie said.

"I love her more than anything, but it might be a pride thing," he admitted.

"Pride is a dangerous thing, son," Valerie told him. "It can ruin a relationship."

"Will she be welcomed into the family?" Brody asked.

"If she loves you as much as you do her. God, Brody,

I can't stand to see you like this. I had no idea that you loved her this deeply," Valerie answered.

"Thank you, Mama." Brody hugged his mother.

The answer was simple. He just had to get to her to deliver it.

*   *   *

Soft, drizzling rain had darkened the Florida skies when Lila pulled into her parking space in front of her apartment. She was close enough to the beach that she could hear the faint sounds of the waves as they splashed against the shore. Leaning on the truck's back fender, she inhaled the salty air and felt the warm rain on her face. She'd miss evenings like this, but it was time to move on.

With a sigh, she opened the passenger door and removed the cat carrier. "Welcome to your two-day home," she said. "It's not as big as the Happy apartment, but it's a heck of a lot more room than you had in the truck. Give me time to get your litter pan out and I'll open the chute."

The word *chute* reminded her of Brody and the way that her heart stopped when he was thrown off that bull. Her mind circled around from that night to when they'd skinny-dipped in the cold water and how he'd looked wearing nothing but a smile in the moonlight. She sighed as she went back to the truck and unloaded kitten supplies. Then she carried them to the kitchen and showed them their food. Neither of them showed as much interest in that as much as snooping around in the new surroundings.

"Make yourselves at home." She yawned.

She sat down on the sofa and called Brody before she passed out from exhaustion.

"I've been waiting all day to hear your voice. Texts just aren't the same," he said.

"Me too. I'm already homesick," she admitted.

"You said home," he whispered.

"Happy has always been the home base, Brody. That doesn't mean..." She yawned again.

"I think it does, Lila, but I'm not going to argue. You sound tired, darlin'. Are you in your apartment?"

"Yes, I am. The cats are set free and happy and I'm going to take a shower and sleep a little bit before I start packing," she said.

"And tomorrow?"

"I got a call from the school in Conway. I've got an interview, so I'll head in that direction. I'm exhausted. I wish you were here."

"So do I, darlin'. You go on and get some rest," he said.

"I miss you so much."

"Me too, Lila."

She took time to send her mother and Molly a text and then she turned off her phone and fell on the bed without even taking off her clothes. She was asleep when her head hit the pillow and it was full dark that evening when she awoke. A black ball of fur rested in the crook of her neck and a white one was sitting beside her shoulder, staring at her.

"I'm awake and I still miss him so much that my heart hurts," she whispered.

Cora meowed loudly, waking Duke, who instantly started to purr. Her stomach growled, reminding her that it had been hours since she'd eaten anything but junk food. She was so hungry, she could almost taste the fish from Margaritaville. She hopped out of bed and headed straight for the bathroom.

Letting the warm water beat down on her back and shoulders for several minutes, she didn't fight the memories of the past month but let them play through her mind on a continuous loop several times before she got out of the shower and wrapped a towel around her body. She dried her hair and dressed in a sundress, applied a little makeup, and kissed both cats on the heads before she left.

With her motorcycle still strapped down on the back of her truck, she drove to one of her favorite places for good local fish. As usual, Margaritaville was noisy and pretty well packed when she arrived. But luck was with her because they had a table in the back corner. A young couple with glimmering gold wedding bands sat to her left. They could have been Brody and Lila in another lifetime. The waiter seated a small couple with a toddler in a high chair not far away. Then an old couple, gray haired and still holding hands as he helped her down the three or four steps into the dining room, was seated at a table for two right ahead of her.

Happy-ever-after was lived out in stages right before her eyes. She wanted that shiny gold wedding ring. She wanted that little blue-eyed daughter in a high chair. And she wanted Brody to hold her hand to steady her as she walked down the steps into a restaurant when they were old and gray.

She studied the menu so that the three couples wouldn't catch her staring at them. A motion in her peripheral vision caught her attention and before she could escape, she saw Belinda drag Clancy by the hand over to her table.

"Clancy told me you're leaving us. I was hoping to see you before you checked out at the school." Belinda stooped to hug her.

The last thing Lila wanted was to share her table but Belinda hesitated so long that it became awkward. "This is a table for four. Y'all can join me if you want."

"That would be wonderful," Belinda said. "So I hear you might be going to Little Rock."

"Conway, actually. It's about an hour from Little Rock. We'll see if they like me and if I like them."

Belinda sat down, crossed one long leg over the other, and then tucked her chin-length red hair behind her ears. "I can't imagine living anywhere but right here. And they have tornadoes in Arkansas."

"Florida has hurricanes," Lila said.

She should have at least a little streak of jealousy, right? But it wasn't there—not even a smidgen. If anything, she felt sorry for Belinda for getting tangled up with a narcissistic, egotistical fool like Clancy.

"But"—Belinda smiled—"they don't have a Margaritaville."

"A sacrifice I'll have to make for their fine Southern cookin' restaurants," Lila said.

"What can I get you?" the waiter appeared at her elbow.

"I'm having whatever the fish of the day is and a bottle of Jäger," she said.

"I want a bowl of gumbo and a glass of white wine," Belinda said.

"And I'll have the eight-ounce sirloin, baked potato,

and salad with house dressing and bring a bottle of red to the table," Clancy said.

"One ticket or separate?"

"Separate," Lila said quickly.

"Separate for all of us," Belinda said.

Lila was suddenly intrigued.

"Okay, then, I'll have that right out," the waiter said.

"I'll have to eat and run," Lila said. "I've got packing to do tonight if I'm going to get my room cleaned out and keys turned in tomorrow."

"We'll miss you," Belinda said.

"We can keep in touch," Lila said. "So how did the summer job go at the T-shirt shack?"

"Great. If I could make a living working there, I'd stop teaching in a minute." She and Clancy exchanged a look and then she sighed. "But minimum wage doesn't pay the bills and..." She let the sentence drop.

"And she's too smart to live that kind of lifestyle," Clancy finished for her. The tilt of his chin said that he was talking to Lila as much or more than Belinda.

"So you think that only stupid people can be sales clerks or waitresses," Lila pushed the issue. "You wouldn't want to introduce Belinda as, 'Please meet my girlfriend who works at the T-shirt shop on the strip,' would you?"

"No, I wouldn't or take home a waitress to introduce to my parents either," he said curtly.

Belinda turned to face Clancy. "That's crazy. It's all good work whether it's teaching kids or making the tourists happy."

"Society makes the rules. I just do my best to live by them." He laid a hand across the back of her chair.

"Oh, well, it's not important," Belinda said. "We are who we are and I'm a teacher. Now, Lila, tell me how did the waitress business in Texas work out?"

The waiter brought a glass of white wine, a beer, and an empty glass with a full bottle of red and set it on the table. He poured the wine and said, "Food should be ready in only a few minutes."

"Thank you," Clancy said. "Now, you were going to tell us about the waitress work, Lila? Still chasing after that redneck cowboy? You're so unsuited to a man like that."

She took a sip of the beer and turned to Belinda. "Being a waitress was amazing. I made a little more than my usual teacher paycheck, actually. And of course, we get all the good town gossip." Her smile faded as she addressed Clancy. "And the cowboy isn't a bit of your business."

Belinda sipped her wine. "Oh, really!"

"Had some good tippers and then some who only came in for a glass of sweet tea but I loved visiting with all of them," Lila said.

Belinda giggled. "I really will miss you. Anytime you want to come back to Florida you can stay with me."

"Thank you." Lila was glad that she'd gotten cornered by Belinda. In Florida she wasn't the wild child; she was a full-fledged bona fide grown-up. Neither of her personalities liked Clancy and that was a good thing to have settled. It wasn't just because she was living a different life in Texas that he'd gotten on her last nerve. He could do it in any state and with either of her twin personalities.

In Happy, she could be that wild child with Brody and still hang on to the grown-up woman. Like Kasey had said that day in the café, she could have both. But the only place she really wanted both was in the panhandle of Texas—that's where both pieces of her heart fit together.

She ate faster than usual and was able to pay her bill and get out of the restaurant in thirty-six minutes. Belinda expressed regret that neither she nor Clancy would be at the school the next day when she checked out but they had plans to visit her parents in Pensacola. Lila faked disappointment and smiled all the way to her truck.

"Here kitty, kitty," she called out at the door of her apartment. Duke and Cora came running from the bathroom and stopped at her feet as if asking if she'd remembered to bring them something.

"I didn't forget. I've got two pretty nice-sized bites of good grilled fish."

Duke growled and slapped a paw down on his bite, practically inhaled it, and then headed across the kitchen floor to help Cora with hers. She sniffed it daintily, walked around it, slapped it a couple of times to see if it would wiggle, and then pranced off, tail held high. Duke grabbed it in his teeth and tossed it into the air like a dead mouse, caught it on the fly, and ate it quickly.

Lila plopped down on the sofa and picked up a notepad from beside the house phone. Call the cable company, the phone company, and the Internet service provider first thing the next morning. Call the Sugar Sands and make a reservation for the next night because her lease actually ran out at midnight on June 30. Her cell phone rang and, hoping it was Brody, she quickly fished it out of her purse and answered without checking the ID.

"I'm awake and ready to talk," she said.

"This is Valerie Dawson and I'm ready to talk too."

The phone fell from Lila's hand and she had to scramble to grab it before it hit the ground. "Is Brody all right?" she whispered.

"Fine when I talked to him earlier today," Valerie said. "I'm butting in where I probably shouldn't but he's my son. You'll understand someday when you have kids."

Lila gulped a couple of times. "Okay, then what do you want to talk about?"

"I'm not sure where to begin or even what to say. I got the number from Kasey and...," she stammered.

Lila was sure that she was about to hear that she should stay out of Happy, leave Brody alone, he would get over his pain, yada, yada, yada. Lila shut her eyes and got ready for the tirade.

"I've judged you and that was wrong," Valerie said.

Lila's eyes snapped open. She was awake and this was not a dream. "Why are you telling me this?"

"My mother-in-law never did think I was good enough for Mitch. Right until her dying day, she awoke every morning and hoped he would divorce me."

Lila chuckled. "Surely not."

"Oh, yeah, she did," Valerie laughed with her. "I swore I'd never make my sons choose between his family and the woman they loved, but I did...and I apologize."

Lila's eyes shot toward the window. It didn't look like the end of the world but surely the apocalypse was on the way if she'd heard Valerie right. "Apology accepted. Why are you telling me this now?"

"Before, you two were so different and so young. Now I see things differently." There was a long whoosh of air on the other end as Valerie sighed. "I want to tell you that I won't be my mother-in-law. I don't know you very well but I'd like to remedy that if you'll come back to Happy for the rest of the summer. I won't stand in the way of whatever relationship you and Brody decide to have."

"Thank you," Lila said. "But I've got an interview in Conway, Arkansas, in a couple of days for a teaching job there. I'll have to find an apartment and get moved in before I can make a trip back to Happy."

"Could we talk again sometime?" Valerie asked.

"Yes, ma'am, that would be great," Lila said, still wondering if she'd awake tomorrow and figure out that this had been some kind of wild dream.

"Okay, then, good night. And before I hang up, Kasey said that she'd love to hear from you, so when you have time would you please give her a call?"

"I sure will," Lila said. "Good night to you too."

She hit the END button, tossed the phone on the pillow beside her, and rolled her eyes toward the ceiling.

Cora climbed the arm of the sofa like it was a tree and perched there. Lila stroked her pretty white fur and said, "Well, now, that should do it for this day. I've dealt with Clancy and Valerie in the same evening. Don't you think that should get me a gold crown even if it's only a plastic one?"

Cora purred an answer and the phone rang a second time. Lila checked it that time.

"Hello, Brody," she said.

"Hi, darlin'," he drawled.

His deep voice sent sweet shivers down her back.

"Gettin' packed and ready to roll out of Florida?"

"Slept all day and am just now getting started, but I

made a list. I'm going to turn in my key tomorrow by quittin' time at the complex office and check into a little place called the Sugar Sands on the beach for one night, then head out on Saturday morning."

"Sounds like you got things under control, then," he said. "I thought after twenty-four hours that the missin' you might get better. It hasn't but at least this time I can call and hear your voice."

"I'm not so sure anything is under control. But I do have a couple of stories to tell you." She went on to tell him about seeing Clancy and knowing that she'd made the right decision six months ago to break it off with him and then about the phone call with his mother.

"Nanny didn't like Mama. We all knew it and it made for tense times when we all went over to their house. I'm glad that Mama is coming around," he said. "I was just listening to Vince Gill sing 'Never Knew Lonely' over and over again. I can so relate to the words of the chorus that say that lonely can tear you in two. I feel like half of me is missing," he said.

"Me too." The lyrics of the song, especially that part about not being able to make up for the times when she was gone, played through her head.

He cleared his throat and she swallowed hard. "I'll try to get things taken care of in Arkansas if I get the job and come back to Happy in a couple of weeks."

"I'm not sure I can survive for two whole weeks," he whispered.

"Well, then, I guess maybe you'll just have to fly into Little Rock if you get to feelin' weak." She fought back new tears. Lord, she hadn't cried so often in more than a decade. "I'll gladly drive to the airport and get you."

"Don't invite me if you don't mean it," he said.

"You're welcome anytime," she said. "How about next weekend?"

"How about this one?"

"Don't tease me, Brody," she laughed.

Chapter Twenty-One

Lila had started out the month of June in Happy, Texas. That Saturday morning, the first day of July, she was sitting on a beach far away from Texas and the only place she wanted to be was at home in Happy.

She let a hand full of warm sand sift through her fingers. The waves were calm that morning, lapping up on the shore peacefully. Seagulls flew around overhead, their beady little eyes looking for food. Sandpipers darted in and out of the edge of the water, leaving their footprints in the sand.

She got one of those antsy feelings that said someone was close by. Glancing to the right, she caught a glimpse of the motel cat, belly to the ground as it stalked a bird. To the left, a seagull was picking at the sand. Then the black and white cat took off for the sea oats and weeds and the gull flapped its wings and joined its flock high in the air.

She looked over her shoulder and blinked several

times. That cowboy silhouetted on the deck looked so much like Brody in the early morning light that it was uncanny. His broad chest and that snowy white T-shirt— it made her ache for Brody. He left the deck and in a few long strides, he covered the distance and sat down beside her. She moved one of her bare feet over to touch his ankle.

He was a real person, not an illusion.

"When you said anytime, I hope you meant it."

"But I'm leaving in a few minutes," she whispered, still unsure if she was imagining things.

"Thought I'd hitch a ride and spend time with you, then fly home from Little Rock to Amarillo."

He was honest to God real, and he was right there beside her. In one fluid motion, she pushed him back and wiggled her way on top of him and then her lips were on his. His arms drew her so close that a grain of sand couldn't have found its way between them. Everything in her world was suddenly all right. Brody was there. He had come to Florida to spend time with her.

"I can't believe you're here." She ran her fingertips over his face and covered his eyelids with butterfly kisses.

"The welcome was a little delayed but…" He pulled her mouth back to his and rolled to one side for a better angle.

"Get a room," a voice above them said.

Lila glanced away from Brody into an old guy's grinning face. "We've got a room, thank you very much."

"Then use it." He moved on down the beach at the slowest jog she'd ever seen.

With a giggle she sat up and grabbed Brody's hand,

afraid that if she wasn't touching him he would disappear. "When did you get here? Where did you stay? Do you have a car? Did you really fly?"

He brought her hand to his lips and answered each question as he kissed her knuckles. "I got here about midnight, then took a car service to the hotel behind us. I stayed in room 101. Since it was a one-way ticket, I'm flying on a prayer that you wouldn't send me packing."

"Mama warned me about picking up strange men." She grinned.

"Well, then." He rubbed his chin. "Would you let just any old cowboy drive your truck?"

"No, I would not," she answered.

"If you let me drive, that would mean I'm not a stranger, right?"

"Seems that way." She smiled. "I could hire you to drive for me and maybe Mama wouldn't get upset."

He gazed out into the water. "I'll take that job. What's the pay?"

"I'm down on my luck, so maybe you'd do it for free meals and a ride to the airport when we get to Conway?"

He pulled his hand free and stuck it out. "Shake on it and it's a deal."

Without hesitation, she took his hand. "We are burning daylight, so we'd best herd the cats into their carrier, check out of this place, and get on the road toward Monroe, Louisiana."

"Is that our first stop?" he asked without letting go of her hand.

She nodded. "It is and then tomorrow morning we'll

go to Conway, get there early, take a look around, and check into a hotel. I have my interview on Monday morning at nine sharp."

"Plans are set in stone, then." He stood to his feet and brought her with him. "So we'd better go chase down Duke and Crazy Cora. Which one of those places are they in?"

"Room 102, right next to where you were last night," she said.

He took the first step across the beach toward the motel. "Only a wall separating us."

"Story of our lives." She stopped at the faucet to wash the sand from her feet.

"Maybe it's time to tear the wall down." He brushed the sand from his jeans and waited his turn.

"That'd be quite a task. You packed and ready?"

"I stay ready." He wiggled his eyebrows.

"I can't argue with that," she laughed. "I'll get the cats in the carrier and meet you at the truck after I check out. And, Brody, this is beyond amazing."

"Yes, it is." He nodded.

*   *   *

The truck bed was loaded with plastic bins in case it rained, and her motorcycle right in the middle of all of it. The backseat held a carrier with two squalling kittens, suitcases, and cardboard boxes. Brody's duffel bag sat on top of it all and he'd never been happier than that morning as he headed west with Lila sitting beside him.

He wanted to say those three words that his mother

said kept her from leaving his dad when things got rough but he wanted it to be a special time. Lila deserved the whole package—flowers, candlelight, and romance—when he finally said that he loved her. She shouldn't have to hear him say it over the top of whining kittens and the sound of traffic all around them.

"Does your mama know about this?" Lila asked after they were on the highway.

"She's the one who told me it's what I should do. She don't like to see her baby boy hurtin'."

"The big tough cowboy will always be her baby, won't he?"

"I hope so. When you have a son, will he always be yours?" Brody made a right-hand turn to head north.

She turned around and stared out the side window for a long time before she answered. "Do you want children, Brody?"

"A dozen wouldn't be too many for me," he said. "You?"

"More than one. I hated being an only child. I envied anyone who had siblings—still do." It was evident by the serious expression on her face that she struggled with the next words. "Do you really think we can make this long-distance thing work?"

"If we keep the lines of communication open, we can make anything work," he answered. "You can come to Happy once a month for a weekend or longer over holidays. I'll fly to Arkansas a weekend out of each month and we can talk every night. Easy has never been our portion, has it?"

She laid a hand on his thigh. "What about the ranch? Can you leave it for two or three days at a time?"

"You're more important to me than Hope Springs, and I can turn some responsibility over to Jace."

She nodded. "I'll have a week at Thanksgiving, two weeks at Christmas."

"We've got an extra bedroom at Hope Springs."

"You mean I don't get to sleep in your room?"

He brought her hand to his lips and kissed the palm. "That's your decision. My door will always be open."

She turned on the radio and leaned her head back on the seat with her eyes shut. "Let's not go to Arkansas or Texas. Let's spend the rest of our lives in this truck, traveling from one place to the other. I can waitress and you can make a few dollars working on a ranch. Maybe we'll get one of those tiny little silver trailers to hitch to the truck and live in it."

"What about all those kids?" he asked.

"When the first one is school age, we'll settle down. I know it's crazy and that it's my wild child talking but let's pretend just for this day that we never have to say good-bye again. Not even for two weeks or a month," she said.

"Sounds good to me. I hate being away from you, especially after this past month. Hey, there's a town not far ahead. Maybe they'll have a trailer for sale."

She straightened up so quick that she grabbed her head. "Wow! That gave me a head rush."

"What? The trailer or making it rock? We should look for one of those signs that says, 'If this trailer is rockin', don't come knockin',' shouldn't we?"

Lila put a finger on her lips and then on his cheek. "Definitely. Or maybe a bumper sticker. We could steal a 'do not disturb' sign from a hotel to hang on the door."

"We do need that trailer for sure. I don't think there's room for us to cuddle together in this truck. If we find one sittin' on the side of the road, then it's a sign that we need to turn this from pretend into real."

Brody allowed himself to indulge in the fantasy for a moment. After his long day being a ranch hand, Lila would come home at night and he'd rub the soreness from her feet. They'd shower together in the warm rain and laugh every time they'd bump into each other in the tiny space.

*   *   *

Lila's imagination went to the only travel trailer she'd ever been inside. The bed took up most of the area on one end and the other was nothing more than a tiny kitchen with a booth for a table. She shut her eyes and visualized Brody's long leg thrown over her in the hot nights of summer. In the bitter cold winter, they'd pile on more covers and make wild, passionate love to keep warm. He'd come home from a day of ranch work and she'd massage the knots from his shoulders.

"What were you thinkin' about?" she asked.

"That travel trailer. Everything you say and do makes me want you," he answered. "You ready for a stop? We just passed a sign that said there's a rest stop at the next exit."

"I'm good, but the kitties might need a bit of dirt to dig in," she said.

He slowed down and parked on the edge of the lot and she bailed out of the truck. She took the carrier with the cats inside to the pet area. She tied the bright red ribbons around each of the cat's collars before she wrapped the other end around the leg of a picnic bench.

Brody headed toward the building and came back with his arms loaded with vending machine snacks. "I'll watch the children while you stretch your legs and go to the ladies' room. I brought breakfast."

She jogged to the bathroom, where she looked at the reflection in the mirror the whole time she washed her hands. There was Dee, the schoolteacher with black hair and brown eyes, staring back at her. But in those same eyes, she could see Lila, who only came out to play when Brody Dawson was around.

"I don't want to be away from him," she whispered. "But there's nothing for me but him in Happy, so what do I do? I have to work and make a living. I really would be willing to throw everything to the wind and go with him if we found a trailer for sale. But he has a ranch to manage and lives depend on him."

She dried her hands and stopped at the vending machine for more junk food and two bottles of cold soda pop to keep them going until lunch.

"Hey, I told you that I bought breakfast," he said.

"We have to keep up our strength."

"And why would we need to do that?"

When he smiled like that, her heart kicked in an extra beat and her pulse raced. "Because you have to drive all the way to Monroe and I get real bitchy when I'm hungry. I don't want you to throw me out on the side of the road. And I promised you food for payment if you would drive."

He corralled the kittens back into the cage and shut the door, picked it up, and headed toward the truck.

"Gettin' to spend time with you is double payment, darlin'. But I am glad you remembered to get us something to drink."

"I saw a sign back there that says there's a truck stop ahead about five miles. We should fill the gas tank there," she said. "And who knows, we might even find a silver trailer for sale."

He resituated the carrier in the backseat. "Remember when we used to sneak away from everyone else and take my old beat-up truck down through the canyon?"

She crawled into the passenger seat and tossed her stash on the console. "And we'd stop at one of those lanes back to a ranch, eat corn chips, drink root beers if we couldn't get real beer, and then make out on that quilt." She ripped open the bag and took a handful out before she handed it to Brody as he drove.

"You do remember."

"Of course I do," she said.

At the gas station, Brody was almost finished filling the tank when a silver trailer showed up. A much bigger truck than hers was pulling it and an old guy got out.

"Want me to ask the driver if he'll sell it?" Brody asked.

"If he'll take twenty dollars for it, we'll call it an omen and see if my truck can move it down the road. If we bog down, then it's a sign that we should stop right here in this place and find jobs," she teased.

Brody grinned and hollered over the top of the truck. "I'll gladly buy that trailer from you. How much would you take for it?"

"My wife would skin me alive if I sold this thing. It's her pride and joy." The fellow smiled. "She likes to go see the grandkids but she needs her space when it comes nighttime." He lowered his voice. "And sometimes even in the daytime when they get rowdy. Why would you want this old dinosaur anyway?"

"My woman over there." Brody nodded toward Lila, who was only a few feet away. "She's wantin' an adventure and we only got a hundred dollars to spend on it."

The guy chuckled. "Son, if me and Mama was your age and we had a few dollars, we'd go rent a cheap hotel, get us a bottle of Tennessee whiskey, and have an adventure that would be a memory maker."

"Well, thanks for the advice," Brody said.

"Anytime. You kids be careful wherever you're movin' to," he said.

"Yes, sir," Brody said as he got into the truck. "I tried, sweetheart. Maybe the next feller will be ready to sell."

Lila giggled. "What did you offer him?"

"I offered a hundred but I would have given him two hundred," he teased.

She crawled over the console and settled into his lap. "It was too big anyway. You could hide from me in that thing. I want one so small that we can't cuss Duke and Cora without spittin' cat hair out of our mouths. But I appreciate you offerin' him more than the twenty dollars I was willin' to pay."

"I'd give him everything I've got to make you happy." Brody cupped her butt in his hands and leaned in for a kiss.

Happy? The town? Her state of mind? What would it take to make her happy? Being with Brody the rest of her life would be a good start and it looked like he was willing to work at a long-distance relationship. Things would be different this time. They'd call every day, text several times, even Skype, so why was her heart so heavy?

Because you want more than that, right? The voice in her head that morning sounded a lot like Kasey.

Yes, I do, she agreed.

Chapter Twenty-Two

The sun was still high in the sky when they reached Monroe that evening. She picked out a hotel that was pet friendly and got them a room on the ground floor with an outside door. He nosed the truck into the slot reserved for room 131 and grabbed the kittens while she got a small suitcase from the backseat.

She tossed the room key across the top of the truck. "What do you need?"

"Just that duffel bag," he answered.

"I'll bring it with me. Maybe we'll get something delivered for supper. I've had all the riding I want for one day."

"I'm fine with that. I'm ready to stretch these old bones out and rest for the evening." He unlocked the door and stood aside to let her go inside first.

"Thirty is not old," she said.

"Tell that to my bones," he said as he kicked the door shut with the heel of his boot and dropped the key beside the television.

She set down the suitcase and duffel bag, then took the carrier from him. "I'll put them in the bathroom while I run out and get the bag with their supplies in it. Then we can turn them loose and decide what we want to order. The places that deliver are usually listed in the folder on the desk."

It took only a few minutes but when she returned, Brody was singing in the shower. The time had come for her to make a very important decision. Tomorrow morning when they left Monroe, they would turn north to the job interview. Or she could tell Brody to drive west and take Molly up on that job offer to do waitress work at the café. Molly said that she could live in the apartment indefinitely, so she'd have a place to live and a job that paid as well as teaching.

She was reminded of an old country song that her dad used to play called "Old Country." She could imagine the whine of the fiddle as the song talked about a country boy comin' to town and the city girl waiting for him in a motel. Humming the melody, she flipped through a folder on the dresser and found a fried chicken place that delivered. She ran a finger down the menu and called in a family order for four. She had fifteen minutes until it arrived, so she unzipped her suitcase and took out a pair of pajama pants and a faded nightshirt.

The bathroom door opened and two fur babies barreled out, one walking sideways with her tail fluffed out and her back arched as if she were hunting full-grown mountain lions. Duke slunk out like a miniature sleek black panther, belly low to the ground and growling as he attacked the dark green bed skirt.

"Mean critters, aren't they?" Brody leaned on the doorjamb.

Jesus, Mary, and Joseph! Forgive me, Lord, if that's blasphemy but he looks like sex on a stick standing there with nothing but a towel slung around his hips. Lord, even the angels' wings would be seared from this kind of heat.

"If they were as mean as they think they are, they'd give old Sundance a run for his money," she said, unable to take her eyes off him. Her tongue flicked out and moistened her dry, hot lips. He took a step forward and she did the same; then the world stopped turning and they were on the bed. The towel got lost and it was as if he snapped his fingers and her clothing fell off. His hands were everywhere but then so were hers. She wrapped her long legs around him and guided him into her. And soon they forgot all about time and circumstances.

"Sweet Lord," Brody groaned afterward.

"Yep." Lila rolled to the side and laid her head on his chest. "Your heart is still pounding."

"So is yours," he panted. "That was intense but it's what I've thought about all day."

"And just think, the night is young," she said.

A hard knock on the door brought them back to reality. "Who..."

"Fried chicken." She grinned.

He rolled off the bed and jerked his jeans up over his fine-looking butt, made sure the cats weren't near the door, and cracked it open.

"Delivery for Lila Harris. I need a signature if you want to leave it on the charge card."

"How much?" Brody reached for his wallet.

"Twenty-one oh two," the kid said.

Brody handed him a five and twenty through the door. "Keep the change and thanks."

He felt something brush against his bare foot and looked down as Duke headed out the door. He grabbed him by the scruff of the neck and quickly shoved him into the bathroom.

The kid handed him the sack and pointed toward the corner. "Best watch that white one too. It's sneakin' out."

"Thanks," Brody said, and quickly shut the door.

"I was supposed to pay for the food." Lila wrapped the sheet around her body like a toga.

"You paid for the room. This smells wonderful." He let Duke out of the bathroom and the kitten went straight to Lila, sat down on the tail of her sheet, and whined.

"No chicken for you, Mr. Bad Boy. You tried to get outside. I saw that stunt. You would have probably told me that it was Cora's idea, wouldn't you?"

"Kind of like a couple of other kids I could name but I won't. The bad boy who always let the blame fall on the girl." Brody set about taking the food out of the bag and putting it on the table. Then he pulled his shirt on and held one of the chairs for her.

"I liked the view better without the shirt," she said.

"Mama would kick my butt from here all the way home if I came to the table bare-chested with a lady present," he said.

"Lady? After what we just did?" she teased.

"My lady no matter where we are or what we just did," he said with a smile. "You still like the thigh and wings?"

"Do you remember everything about me?"

"Yes, darlin', I do." He put two pieces of chicken on a paper plate and handed it to her. "And you like potato salad but not coleslaw and fries with ketchup. You like corn chips better than potato chips and root beer better than cola but if you have a choice you'd rather have a longneck beer."

"Good grief," she exclaimed.

"I've lain awake many nights reliving the past. But not once were we sittin' in a hotel or were you wearing a sheet while we ate fried chicken with our fingers."

"Oh, really! Well, I had that vision lots of times."

He straightened up enough to brush a kiss across her lips. "They say out of sight, out of mind. Promise me that won't happen."

"I promise," she said seriously.

*   *   *

Lila slept like a baby until about two-thirty in the morning. She awoke to find Duke and Cora both sleeping on the foot of the bed. She eased out of bed without disturbing either the cats or Brody, pulled a wing-back chair over to the window, and cracked the curtains enough that she could see out.

A half-moon hung in the sky, one side brightly lit and the other side dark—exactly the way she felt as she faced the idea of two pathways, come time to leave. Only a little way on their journey tomorrow there would be a ramp pointing them from Interstate 20 toward Little Rock. That would take her to the job interview. But if she told Brody to go on straight ahead, she'd be making the decision to leave her way of life behind and walk into territory that she was running from just days before.

Which side is the light one and which one is dark? *Daddy, you could pop into my head and give me some advice,* she thought, but there was nothing to help her out.

It might spook the devil out of Brody if she told him to forget about turning north and take her to Happy. Right now he was all for this long-distance relationship thing. Maybe he needed time and space to be ready to take it from a visit every couple of weeks to something more permanent.

At four o'clock she fell asleep in the chair and awoke with a knot in her neck when Brody kissed her on the forehead. "Good mornin'," she said.

"Mornin'. Did I snore?"

"No, I just had a lot of thinkin' to do," she said honestly.

"Want to talk about it?" he asked.

She shook her head. *Tell me you love me and we might have something to talk about but right now it's probably best if I go to Conway and we give this a year.*

"Are we ready to get on the road, then?"

"Soon as I get the cats in the carrier and get a shower. There's not a silver travel trailer out there that's better than this hotel. You want to just stay here for a year?" she teased.

"Yes, I do, but I don't reckon that's an option, is it?"

She smiled and shook her head. "No, but you can't blame the wild child for wishin'."

"Or me neither."

"Well, now that we know we have to check out, then

let's go down to the dining room and have some of that free breakfast they're offering."

Just give me a sign, Lord. It's still not too late for me to change my mind. I'll drag my feet right up until the time to put my name on the contract but he's got to make a move here.

"Aha, hot breakfast. This is great," Brody said when they reached the dining area. "Should we take a piece of bacon back to the children?"

"I'm sure they'd love it," she said.

I don't want to talk about food. I want you to tell me that you won't skitter like a Texas jackrabbit if I spring the news on you that I'm going to Happy.

"Are you okay? Are you worried about this job thing? Honey, I'm sure this interview is just a formality. They've already called your past employers and gotten good recommendations." He heaped a plate with food and carried it to a small table for two.

It wasn't what she wanted to hear but was probably what she needed. She'd asked for a sign and she'd gotten one. It pointed north in a very definite way, whether she liked it or not. She poured batter into the waffle iron. Two minutes later she removed it, dumped a container of yogurt on the top, and then covered that with fresh strawberries.

"Never seen anyone eat a waffle like that," he said.

"I don't like syrup, so I improvise," she said. "I'll come to Amarillo for fall break and Thanksgiving but Christmas always belongs to Mama unless I can talk her into coming to Happy."

"That was a change of subject." He grinned. "But I like that you're plannin' to come home. I've been scared that you'd forget all about me after we say good-bye at the airport."

"Not a chance, cowboy," she said.

He'd said "come home." Was that a sign? Or was the sign the fact that she didn't want to ever say good-bye to him again?

They finished breakfast and went back to the room to get packed and ready for the next four-hour leg of the journey to Conway. The cats carried on with pitiful meows when they had to go back into the cage. The bags were packed and in the truck and she'd made a call to the office to tell the day clerk that she'd left the key in the room. There was nothing to do but get in the truck and make that turn. Brody started the engine and got back out on the highway.

She gripped her clammy palms in her lap. She didn't want to go to Conway, not even to check out the place and interview for the job. Waitress work at the café sounded so much better. *But you worked so hard to be a teacher. You love your job,* her mind argued with her heart.

He caught the exit back onto Highway 20 and pointed to the big sign that said their turnoff was a mile and a half up the road.

Her breath came in short bursts and her heart thumped so hard that any minute it was going to break through her ribs and fall out on the floor of the truck. Visualizing kissing him good-bye at the airport didn't help at all. It might be risky and stupid but she had to listen to her heart and not her mind.

He slowed down and she touched him on the arm. "Keep going, Brody. I can't go to Arkansas. I want to go home and I never want to tell you good-bye again. I can't live with a long-distance relationship. I want it all and if that terrifies the bejesus out of you, then you'll just have to be scared," she said.

He braked and pulled over to the side of the highway. When he turned to her, there were tears in his eyes. "I love you, Lila. Plain and simple, I love you so much that I can't bear life without you."

"You love me?" She brushed away the tear that made a path down his cheek.

"I always have," he whispered. "I was afraid to say it for fear that you wouldn't say it back and my heart would..."

"I can't remember when I didn't love you, Brody Dawson," she said.

"Then let's go home, darlin'."

"I'm ready."

*   *   *

Brody put the truck in gear and started down the road, then pulled off at the next ramp and parked beside an old vacant service station. He got out of the vehicle, circled around the front of it, and opened her door. "May I have this dance, ma'am?"

She put her hand in his as Dolly Parton sang "Rockin' Years" on the radio. "How did you know this would be comin' on right now?"

"I didn't care what came on as long as I could hold you, but this is a sign for both of us. I need to kiss you. It's important that you know that I love you and that I'll stand by you forever just like the song says." He took her into his arms and danced with her in the hot morning sun with nothing around them but a couple of vintage gas pumps and a building with no windows.

She laid her head on his chest and looped her arms around his neck. "I love you, cowboy."

"I love you, Lila, and I'll never get tired of saying it."

When the song ended, he kissed her tenderly. "I'm glad we won't get home until tomorrow because I want this day with you and only you."

Two hours later, they reached Shreveport and a few minutes past that he pulled over again right near the Texas line. He stopped the truck and got out.

"What's wrong?"

"Not one thing," he said.

He opened her door and held out his hand. "Would you please get out?"

"Why?"

"Because I asked," he said.

She hopped out and he dropped down on one knee. "Dee Harris, I love you. You're my soul mate and the miracle that makes my heart beat. I don't have a ring, but I'm not kidding and I'm very serious. Will you marry me? It can be in a week, a year, or even longer, as long as I know you'll never leave me again."

"Yes," she said without hesitating one second as she dropped down on the grass beside him and wrapped her arms around his neck. "I want to spend the rest of my life with you, Brody."

An old fellow in an older model truck stopped and yelled out the window, "You kids need some help? Everyone okay?"

"She said yes!" Brody yelled.

"Congratulations. Looks like you got it under control," he said, and drove away.

"Yes, we do have it under control—finally," Brody said as he helped her back into the truck.

A mile down the road, he stopped beside the WELCOME TO TEXAS sign and stopped again. He jogged around the back side of the truck, opened her door, and stretched out his hand.

"You can't undo the proposal. I said yes." But she got out of the truck again without arguing.

He dropped on a knee again. "Lila Harris, the wild child who I fell in love with all those years ago, the person who has carried my heart in her pocket for twelve years, will you marry me?"

"Yes," she said again without even a moment's pause as she fell to her knees. "But why twice?"

He cupped her face in his hands and kissed her in a wildly passionate way that was so different from the first one. "Because I want both of you. I want the wild girl I fell in love with and I want the woman that girl has become. I love both of you and I never want you to think that I proposed to one or the other."

"You're crazy, Brody," she laughed.

"Crazy in love with you." He kissed her again. "Let's come back to this very place when we've been married sixty years." He started the truck and headed west toward Happy.

"You mean you think we'll still be kickin' when we're ninety?"

"We'll still be going skinny-dippin' in Hope Springs when we are a hundred," he said.